THE RED-HOT BLUES CHANTEUSE

A VIOLA VERMILLION VAUDEVILLE MYSTERY

ANA BRAZIL

Rhymes with
Razzle Press

This is a work of fiction. Names, characters, places, and incidents either are the product of the author's imagination or are used fictitiously. Any resemblance to actual persons, living or dead, events, or locales is entirely coincidental.

First paperback edition October 2023

First digital edition October 2023

Cover design by Dee Marley

ISBN 979-8-8621266-5-5 (paperback)

ISBN 979-8-9889545-0-7 (ebook)

Published by Rhymes with Razzle Press

For Tim

THE RED-HOT BLUES CHANTEUSE

~ A VIOLA VERMILLION VAUDEVILLE MYSTERY ~

Ana Brazil

Rhymes with
Razzle Press

PANTAGES THEATER

SAN FRANCISCO

Presenting the Week of FRIDAY, March 21, 1919

================================

14 All-Star Acts

TIME TABLE

MATINEES / EVENINGS

Kitty LeBlanc – French Poodle Acrobats

1:30 / 7:30

The Seven Nolan Sisters – Dance Specialty

1:35 / 7:35

Hagan & Wescott – Irish Singing, Dancing, and Comedy

1:44 / 7:44

Seymore & Hill – Card Tricks

2:00 / 8:00

O'Toole Brothers – Sophisticated Dual Piano Song and Dance
2:10 / 8:10

Ugo Baldanza – Accordionist
2:23 / 8:23

Viola Vermillion – Red-Hot Blues Chanteuse
2:34 / 8:34

Gallagher & Shean – Sketch Comedians
2:49 / 8:49

Officer Tuck & Champ the Drunken Dog
3:00 / 9:00

Adele Herman – Magic and Hypnotism
3:14 / 9:14

The Darling diLorenzos – Dancers Extraordinaire
3:32 / 9:32

The Sensational Audrey Merrick – World-Renowned Female Impersonator
3:50 / 9:50

Ling Ting Tumblers – Acrobatics
4:40 / 10:40

Morriscope – News of the World
4:50 / 10:50

PANTAGES THEATER

CURTAIN

5:00 / 11:00

CHAPTER
ONE

SAN FRANCISCO ~ MONDAY, MARCH 24, 1919

STU COVERED my eyes with his long fingers and I couldn't see anything.

"No cheating," he whispered against my ear.

I was trying not to look, but since we stood across from the Pantages Theater, I'd already guessed what the surprise was. I tingled from head to toe, barely able to stand still.

"A-a-a-a-and now, ladies and gentlemen." Stu's voice reached almost stage level, as though he was trying to command the people rushing past us on the sidewalk to stop and enjoy the show. "Pre-e-e-sen-ting . . . the Pride of the Pantages."

He removed his hands. Slowly. "You can look now, Vi."

The first thing I saw—the *only* thing I saw—was the Pan's elaborate marquee, a huge sign extending over the sidewalk. The marquee was a small part of the seven-story theater, but it was the only thing that mattered to me. From the moment our troupe arrived in San Francisco last week, I'd been desperate to see my name on it.

Stu lowered his voice as he read the sign's bottom row. "Viola Vermillion, Red-Hot Blues Chanteuse!"

"Red-Hot Blues Chanteuse!" I squealed in delight at my act's new name. I shook my shoulders, too, and almost launched into the choreography for Stu's song "Kiss Mama, Kiss Papa" even though I was in public. I had no idea how Stu'd managed to get my name on the marquee, but once we got back to our hotel tonight, I'd make sure Papa knew how grateful Mama was for her present.

"I'm really up there." I wanted to grab everyone walking past us—these men and women with their heads down, shuffling off to their humdrum offices and shops—and invite them to my two shows today. I wanted to prove that the war and the influenza were over, that we could sing and dance and enjoy ourselves again.

Stu clutched me to him and kissed me hard, his lips smacking my temple. "You did it, Viola. Your name in lights."

Or against the lights, since the bulbs behind the solid black letters of my name wouldn't be turned on for a half hour. But I'd take my name in big black letters any time.

"Too bad we don't have a Brownie," I said. "This'd look great in my scrapbook."

"You mean you won't remember this moment always?" Stu kissed me again. "You, me, and the grand unveiling of your new act?"

"Of course, I'll remember it forever." And I meant it. I'd also be grateful to Stu forever—grateful for helping me get my voice back after I almost died from the flu, and grateful for writing songs that showed off my talents.

After we'd blocked traffic on the sidewalk for another minute, he asked, "Had enough?"

I hadn't, but there was work to do. Vaudeville was so much more than eight or fifteen or fifty minutes on stage twice a day. It was everything that came before and after: the song decisions and rehearsals and costume selections, the endless negotiations with the stage manager and crew and house orchestra.

"Do you think they updated the playbill, too?" I asked.

"Only one way to find out." He nodded toward the front doors of the Pan, where the playbill was posted.

Because I really couldn't stop looking at my name, Stu guided me over the metal bus rails that ran along asphalted Market Street, which had to be San Francisco's busiest street. As we approached the theater, my name got bigger and bigger, until I stood directly in front of the building, where *Viola Vermillion* was huge.

I tugged on Stu's sleeve. "This is really real, isn't it?"

"Sure is, Mama." His grin was wide, almost contagious. "As real as sharing a dressing room with fifteen other people."

I returned his smile. We'd been playing this game of woe-is-me since we'd started traveling out west from New Jersey. "Or eating chicken chow mein for breakfast, lunch, and dinner."

"Or trying to sleep on a train for twelve hours sitting up."

Then I countered with something that was all too real for me. "Or singing your heart out to an audience that's half asleep."

Yes, we'd practiced this litany of life in a vaudeville troupe for so long that we had the patter down. Yet no matter how hard we complained, vaudeville was our chosen life. We couldn't be happy without it. Stu loved to write words and music, and I loved to sing his songs. We were both driven by the same demon—the desire to touch an audience and make them love us.

But as we approached the theater entrance, with today's matinee just an hour away, my confidence faded. What if I wasn't really red-hot? What if the audience didn't love my act? And who was I to call myself a *chanteuse*? I'd heard the word for the first time in Portland last week and warmed to it immediately, especially since it rhymed with *blues*. Stu liked it also, and since he knew words, I trusted him that we'd made the right decision.

Pinned up in a glass case on the entrance wall, the Pantages playbill was almost as large as a full newspaper page. Stu was too late to cover my eyes, and I immediately saw that *Viola Vermillion, Red-Hot Blues Chanteuse* had been included. With dark red letters almost one inch high, my name definitely commanded attention.

Stu took my arm and we walked to the stage door alley. "How about we celebrate with dinner tonight? There's a special place I heard of in North Beach."

"North Beach?"

"It's like Little Italy. Meatballs so big you can't finish more than one. And so much wine you'll forget the Thirsty First is coming up."

I groaned when he mentioned the upcoming wartime liquor restrictions, still in effect even though the war was over. To protect my voice, I didn't drink much alcohol, but Stu kept a flask full of gin. Once the liquor laws changed in July, his gin might be hard to find. Just another woe-is-me.

As we approached the stage door, I put my hand in Stu's jacket pocket in search of the lemon drops he kept for me. But the only thing in his pocket today was a dog biscuit, his daily treat for his best buddy, an oversized terrier mix named Champ. I slipped my hand into Stu's trouser pocket, but instead of finding candy, my fingers landed on his money clip. And a whole bunch of folded bills.

With the cost of our hotel rooms and my costumes, our train fares and eating in restaurants, not to mention the 5 percent we sent to our booking agent every week we got paid, Stu and I never had much money between us. Certainly not a wad as thick as this one.

I removed the clip and money from his pocket, turned away from possible prying eyes, and counted out the stiff bills. Seventy-five dollars.

I thought of all the clothes, hats, stockings, and handbags that seventy-five dollars could buy. Most of my street clothes were meant for a New Jersey winter and had been fine for Seattle or Tacoma. But spring had blossomed the first day we hit San Francisco, and even though Stu'd bought me the new dress I wore today, I lusted after every pastel frock I saw in the department stores in Union Square.

Stu's chest seemed to puff out in pride, like a proud Papa who gave his Mama everything she needed. "I was going to tell you about that tonight."

He opened his hand, but I kept the money in mine, a little in awe of its heft. "How 'bout you tell me now."

"Tonight," he said. "At dinner."

I wasn't mad at him—who could be mad at an extra seventy-five dollars?—and I plunked the bills into his still-open hand.

"Look, Stu." I spread my hands on his chest to gain his complete attention. But instead, he got mine. Because that's when I realized he was wearing a shoulder holster.

I pushed my hand under his jacket and slowly traced the

barrel and cylinder of my own Savage M1907. The gunmetal was warm and reassuring. Confident, like I was.

"What's wrong?" I wanted to know, wondering how I was going to get my heart to stop pounding. "Why do you have Mademoiselle Savage with you?"

"Nothing's wrong."

Except it had to be. Because Stu'd never holstered Mademoiselle Savage before.

"You know Blanche gave her to me," I told him.

I suddenly felt silly mentioning my dead sister. Just like I felt silly giving my gun a feminine name. I felt sillier still when I said, "I didn't know you had a holster."

"I served in the army, Vi." Stu shook his head, as if I'd already forgotten we'd lived through the war to end all wars. "And I kept my holster."

"But why do you need her?"

"Why do *you* need her?" he countered.

I had my reasons, but I wasn't sure I could explain them to him. I wasn't sure if I should. I searched his eyes, wondering if the time had come to 'fess up, but all I said was, "It's different for a girl on the road. You know that."

"But I'm here now, and I'm taking care of you."

All the humor drained out of me. "You mean I'm in danger?" *Because I might be,* I wanted to tell him. *Something happened in New Jersey before I met you. Something that made me bring Mademoiselle Savage with me out west.*

But before I decided anything, he put his arms around my waist and nuzzled my neck. "The only danger's from me, Mama."

Like he'd done so many times before, Stu turned a moment when I was almost going to tell him the truth into something playful. He got this way sometimes, twisting the meaning of words on me. Like he was working out the lyrics of a song right then and there.

With my fingers still on Mademoiselle Savage and my thoughts on the money in his pocket, I asked playfully, "You didn't rob a bank, did you?"

"Of course not." Stuart pulled my hand from under his jacket, but instead of holding it close, he let it drop.

I thought back to the day my sister Blanche gave me the Savage, insisting she wanted me to be safe. She told me that a woman had to take care of herself. Blanche had been right, and as much as I depended upon Stu, I was still a woman on my own.

Suddenly, having my name on the Pantages marquee seemed less of a triumph. Because no matter how much I succeeded in vaudeville, my sister'd never know.

"I promise I'll tell you everything at dinner, Vi." Stuart took my hand gently, as though he realized how abruptly he'd dropped it. "And I promise you're going to like it."

"I hope so."

We entered through the stage door together, neither of us surprised to see Charlie, the doorkeeper, sleeping at his desk. As we checked for our mail in the boxes by the stage manager's office, Kitty LeBlanc rushed over to us.

"Such news, Viola! Stuart!" Despite her enthusiastic greeting, Kitty kept her voice low, as though she were talking only to the snow-white poodle cradled in her arms. "The Orpheum's sending a scout to today's matinee."

Kitty was right to speak softly because the Pantages and Orpheum circuits competed fiercely for talented acts. If the Pan's management knew there was an Orpheum scout in the house, he'd be kicked to the curb quickly.

"He's coming for the entire show," she said. Good news

for Kitty, because her poodles opened the show in the one spot. I wanted to find out where Kitty had gotten her gossip, but she'd already moved on, pointedly ignoring Officer Tuck and Champ, the troupe's other dog act, but eagerly stopping to share her news with the piano-playing O'Toole Brothers.

"You think it's real?" I asked Stu. "Do Orpheum agents come to the Pan to poach acts?"

"Everybody poaches in vaudeville, although I'm guessing he's coming—if he's really coming—for just one act."

"Our act, maybe?" My name was on the playbill and marquee, but both of us knew that a singer was nothing without a wordsmith and composer behind her. Stu's songs were as good as any I'd heard in a New York City show, and much better than anything used by our fellow Pantages troupers.

Stu answered with the title of one of his novelty songs. "M-M-M-M-Maybe."

The theater's curtains—rich, royal blue velvet panels that made my costumes shimmer—were open, and I walked past Stu to stand center stage. I gazed into the house, luxuriating in the full grandeur of the San Francisco Pantages.

While the outside of the theater looked like any brick office building on any main street, inside, the Pan was a wonderland of garlands, arches, stars, and colors. The ceiling was painted with large bouquets of flowers and greenery, and the proscenium arch above the stage featured larger-than-life statues of cherubs throwing flowers and boys blowing trumpets. All of this decoration was arranged in a swirl of white, blue, pink, and gold. Lots of gold. The Pan was more beautiful than any church or train station I'd seen, although the best part was the seats. Between them, the main floor, loge, and balcony seated over seventeen hundred people. Not to mention the three private boxes on each sidewall, just feet from the stage.

Imaging those seats filled with men, women, and children, imagining how they'd gaze at me when I performed, how my songs would make them smile and laugh and shed a tear, thrilled me from head to toe. I was never as happy, as *me*, as when I was performing. And this afternoon on the Pantages's full stage, I was so complete with happiness it was almost like my sister Blanche was still alive. Almost like the two of us were still performing together.

As I wiped a tear from my eye, Stu joined me on stage. He looked a little uneasy, like he didn't belong there and wanted to hurry down to the orchestra pit.

I took a deep breath. "Where do you think he'll sit, the Orpheum agent?"

I searched the vast sea of seats, wondering about today's audiences and how to make them love me. Which song would break a fella's heart? Which movement would make him shiver and take his neighbor's hand? Which woman would welcome my wink?

"Any idea?"

"Center Main," he said simply. "Best seat in the house."

I studied the seats in Center Main, selected one, and decided I'd sing directly to it. "What do you think about my set? Should we change it? Add another song? Maybe—"

Stu shook his head. "It's too late to throw any changes at the orchestra."

He was right. The Pan house orchestra was composed of thirteen men who'd been too old to serve in the war and were known more for their sour notes and fumbling fingers than their virtuoso sight reading. Throwing anything new at them was asking for failure.

Stu put his hands on my shoulders and turned me toward the back of the stage, facing the spiral staircase that led downstairs to the ladies' dressing room.

"Start your warm-ups, fluff your hair, and wear your shortest skirt. You've got the talent no matter who's in the audience." He pressed my shoulders just a little tighter and spoke so low that only I heard him. "The Orpheum's going to come begging for you someday, Vi. And the Palace will be right beside them."

With that almost-benediction, he pushed me toward the staircase. I took the rail but turned back when I realized he wasn't behind me.

"Where are you going?"

"To get some lemon drops," he said. "I'll be back in time for warm-ups."

"But you never—"

He was out the stage door before I finished. Before I told him my throat was fine and I didn't need any lemon drops today. But mostly, before I could ask him again why he had Mademoiselle Savage strapped to his shoulder.

CHAPTER
TWO

News of the Orpheum scout's visit had reached the ladies' dressing room, and it was every performer for herself. Fourteen ladies were on the bill—singers, dancers, even a mesmerizer—and today everyone ended up in the room at the same time. Only Kitty and her nine poodles were missing because they had a dressing room reserved for animal acts.

Each one of us—including the youngest performer, all of seven years old—had an assigned dressing table and mirror. But today everyone wanted more. More light, more table space, more time at the only full-sized three-panel mirror.

I hung my coat and hat on my costume rack. I'd lost a lot of hair while I was sick, and after I got better and saw that bobbed hair was all the rage, I'd had mine cut off, just to the middle of my neck. Fortunately, I hadn't lost my curls or my natural almost-vermillion hair color, although I still used henna once a month.

"Fluff your hair," Stu had said, knowing my fashionable locks would reassure me. But as I put down my hairbrush and looked inside my dressing room drawer, I realized my small can of vermillion lip rouge was missing. It wasn't labeled *vermillion*, of course; it was called *orange-red*, but it perfectly complimented my hair and made me feel *red-hot*.

I knew the rouge had been in my drawer last night, but I still searched my dressing table. Then I realized I was the latest victim of the ladies' dressing room bandit.

So many things had gone missing from our dressing room, not just in San Francisco, but in every city. Small things that gave each of us confidence on stage, like an eyebrow pencil or curling rags or a can of talcum powder. Or orange-red lipstick.

I'd counted up all of the thefts when we played Portland and realized that everyone had been touched except Jeanette diLorenzo, the bottle-blonde dancer who performed with her husband, Rocco. Once I'd guessed that Jeanette was our thief, I started watching her in the dressing room, but so far, I hadn't caught her in the act.

Jeanette'd been watching me too, ever since Seattle when Stu and I joined the troupe. She'd asked me a lot of questions that first week, and from then on, I'd caught her studying me. Not just in the dressing room, but backstage, on stage, at the hotel, and, last week, at Fong's Café. For a while, I'd thought she was trying to lure Stu away from me to compose music for her act. Then I realized she couldn't carry a tune.

Ever since the thefts began, I'd wanted to search Jeanette's dressing table while she was performing, but I hadn't worked up the courage. And I couldn't do it today, not with a full house in the dressing room.

But, like Stu said, I could start my warm-ups.

So I began exercising my chest voice as I put on my

makeup. Despite being laid low by the influenza last year, my voice was gaining more volume and range every day. Stu's music had improved over the last months, too. His novelty songs were funnier, his ballads more heartbreaking, and his love songs more suggestive. Together, our talent would knock the socks off the Orpheum scout.

As I put on my costume—a stunning concoction of gold chiffon featuring three thousand silver spangles—I fantasized about charming the scout today, negotiating a contract with him tomorrow, and starting at the San Francisco Orpheum down the street on Wednesday. Until I remembered that our Pantages contract ran through mid-May when we finished up in San Diego.

Still, a girl could dream about more money, a private dressing room, and an in-tune full orchestra, couldn't she?

As I glanced at the other performers' reflections in my mirror, I guessed I wasn't the only one dreaming. Each of us had our ambitions. Mine started when my sister Blanche thrilled the audience with her song routine at the Masonic Hall in Passaic. Seeing her command that small stage—despite the out-of-tune piano—made me realize that I wanted to be a vaudeville performer just like her.

My lovely reverie was shattered by Jeanette's screeches. "If you step in my light one more time, I'm going to tear your hair out."

I adjusted my mirror to locate Jeanette and whoever she was picking on. Her prey was Gladys Nolan, the oldest and bossiest of the seven Nolan Sisters.

"What do you care? I thought you hated vaudeville." Gladys paused as though she expected a reaction from the other troupers. And she got it. Everyone stopped their preparations to listen, although the littlest Nolan sister fixed her hands over her ears. "Ain't you going off to the moving pictures? Be a big star. Just like Mary Pickford?"

"That's right, Glad-ass. I'm gonna be in pictures. 'Cause that's where the real talent goes these days. That's where the money is."

"Real talent, huh?" Gladys looked like she was about to roll up her sleeves, like she wanted to show Jeanette a thing or two about talent. "You call what you got talent?"

"I got talent," Jeanette almost barked. "And better than that, I got *photogenic*. Cameras love me. Something you and your brats will never have."

As much as I distrusted Jeanette, she wasn't all wrong. Every Pantages house we'd played along the West Coast had a huge projector room in the balcony, and they all showed a Morriscope *News of the World* reel at the end of the show. It was just a ten-minute short, but most of the audience stayed to watch it. Even worse, some vaudeville houses were showing half live and half moving picture performances. Vaudeville and the pictures were already competing against each other, and there was no way to tell which was going to win.

I knew which I wanted to win, of course. All of us in the dressing room did. And I couldn't let Jeanette get away with insulting us. We all had talent, and some of us were photogenic, too.

I stood up, turned my back to my mirror, and clutched my table with both hands for support. For the first time since I'd joined the troupe, I was going to say something to everyone. Not only that, I was saying it to Jeanette.

"You can't compare us and them." I wasn't surprised when Jeanette met me glare to glare. "Because we're live and the pictures aren't."

She was quick to answer. “Sure, you can squawk on stage, but you’re nothing more than a tiny speck. So tiny that no one in the cheap seats can see you. Or hear you.” As I tried to figure out what to say next, she continued, “I’m going to be seen. I’m going to be full stage, and only the pictures do that.”

“They see us because we give them a show,” I said. Suddenly I knew I wasn’t talking just for myself, but for the other women in the room who loved performing. “In color, and with music.”

“That’s right,” Gladys added. “We got sound. Pictures don’t.”

“Pictures got subtitles and they work just fine,” said Jeanette. “Unless you’re stupid and can’t read.”

Gladys bristled. “We can read and we can count, too. And we’ve got rhythm. We’ve never tripped on stage.” Gladys smirked, reminding everyone about how Jeanette’d fallen in Tacoma when she couldn’t keep up with Rocco’s footwork. “No one ever dumped the curtain on us because we fell on our ass.”

Jeanette’s high-and-mighty air dissolved and her face went red. Within seconds, she headed toward Gladys, hands raised as though she was going to take her by the neck. But just when it seemed she was going to sink her teeth into Gladys, all of the fire left her. Jeanette stopped to stare at Stu, who must have pushed open the dressing room door to get my attention.

It was strange, Jeanette looking at Stu for that long. Like he was as handsome as picture idol Douglas Fairbanks or as rich as munitions tycoon Thaddeus Rutherfurd. Stu always looked good to me, especially when he wore his tuxedo like he did now, but I’d be the first to admit his looks wouldn't stop a show. Or a tirade from a spoiled dancer.

Then the stage manager's assistant pushed between Stu and the door. "Ten minutes to showtime, Nolan Sisters. Ten minutes to showtime."

Gladys collected her six sisters quicker than I'd ever seen and scooted them out the door. I remained standing, just in case Jeanette started up on someone else. After a few seconds, she sat down at her table and clattered through her drawers.

With Stu still waiting at the door, I fluffed my hair one more time and collected my plume of peacock feathers. I followed him up the spiral stairs to backstage, never suspecting the dressing room had been a rehearsal for the real drama that waited in the wings.

♫

Backstage wasn't any friendlier than the women's dressing room; at least three acts stood by, each of them sneering at the others, each of them intending to shine in front of the Orpheum scout. Even our headliner, female impersonator Audrey Merrick, and his manager, Lionel Fisk, were backstage, making everyone stand three feet away from them as they watched the stage.

At least I had Stu with me. I still had questions about why he needed Mademoiselle Savage and where he'd gotten that seventy-five dollars. And whether he'd really gone out for lemon drops.

Still unsettled about my quarrel with Jeanette, I smoothed down Stu's lapel before asking, "Where'd you go?"

But at the same time, Stu asked, "What'd she want?" He put his hand over mine. "Jeanette? What'd she want? What was that argument about?"

"She thinks moving pictures are better than vaudeville." I wanted Stu to know what a traitor Jeanette was. Except even as I'd been defending vaudeville to everyone in the dressing room, I had to wonder if maybe she was right. Maybe all the public wanted were black-and-white images flickering in front of them. Maybe the human connection didn't matter anymore.

But no, that just couldn't happen. We'd lost so much of our lives during the war and the epidemic—we couldn't lose vaudeville, too.

Stu clutched my hands harder, making sure I looked up at him. "Stay away from her. She can be trouble."

"Why?" I already was staying away from her, although I'd never told Stu, because why would he care?

"Just do it for me. As a favor."

"Fine." I folded my arms across my chest. "Now, how about you tell me where you've been."

He pulled a lemon drop out of his pocket and dangled it between us. He unwrapped the candy himself, all the while looking at my lips. He brought it close to my mouth, but still far enough away that I wondered if he expected me to beg for it. All that fuss about vaudeville dying and everyone wanting moving pictures faded fast. All I thought of was how I'd missed being in Stu's bed last night. Now I knew he'd missed me too.

I opened my mouth, and as he pushed the drop onto my tongue, I licked his finger. Just when I felt like easing Stu into the darkest corner backstage, a harsh whisper edged toward us.

"Help me, please!"

We both turned to see Owen Tuck carrying Champ in his arms. I'd seen Champ play dead a few times, but it'd been nothing like this. His legs were limp and his tongue hung out of his open mouth. Stu was at Tuck's side quickly, trying to support Champ's legs.

Even in the backstage darkness, I saw the tears running down Tuck's face. He loved Champ with his whole heart, so much that he'd turned his talented pet into an almost-headliner. Their Officer Tuck and Champ the Drunk Dog act featured Tuck dressed in a police uniform trying to arrest Champ for drunk and disorderly behavior. Against all odds, Champ had learned how to imitate a drunk's walk and demeanor, and his hilarious hiccups captivated audiences. Talk about encores.

"What is it? Can I do anything?" I stared at Champ's chest, hoping to see it go up and down, but nothing moved. "Maybe he's nervous because there's an Orpheum scout in the house?"

"That's not it." Stu had the strangest scowl on his face. "Champ's as good a trouper as the rest of us."

Suddenly our stage manager, Mr. Steccati, stood beside Tuck. "Get that dog downstairs or outside. And stop gossiping about an Orpheum scout. This is a Pantages house, and you should be grateful you're playing here."

Tuck wiped the sleeve of his uniform across his face, smearing his black-penciled eye makeup until he looked more like a masked bandit than a police officer. "I gotta get him to an animal hospital. Or find a doc somewhere. I can't lose him."

"A cabbie will know where to take him," said Stu. "Let's get him in a taxi."

I ran to prop the stage door open—even though Mr. S glared at me as if the outside sounds would carry to the stage—and Stu led Tuck and Champ down the stairs and through the alley. They waited on Market Street, searching for a taxicab. I watched as long as I could, which was until Mr. S. pulled the doors closed.

Mr. S's assistant was soon at my side. "Five minutes before the seven spot, Viola Vermillion. Places, please."

All of a sudden, I was minutes away from singing in front of an Orpheum scout. Except that I had no idea if Stu would make it back to the theater.

I was surprised to see Kitty backstage and still in costume. I was really surprised to see her standing close to the stage, almost peering into the audience. Her one spot had been over an hour ago, and she usually would have been out of the theater by now, giving her dogs their evening stroll or cooking dinner in her hotel room.

I elbowed past the O'Toole Brothers and stood next to Kitty. We were too close to the stage to even whisper, but maybe because she was about Blanche's age, or maybe because I knew that her poodles and her son adored her, just standing next to her made me feel better. She took my arm and drew me to her. She smelled of greasepaint and dog biscuits, and I was suddenly sure that our crazy, competitive world would be all right. Kitty's friendship was exactly what I needed to help me forget about Jeanette and moving pictures and Mademoiselle Savage and almost-lifeless Champ.

Because right now, I had to give my heart and soul to my act. This might be my big break. I had to make the Orpheum scout love me.

Kitty and I watched as the six spot—Ugo Baldanza,

Accordionist Extraordinaire—made the final run up his keyboard. As the orchestra took up "Italian Love Song" to move Ugo off the stage, I rolled back my shoulders. I took a deep breath, inhaling a snootful of sawdust, acrobat's chalk, spoiled chop suey, and sweaty comedians.

But even as the orchestra played him offstage, Ugo launched into another song. It was a tricky extravaganza of elaborate pushes and pulls, runs and chords. Finally, he drilled out one last chord. As the audience rallied with applause and the curtain closed, Ugo strode off the stage opposite from me. He caught my gaze and I read his lips. "Beat that."

Sure, Ugo had talent, but so did I. And I had every intention of making the audience forget all about him and his accordion. I winked at Kitty.

"Orpheum circuit, here I come."

With the orchestra vamping my entrance music, I strutted out in front of the curtains, knowing my gold costume with silver spangles shined like a star. This costume was my favorite. It had a scooped neckline, no sleeves, and, as Stu had suggested, my shortest skirt. It showed off my legs and décolletage to perfection. As I eased my long peacock-feathered fan behind my back, I realized I needed a manicure, but I also knew the audience wasn't close enough to know.

To my relief, Stu'd made it back to the orchestra pit. But he wasn't giving me his big start-the-show smile. No, he definitely had a my-favorite-dog-is-sick look. My heart went out to him.

At Stu's nod, Maestro Mitch directed his orchestra to launch into the opening of my five-song set. The clarinets rang out a brisk toot and I let the audience get a good look at me. I reached center stage and marked the Center Main seat dead in my sights. I couldn't see the Orpheum scout, not with the lights blasting in my eyes, but I'd still sing my heart out.

I looked up to the balcony, the highest tier of the three seating areas. Set back in the theater, the balcony was where the loneliest of ticket holders seemed to take their pleasures. I winked up at them. No sir, your Red-Hot Blues Chanteuse doesn't want anyone feeling neglected this afternoon. After that, I saluted the loge.

I stepped up to center apron and let the one-thirty-in-the-afternoon audience at the San Francisco Pan know exactly what I thought about men and love:

I'm worried, I'm worried, Thinking about you,
And there's a reason why
It's all on account of the things that you do
You know you're naughty, and I know it, too
You made me love you right from the start
Why do you play with my heart?

As I vamped between the verse and chorus, I got a better sense of today's audience: the glare from a pair of spectacles; the stringent odor of a bottle of cheap booze; the hint of a spicy hotdog. I even saw the arch of a broad-brimmed lady's hat in the audience. I turned toward the hat as I launched into the chorus:

Naughty! Naughty! Naughty! Can't you be
good?

I advised my newfound female friend on her love life through two more verses and ended the chorus with:

If you keep on worrying me
I'm goin' to take you right across my knee
Because you're naughty! Naughty! Naughty!
Oh so naughty to me!

Ugo might have thought he won the audience's loyalty, but my applause—and whistles and hoots—was twice as loud as his. Yet, just as I shook my hips back and forth and released the feathered plume behind me, the orchestra stepped on my moment and set up my next song. Way too quickly.

I was forced to sing "I Hold His Hand and He Holds Mine" like it was a comedian's patter. Neither Stu nor Maestro would look at me, and I was almost out of breath when I finished. Before the audience could applaud, the orchestra started "Ooo-gie Ooo-gie Wa-Wa," my closing number.

What the hell? This was a five-song set and I needed every emotion in every song to impress the Orpheum scout.

I was barely able to "Ooo-gie Ooo-gie Wa-Wa" all the way through. I certainly wasn't able to shimmy, strut, or engage the audience with my peacock feathers. As I swallowed my rage, I couldn't get to the closing verse soon enough.

But because I was Viola Vermillion, Red-Hot Blues Chanteuse, because my name was now on the Pantages marquee, in a gracious gesture worthy of a headliner, I bowed regally. I extended my plume of peacock feathers toward the orchestra and the musicians rose in response. Maestro bowed in my direction but refused to look at me.

Then I saw the piano stool, unoccupied and revolving in slow circles. Stu had left the pit.

I exited stage left and comedians Gallagher and Shean barreled up to me. As Shean marched on stage, Gallagher politely tapped his derby. “Never you mind about your encore, Miss Vermillion, we got this! We’ll always take five more minutes when there’s a scout in the house.”

Seconds later, as I tried to contain my frustration, Stu tried to sneak past me, already changed into street clothes and with his fedora in hand. I grabbed his sleeve before he slipped out the stage door.

“You cut me down to three songs! With an Orpheum scout out there!”

“Shhhh . . . take it easy, Vi.”

“Don’t tell me to take it easy. This was our big break!”

“There wasn’t an Orpheum scout out there. Not on a Monday.” He smudged his lips against my forehead. “I have to go.”

Before I could stop him, he slipped past sleeping Charlie and out the stage door.

I followed him through the alley and out to Market Street, sure I knew where he was going. Stu’d been charmed by Champ since the first day they met, and his affection for the dog had only grown during our tour. But how could he choose Champ over me?

I watched Stu weave through the pedestrians and buses and motorcars like he’d been fighting San Francisco traffic his entire life. He darted toward the cable car turnaround, where I lost sight of him.

“I hope Champ makes it,” I said to no one.

What could I do except change into my street clothes and go in search of my orange-red lip rouge? And purchase a new pair of stockings? And get a manicure? Because when I got Stu all to myself tonight, I wanted my claws to be as sharp as possible.

CHAPTER THREE

I FOUND my lip rouge in a small shop on Sutter Street and had enough time for a manicure and a hand massage at the City of Paris. After those indulgences, I returned to the Pan for my solo rehearsal time. The matinee had let out and the entire theatre was dark; vaudevillians left the theater soon after their spots were finished, of course, and between shows, most everyone else went for dinner. But I didn't mind the quiet darkness or the almost-empty Pan.

I did mind that I had to cut my rehearsal short due to Rocco diLorenzo's unwanted advances during my practice. I took my frustrations out on Rocco's feet, shins, and groin, which diminished my irritation some. Then I braved the darkened house and went to look for Stu in the balcony.

Stu loved balconies. Wherever we played, he always gravitated to a certain balcony spot between shows. I didn't know why, but since it was too dark to write up there, I always suspected he went up there to nap.

The San Francisco Pan's balcony looked like every other balcony in every other Pan we'd played. Perhaps the room for the Morriscope film projector was larger? Perhaps the ceiling was lower? Perhaps it smelled more heavily of cherished sexual liaisons?

I sniffed silently for a few seconds to be sure. Yes, something musky and mean, something tinged with sour smoke and sadness assaulted my nose. These odors were not unique to the balcony, of course. I'd smelled spent passion all over the Pan. In the rehearsal hall, in backstage cubby-holes, in the boxes, even out in the alleyway. All over the theatre, it seemed, sex was unavoidable. But even though passion's odor was sharp in the balcony this afternoon, I always knew that Stu was true to me.

As my eyes grew accustomed to the low light, I saw the outline of his fedora slouched in the corner seat eight rows down. Stu's usual spot. Damn him for being able to sleep when I was mad at him for rushing my act.

As I made my way down to him, the heavy cling of passion gave way to an odor of urine. And then blood.

My anger turned to fear and I almost backed out of the balcony. As my heart began to throb, I mumbled his name. Then I yelled it. He could laugh or swear or yawn in my face, I just wanted him to turn around. I needed to know the blood I smelled didn't belong to him.

But it did. Blood soaked through his white shirt and his tie and vest, right in the middle of his chest. He slumped in the seat, his eyes closed and his mouth open, as if he wanted to tell me something. As if he *needed* to tell me something.

"No." I stared at his bloody, sunken chest, begging it to move. "No, no, no, no."

I knelt by his side, grabbed his right hand, and pressed my fingers to the inside of his wrist. I searched for a pulse, but I couldn't find one. I held his hand, still so strong and supple that it seemed as if it could launch into a jaunty melody at any time. Despite the blood that soaked his shirt and vest, I pressed my hand against his heart, still hoping to feel his chest lift. Hoping the warmth of my hand could make him breathe again. But it couldn't.

"Oh, Stu."

His head rested against the back of the seat, as though he'd been standing and fell backwards. *When he was shot,* I thought. *Because that's a gunshot.* For the first time, I realized that blood had passed through a hole in his left shoulder. *That's another gunshot.*

If I kept my eyes only on his face, I might have thought he was napping, if not for the blood that stained his mouth and chin. I grabbed Stu's handkerchief from his breast pocket, thinking I'd wipe the blood from his lips. But before I did, I realized that something else was wrong.

The notebook he carried in his inner pocket was gone. The red leather notebook I'd asked Stu to safeguard for me, the one that I'd felt in his pocket hours ago, was gone.

I *needed* that notebook, and although it was the last thing I ever wanted to do, I plunged through Stu's pockets trying to find it. I came up with lemon drops, a dog biscuit, his money clip, and his pencil. But no notebook.

Then, from the corner of my eye, I saw my gun on the floor, just beyond Stu's feet. My eyes filled with tears as I stared at Mademoiselle Savage until she dissolved from my sight. I'd trusted her to protect me, to protect *us*, but instead, the bitch had killed my lover.

CHAPTER FOUR

I'd never been inside the theater manager's office before. Never been close. I'd only seen all-powerful Thomas Zimmerman—whom everyone called Mr. Z—once, when he scrutinized me and Stu during our first run-through. In his office today, he reigned once more, nodding for me to enter.

The policeman at my side tightened his grip on my elbow and steered me toward Mr. Z's desk like a tugboat. It'd been less than an hour since the police arrived at the Pan, and my body was numb. I'd wrapped my coat around me to keep from freezing, but no matter how hard I rubbed my hands inside my pockets, they wouldn't warm up. I was so cold, so brittle, I wondered if my arm might shatter under the policeman's pressure and break into bits. But what would it matter now? After finding Stu dead, my heart was already broken.

No, I corrected myself. *Not dead. Murdered.*

Despite the anguish that pulsed icily through my body, I was awestruck by Mr. Z's office. Every wall was covered with photographs of vaudeville acts: clowns and dogs, bicycle riders and high divers, minstrels and magicians. On the credenza behind his desk were autographed photographs of some of the brightest stars of vaudeville—Ed Wynn, Nora Bayes and Jack Norworth, and the woman I'd vowed to replace someday: Eva Tanguay, the Queen of Vaudeville.

Eva posed casually on top of a grand piano, her legs crossed, leaning forward to allow her neckline to expose her cleavage, smiling directly at the camera. Eva was aces, all right, and how I knew it. I'd stolen every detail of her pose and used it in my own publicity photos, the ones in Mr. Z's lobby. I might have stolen her every dance step if Stu hadn't stopped me, hadn't insisted he'd help me find my own dance sweet spot.

Mr. Z also had a photograph of Mr. Pantages, the founder of the Pantages Vaudeville Circuit. Mr. Pantages appeared in an almost life-sized headshot, and Mr. Z stood so close to the photo it looked like the two men were talking to each other. I imagined them standing in judgment of me right now, exchanging notes about today's rushed performance or blaming me for Stu's death.

There were four other men in the room: a tall man who was folding himself into the chair behind Mr. Z's desk, two men in suits, one on either side of the doorway, and my own personal policeman, a short man with a grip as tight as that of a traveling salesman making change.

The police—minus the tall man taking over Mr. Z's desk—had questioned me outside the balcony, so I guessed that bringing me up to Mr. Z's office meant they suspected I had something to do with Stu's death.

Which I had, of course. If I'd never shown Mademoiselle Savage to Stu, he might still be alive. Or if I'd kept Stu from leaving the theater or suggested we return to the hotel for a snuggle, he might still be alive. If I'd done any of a hundred things differently, Stu might still be alive.

But he wasn't, and all I wanted was to crawl into a warm bed with a full flask of gin. Despite the allure of Mr. Z's photographic gallery, I'd do whatever I could to escape his office as quickly as possible.

I pulled my elbow from the policeman's grasp and straightened my shoulders. Taking my cue from the lyrics of one of Stu's songs ("I'm Nobody's Fool, Not Even His"), I leveled my eyes, parted my lips, and sat down directly across from Mr. Z's desk. I tried to cross my legs—just like Eva and I did in our photos—but they were frozen straight.

By the time the man in Mr. Z's chair introduced himself as Detective Petersen, I'd committed myself to giving a performance that'd make Stu proud. I'd be confident and sassy, stay on key, and hit all of my marks.

But first I blurted out, "I didn't kill Stu."

"Do you know who did?" The detective removed a small notebook and short pencil from his pocket.

I sniffed back the tears that welled in my eyes and shook my head.

"Then let's start at the beginning. What's your name?"

I sniffed again. "Viola Vermillion."

"Is that your real name?"

"No. It's Viola Clark."

"Where're you from?"

"Paterson, New Jersey."

"How long have you been in San Francisco?"

"Since last week."

"They're part of a thirteen-act troupe put together by Mr. Pantages, traveling down the West Coast." Mr. Z's head veered toward Mr. Pantages' headshot. "They started out in Seattle in February, played Tacoma and Portland, and now they're here for two weeks before going on to Oakland."

Remembering those happy days on the road, the chill that threaded through my body began to thaw. I opened my coat and exposed my new springtime dress, a sweet mint-green georgette frock with a demure neckline.

The detective turned from Mr. Z and back to me. "Where were you this afternoon?"

"I had breakfast around noon at Fong's Café next door."

"Was Mr. Wiley with you?"

"No."

"Was he with you after breakfast?"

"After breakfast at noon," snickered one of the suits standing near the door.

I ignored the insult, thinking only of those magical moments just a few hours ago when Stu and I had gazed at my name on the marquee. "We got to the theater together to prepare for the matinee. I'm a five-song act in the seven spot." I looked up at Mr. Z, expecting he might want to add something, but his lips were pursed.

"What'd you do after the show? Did you see him then?"

I clutched at a soft tassel of my skirt and resisted the urge to wrap it around my finger. And maybe pluck it out and tear it apart. But then I decided that *I could do this.* Speak about Stu without going to pieces.

"Just . . . just for a few seconds." That was the last time I saw him alive, and the moment when I should have done every one of those hundred different things to keep him alive.

"What time was that?"

I was surprised to hear Mr. Z answer for me. "Her spot

ends at two forty-eight. Except I'm told today it ended at two forty-four."

"That's right," I answered slowly. "Stu rushed me and I only sang three songs."

The detective made a mark in his notebook. "You know why he rushed you?"

I shook my head.

He asked, "What did you do after that?"

"I had a manicure at the City of Paris. It's a department store." I looked down at my hands, surprised to see my polished nails. "After that, I rehearsed."

"You and Stuart?"

"No. I didn't need Stu—" The words froze on my lips. Of course I needed Stu. I'd always need Stu. "I rehearsed solo."

"Anyone with you?"

"Yes," I replied reluctantly. "Rocco diLorenzo."

"Rocco's part of the Darling diLorenzo Dancers," said Mr. Z.

"Rocco . . ." Saying his name once more made me want to knee him in the groin. Again. "Showed me a new dance step." *His* kind of dance step, where he slid his hand under my skirt, pulled me toward him, and pushed his tongue into my mouth. I felt like such a fool asking Rocco for instruction only to be mashed at the end.

"Rocco and his wife Jeanette play the eleven spot," Mr. Z told the detective. "My secretary's getting you a list of the troupe."

"You found Mr. Wiley today, didn't you?" asked the detective.

I glanced over at the wall of vaudeville greats, wondering if they might help me out, but in the end, I looked down at my own hands for direction. My freshly painted scarlet nails flashed back at me. After touching Stu's chest, I'd wiped my bloodied fingertips on the hem of my slip, but was that blood around my fingertips? I curled my fingers to keep from looking at them.

"Yes," I finally answered. "Stu always went to the balcony between shows, so I went up there to find him. I thought maybe he was sleeping . . . until I smelled . . . until I saw his blood."

I replayed those moments in my heart, the moments when I knew Stu was dead but hoped he wasn't. When I checked for a pulse and put my hand to his heart, like they taught us in Red Cross training. They never trained us to move hair away from anyone's eyes, but I did that too. Just before I kissed his forehead.

"That's when you called the police?" asked the detective.

"No." How could I? I couldn't leave Stu. "I went to the railing and called down to the stage. It took a while, but one of the stagehands came out. I think he'd been eating supper with the others in the back alley. He got Mr. S to the stage, but that took a while too."

"Mr. S," said Mr. Z. "That's Caesar Steccati, my stage manager."

"You didn't look for someone else to help you?"

"It's between shows. Suppertime. Nobody's here," I told him. "Once I got Mr. S to come up to the balcony, he called the police."

"What about the gun? You found that, too, didn't you?" Petersen laid Mademoiselle Savage on the middle of the desk, the barrel pointed at a space to my left. "Tell me about the gun."

I dug my thumbnail into my index finger, trying to

distract myself from the fresh surge of tears building at the base of my throat.

"It's mine. Stu said he needed her this afternoon."

"Did he say why?"

I shook my head, remembering the solid sureness of the gun in Stu's shoulder holster and wondering who strong-armed the gun from him. Because the person who took the gun from him must have killed him.

"Why do you have a gun with you?"

As much as I needed to know who shot Stu, I couldn't tell the detective the truth. Couldn't tell him about the red leather notebook, or that Thaddeus Rutherfurd—owner of the notebook—wanted it back. And how I needed the gun to protect myself from Rutherfurd.

"I'd be pretty stupid to shoot Stu," I replied honestly. "Without him, I can't—" A shiver ran through me, and I let it settle before I continued, thinking about a dozen men in the theater who could have taken the gun from Stu. And maybe could have shot him.

Almost to myself, I said, "There's friction in any theater. Everyone is so compe—"

"You're saying someone working in the theater killed Mr. Wiley?"

It was subtle, but I caught a change in the detective's tone. A possibility that he wanted to believe me. That he'd welcome finding out that someone besides me killed Stu. Perhaps at his core, he was an old-fashioned gent, a detective who liked his women innocent and his murderers male.

"Everyone was jealous of Stu's talent," I offered truthfully. "Lots of people tried to hire him away from me."

From somewhere in the room, I heard the tinny strains of the orchestra performing its opening musical selection.

As the trumpets tooted the first notes of "I'll Say She Does," I imagined Kitty lining up her poodles, ready to start the show. Despite Stu's murder, it was still seven-thirty. *Show-time*. But how could anything continue when Stu was dead?

Mr. Z went over to a large knob on the wall and turned it all the way to the left. The orchestra went silent.

The detective shoved back his chair and unwound to his full height. He leaned over to Mr. Z and they whispered. Finally, the detective headed toward the door.

I bolted from the chair. "What happens now?"

Images of white lilies and black-suited mourners floated through my thoughts. Stu'd need a funeral; he'd need to be buried. He'd need a suitable obituary in *The New York Clipper Theatrical Weekly,* and as his partner, that was my responsi-bility. "When can I see him again?"

"Does he have family to notify?" asked the detective.

"I'm his family," I replied forcefully.

"Then I'll have to let you know."

"But what are you going to do?" Now that the police suits were easing out of Mr. Z's door, I realized how much I wanted to talk about Stu. I wanted to tell them how wonderful he was and how much they needed to find the brute who took him away from me.

Mr. Z put his hand firmly on my sleeve. "No need to worry about that, Miss Vermillion. The San Francisco Police always find their man."

"That's right." The detective looked me in the eyes, as if he knew what I'd lied about and what I hadn't. "And if I don't find my man, I'll definitely find my woman."

♫

Mr. Z reclaimed his chair and his desk. Now it was just the two of us. "Miss Vermillion, you need to lay off for a while."

I wrapped my coat around me, chilled to the bone once more. "But—"

"Neither Mr. Pantages nor I expect you to perform now." Mr. Z pulled a key from his vest pocket. "I'll pay you up front for this week, of course."

He opened a lower desk drawer. I heard him scratching around in a metal box and watched him bring a stack of bills to the desk. He counted out the money in front of me. Two hundred and fifty dollars; our contracted weekly amount. He took another ten-dollar bill from the box and placed it on top of the pile. He put the money in an envelope, rose from his chair, and came around the desk to where I sat. "You're not the first person to lose someone in their act. Not with the war and the influenza."

"But Mr. Zim—"

"Face the truth, Miss Vermillion. You need a new piano player. Come back when you have one and we'll talk."

But Mr. Z was wrong. I didn't need *a* piano player; I needed Stu. Right then I heard Stu's voice in my head, his deliberate, encouraging voice, instructing me to fight for my spot on the bill. Commanding me to promise Mr. Z anything to get back in the spotlight.

I took Mr. Z's money, looking inside the envelope to make sure there was no pink slip included. Maybe he was playing straight with me. Maybe being pulled from the show was only temporary.

But all I really heard was Stu's voice, and his words were louder than anything I'd heard from Mr. Z.

In a voice that was all Stu's, I heard myself say, "Then I'll go out and get another piano player. I'll be ready to be on stage in a few days. Tops."

♫

The seven-story Hotel Henry (*Theatricals welcome! Rates by the Week and Month!*) sagged on the corner of Mission and Sixth Streets, a few blocks from the Pan. The rooms had mismatched furniture, thin walls, loose locks, a sink in the corner, and two full bathrooms at the end of each floor. For two bucks a week (two bucks and four bits for the luxury of my very small bathroom), it was perfect for vaudeville folk.

In my room on the sixth floor, I fell face down on my bed, not even changing into my kimono, not needing gin to help me sleep. When I awoke, I knew I was in a hotel and I knew I was in San Francisco, but for a very few moments, I thought Stu's murder was all a bad dream. I pulled the blanket over my head and hugged my knees to my chest. I'd lost my lover, my job, and that red leather notebook—the only things in the world that mattered to me.

The thin blanket scratched my cheeks and hardly covered my toes, and despite my desperation to fall asleep and stay asleep, my thoughts flailed wildly about. Stu was really dead, wasn't he? And why? Why would anyone shoot such a sweet, talented guy?

I stared at the door connecting my room to his. We always left this door unlocked, so I slipped inside and turned on the small lamp by his dresser. His room was smaller than mine and his furniture was just as shabby, but we never cared about a wobbly dresser or a moth-eaten rug. Not when we spent most of our hotel time in his bed or mine.

I slumped on his narrow, unmade bed and shimmied to sit against the headboard. I hugged his pillow to my chest as though it were Stu himself. From the hallway, I heard the unmistakable sounds of the troupe members arriving on the floor and guessed that the seven-thirty show had wrapped up.

I crunched his pillow hard, and little feathers escaped from a hole in the case, teasing my nose into a sneeze. The sneeze provoked a tear, and soon tears ran down my cheeks without stopping, great streams of tears that fell from my chin to my chest no matter how hard I tried to brush them away.

Someone knocked on the hall door to my room. Another set of three knocks and then silence. Seconds later, someone knocked on Stu's door. The doorknob shook and Kitty LeBlanc said, "Please, Viola, let me in. I know you're in there."

Although I wanted to collapse into Kitty's motherly embrace, I knew she'd have questions and I needed to be alone. I raised Stu's pillow to my face and was unexpectedly welcomed by the familiar tang of his lime-scented hair salve. Inhaling his fragrance lulled me back into thoughts of his tender lovemaking and, for the moment, my tears stopped.

We'd had something special, Stu and me. Plenty of troupers shared a bed when they were on the road, but Stu and I had found our romantic pace when we'd started rehearsing in New Jersey. As we crossed the country to reach the Pacific Coast, we'd perfected both our act and our love-making. Even though we'd agreed to not share a room, we slept together almost every night. Except last night. Stu's thoughts had been so tied up in something that he hadn't even looked up when I sat on his lap and purred at him to unroll my stockings.

I melted into the citrus scent escaping from Stu's pillow, imagining him beside me. Then, through his scent, I caught an entirely different perfume, something soaked in the sizzle of hot, sultry carnations. It wasn't my perfume; it wasn't one I'd wear in a million years, and even though I knew its name—L'Amour Bleu—my crushed heart began to beat harder and faster and my head was flush and hot.

I wanted to rip the case off the pillow and tear it to pieces. Stu and I'd never talked about what we had together, but I never thought he'd cheat on me. Not just cheat, but leave me to find the evidence.

I smacked the pillow hard and hurled it across the room, wishing I could do the same to whoever'd been in Stu's bed.

CHAPTER FIVE

Kitty walked two of her poodles along the alley outside the Pan's stage door. "I was worried about you last night, *ma chère*."

I'd slept twelve hours straight and stayed in bed for another three, too numb to start my day. Only my hope that Kitty had news or gossip got me out of bed and to the Pan before the one-thirty show.

But after ten minutes together, I hadn't asked Kitty if she knew who might have been in Stu's bed. Or who wore L'Amour Bleu. I wasn't ready to admit Stu had cheated on me.

As the petite Frenchwoman and I stepped through the alley, her son Pascal followed behind us. At nine years old, Pascal was almost as tall as Kitty, but he strained to hold the leashes of the seven dogs in his charge.

"I came to your room after our last walk," said Kitty. "But you—"

"I know . . ." I stepped on some colored strips of confetti from one of San Francisco's recent Welcome Home Soldiers events and felt a sense of satisfaction as I ground the paper into the pavement. Even remembering that the war was over didn't brighten the day for me. "But I needed to be alone."

No, not true. I needed Stu beside me, holding my hand, rubbing my shoulders, assuring me that he hadn't betrayed me, that he was still as true to me as the songs he'd written.

"We all got questioned last night about Stuart, after our spots in the evening show." Kitty rewarded her dogs with a snip of biscuit. "We couldn't leave until they were finished."

"Everyone?"

"Yes. The troupe, the orchestra, the stage crew, and even those working front-of-house."

My heavy heart lightened just a little. If *everyone* was questioned, maybe the police knew who killed Stu. "What did they ask?"

"Where I was between five-fifteen and six o'clock." Kitty made sure Pascal was not listening when she said, "I think that's when Stuart was killed."

"I had the rehearsal room from five-thirty to six," I said. I wanted Kitty to know.

"Did anyone see you?"

"Uh-huh." I took a breath before continuing. "Rocco."

"Rocco?"

But I wasn't ready to talk to her about Rocco. "Did they take you up to Mr. Z's office?"

Kitty studied me before answering. "They took us into Mr. Steccati's office, one at a time. Except for Mr. Merrick. Him, they escorted up to Mr. Z's office. With Lionel protesting the entire time."

Kitty shook her head, always critical about the special demands made by Lionel Fisk, the Sensational Audrey

Merrick's finicky manager. But how could I blame Kitty for her disdain? Lionel constantly reminded the troupe members that we wouldn't have an audience—or even have a job—if it weren't for Audrey's genius as a female impersonator.

Of course, Lionel's claim wasn't true; there was lots of talent in the troupe. But it sure seemed true that whatever Lionel demanded for Audrey, Lionel got. And the rest of the troupe resented both of them for it. Some members of the troupe even whispered backstage that Lionel and Audrey were lovers. Or that Lionel liked to dress up in Audrey's costumes and wigs.

It was great gossip, but who knew the real truth? Even so, Stu and I tried to mind our own business and always stayed out of Lionel's way.

"The police wanted to know about you and Stuart," Kitty offered gently. "If you had quarreled recently."

I thought the police believed I hadn't killed Stu, but that question sounded like they were trying to prove Stu and I were on the outs. That I might have reason to kill him.

Kitty looked away from her dog as it squatted regally. She turned her attention to me. "They asked me that three times. 'Did they fight a lot?'"

I breathed a little easier. A lot easier. Although Stu and I might fuss about tempo and volume and syncopation—just like all artistes do—we never fought.

"But of course, I told them nothing about it," she said.

Kitty responded in such a low, conspiratorial tone that I had to ask, "About what?"

"That argument you two had." She lowered her voice even more and put her hand on mine. "That blowup in Portland."

"What—"

"The argument at the hotel, the day after we got to town."

I tried to remember that week. I'd lost my raccoon collar —the one Blanche had given me last year for my twenty-sixth birthday—on the jump from Tacoma to Portland. Despite the rain showering the city, I searched for that collar every day by rewalking the path from the train station to the theater and the hotel room. I'd only seen Stu at rehearsal and on stage, but I'd found my collar.

"That wasn't me. I hardly saw Stu in Portland."

"It sounded like you, *ma chère*. And . . ." Her voice drifted off.

"And what?"

Kitty looked aside to Pascal, who was untwisting himself from the dogs' leashes. "The lovemaking in Stuart's hotel room. After the argument. That sounded like you also. I had to move Pascal's bed away from the wall; he was giggling from all of the bed bumping and moaning."

From my toes to my nose, my body flared with embarrassment. Yes, the walls in our cheap hotels were thin and Stu and I were enthusiastic lovers, but we'd always done whatever we could to maintain our privacy. We'd even mastered the rigors of silent sex. Or so I thought.

When I recalled the spicy scent of L'Amour Bleu on Stu's pillowcase, my embarrassment turned to anger. He must have cheated on me in Portland *and* San Francisco. I'd been too overwhelmed last night to react to his cheating, but this afternoon, I was ready to demand an explanation and an apology from him. Except he needed to be alive for that.

As much as I wanted to confront Stu, I reminded Kitty, "Stu and I never fought. You know that."

“I do, and I was surprised. For a moment, I thought it was Jeanette and Rocco.” She shook her head and looked heavenward. The diLorenzos’ gin-fueled shouting matches and follow-up lovemaking were a constant source of irritation for the troupe.

“Rocco and Jeanette pick fights with each other just to make up,” I said. “And even then, they still seem to hate each other.” And almost everyone else in the troupe.

As soon as Stu and I joined the troupe, we both saw that Jeanette and Rocco had alienated everyone else. Maybe it was Jeanette’s complete disdain for sharing a dressing room, or maybe it was her constant quips that she was destined to replace Mary Pickford. Or maybe it was how Rocco belittled every man and eyed every woman. Rocco’d even picked on Kitty’s poodles, threatening to dose them with rat poison if they bothered him backstage. Everyone seemed to blame Rocco’s crudeness on being Italian or his love of gin, but after I saw him shake a box of rat poison in Kitty’s face, I knew his temper was his own.

“I don’t suppose you heard what the argument was about?” I asked Kitty.

She shook her head. “I wish I had, if it would help you out.”

I knew I should ask Kitty more about Stu’s Portland lovemaking, maybe even share what I’d learned about his infidelity, but my whole body dragged with defeat. I was about to brace myself against the brick walls for support, but then I remembered how many dogs and men had saluted it. So instead of lingering over my broken love life, I did exactly what Stu would have told me to do if he were here: get back to business.

“Mr. Z said I need to replace Stu before I can go back on

stage," I told Kitty. "But I've never looked for a piano player before. Stu's been my one and only."

Kitty put her arm around me. "I liked Stuart very much; I think you know that. But you're the talent of the act. You're the sizzle."

I'd heard it before, that Stu was lucky to write songs for a singer like me, but I'd always reminded everyone that we were a team. Partners. Equals.

This time, when I got back on stage, I'd be the boss. And I wouldn't give my heart to my piano player. No, not this time.

"How do I even start to replace him?" My mind flew to members of the troupe who played piano. But even if I were the kind of girl to poach from another act, there was so much more to Stu than just his piano playing.

No one put together words like Stu. No one crafted a story that twisted your emotions to shreds in sixteen bars and then, in the chorus, tore your heart out. Stu's lyrics were the most important part of our act, no matter how Kitty downplayed them. What did she know anyway? As talented as her dogs might be, she and her dogs had the one spot, working in silence as the audience settled in their seats. Before the *real* show began.

Still, Kitty had been working in music halls and vaudeville for years. She knew the ropes, and she didn't fail me now. "Go see the Pan's talent booker on the sixth floor. He'll know someone. Or try the Orpheum booker down the street."

"Wouldn't a booker charge—"

"*Merde!*"

Lionel Fisk stood at the alley entrance, his feet fused to a pile of poodle poo. The largest of Kitty's dogs had escaped from Pascal's grasp and was pawing at Lionel, leaving muddy marks on his suit.

Kitty whistled and the dog trotted to her. Lionel wiped his shoes on the ground and then headed toward Pascal, who was trying to hide the poodles behind his slim figure. Kitty marched to her son and met Lionel face to face. Just over five feet, she put her hands on her hips and dared the foot-taller Lionel to take another step.

Perhaps Lionel understood how fiercely Kitty protected her own, because he backed away. Still, he warned her, "Keep your dirty animals away from me before one of them becomes dogmeat."

Wise woman that she was, Kitty allowed Lionel to have the first and last words. She even gave him a few minutes inside the Pan before following him.

"*Bon chance*, Viola," Kitty opened the stage door wide for her son and dogs. "If I hear more, I'll let you know."

And so I set out to find a new piano player, stepping carefully to avoid any poodle poo.

♫

Market Street was crowded with motorcars, electric streetcars, and even a few horse-drawn wagons. Most of the men wore uniforms in varying shades of army green or navy blue. Most of the women wore black. Many people still wore large white cotton masks across their noses and mouths to protect themselves against the influenza. *Good luck,* I wished them. *I wore a mask and still almost died.*

I ran across Market Street and turned to inspect the Pan marquee. Yes, my name was still up there. Maybe being laid off really was temporary.

I was so relieved to see *Viola Vermillion, Red-Hot Blues Chanteuse* that the world seemed to brighten—just a bit—around me. I stood on the sidewalk for seconds, hugging myself with hope. Maybe my path to stardom was still before me—the path to being the singer Blanche and Stu told me I was.

Except that I needed a new piano player. A booking agent might come through, but he'd charge me for the referral. And I'd heard horror stories about agents who demanded money before they found the talent. *Months* before they found the talent.

I couldn't wait that long to get back on stage, so to the newspaper office I went.

I read the local papers—usually retrieved from underneath one of the theater seats—every day to make sure the papers reviewed my act. Since arriving in town, the *Examiner*'d given me the most ink, but the *Chronicle* printed my photograph *and* gave me a headline: *Miss Viola Vermillion, Vivacious Vaudevillian.*

I found the *Chronicle* building quickly enough and headed toward the *Place Your Advertisement Here* sign. Even though I was there for a Help Wanted ad, all I thought about were obituaries. Stu should have one, and I should write it. I should tell the world about what a wonderful lyricist and piano player he was. How he helped bring my voice back after the influenza and got me back on stage. I wanted to write all of that in Stu's obituary, but I couldn't—not today. My heart was too sore.

As I reached the sign, a man in short sleeves leaned toward the counter grillwork. "Looking for love? Selling your stocks? Buying books?"

"Pursuing piano players," I replied. "How soon can I get my ad printed?"

"Deadline's passed, doll," he moaned sympathetically before pushing a pen and paper toward me. "But if you finish in five minutes, I will personally get your advertisement in tomorrow morning's edition."

I took the form and pencil he passed me and wrote *Help Needed: Big-Time Music Conductor.*

Sure, *Big-Time* was a stretch. With a couple of dozen theaters in Canada and the West, the Pantages Circuit was strictly small-time. Still, Stu and I had Big-Time plans for our act. We'd leave the Pantages Circuit for the Orpheum and then move up to the Keith-Albee. From there, I'd headline the Palace Theater in New York City.

The pencil scratched plenty as I scribbled, *Talented piano player.*

No one would ever be as good at Stu, but I had to hope.

Vaudeville stage experience required.

Naturally.

Excellent pay and management.

I cringed slightly. Nobody got rich playing the seven spot, and I'd never managed anyone in my life. But Stu's voice in my head told me that boldness was better than honesty.

I finished the ad and paid my money. Now that one piece of business was done, it was time for another. "Where's the closest pawn shop?"

The man in short sleeves answered like he heard the question hourly. "Out the door, turn right onto Kearny, and walk two blocks. Feldman's. Tell 'em, Sam at the *Chron* sent you."

I reached Feldman's in ten minutes. The large glass window was broad and packed with goods. After searching inside through the rows of musical instruments, suitcases, and magic lanterns, I saw what I needed in a locked case on the back wall.

Before the shop owner tempted me with something from his case of jewelry, I asked, "What's the action like on that Savage 1907?"

♫

As much as I despised Mademoiselle Savage for her role in Stu's death, I still needed to protect myself.

With my new gun—I named her Madame Savage—buttoned in the side pocket of my handbag, I slipped into a moving picture show to see Harold Lloyd's five-reeler *Be My Wife*. I was yearning to distract and comfort myself, but the piano accompanist butchered every tune, and an actor in the first reel had a slight resemblance to Stu. I cried my way through the rest of the reels.

After the picture show, I walked down the street and paid ten cents at the Orpheum. I sat through the entire fourteen-act show to hear Grace La Rue, their songbird-of-the-week and my competition. I left with my confidence high. I hadn't recovered all of my verve, but I certainly had more sizzle than Grace. My costumes were better than hers, too. I'd had mine specially made in New York City, in materials that shined, shimmered, and showed a significant length of my leg. It cost a pretty penny, but Stu said it was well worth it because sex sells in vaudeville.

I slipped backstage at the Pantages about a half hour after the evening show ended, already fighting the shivers. The ghost light stood sentry in the middle of the stage, and even though everyone should have been gone, I heard dice hitting against a wall somewhere in the back. Good. The stagehands or orchestra were not far away, gambling. Only a crazy person would want to be alone in a dark theater late at night. Especially after someone was murdered in it.

I didn't need long in the dressing room. I'd left the theater yesterday without putting my costumes and makeup away, and I didn't want to make it any easier for the dressing room bandit to steal my stuff.

It was just as dark downstairs in the dressing room as it was upstairs, and I turned on every light I found. I greeted each frock, fan, and headband on my costume rack with an affectionate stroke. Someone had placed a folded newspaper on my dressing table, and I picked it up, anticipating a glowing Sunday review of my act. But when I saw the heading DEATH NOTICES, I let the paper fall from my fingers.

Stu's notice couldn't be in there—who else could write it but me?—but I was still tempted to look down the page, just to make sure. But then I realized there should be *something* about Stu in the newspaper. Or something about *someone* being killed in the Pantages. As I rustled through the paper to find that news, the smooth glissando of a solitary piano floated into the dressing room. I held the paper stiffly, wondering what I'd really heard, when there came another glissando and then an obvious vamp.

I knew the song right away. It was "Till We Meet Again," a love ballad written during the war, and one of Blanche's favorites. When the verse came around, I couldn't help but sing:

Tho' goodbye means the birth of a tear drop
Hello means the birth of a smile.
And the smile will erase the tear blighting trace
When we meet in the after awhile.

Before memories of Blanche and all the friends I'd lost during the war overwhelmed me, the pianist launched into another song. I recovered from my reverie with a bolt. It was a song Stu had written for me, one I'd performed the last week of our Seattle show: "After You're Gone." As the piano player vamped to the chorus, I whispered the words.

After you've gone and left me crying
After you've gone
There's no denying you'll feel blue
You'll feel sad
You'll miss the bestest pal you've ever had

Every note was played just as Stu would play it, but Stu and I'd never recorded that song, and we'd never played it in San Francisco. No one had the piano music to it except for Stu. Nobody here should know this song, and they certainly shouldn't be able to play it with such gusto.

What the hell was going on?

I walked up the stairs to the stage floor, reassured by the weight of Madame Savage in my handbag. Blanche had warned me to be careful in a theater—she'd never trusted a stagehand closer than she could kick one—and despite my confusion, I felt oddly confident.

The stage was the same as it had been earlier: curtains opened to the house, a single ghost light in the center. A few stagehands had emerged from wherever they'd been throwing dice and stood open-mouthed, gazing at the darkened orchestra pit. I motioned to one of them to turn on the house lights, but he was planted in place, hardly able to make a slow sign of the cross along his chest. He might have thought Stu'd come back to haunt the Pantages, but the music was much too vibrant, too confident for a dead man.

Although the house was dark, I knew my path. Down the stairs to the pit I went, feeling my way along the wall. Piano light spilled up on the music stand, finally illuminating the man at the piano.

CHAPTER SIX

It wasn't Stu; of course, it wasn't Stu. No matter how hard I closed my eyes and wished that Stu—or his ghost, even—were seated at the piano, it wasn't him.

But I had no idea who the man on the piano bench was, and I couldn't imagine how he'd learned to play "After You're Gone." All I could do was stare at him: younger than Stu and me, almost a kid, golden blond, and pale. He'd removed his jacket and rolled the sleeves of his white shirt up to his elbows. His muscled forearms seemed to be the only thing he had in common with Stu. I wondered if he also had Stu's long fingers and if his hands stretched a full octave and two notes.

My mouth was dry and I swallowed hard. "Who are you?"

"Jimmy Harrigan, ma'am." He drawled slightly in a Southern accent I couldn't place. "I hear you're looking for a piano player."

Jimmy Harrigan slid off the piano stool, grabbed one of the chairs in the pit, and set it up on stage a few feet in front of me. He expected me to sit down, but I was too wary. I stood as firmly as my legs would allow, ready to bolt if I needed to.

Without additional introduction, the kid sat down at the piano and ran through the songs in my act. "Kiss Mama, Kiss Papa"; "For Crying Out Loud"; "You're a Good Old Car"; he knew them all.

The shivers I'd been trying to manage since I arrived at the theater finally caught up with me. I bundled my coat around my chest, wishing it were as strong as an armored tank and could repel anyone who tried to replace Stu in my life. Because he was one-of-a-kind and always would be.

The kid ran through eight of my songs before I stopped him. "Come with me."

"Yes, ma'am." His response was so crisp I almost expected him to salute.

The kid met me in the wings, sleeves rolled down, jacket on, and a fedora in his hands. He followed me downstairs to the ladies' dressing room, where I sank into my chair. Before he even thought I'd let him sit down, I said, "Where've you played, kid?"

"Around."

"That's all?"

"All around." He seemed pleased with his answer, lightly hanging his fedora on his index finger.

"You know my songs, that's for sure."

"I've heard your act a few times."

"I only placed an advertisement today. How did you find out—"

"Everyone was whispering about it last night at the seven-thirty show. That your piano player was dead and that's why you missed the show. Which made me realize you needed another one." He cast his eyes downward before asking, "So do I have a job or not?"

This was like manna from heaven, having a talented piano player show up just when I needed him most. But I didn't believe in manna, at least not for me. Losing Stu had turned my world upside down, and there was something strange about this kid's sudden appearance. I didn't have the stamina to imagine what it was. But my gut—which Blanche had always told me to trust—told me I shouldn't replace Stu so quickly.

I held firm. "I'm holding auditions Thursday morning."

"I need the money tonight." With that confession, a little of the kid's cockiness evaporated. The lights flickered in the dressing room, and he looked around to make sure he hadn't touched anything.

We were interrupted by a stagehand's shout. "Locking up in five, Miss Vermillion."

The kid took a step in my direction. "Whaddya say, Miss Vermillion? How about a job?"

I hadn't remembered my new Savage until the kid stepped toward me. Now I wished I'd let the pawnshop owner load it like he offered. I didn't feel threatened, but I didn't feel exactly safe. I was sure the stagehands would come to help me if I yelled, but I preferred to fix my own problems.

"I'm holding auditions on Thursday morning," I repeated.

Jimmy put his hat on his head a little too firmly. "Then I'll be back Thursday."

The lights flickered again. I listened as the kid walked upstairs to the stage floor. I knew the hands would make sure he left the theater, but I still waited in my dressing room for a while, making plans to clean and load Madame Savage as soon as possible. Even though all I wanted was to sleep for another twelve hours.

When I left the theater, the kid wasn't waiting for me. But Detective Petersen of the San Francisco Police Department was.

♫

I joined the detective under the lamplight at the end of the alley.

"I've been looking for you," he said.

A sudden hope spread through me. "You found out who murdered Stu?"

"No," he replied. "I found out a few other things. Can I walk you back to your hotel?"

"You'll tell me what you've found?"

The detective stepped toward Market Street like a well-trained workhorse who knew the way home. I had no choice but to walk with him.

Despite my glances, the detective remained silent. I understood his technique; the best way to get someone to tell you something, to get them to spill the beans, was to be silent yourself. But after sparring with Jimmy Harrigan, I was too exhausted to play the detective's game. The kid's ghostly appearance and prowess with Stu's music rattled me. How could he play Stu's music so well? How could he know I was going to be at the Pan tonight?

As we reached the Hotel Henry, the detective finally spoke. "It turns out your piano player's name wasn't Stu Wiley. It was Stuart Wilson."

"So?" I clutched onto the door handle with all the determination I had, hiding my surprise. Stu'd never mentioned changing his name. "Stu had a stage name. I have a stage name. Almost everyone in the troupe has a stage name. There's no law against it, is there?"

"No law against *that*, but having an alias to evade the law is another thing entirely."

"Stu was evading the police?" The police had to have it wrong. There must be two Stu Wilsons. My Stu'd always been a straight arrow. Aboveboard. At least he'd been until I'd inhaled the carnation fragrance on his pillowcase and Kitty told me about his cheating in Portland.

"Did you know he was from San Francisco?" asked Petersen.

"He was evading the *San Francisco* police?" This time I couldn't hide my surprise. We'd both known from the beginning that San Francisco was on our itinerary, and he'd never mentioned he knew the city. "What for?"

A bright light illuminated the area in front of the elevator, and I stared at the beam, focusing on it like a ship seeking out a lighthouse, hoping it would keep me from crashing into little pieces. How many more secrets had Stu kept from me?

"Did you know?" the detective persisted.

"That he changed his name and was from San Francisco? No. How did you find out?"

"He had a postcard of Seattle in his coat pocket, addressed to—"

"If Stu was from here," I said, more to myself than the detective, "that means someone from here might have killed him."

"It could," he said. "But it also means something else."

"What's that?"

"Stuart Wilson's mother wants to see you."

"Stu has a mother here?" And then I knew. "The postcard was addressed to Stu's mother?"

"It was, and I'll come by for you tomorrow morning at seven."

"You'll what? For what?"

"Because Mrs. Wilson wants to meet you."

"She does?" Meeting Stu's mother was too much to think about. It was hard enough to lose Stuart, but what would I say to his mother? "What if I don't want to meet her?"

"Would you really refuse to meet a mother who just lost her son?"

I had so many responses on the tip of my tongue. In the end, I just said, "But I don't wake up until ten."

"Fine with me," said the detective. "But if you don't meet me right here at seven tomorrow morning, I'll come up to your room and haul you out."

CHAPTER SEVEN

From a darkened alley across from the Hotel Henry, Jimmy Harrigan watched as the thin curtain of room 601 illuminated with soft yellow light. Viola's figure appeared between the curtain and the lamp and he steeled his eyes. She raised the sash a few inches, but not enough to lean over the ledge.

Jimmy released his breath, not even knowing he was holding it. He hadn't taken her for a jumper, but you never knew. He still wasn't certain that ambushing her with Stuart's music had been the right play, but he didn't have much of a choice. Someone had murdered her piano player and she was alone in the world. Joining her act and keeping her on stage was the best way to protect her and make sure she didn't leave San Francisco.

Jimmy'd been following Viola for weeks but had never gotten as close to her as he had tonight. On stage, she appeared vivacious, in control, commanding. Only up close did he see the dark circles under her eyes and the fatigue in her shoulders.

As Viola turned from the window, Jimmy could only imagine what she did next. Like all the other times he'd watched her, his imagination didn't let him down. Was she rolling down her stockings? Working off her corset? (If she wore a corset, and Jimmy's two bits were on *no*.) Securing her money belt underneath her mattress? He lingered on the last image, wondering how much money she had now that Stuart was gone.

There'd been six whole paragraphs of information about Stuart's death in today's *San Francisco Chronicle*, but none of them mentioned if his wallet had been emptied or stolen. The article did mention that the police questioned everyone who had been at the theater around the time of Stuart's death, although Jimmy knew of at least one person who had eluded the police. Besides himself, of course.

A few minutes after Viola turned off her light, Jimmy entered the Hotel Henry and sprinted up the broad dogleg staircase that wrapped around the tiny elevator. He was almost to the third floor when the elevator cage began to chug downward. He hid in the staircase's dark corner, ready to follow the elevator down if Viola were inside.

As the bottom of the elevator came into sight, a man's voice cooed, "How's my baby tonight? Feeling better?"

Unable to place the voice, Jimmy strained to see the man's footwear and who was with him. The last thing he expected was a single pair of scuffed brown shoes. Or that the solitary man's sweet talk would get bolder. "You stick with Daddy, baby-mine. I'll take good care of you."

Jimmy finally saw the man's back, but his clothing—brown pants, a worn plaid overcoat, and a brown hat—told him nothing. He followed down the stairs as the elevator descended and was at the top of the last flight when the elevator opened on the first floor. A terrier mutt wobbled uneasily onto the worn carpet, the man in brown shoes and pants just behind him.

Jimmy was sure the terrier was Champ the Drunk Dog from the Pantages show. Which should make the baby-talking lover-man his owner, "Officer" Owen Tuck. As Jimmy watched the two walk slowly through the lobby, he remembered that something had happened to Champ or Tuck before yesterday's matinee. Something that prevented them from performing, something the ticket seller couldn't talk about to Jimmy. That had been the same show where Viola's spot had been cut to three songs. It was also Stuart Wilson's last show.

Of course Stuart's murder worried him—had kept Jimmy up and thinking most of last night—but finding Stuart's murderer wasn't his job. Finding, following, and protecting Viola was.

Jimmy resumed climbing the stairs. He reached Viola's floor and paused outside her room, watching the space under the door for any light, listening for any sounds of activity. He did the same at Stuart's door. If she went into Stuart's room, she went silently and in darkness. Satisfied that she was in for the night, Jimmy walked down the hallway, past the rooms of the other troupers, and took the stairs up to his own room on the seventh floor.

CHAPTER EIGHT

Detective Petersen knocked on my hotel room at 6:45 a.m., and I was sure I was the only trouper awake on the floor. Despite the early hour, he was shaved clean and his suit was sharply pressed. But what I noticed most were his shoes, highly reflective and probably spit-polished, just like a soldier preparing for inspection.

I'd thrown away my one black dress before Stu and I left New Jersey, and I had nothing suitable to visit a mother in mourning. So I wore the most modest ensemble I possessed, an orchid-colored georgette dress, a matching feathered felt hat, and my raccoon-collared coat. After a short debate with myself, I decided to keep Madame Savage in my handbag. I placed a few bullets in my pocket for good measure.

I'd fallen asleep quickly last night but woke up when I heard someone shuffling past my door—the not-unfamiliar sound of someone heading for the washroom at the end of the hallway. My thoughts ricocheted from wondering who was out there, to Detective Petersen's information, to curiosity about Stu's mother, to the mouthy blond kid who knew all of Stu's songs, to knowing I'd give anything to back up against Stu's warm body, to wondering why anyone would kill Stu.

So even though I'd seen him late last night, I greeted the detective with, "Did you find out who killed Stu yet?"

Petersen shook his head.

As we took the elevator down to the lobby, I asked, "Where are we going, and why so early in the morning?"

I was surprised when he actually answered. "We have to catch a boat."

"A boat? To where? How long will we be gone?" I looked around the elevator cage, ready to grasp onto the grillwork with both hands and refuse to leave. "Because I have a matinee—"

Which is when I remembered I didn't have a matinee to perform, or an evening show either. I couldn't work until I got a new piano player.

The detective guided me out of the hotel and through the light fog to Powell Street and then up to O'Farrell, where he led me to an inside bench at the front of a waiting cable car. The car quickly filled up with men, and I knew they were looking me over, as if my hennaed hair made me some exotic creature. I was used to being watched on stage and even during my daily jaunts about town, but this close of an inspection in the morning unnerved me. Especially when I couldn't turn on my stage smile and invite them to catch my act at the Pan.

Yet despite my discomfort, as our car crept up the torturous hills, the bell clanging twice at every intersection, I was excited to see more of the city. I'd already seen a little of it when Stu and I arrived last week. Fresh off the Shasta Route, we'd checked in with the Pan's booking manager, met with the orchestra leader, unpacked in our dressing rooms, and gotten our rooms at the Hotel Henry. Then we strolled our new temporary city.

I'd been amazed at the height of the hills, the bold sunlight on the white, stuccoed buildings, even the crumbling dome of the Palace of Fine Arts. Throughout our rambling, San Francisco revealed itself as a marvel of beauty and vigor. But how could Stu have walked around beautiful San Francisco with me for hours, never telling me he was from here? And what made him keep his mother a secret?

The cable car turned left and ascended a narrow street. I turned to Petersen, figuring I could pull some piece of information from him. "You said last night that Stu changed his name to evade the San Francisco Police. I want to know why."

To my surprise, Petersen responded. "Stuart Wilson was the son of the lighthouse keeper on Alcatraz Island, and he worked there—"

"Wait a minute. What's Alcatraz Island?"

"It's an army disciplinary barracks in the bay."

"Stu lived on an army island in the bay?"

Petersen looked at me like I was the slowest student in the class. Then he repeated himself. "Stuart Wilson was the son of the lighthouse keeper on Alcatraz Island, and he disappeared on December 4, 1915. He was attending the closing night of the Pan Pacific Expo in the city." He nodded as though the Expo was still going on, just over his left shoulder. "He never made it back to the island. Weeks later, a body fitting his description washed up on Baker Beach." Petersen's eyes eased toward the general direction of the bay.

The detective had spoken four sentences in a row. He

was on a roll and I wasn't going to stop him with questions about Baker Beach.

"The body had been in the water too long to know who it was for certain. But a packet wrapped in waterproof material and holding some of Stuart's music washed up on the same beach a day later."

"Everyone thought Stu drowned?" A shiver of sadness ran through me and I slumped against the wooden seat. "Everyone here thought he died back in 1915?"

"Mostly. Except I sent photos and descriptions of Stuart to police stations across the country, trying to locate him, just in case he was alive. But now that I know he changed his name, that he willfully evaded the law, I'm wondering if he purposely faked his death, too."

The cable car turned right and descended the hill quickly. We ascended again and stopped at the top of the hill. Finally, just as the sun came out, the bay waters peeked through at the bottom of the street. In the water, I saw a small island dominated by a massive stone building perched like a fortress.

Petersen followed my gaze. "That island out there is Alcatraz. And that big building's the disciplinary barracks."

"Stu lived on an island?" Even in the distance, the tall white lighthouse looked beaten and worn. I couldn't imagine my lighthearted Stu living on such a forlorn rock.

"You didn't know Stuart Wilson that well, did you?" Petersen stood up as the cable car made its final stop.

"I didn't know Stuart *Wilson* at all," I whispered to the chilly wind drifting toward me from the bay. "And now it feels like I didn't know Stu Wiley, either."

♫

At the end of the cable car line, the detective walked me to a pier a few blocks away. Within minutes, we were on the *General McDowell II,* a small white boat that tilted dangerously as we came aboard.

As the boat chopped through the bay, I held down my hat with both hands, trying to protect the curls I'd carefully shaped at dawn. Little rays of sunlight cut through the fog, shedding just enough bright light that the boat almost sparkled, but the air was cold and the wind stiff. Even my raccoon collar couldn't keep out the chill. I wished I'd brought a thick scarf to protect my neck and prayed the weather wouldn't harm my throat. It was hell singing on stage with a bad cold.

The island emerged from the fog, the white lighthouse on the plateau at the very top. I tried to imagine what being the son of a lighthouse keeper was like and how it felt to live on an island, being teased every day by a beautiful city like San Francisco. If the Stu of 1915 was anything like the man I knew, he'd hate being on that island, hate knowing there were theaters and moving pictures and nightclubs so close, yet so far away. He'd hate it so much he'd do anything he could to escape.

Suddenly, I hated that stern island. I didn't care who wanted to talk to me—I didn't want to step foot on it. I grabbed a rail, and as Detective Petersen approached, braced my arms against my sides.

The detective stood back for a few moments before speaking. "I found the body back in '15. It was just before New Year's and I had to come out to the island in a rainstorm to tell Stuart's parents." He paused, ensuring that he had my full attention. "I've never seen a woman so bereft at losing a child. And I've done plenty of notifications since then."

I knew he was talking about the war, about having to visit family after family to inform them that their son had been killed. I couldn't imagine how awful that part of Petersen's job was, but that was his grief to shoulder, not mine. Mine was that I'd lost my lover and our life in vaudeville.

"It's only natural that Mrs. Wilson wants to see you," he said. "He was her only child and she didn't lose him just once, she lost him twice. Put yourself in her place. She just wants to meet you."

But I couldn't put myself in her place. I hadn't even known Stu had a mother until last night.

"Or put yourself in Stuart's place." The detective seemed to read my thoughts. "Don't you think he'd want you to comfort his mother if you could?"

I hated the detective for suggesting he knew what Stu wanted. Then I hated him more because he was right. I had been thinking the same thing about Stu, almost since the hour that I found him dead. What did he want me to do? Did he want me to keep performing? Did he want me to trust his music to another piano player? Or did he—as he'd seemed to whisper in my ear this morning—really believe I could find out who murdered him?

Once on the island, the detective and I followed a guard up a hairpin path. I stopped frequently on the trip up the hill, slow of breath and needing air, and also out of concern for my poor Cuban heels. I'd never walked on such rough ground in these shoes, and I was sure I'd have to get them resoled before wearing them again.

Finally, after the toughest walk of my life, the three of us reached three buildings that looked almost like houses.

"Officer's Row," reported Petersen.

A sentry outside one of the houses looked me over and opened the door wide. "In here, miss."

Petersen strolled away from me, cigarette in hand.

I stood alone in the foyer. A large hall tree hugged most of one wall and I took a hard look at myself in the mirror. The curls that had so gently circled my face earlier had been blown into snarls, and my cheeks were as red as my still-rouged lips. I sneered at my grotesque image, my cauldron of emotions—surprise, curiosity, and sorrow at losing Stu—perfectly suiting my disturbed appearance.

Still, the woman in the mirror needed a plan. I had no idea what Stu's mother wanted to know, but I was already feeling stingy. My memories of Stu were *mine* and I wanted to hoard every one of them, keep them all to myself. Besides, would anything I tell her make her feel better? Could anything lessen the pain of losing her son?

Then a young woman's voice called out, "We're in here."

I followed the voice into the nearest room, where two women—one old enough to be Stu's mother, the other young enough to be his sister—sat side by side on a green settee. Both women were dressed in black, with white lace collars and cuffs attached to their mourning. The older woman's head hung down and I couldn't see her face at all, couldn't tell if she favored Stu or not. I had no idea who the girl was—the detective had said that Mrs. Wilson had only one child. The girl held Mrs. Wilson's hand firmly in hers, as though keeping her anchored to the furniture.

The girl nodded toward a low stool a few feet from the

settee, but I remained standing. I wondered if she'd selected the heavy, masculine furniture upholstered in battered burgundy or the dark curtains that shrouded the windows. I wondered if she ever touched the small grand piano, covered with a damask cloth, the keyboard closed up tight. It was a harsh, uncomfortable setting for two women in mourning. Only the sparking logs in the fireplace added any warmth.

"I'm Dorothy Garrard. My father's the commandant of Alcatraz." The young woman addressed me as though she were interviewing a new maid. "And this is Mrs. Margaret Wilson, Stuart's mother."

Despite being in this strange house on this strange island, I was sure of my opening line. "I'm Viola Vermillion." I made my entrance, stopping in front of Stu's mother, offering my hand. "I'm very sorry for your loss, Mrs. Wilson."

Stu's mother looked up, her tears so silent and soft they were almost invisible. Dorothy leaned against the older woman as if her young body could absorb all of Mrs. Wilson's pain. She pulled a handkerchief from inside her lace cuff and dabbed at Stu's mother's tears. It was obvious that Mrs. Wilson was too upset to meet anyone, that any words I might offer her were no comfort.

Dorothy whispered a few words before helping Stu's mother stand. Mrs. Wilson listed against the younger woman as though she'd been worn down by years of mourning.

I stepped back and let them pass.

Mrs. Wilson turned around suddenly, her hollow eyes staring at me, her lips—looking just like Stu's, if that was really possible—moving in mumbles, as if she wanted to say something but had forgotten how to speak. Dorothy clutched Mrs. Wilson to her side. She nodded once more at the low stool before walking Stu's mother into the hallway.

Dorothy wanted me to sit and wait for her, but I walked over to the baby grand and a pile of handwritten sheet music. The corners of the sheets were curled and the penciled notes and lyrics softened from years of handling: *San Francisco, you lovely city. We're all fond of San Francisco.* I knew that handwriting; these were Stu's lyrics and notes. After fingering through the songs, I knew none of them would have been suitable for the stage—even four years ago. But they definitely showed his early enthusiasm.

Dorothy quietly joined me at the piano, explaining the obvious. "Those were Stuart's."

I listened hard to those three words, trying to hear something in their inflection. Did she love Stu or did she hate him? Were they friends or rivals? Had she even lived here, known Stuart, before he went missing?

Dorothy reached in front of me to collect the sheet music I'd been looking through. I caught her fragrance, a strong, harsh odor that could hardly be called perfume, an odor that reminded me instantly of the cramped influenza wards of St. Joseph's Hospital. I edged away from her, needing to erase the memories of being locked up with those other dying women, but Dorothy put her hand on mine to keep me in place.

"Did he . . . did Stuart ever talk about me?"

"No." I wasn't sure why, but I hoped the denial hurt her. How important could she have been if Stu never mentioned her?

But the truth was that Stu hadn't mentioned anyone from his past, and I'd never asked him. I realized now how selfish that was of me. Stu knew all about my sister

Blanche's comedic singing talents, about how she'd given up vaudeville to make munitions during the war, and how she'd died months before he and I met. The most I knew about his past was that he'd had at least one lover—someone self-centered and even a little cruel—although he never mentioned her by name. I wondered now if that lover was Dorothy.

A loud whistle pierced the silence. When it ended after a few seconds, Dorothy said, "The *General McDowell's* heading back to the city. You should be on it."

I had never been so grateful to be dismissed, until I realized I'd only been here for ten minutes. Was that the plan all along? Just to let Mrs. Wilson have a look at me?

Before I could find out, Dorothy asked, "Did you leave Stuart's things at the dock?"

"His things?" I couldn't even imagine what she was asking about. And who cared about his things when Stu was dead?

"His books and papers and letters. You were supposed to bring them today."

"I was?" I'd been cocooned in my own grief, but I would have remembered if Petersen told me to pack up and bring Stu's things today. Not that I would have done it.

Dorothy scowled with such frustration that I finally understood why I'd been summoned to Alcatraz today. Stu's mother didn't want me here; Dorothy did. Because Stu had something Dorothy wanted, and I had everything that belonged to him.

"All of Stu's things are at the hotel." I laid his music on the piano and headed toward the door, where the sentry stood at attention. The whistle blasted again, and I guessed I'd need to rush down the hill to make the boat. I also guessed there was only one way Dorothy would let me leave her father's house.

"What do you want?" I asked her.

"Only what's mine. I wrote Stuart a letter and I want it back."

It took a few seconds for me to understand what she'd said, and then a few seconds more to *really* understand. "You wrote him a letter when everyone thought he was dead? You knew he was alive?"

"He wrote to me first. Last month."

"Did you let his mother know?" I remembered how Detective Petersen had found out Stu was from San Francisco because of a postcard in his pocket addressed to his mother. Once I recalled that, I didn't wait for her answer. "You didn't, did you? You let her believe her son was dead."

"No, I didn't tell her." The girl faltered a bit. "She's . . . she's got a bad heart. I didn't want to shock her. That's why you were supposed to bring Stu's things today . . . to help her through it."

And then I realized that Stuart's things really did belong to his mother. I'd need to go through them, pack them up, deliver them to her. It was the right thing to do. Was this what Detective Petersen had really meant by *putting myself in her place*?

But that didn't mean I had to give Dorothy any satisfaction. "Now that I know about your letter, you can be sure I'll go through his things. And I'll let his mother know what I find."

"No! *You* can't go through his things! You're not family!"

She couldn't be more wrong. "Yes, that's exactly who I am."

I settled my sternest look on her, the look that reduced

flirtatious stagehands to shivers. "I'll read everything and give what I find to Stu's mother. Because she probably wants to read it also."

I didn't wait for Dorothy to respond; I didn't wait for her to protest. I left the house quickly, hoping that walking downhill would be easier than walking up.

CHAPTER NINE

The *General McDowell II* launched from Alcatraz and I planted myself in front of Detective Petersen, balancing precariously as the boat rolled beneath me. The wind picked up as we crossed the bay, chilling my cheeks, freezing my ears, and making my head ache like I'd just listened to a pair of bagpipers auditioning.

"Where were you?"

"I was paying my respects to Stu's father. He couldn't leave the lighthouse." The detective folded his handkerchief into small quarters and wiped his nose. "It wasn't easy for Mr. Wilson, four years ago. He had to identify the body we found on the beach."

"It wasn't easy for me either," I told him. "I found Stu dead. Really dead."

The detective gave me a look like he knew what it was like to find someone you loved dead. It was almost like seeing a reflection in a mirror; he knew how I felt, I was sure of it. Which gave me the courage to press on.

"Was Dorothy Garrard on Alcatraz in 1915? Did you talk to *her* when Stu went missing?"

"She was just a girl, but yes, I talked to her, and she didn't know anything."

She didn't tell you anything was probably the real truth. Being a girl had never stopped me from knowing things. Or from getting into trouble because of what I knew.

After the boat landed, the detective and I walked together toward the cable car. I realized I'd met my obligation to Stu, and I could go anywhere I wanted. Like that cozy saloon on the corner. They had to have a cup of hot coffee—maybe with a slug of whiskey—to warm me up.

Except that I was warming up to a new idea.

"Is it possible someone from Alcatraz killed Stu? Someone who didn't like him back in 1915?"

"He was killed in the Pantages vaudeville house, so it's more likely someone working in the theater killed him." The detective hopped on the cable car and I knew the only way to get more information was to take the hand he offered and join him. This time there was no room inside, so we were forced to freeze outside—and I silently bade farewell to the cheery Buena Vista Saloon and the coffee I wanted so badly.

"We investigated Stu's disappearance as a murder," the detective said as the car climbed a steep hill. I grabbed the brass pole next to me and clung on for dear life. Petersen swayed, leaning away from me. "The commandant—Dorothy's father—insisted that we did. But we couldn't find any reason someone would want to kill him."

"What if you missed something, someone, back then?"

"Four years is a long time to hold a grudge."

"Not in vaudeville it ain't." The words came out of my mouth before I thought them through. It was true, of course.

I'd heard stories about lifelong grudges between performers. "But that still doesn't mean it's one of us that killed him."

The car crested the hill and I glanced back. Alcatraz was lightly shrouded in fog, although I could see the outline of the buildings and the slow rotation of the lighthouse lamp. I still couldn't imagine my Stu living there.

The car stopped at a large green square of park and the detective jumped down.

"You're leaving?" I asked.

"Hall of Justice is that way." He nodded. "End of the line is just a few blocks away."

"What happens now? How soon will you catch Stu's murderer?" I remembered Mr. Z's confident boast about the police. Did they really always get their man?

"As soon as I find out who can't keep their stories straight," he replied, "that's when we'll catch him."

♫

As soon as I returned to the hotel, I went into Stu's room, pulling open the curtains as far as possible. I stood in the soft sunlight, flexing my hands over the hissing radiator beneath the window, trying to warm up from the chill of Alcatraz and the cable car. I dared the wild carnation fragrance on Stu's pillow to waft toward me, and for the moment, the scent behaved.

I started my search for Dorothy's letter with Stu's dresser. I sifted through socks, underclothes, and handkerchiefs but found only a single lemon drop, just like the ones he gave me before every performance. With the candy on my tongue and tears in my eyes, I searched through his box of collars and the pockets of his trousers.

I lingered over Stu's masculine essentials, running his shaving brush across my own jawline, knowing I'd never again get to tickle him while he shaved. I opened—and quickly closed—the cap of his lime-scented hair salve. Then I set aside his pouch of gun-cleaning materials.

The contents from Stu's favorite suitcase were already in his dresser, but he had two more cases, neither of which I'd seen open. Just the places to keep something to himself.

I lugged the largest and heaviest case onto the bed, relieved that it was unlocked and opened easily. I gasped at the contents. I couldn't help it. The case was packed with sheets of music and lyrics, all in Stu's hand. I touched one sheet and burst into tears, desperately wanting Stu to be alive and knowing he never would be.

I don't know how long I cried or how long I slept after falling asleep on Stu's bed, and when I awoke, I couldn't even look at the sheet music. But I still needed to find that letter, so I grabbed the smaller suitcase. It was much lighter than the first case, and it was locked. After a little expert jimmying—stock knowledge for any traveling vaudevillian—the case yielded to my hairpin.

Stu's neatly folded woolen army tunic and breeches were on the top. I lost my breath for a moment, overwhelmed by memories. He'd been in uniform the first time I saw him, and I remembered how thrilling it'd been to hear him perform on stage at Fort Dix.

I even remembered the first song I heard him play, "Keep in Line, Soldier Boy." I hummed the tune as I lifted his tunic and breeches out of the case and hung them on a wooden hanger. I could languish in memories of Stu all day, but I had a job to do. I gave myself a big shake before patting down the tunic's outer pockets. Nothing. I unbuttoned his tunic and dug into the deep inside pockets. My fingertips immediately touched something stiff, and even though this was sober business, a thrill ran through me.

A letter! A heavy, formal, cream-colored envelope edged in black and addressed to *S. Wilson* at a post office box in New York City. It was postmarked *Alcatraz*, but the date—faint and almost blended into the stamp—looked like 1916, not 1919.

I held the letter under my nose, daring it to display a hint of carnation fragrance—even three years after being mailed—but it smelled only of being stored in Stu's wool uniform.

The envelope had been slit on the top, and I pulled out a piece of stationery and a newspaper clipping. I gasped when I saw *Stuart Wilson* as the headline. I leaned against Stu's bed, my triumph at finding the letter suddenly spent. Anchoring myself against his headboard, I quickly read his January 1916 obituary.

> WILSON—In San Francisco, December 4, Stuart C. Wilson, son of Ronald Reece Wilson and Margaret Smith Wilson, a native of San Francisco, aged 21 years. Funeral services tomorrow (Monday) at noon at the chapel of Halsted and Co., 1122 Sutter St.

The unsigned letter was short.

> *I'm taking good care of your mother. She has everything she needs. Don't worry about her.*

I noted the curled, feminine script and wondered if a

younger Dorothy Garrard had written it. If she had, then she'd written Stu at least twice after his "death" in the bay. But why would she send him his obituary, and how did she know where he was? And where was the letter she really wanted?

I returned to Stu's tunic, but the rest of the inside pockets were empty. I went back to the larger case of sheet music, took a deep breath, and sifted through it quickly. I didn't even look at the sheets, knowing that one title, one phrase, would sink me into an evening of tears.

By the time I put Stu's suitcases back into his closet, I'd stopped wondering about why Dorothy sent Stu his obituary or how she knew where he was. What I really wondered now was how long Stu carried that letter against his heart and whether its message brought him pain or solace. Or both.

CHAPTER TEN

Jimmy Harrigan was waiting outside the stage door when I arrived on Thursday morning. He leaned casually against the railing and tipped his hat at my arrival.

I carried the portfolio containing Stu's sheet music, both the songs in our current routine and things we'd been working on. I clutched the music to my heart, not sure I wanted to share it with anyone else. Especially someone as brash as this kid.

Charlie, the stage doorkeeper, slumped and snored against the wall, and Jimmy and I passed him without signing in. The curtains were open to the house and the solitary ghost light stood on a pole at center stage. Then the stage lights flickered on.

"Thank you, Mr. Steccati," I shouted toward the stage manager's office. He didn't have to help me out this morning, and I was appreciative.

Jimmy stood with me at center stage. Since my act takes place *in one*—in front of the curtain—I seldom stood center stage. Not for the first time, I wondered what it was like to have all of the stage to perform on. What was it like to be Rocco and Jeanette, who foxtrotted and waltzed across every inch? Or Audrey Merrick, who commanded the entire stage for his act? No wonder the three of them acted like they were superior to me. Once I made it to the Big Time, of course, I'd have the entire stage to myself. That was one of the big rewards of being the best in vaudeville.

The only pianos I saw close to the stage were the baby grands reserved exclusively for the O'Toole Brothers. I knew better than to let anyone audition on those instruments, so I told Jimmy to use the piano in the orchestra pit.

Jimmy jumped from the edge of the stage and into the pit, opened the lid of the upright piano, and positioned the stool to his liking. Before I could tell him what I wanted to hear, he played all five numbers of my San Francisco routine in sequence, without missing much except a vamp here or a fancy ending there.

Then—just to show he could, I suppose—he played through a selection of popular songs. Starting with "Everything Is Peaches Down in Georgia" and running into "From Here to Shanghai," he finally erupted into "K-K-K-Katy." Jimmy played them perfectly, and in my key. I had to steel myself to just stand there—not singing, not swinging, not humming, and definitely not dancing—when all of that music, even so early in the morning, was making my blood rise and shine. And somehow, despite the ache in my heart for Stu, Jimmy's tunes turned my blues just a shade lighter.

Before I could ask him to play my songs a little more slowly, a little more *dolce,* Jimmy moved on to ragtime, shaking that St. Louis beat out of his fingers at an alarming speed. He didn't have Stu's precision, but he did have an undeniably sensual swagger. And how he knew it. The kid was so impressed with his playing that he didn't even look at me, didn't see me shaking my head for him to stop, didn't realize how much it hurt to hear someone else playing Stu's music so well.

That's when I knew that I had to get rid of him.

I saw the answer to my anyone-but-Jimmy-Harrigan prayers standing at the entrance to the main aisle: a stoop-shouldered older man clutching a battered music portfolio. He stepped confidently down the carpet until the full sound of Jimmy's playing reached him. The older man paused for a few seconds, put his hand on the arm of the closest seat, and turned back to the lobby. I couldn't blame him; Jimmy's performance would be hard to beat.

I joined Jimmy in the orchestra pit just as he finished his wild rendition of "The Memphis Blues." He swiveled the piano stool to face me, looking even younger than Tuesday night. He couldn't be more than twenty-two. Twenty-three, tops.

His blue eyes were clear and piercing; his blond hair was freshly slicked down. His tan suit was linen and he wore a fresh collar. At the sight of his collar, I realized why his features—the tall forehead, sharp jaw, and chiseled cheeks—had looked so familiar on Tuesday night. Jimmy was the spitting image of the Arrow Collar Man.

I folded my arms across my chest. "Where'd you learn to play like that?"

Jimmy closed the lid on the piano as he drawled, "Places that aren't mentioned in front of nice ladies like you."

I refused to flinch. I knew that many jazz musicians learned their chops in whorehouses and that lots of vaudeville sketches started out as bordello entertainment. But I wouldn't let this kid play me for a fool. "Just what part of the South are you from?"

"That would be N'Awlins, ma'am."

"What are you doing out here?"

"Just trying to make a living."

"Ever played vaudeville?"

"Yes, ma'am."

"Really?"

"Well, not *real* vaudeville. I've been picking up work with bands here and there. The last one—the Magnolia Voodoo Brawlers, you may have heard of us?—brought me all the way out to Oakland. It was a swell band . . . until the 'bone player got religion last Sunday. Seems there's no voodoo brawling once you become a Holy Roller."

I'd never heard a more unbelievable story in my life. In addition to his unquestionable talent on the piano, Jimmy Harrigan was a bona fide storyteller, just like Stu.

"Do you write, too?" I shivered, suddenly feeling like a traitor to Stu's memory. "Music and lyrics?"

"No, ma'am," said Jimmy. "No music. No lyrics. No singing. No carrying other people's instruments. All I do is play piano."

His answer pleased me. Jimmy might have a superior playlist, but if he didn't compose music or write lyrics, he'd never compare with Stu. Not that I needed anyone else to write for me. From the sheets of music I'd found yesterday in Stu's suitcase, I had enough material for the rest of the year. Maybe even enough to get me to the Big Time.

Jimmy stood up. I was exactly five feet eight in my heels and I liked the presence my height gave me. Jimmy was just an inch taller than me, but suddenly, the orchestra pit was not large enough for both of us. I stepped out of the pit and looked around the empty theater. No other piano players were waiting to audition.

Jimmy Harrigan would do for now, but I doubted I'd keep him for long. There was something a little too sly about him.

"We do two-a-day here. I'm on at two thirty-four and eight thirty-four. This Sunday, we're playing a special show at some playland across the bay. It's a big bash for soldiers and sailors." I looked him over. "Which were you?"

"Army." Jimmy stood a little taller as he answered.

"Good. Mr. Pantages is careful about not letting any slackers work in his theaters." With his piano skills, I wondered if Jimmy, like Stu, had been assigned an entertainer's slot at some American army fort. But I didn't want to get too friendly by asking something personal.

"Don't worry about me," he said. "I did my bit. So am I hired? Twenty-five dollars a week?"

"That's right." I forced myself to agree, feeling sure in my heart of hearts that Jimmy Harrigan was too perfect to be true and that trouble was on the way. But what choice did I have if I wanted to get back on stage?

"The job is yours." Then I asked, "Have you been backstage before? I mean before Tuesday night?"

"Sure have. The Magnolia Voodoo Brawlers played only the finest—"

"Okay, then. The Pan's set up like most other theaters. The only places you'll ever need to go are the men's dressing room and the rehearsal halls. And there are places you shouldn't go, of course. Mr. Steccati—our stage manager—doesn't like anyone around his office. And you need to stay out of the stage crew's way. They're always moving things around; it's dangerous back there. And also up there." I looked into the rafters above the stage, although I was really thinking of the balcony where Stu was murdered. "Stay away from there."

My heart beat ever so faster as I explained the rest of the backstage rules. As much as I loved being *on* stage, I also loved being *back*stage. It was an exotic world of riggers and stagehands, flats and props, ambition and nerves, all creating a special camaraderie between the crew and troupers. Every moment backstage invigorated me, even the temper tantrums from headliners like Audrey. We were a family, this troupe of thirteen acts playing the Pantages theaters across the American West, and it all came together backstage.

No, I corrected myself. We weren't a family anymore, not with Stu dead. And especially not if what the detective said was true—that someone from the theater killed Stu.

But I couldn't let Stu invade my thoughts. I had to continue with my new piano player. So I did.

"Most theaters took a beating during the war, with all the men gone. So the lighting in the hallway still flickers and there's a puddle in the corner of the rehearsal hall and . . . well, despite being in the center of San Francisco, the Pan is still small-time."

It was so small-time and the pay was so bad that guys in the orchestra ran a regular poker game on the side. I could tell from the four men shuffling wearily toward us that last night's game was just winding down. I nodded toward a balding man who had just lit one cigarette from another. "That's Maestro Mitch. He leads the orchestra."

Mitch was an untalented dictator who hated change and refused to take orders from a woman. You didn't tell him how you liked your music played, you begged him to please play it. Somehow Stu had been able to handle Mitch, and if Jimmy could also, he might be worth his twenty-five dollars a week. "I'll introduce you after he's had his coffee and eggs."

Ignoring me, Jimmy strode toward Mitch, greeting him in tones I could not hear. Jimmy put his hand out and Mitch shook it without hesitation. Somehow, Jimmy Harrigan had made quick friends with Maestro Mitch, something I could never do.

Jimmy swaggered back to me. "Mitch and the orchestra'll meet us in the pit forty-five minutes before the show starts. To run through everything."

♫

I led Jimmy downstairs to the men's dressing room where early-risers Gallagher and Shean—the comedians right after me, in the eight spot—were hunched over a checkerboard.

I knocked gently on the door. "Good morning, gentlemen."

Without missing a beat, both men scanned the room, baffled and bewildered, glancing high and low, searching for a gentleman. I grinned at their joke even though I'd seen it before. Dozens of times. Despite their broad humor on stage, Gallagher and Shean were two classy guys and had clutched me in their arms when they heard about Stu's murder.

"This is Jimmy Harrigan. He's joining my act." I swallowed hard, unable to call him *my new piano player*.

The comedians shook Jimmy's hand so vigorously I was afraid they'd damage his fingers. I extracted him from their grip and walked him over to the wall where Stu's tuxedo and pleated shirt hung on a hanger.

When I saw Stu's tux, I saw *him*. His warm brown eyes and short brown hair. The small scar on his right thumb and the larger scar on his left leg. The dark blotch on his right bicep that looked like a tattoo but he always swore wasn't.

Jimmy removed the tux jacket from the hanger. He stood before the full-length mirror, holding it to his shoulders. He might fit in Stu's trousers—if he rolled up the legs—but his broad shoulders would break the back jacket seam the first time he spread his fingers over the keyboard.

Jimmy understood immediately. "Doesn't matter. I've got my own."

"A tuxedo?"

"Of course. No self-respecting Magnolia—"

"Fine." I reached to take the tux, but I could only grasp the satin lapel between my fingers. Just the touch of Stu's tux undid me.

Jimmy eased the lapel from my grasp and placed the hanger back on the peg. "We'll just put this here for now." His sudden authority surprised me, but I didn't resist.

The four of us studied Stuart's tux until Gallagher slapped Jimmy on the back. "Don't worry, Viola. We'll take care of him."

I nodded my thanks—with my thoughts on Stu, it was the most I could do at the moment—and led Jimmy upstairs and down the main aisle of the theater. As he opened the door to the lobby, he asked, "So, how'd it go yesterday morning? With the police?"

As the harsh morning light streamed into the lobby, I saw Jimmy in full for the first time. "You were in the cable car yesterday?" *Watching me*, I stopped myself from adding.

"Yes, ma'am, I was," he replied. "I thought if I had an opportunity to do something gallant—like escort you from the cable car or something—I could convince you to hire me a day earlier. Except you already had an escort."

As I calculated whether I could possibly find another piano player as talented as Jimmy, I stopped dead, unable to turn away from the glass cases along the wall. My best photograph—a large headshot that played up my kohl-rimmed eyes and pouty, vermillion-colored lips—was still in place. But the equally-large photograph of me and Stu—Stu seated at the grand piano keyboard, me draped along the top—had been torn into pieces and left to rot at the bottom of the case.

I stormed up the elegant curved stairs that led to the third floor, marched past the desk of Mr. Z's secretary, Clipboard Clippy, and was ready to bolt into Mr. Z's office when Jimmy put his hand on my arm.

"I don't know how they do things here," he said quickly. "But where I come from, you don't bust into the boss man's office over a shredded photograph."

I glared at him hard and he released his grip. Who was Jimmy Harrigan to tell me how to manage myself? Seeing Stu's photo torn up was like ripping a piece of him from my heart.

"Maybe you should sit and think this through." Jimmy nodded to the chair next to Clippy's desk. "I mean, aren't you trying to get back on stage? Shouldn't you be sharing the sugar with the boss man instead of yelling at him?"

I had no idea at all what *sharing the sugar* meant, and I was sure Jimmy's intervention was all about his paycheck, but I got his point. I even followed his suggestion and sat in the chair beside Clippy's desk.

As I tried to gather my thoughts, I saw a stack of newspapers on the desk. Guessing that they were the latest notices about the Pantages, I slid the stack my way. I could use a glowing review of my act right about now.

But I wasn't at all prepared for the paper on top: Stu's obituary circled in pencil.

> WILSON—In this city, March 24, 1919, Stuart Wilson, a native of San Francisco, aged 25 years. Funeral services tomorrow (Thursday) at 10 A.M. at the chapel of Halsted and Co., 1122 Sutter St.

Thursday. Today.

"No," I mumbled, unable to believe that Stu was getting laid to rest and we didn't have one last goodbye. "No, no, no."

"What is it?" asked Jimmy. Then, "Oh." Then, "I'm sorry, Miss—"

"They're burying him without me." I clutched the paper, still unable to believe it. Didn't everyone know how much Stu meant to me? Didn't they know how much I meant to him? "How could they do that?"

Jimmy eased the paper from my hands. "It's past ten. Too late—"

"Of course it's too late." My confusion about not being told about Stuart's funeral was quickly turning into something stronger. And angrier. Who would deny me a last look at my lover?

I peered at Mr. Z's closed door, wondering if he'd had any role in keeping me from Stuart's funeral. There was only one way to find out.

As I approached his door, Jimmy put his hand on my

arm again. This time he pulled me back and walked me toward the stairway.

"I'm sure it hurts, Miss Viola," he said. "But you got to think of yourself right now. About your career. And maybe even about what Stuart would want you to do right now."

I really wished men would stop telling me to think about what Stu would want me to do because it was never what *I* wanted to do. But before I decided anything, Clipboard Clippy appeared, hat in hand and huffing hard. He stopped to catch his breath, and I took a moment to breathe along with him. In those moments I knew what Stuart would want me to do. So I did it.

"I wanted to let Mr. Z to know I'm back in business." I tried out a smile on Clippy. A big, confident smile proclaiming that I was once again *Viola Vermillion, Red-Hot Blues Chanteuse*. "I've got a new accompanist, and we're good to get back on stage."

"I'll give Mr. Z your message and let you know what he says." Clippy worked the crease in his hat, not even looking at my big smile. "Although I wouldn't get your hopes up."

"What do you mean?"

"Mr. Merrick took over Champ's minutes on Monday afternoon and yours on Monday night. Now he wants Mr. Z to give him yours for the rest of the tour."

"But I've only got a fourteen-minute act," I protested. "Mr. Merrick can't take my minutes, can he?"

But even as I asked, I knew the answer. As the Pantages headliner, Audrey could take just about anything he wanted.

But what about me? I wanted things, too. I wanted Stu's songs to shine. I wanted people to love and applaud him. Getting back on stage was the most important thing in my life.

“Between you and me,” Clippy said, lowering his voice. “Unless you can change Mr. Merrick’s mind—”

“Then that’s what I’ll do.” I took a final look at Mr. Z’s closed door, promising Stu that his songs would be sung once more in San Francisco. “And then I’ll get back on stage.”

CHAPTER
ELEVEN

I HAULED Jimmy down to the basement rehearsal room, figuring that he was my best hope to get back on stage. Jimmy sat at the piano, ran his fingers over the keys, and tested the pedals. He looked up eagerly, reminding me of Kitty's poodle Romeo, always ready to perform.

Jimmy finished an arpeggio before asking, "What do you want to start with?"

I placed Stu's portfolio on the top of the piano, suddenly realizing that he'd been the last to touch these papers and that this portfolio—these notes and lyrics—was Stu's legacy to me. But how could I perform without him?

Because I had to, that's how. I didn't even need Stu's voice in my head to know that I could do it. I *could* perform with a new piano player. I could keep my act going. I could even keep Audrey from getting my minutes.

Each song in the portfolio jolted me with images of Stu —looking swell in his tux, or steepling his long fingers together, or winking at me just before I took my first big breath. The portfolio held so many songs, so many memories of Stu, that all I could do was hand Jimmy the top piece of music, one that we'd premiered in Seattle.

"Okay." Jimmy anchored the sheets above the piano keyboard. "'Someday Sweetheart' it is."

Jimmy played the vamp and my throat went dry. My mouth wouldn't open; I couldn't sing a note. I closed my eyes to keep my world from swirling out of control and steadied my hand on the piano.

Just hearing Stu's notes bought back the first time he'd played "Sweetheart" for me, way back in Jersey. He'd sketched out the song and made me sit next to him as I sang it the first time. I'd struggled through it, needing to get closer to the music to read the penciled-in words, until we sat thigh to thigh. As I sang the last note, holding it for two bars, Stu finished the piece by running his right hand up the keyboard in a grand flourish. As we both released our last notes, he gazed into my eyes and looked down at my lips, and we kissed for the first time.

It was far from our last kiss that evening, and as I remembered every single kiss—and the bright rash on my face the next day from Stu's stubble—it was almost like he was beside me.

Until the stranger playing Stu's music asked, "You want to sing this or not?"

Nope, I sure didn't. All I wanted was to run from the rehearsal room, the theater, even my longing for Stu. But at the same time, remembering how the audience had applauded "Someday Sweetheart," I wanted to own that triumphant feeling once again. I wanted to get back on stage, pull the audience into my songs, and entertain them like no one else had before.

"Yes," I whispered. "I want to sing."

Before Jimmy vamped again, I opened my eyes and launched into the verse. He came in after a few bars, looking surprised that I'd started on key.

When we took a breather after the third song Jimmy asked, "Does it happen all of the time? Headliners like Audrey stealing minutes from other acts?"

"Sure. Not just minutes, but jokes and songs and moves and other bits," I replied. "You've got a lot to learn about vaudeville, kid."

Jimmy looked a little bruised when I called him *kid*, but I enjoyed it. Especially if it kept him in his place.

"Look, kid." This time he scowled at me. "It's a long hard road to the top and a performer does what they gotta to get there. I understand what Mr. Merrick is doing, but I'm not going to let him do it to me." Jimmy had no idea the big dreams I had for my future, and I wasn't about to share them with him. So I said, "Let's get back to work."

I knew exactly what I wanted to work on next. "Welcome Home, Battling Boys" was a rousing anthem that Stu'd dedicated to our returning soldiers, and it was good enough to compete with the popular "How You Gonna Keep 'Em Down on the Farm." We'd even thought "Battling Boys" might be our big break—the record that everyone had to hear on their Victrola, the music that everyone needed for their piano.

I was about to give Jimmy the sheets when he asked, "How'd you get into the business anyway?"

It was a peace offering, of course. The kid was trying to get back into my good graces.

"My sister started me," I told him. "Blanche said I had a voice that carried out to the last seat in the—" The word *balcony* stuck in my throat. I couldn't think about balconies without thinking about Stu's lifeless body. Although it wasn't much easier thinking about Blanche, I answered, "She said I was a natural."

"How come she's not performing with you?"

"She died." I pushed the sheets at Jimmy and swallowed hard. "Last year."

Instead of spreading out the music on the piano top, the kid stared at me. Like he wanted to say "I'm sorry" but knew he shouldn't. He began to play the melody of "How You Gonna Keep 'Em" and then brought in a strong bass with his left hand. "Can you really reach the last seats?"

"Sure can. Get me going and I can out-blast Sophie Tucker, Nora Bayes, and Marion Harris singing together." It was an exaggeration, of course. One that Stu and I created together and thought would sound good—someday—in my publicity materials.

Jimmy segued from the chorus into the vamp before the verse. "Then let me hear it."

I was a little miffed at his request—and myself for boasting—because even though I'd been recovered from the influenza for months, my lungs were still sludgy. The flu had almost killed me, and my career with it. But maybe I should show Jimmy who he was working for.

I started out in my normal stage voice, savoring the jaunty tempo, before building my volume. Jimmy set up the chorus with a rumble like thunder, just like the piano players did in moving picture shows. Just as I was about to let loose, crossing my fingers behind my back that the notes I wanted would be the notes I got, Clipboard Clippy appeared in the doorway.

"There you are, Miss Vermillion." He held a white envelope in his right hand—an envelope that could contain a pink slip with my name on it. I was ready to challenge a permanent layoff, ready to beg that I'd do anything to get back on stage, when Clippy said, "Mr. Zimmerman says to tell you you're in the matinee today. In the two spot."

"The two spot? But—"

"You've got the two spot this afternoon and maybe at the seven-thirty tonight."

"But—"

"You weren't going on at all until—"

"We'll take it." Jimmy stood up and came to attention, his posture so erect that I thought he was going to salute. Instead, he offered his hand to Clippy and the two men shook on it.

As Clippy walked out, Jimmy leaned toward me. "The two spot's good, right? Not quite the one spot, but still good?"

I couldn't believe how much I had to teach him. "Listen, kid, anything before the six spot is bad news. If we get stuck in the two spot for long, I might as well quit vaudeville forever."

♫

A few hours later, Jimmy and I waited in the wings as Kitty—in the one spot—commanded her poodles to jump through seven consecutive hoops, each hoop smaller than the last. It was the first trick of their performance, which meant that I'd go on stage in four-and-a-half minutes.

Jimmy'd retrieved his tuxedo—a sad, shiny suit that looked patched under the left arm and thin at the knees—and was cracking his knuckles and breathing hard. He shifted from foot to foot, and I couldn't tell if this was his warm-up routine or if he was really nervous. I was tingling myself, but then I always do just before my spot. Knowing I'm about to perform always gets my blood pumping.

Suddenly, Rocco diLorenzo positioned himself a few feet away from me, like he hadn't tried to mash me on Monday, like he hadn't yelped when my teeth bit his probing tongue.

Always fiercely groomed and elegantly dressed, Rocco considered himself God's gift to women. It didn't help that he really was one of the more attractive men in the troupe, and his glossy, dark hair, smooth complexion, and perfect posture won him a considerable amount of admiration from both ladies and gents. He'd been teasing me since I joined the troupe, but Monday was the first time he'd tried something. I'd shut him down quickly enough, and he hadn't bothered me since. Nor had he offered condolences about Stu's death.

I didn't think Rocco'd try to mash me here in the wings, but I looked around for something to slug him with. If I needed to. I saw one of the Nolan Sisters' wooden rifles on the prop table and estimated how many steps it'd take me to reach it. That's when I realized Jimmy was leaning against the table, still cracking his knuckles but breathing more heavily than before.

"So . . ." Rocco's voice was low. "You've found someone to replace Stuart."

His words pierced my heart. No one could ever replace Stu.

"Let's hope this one doesn't get himself murdered," said Rocco.

I threw myself at Rocco, ready to pull out his pencil mustache hair by hair, but Jimmy wedged himself between us, facing Rocco.

"Listen here—"

With Jimmy defending me, Rocco took a step back. Then Jimmy took two steps forward, landing inches from Rocco. They stared at each other for seconds, and then Rocco turned and walked toward the stairs.

"I'll be right back." Jimmy started off in Rocco's direction, but I grabbed his sleeve and pulled him to me.

"Leave it," I said. "I go on in two minutes. You need to get down to the pit now."

To my surprise, Jimmy raised his fingers to his forehead in a chauffeur's salute and jaunted down the stairs to the orchestra pit.

As I waited to make my entrance, Rocco's nasty comment kept running through my head. *Get himself murdered.* What did that even mean? Everyone in the troupe liked Stu. Some of them—like Tuck and his dog Champ—*loved* him. Oddly enough, the one person in the troupe who didn't care for anyone—Rocco—had me as an alibi.

Moments later, our headliner, Audrey Merrick—shadowed by Oscar, one of the three in-between boys who entertained the audience while Audrey made his quick costume changes—glided into the spot where Rocco had stood.

Audrey wasn't in costume yet, but his face was made up and he floated in his emerald silk dressing gown, the same gown I'd wanted to steal the first time I saw it.

"That was quite a tussle, wasn't it?"

Despite being on the same playbill for weeks, this was the first time our headliner had spoken to me. I was surprised to hear his feminine stage voice used backstage, until I wondered if maybe his stage voice *was* his real voice.

"Two men battling over you?" he continued. "A girl's got to love that."

Earlier today I would have doubted that Audrey knew my name, except now I knew he wanted my minutes. But why was he being so cozy with me?

"Fighting with each other, Mr. Merrick." As wary as I was of him, as the headliner, he required respect. Plus, he might be the first one of us to hit the Big Time, and it was always possible he'd take one of us along. Not likely—so many vaudevillians were only out for themselves—but still possible.

"I'd heard you got a *sizzling* new piano player." The headliner hissed the *s* in *sizzling* like a snake. "But what an understatement."

I glanced at the stage, trying to gauge where Kitty was in her act. I was getting nervous about performing. I wanted to move away from our headliner, but Audrey's lilting voice—higher and thinner than mine—held me close.

"How did you know about my new piano player, Mr. Merrick?"

"Everyone shares tidbits with the headliner, my dear."

"Is that true?" I put my head toward his, suddenly brave. "Anyone told you who killed my Stu?"

"No one's confessed to me, but everyone's got an idea." Audrey played our scene like a true professional, even taking my hands and staring into my eyes. "I'm sorry to tell you, Miss Vermillion, but the leading contender for his murderer is you."

After delivering a punch line that would make a Broadway thespian proud, Audrey dropped my hands, swept up his gown, and swished toward his dressing room. Oscar swished in his wake. Lionel emerged from the shadows a few feet away and followed Audrey inside the dressing room, shutting the door so deliberately that the large gold headliner star nailed on the door slid back and forth.

Right then, Kitty and her dogs jogged off stage. Her son Pascal quickly took command of the animals and handed his mother a white towel. As Kitty's scattered applause died down, the orchestra intro'd my opening number.

The orchestra sound was full, the tempo was perfect, and the piano melody came through strong. I would have sworn Stu was playing the piano right now. Normally, I would have bounced onto the stage, but today I stalled. As much as I wanted to believe Stu was out there, I knew he wasn't. I was on my own, and, for the first time in my career, I was sure I'd fail.

Kitty put her hand on the small of my back as though she was ready to push me on stage. "You can do this, Viola. You have to do this."

Kitty's encouragement—and the thought that if she pushed me, I'd end up face down on stage—did the trick. I breathed deeply, shook my shoulders into place, and walked on stage to my mark.

Then the spotlight flared up on me and I froze. I forgot every note, every word, every sultry shimmy of my act. I looked out into the seats, wondering who all of these darkened silhouettes were and why they were staring at me.

I'd been avoiding the balcony since finding Stu up there, but now I was drawn to it. Couldn't take my eyes from it. Stu'd been there, in that seat, looking down at the stage where I stood, when someone put two shots in him.

At my feet, I heard horns braying in double-time and I looked down to see two trumpet players aiming their instruments right at me, as if they were trying to wake me.

It worked. Something suddenly clicked, and I turned

away from the balcony and toward the audience. I opened my mouth and sang. My voice came out thin and unconvincing, hardly reaching the orchestra. I sounded worse than my first rehearsal after surviving the influenza, but at least lyrics were coming out of my mouth.

Then I remembered that I couldn't give Mr. Z any reason to give my minutes to Audrey. If I didn't deliver now, this moment, Mr. Z might cut my entire act.

So I went big, blasting on stage as fiercely as Eva Tanguay. The matinee audience woke up, paid attention, and applauded their approval. I sang one encore and sauntered off the stage, looking to the audience like my sassy stage self.

Kitty met me in the wings, offering me a dry towel. I jolted past her and ran out the stage door, needing . . . I don't know what. I grasped the iron railings leading down to the alley and gulped for fresh air.

I'd done it. I'd returned to the stage. I'd sung five songs and one encore, but I felt anything but triumphant. By performing without Stu, I'd proved that I didn't need him anymore, that life would go on without him. But being in vaudeville without Stu seemed terribly wrong.

I stood at the stage door landing for some time, watching people scurrying along sunny Market Street. How could the city keep moving when my heart kept breaking? How could anyone walk down the street and live a regular life when the man I loved had been murdered?

As a torn newspaper tumbled in the wind, I saw a woman dressed in black head to toe count out money for her taxi driver. I'd hardly looked Margaret Wilson in the face yesterday, but still, I knew it was her.

She caught me watching her and walked toward me. I

met her in the alley, wiping away my tears with Kitty's towel. I tried to manufacture a false smile and a handshake, but Margaret grabbed my hands and held them to her chest.

"Tell me everything you know about Stuart," she said through tear-filled eyes. "Tell me everything about my boy."

CHAPTER TWELVE

I WAS ready to tell Margaret Wilson anything she wanted to know, but as we sat with our tea at Fong's Café, she did all the talking.

"Stuart already had a headstone in Colma, so we buried him there." Margaret's fingers clutched the small cup of oolong tea. "The detective explained that Stuart had been in the army and we could bury him at the Presidio, but it's . . . it's so large."

"I'm sure that Colma is lovely," I replied, having no idea where Colma was or what it looked like. I wanted to crawl into the corner of the booth, pull my coat about me, and sniff back my tears. Being with Margaret made me miss Stu even more.

"At least my boy came back," she said. "I know where he's buried."

I knew just what she meant. Thousands of American soldiers in Europe had died in the war or from the influenza and were buried where they fell. Burying your loved one in a grave of your own choosing was almost a privilege these days.

"I always hoped that Stuart was alive. I waited for him to write me. Or call me on the telephone, or come home." She looked at me with red-rimmed eyes, as though I might have an answer. But I had no idea why Stu would play such a dirty trick, not letting his mother know where he was.

"And now," she twisted the napkin in her lap, "to know that he was alive all those years . . ."

Very much alive. I fought my anger at Stu and refocused it on Dorothy. *And if Dorothy sent the letter with the obituary notice to Stu, she knew exactly where to find him in 1916 and never told you.* For the second time since we'd nestled into Fong's back booth together, I wondered at a mother's strength. How could Margaret endure losing her only child, especially when that child had been murdered and the murderer was not yet caught?

"And all those years," I said, "When Stu was gone, was Dorothy—"

"My rock," Margaret replied. "She stood with me through everything. Never let me out of her sight. Poor girl, she lost her mother when she was young; I lost my son a few years later. We almost seemed fated for each other."

I was not a big believer in fate, but Margaret seemed convinced. "Dorothy and Stuart grew up together, you know. Almost like brother and sister. But all that ended when he started writing music. He was going to be the next Irving Berlin and didn't have time to play with Dorothy anymore."

At Mr. Berlin's name, I had something to add. Something delightful that she didn't know about her son.

"Stu met Mr. Berlin. At Fort Dix during the war. Fort Dix,

New Jersey, that's where Stu served." I stopped myself before the pain in her eyes dissolved into full-on tears. I realized now why she did all of the talking—it kept her tears away. Still, I guessed she'd like to hear Stu's story, even if she wept during the entire telling.

"Mr. Berlin came to entertain the troops and Stu played his own songs for him. Mr. Berlin told him to keep composing. He said the best thing Stu could do for his composing was to see the world. Get a real sense of what people wanted, what they missed, how they wanted their lives to turn out. That was what Stu should write about. Mr. Berlin even told him that once he'd seen the world, once he had a suitcase full of songs, to come back to New York and play them for him."

"He did?" She wiped a tear with her handkerchief, but her voice was strong and proud.

I nodded. "If you like, I can play you one of his recordings. We made them before we left New Jersey. I've got them at the Pan."

"Yes, I'd like that." Stu's mother took her first sip of oolong, wincing slightly at its bitterness.

♫

Backstage at the Pan, the Ling Ting Tumblers were performing the show's last spot, just before the Morriscope movies began. Even though I had my arm in Margaret's, she veered toward the curtain to watch the acrobats. She seemed excited, but I had to wonder: Was I an idiot to bring her back to the Pan? How could she be here, in the theater where her son was murdered, and not be overwhelmed?

I was prepared to hustle Margaret downstairs when I

realized she was gazing up at the balcony. She searched each seat—empty and occupied—as if she might see Stu in one of them. Almost against my will, I looked up at the seat Stu had died in and was surprised to see someone in it. Someone who hadn't been there when I performed earlier in the show. It wasn't Stu, of course. Unless his ghost wore spectacles the size of goggles.

As the orchestra set up the acrobats' big finale, I knew that in seconds, the tumblers would be rushing off the stage and directly into Margaret.

"Better come away now," I whispered in her ear. "There's gonna be a stampede."

As I walked her toward the staircase, her voice was softer than before, as though she had swallowed back tears. "I wasn't going to ask, but—"

Although our conversation had been about Stu, I had carefully avoided any mention of his murder. I guessed that Detective Petersen had assured her I was not a suspect, because I couldn't imagine anyone being so cruel as to let Stu's mother meet her son's killer. I just wished the detective had informed the troupe about my innocence. It still stung, remembering how Audrey had suggested that some of the troupers thought I murdered Stu.

I took a deep breath. If Margaret asked about me finding Stu in the balcony, I'd have to tell her. I wouldn't want someone lying to me about a loved one, and I wouldn't do it to her.

But instead, she offered me a real smile. "Stu loved being part of all of this, didn't he? Being here, working in a big theater act. It's all he ever wanted, and he got it."

She didn't need an answer from me because she'd found

it herself. "His music always made me so happy; I always thought it'd make others happy, too. I hope you are on some of those records, Miss Vermillion. I'd like to hear how you and Stuart sounded together."

She had no idea how happy her request made me. She must have guessed that Stu and I were lovers, but she didn't treat me any differently, didn't treat me like a tramp or a temptress.

I retrieved our recordings from the dressing room and escorted Stu's mother to the rehearsal room where Jimmy and I had worked earlier. The phonographic machine there wasn't very reliable, although it might work if you were really sweet to it. But wooing the machine would have to wait, because when we reached the room, I heard a knock-down-drag-'em-out shouting match between two women behind the closed door. Despite their shrieks—or maybe because of them—I only made out a few words, none of them pretty.

I normally didn't interrupt fights unless someone was being mashed or bullied, but these were not normal times. Stu had been murdered and the police hadn't arrested anyone. And I couldn't recognize the voices, which meant that we might have a stranger in our midst, a stranger that might be Stu's murderer.

With the records pressed against my chest and Stu's mother behind me, there was only one thing to do. Go inside.

It took only seconds to open the room and see who was yelling at whom. But it wasn't two women; it was one woman and two men—Jeanette diLorenzo, Audrey Merrick, and in-between-songs-boy Oscar.

Although none of them seemed to know I was watching, the screaming had stopped. Audrey and Oscar stood in the middle of the room, facing the mirror on the far wall, as though they were practicing a duet. Jeanette stood inches from Oscar, her hands on her hips. "You screw this up for me and I'll—"

"You'll what?" Oscar leaned in toward Jeanette. "What'll you do? Kill me? Shoot me like Stuart?"

Audrey put his hand on Oscar's shoulder as if to pull him away, but Jeanette grabbed the boy's lapels and jerked him toward her until they were face to face. "You don't know what you're talking about, sonny."

"I know more than you think," Oscar told her. "I know it takes real talent to make it in the moving pictures, and you don't have it!"

Suddenly, Lionel Fisk hissed at me from behind. "Step aside, Miss Vermillion. This doesn't concern you."

Jeanette swept past us, grumbling under her breath, "I'm gonna be bigger than Mary Pickford ever was."

All at once, Margaret's calm bravery shattered. Her eyes filled with tears as she grabbed my arm.

"Who shot Stuart?" she moaned. "Who killed my boy?"

I was torn between wanting to find out if Oscar really knew anything about Stu's murder and getting Margaret out of here. I chose Margaret.

I eased Stu's mother upstairs and out the stage door, then walked her down the alley, not sure if she still wanted to hear Stu's recordings. Ugo Baldanza traveled with a small phonographic machine that we might be able to use, but if I took her back to the hotel, there was a risk she'd ask about Stu's things. And I wasn't ready to let any of his things go.

"Can I help you ladies?" Jimmy appeared at my side, looking at the records in my arms. As if he read my thoughts, he said, "I heard there's a grafonola shop just down the street. If you're really polite, they let you bring your own recordings and listen to them."

I sought the words to introduce Jimmy to Stu's mother, but how could I say that I'd replaced her son? As I debated with myself, a taxi screeched to a stop in front of us. Dorothy Garrard barged out of the back seat.

"Mother Wilson!" Dorothy's voice was low and thick. "I've been looking all over for you!"

The girl pushed past me to put her arms around Stu's mother, embracing her as though Margaret were a long-lost child.

Stu's mother let Dorothy hug her without complaint. "I'm fine, Dorothy. I just wanted to—"

"I was so worried!" Dorothy pulled Margaret toward the taxicab.

But Margaret put out a hand toward me and I took it, surprised that her farewell was so firm. "Thank you, Miss Vermillion."

Dorothy grudgingly allowed us that short goodbye before making sure Margaret was in the taxicab. Then she scooted in next to her. I came up to the open window, not quite ready to let Margaret leave, not when there was so much more we had to share about Stu. "Mrs. Wilson . . . do you think . . ."

Dorothy poked through the window, blocking my view of Margaret. "Haven't you done enough to her already? Just leave her alone!"

Jimmy pulled me away from the taxicab and back onto

the sidewalk. For once, Market Street was almost bare of traffic, and the taxicab quickly drove down the street. When it finally disappeared, I gave Dorothy my response.

"I won't leave her alone. Not until I know who murdered her son."

CHAPTER THIRTEEN

THAT NIGHT I GAVE A SOLID, shimmering performance in the two spot, never looking up at the balcony, never giving Stu any reason to haunt me. I performed my final curtsy to a barrage of applause, whistles, and approving hoots, appreciation almost unheard of in the two spot.

How ya like them apples, Mr. Z? Let me keep all of my minutes in the seven and you won't be sorry.

But the euphoria of my performance dulled once I reached the wings. Success didn't matter if Stu wasn't here to share it. I switched my shoes, grabbed my coat, and headed out of the theater.

I took a long walk down Market Street, ending up at the Ferry Building, where I stood over the railing watching the bay waters and longing for Stu. The night grew colder, and I turned and walked down the other side of Market Street, bound for Fong's Café. As I reached the Pan, I glanced at the marquee—my name was still up in lights—and ran straight into Detective Petersen.

A taxicab drove up and the detective motioned for me to enter. Which I had to, because he'd put his hand—his large, firm hand—under my elbow. Before he joined me in the back seat, I jiggled the door handle. Unlocked. If I needed to, I could jump out. I wasn't much of a runner and my French heels would fall apart after a block, but I had an exit if I needed one.

I knew as the car turned left on Market that we weren't headed to my hotel, but I had no idea where we were. Thoughts of the police station loomed large.

"Are you arresting me?" I asked. Then I told him, "It wouldn't solve Stu's murder, locking me up."

"I'm not taking you in tonight," he replied. "But you've got to be straight with me. You knew him best, and there's something you're not telling me. You know it and I know it."

I've told you everything I know died on my lips, because I definitely hadn't. I'd found out two things since Stu's death. That someone—probably Dorothy—had mailed him his obituary in 1916, and that another someone wore L'Amour Bleu in his bed. There was also Kitty's story of Stu making love to someone in Portland, but why would the police be interested in that?

And what did any of those things have to do with somebody shooting Stu?

But I could tell the detective one thing, something I'd forgotten when he questioned me in Mr. Z's office. "A few hours before he died, Stu had seventy-five dollars in his money clip. After he died, the money was gone."

"You went through Wilson's pockets?" Petersen didn't hide his scorn, and I shriveled slightly, realizing that going through a dead man's pockets made me look bad.

But I'd already put my foot in my mouth, so I kept going. "If you find Stu's money, you'll find his murderer. Right?"

"If you'd told me earlier, maybe. But that money is long gone now and that trail is cold."

"You don't know that."

He said, "What would you do if you stole seventy-five dollars? Would you keep it around?" Then he asked, "Is there anything else you'd like to tell me?"

"I want Stu's murderer found more than anyone." I almost dared him to challenge me. Then I recalled Margaret Wilson's anguish this afternoon and realized she needed justice as much as me. So I added, "More than Dorothy Garrard, that's for sure. You are here because of her, right? Because her father's a bigwig?"

"He's commandant of the Alcatraz Disciplinary Barracks," the detective corrected me. "A good friend of the chief of police. And the mayor." His tone was clear. Dorothy Garrard had the power of the San Francisco elite on her side. I did not.

To my surprise, the taxi stopped in front of my hotel.

"Do you believe in instinct, Miss Vermillion?"

"A woman's instinct, Detective?"

"Just instinct. Because mine tells me that Miss Garrard wants something from you. And the sooner you give it to her, the sooner she'll leave you alone. Which will make life a lot easier for you and me both."

The detective eased out and held the door for me. He walked me to the front door, just as he had two nights ago.

"One more thing," he said. "Don't leave town until I give you the word. Don't even think about it."

From the way she'd glared at me hours earlier, I'd

thought Dorothy wanted me run out of San Francisco on a rail. But maybe it was just the opposite. Maybe her only way to get the letter she wanted was to keep me in town. By putting me in jail.

Inside the Hotel Henry, of course, all I thought about was leaving town. Then, because Stu's lyrics had been popping up in my head since he died, I decided to ask him what to do. Of course, I didn't ask him as much as stand in the lobby and wait to hear him whisper in my ear. But no matter how tightly I closed my eyes and wished for Stu's wisdom, I only heard the night manager mumbling to himself.

So I was forced to think for myself. Starting with how Dorothy wanted the letter she'd sent to Stu weeks ago and how she'd gotten her father to lean in to the police to threaten me until I gave it to her.

But I hadn't found that letter; I'd found the other letter. The one written in a girlish hand, mailed from Alcatraz in 1916, letting Stu know that *I'm taking good care of your mother.* If Dorothy'd sent *that* letter, why didn't she want it back also?

There was only one reason I could think of—Stu never answered it, which had left Dorothy to believe that he really was dead. Except that three years later, Stu wrote to Dorothy, and she wrote him back.

Or so she said. I had no reason to believe Dorothy had told me the truth about anything. All I knew was that she was protective of Margaret. Or was that just her way of *taking good care of his mother?*

My mind was stuffed with unanswerable questions, and all I wanted was to reach my room and fall asleep.

As the elevator car rumbled me up to the sixth floor, a

red rubber ball bounced down the carpeted steps surrounding the elevator. I watched the ball roll, expecting a speedy flex of fur to run after it. Sure enough, feisty fireball Champ dashed down the stairs, retrieved the ball, and ran upstairs. As I arrived on the sixth floor, Owen Tuck opened the elevator gate for me.

"Hi, Viola."

"Good evening, Officer Tuck." This—along with a crisp salute—was how Stu always greeted Tuck, and somehow it came out naturally for me tonight. Minus the salute. "How are you?"

Tuck took off his hat and held it in both hands. "I wanted to tell you how sorry I am about Stuart. He was a good man."

I'd received numerous condolences from members of the troupe, but the tears welling up in Tuck's eyes were the most heartfelt.

I sniffed away my own sudden tears. "He was, wasn't he?"

Despite his stage training—and I had no idea how you got a dog to play drunk—Champ never sat still for long. He made his presence known now by putting his paw out to me. I bent to shake it, feeling as though it was his solemn tribute to Stu.

"Thanks, Champ. You were a real pal to Stu, and I appreciate it." Unlike Kitty's precious poodles, Champ was a hearty, knock-around terrier mutt who made friends easily. He and Stu had been buddies since the first time they met, and I was just a little jealous that Stu bought a daily dog biscuit for Champ and kept it in the same pocket as my lemon drops.

Tuck bent down to scratch the back of Champ's ears,

and only then did I remember that Champ had taken sick at the Monday matinee, just hours before I'd found Stu dead.

Before I let memories of finding Stu overwhelm me, I asked Tuck, "How's he doing?"

Champ looked at me as if to say, *It's about time you asked.*

"It's been a rough couple of days." Tuck's eyes filled with tears. "I almost lost him."

"To food poisoning?" Almost all of us had suffered it while eating at strange restaurants on the road, but I'd never heard of anyone—even an animal trouper—almost dying from it.

"It wasn't food poisoning. The doc said it was real poison. He just didn't know which." Tuck wiped his sleeve over his face. "Champ knows he's not supposed to take food off the floor, but I turned my back for a few seconds and there he was, sick as a dog."

Champ yipped loudly, like he was agreeing.

"Just our luck, too," said Tuck. "The one day we got an Orpheum agent in the house, Champ gets sick. So sick that Mr. Z sent a get-well bouquet."

"You got flowers?" I asked.

"*Champ* got flowers. Yellow and white daisies. Didn't you, boy?"

"Is he ready to go back to work, or are you laying off for a while?"

"We're back in the eight spot starting tomorrow," he replied. "How about you? I heard you found a piano player."

"I got the two spot. At least for tomorrow."

"Atta girl, Viola. That'd make Stuart proud, you getting back on stage so soon. It's a dog-eat-dog world, but vaudeville's all we got." Tuck patted his chest, right around his heart, and Champ jumped into his arms.

"I hope you don't mind," Tuck stifled a yawn, "but it's time for us to get our beauty sleep. So good night, sleep tight, and see you on stage."

CHAPTER FOURTEEN

I UNLOCKED my door to find Jimmy Harrigan in my chair, feet on my footboard, hat hanging on the handle of my bathroom door.

Although my act celebrated the sizzle of sex, an uninvited man, whether in my dressing or hotel room, put me on edge. I drew my handbag to my chest, reassured by Madame Savage's solid heft.

"How the hell did you get in here?"

"The porter let me in." He nodded to a square-shaped gold-papered box, a green bottle, and two mugs on the dresser. "I brought you chocolates and champagne to celebrate our new act."

He stood and offered me the box of chocolates like he was presenting a glass slipper on a cushion. It was a doozy. Small but heavy with a wide red velveteen ribbon tied in a bow on the top. I smelled the chocolate inside the box and my mouth watered with delight.

But I couldn't give in so easily. I couldn't give in at all.

The last thing I wanted was to play games with my new piano player.

"I thought you were broke," I said. "Isn't that what you said Tuesday?"

"I *was* broke Tuesday. And today I discovered that Maestro Mitch can't drink and play poker at the same time. So he drank and I won. Now I'm not broke, but I am thirsty." He eyed the champagne on the dresser but made no move to pop it open.

I kept my eyes on him. "So you're a gambler now?"

"I gamble when I need to, that's all."

I pushed the box back at him, once again aware of his crisp Arrow Collar Man appearance. It even looked like he'd shaved after tonight's show. A slow dread spread through me. What else was Jimmy Harrigan gambling on winning tonight?

He untied the box's red ribbon and lifted the top. Chocolates all right. Three rows of three. Milk and dark. Squares, rounds, and hearts. Despite my uneasiness at his appearance, I selected a chocolate and popped it into my mouth.

"These are mighty fine, but—" At least, that's what I tried to say. The sweet, sassy chocolate coconut chew was getting the better of me, keeping me silent. Finally, I asked, "What are you really doing in my room?"

"Looking for a woman."

I put my hands on my hips, making sure not to mess my coat with any chocolate. "Listen, Jimmy. If you're going to work for me, we've got to get one thing straight. There's no hanky-panky between us. Ever. This is a business relationship. I'm the boss and you're the hired help."

Jimmy smiled. Well, actually, his blue eyes smiled.

"You've mistaken my intentions, ma'am. I'm looking for a very specific woman."

"Who is she, this very specific woman?" I tossed a caramel into my mouth and chomped down on it.

"Her name is Eleanor Rutherfurd."

The caramel stuck between my teeth; even my tongue couldn't dislodge it. I went into my tiny bathroom and looked at myself in the mirror. My lips were stuck in a caramel frown. I put my fingers in my mouth to work it out and threw the caramel in the sink. I rejoined Jimmy, made sure he hadn't closed the door to the hallway, and used every ounce of control to keep my voice even.

"Eleanor who?"

"Eleanor Rutherfurd. She's the wife of Thaddeus Rutherfurd, and he's—"

"I know who he is." Because oh, boy, did I.

Jimmy had no idea how much I knew about Thaddeus Rutherfurd and how much I hated him. But for the moment, I played along.

"Thaddeus Rutherfurd." I hadn't said his name in months, but it was still as distasteful as ever. "Mr. High-and-Mighty Munitions Manufacturer. The man who made the bullets that won the war." *The man who wants his red leather notebook back.* "The entire country knows who he is," I added.

"But the entire country doesn't know his wife ran away from him."

"You think his wife—"

"Eleanor," he said.

"You think Eleanor ran *here*, to San Francisco?" I folded my arms across my chest.

He folded his arms as well. "I think she's in this room."

Was the man crazy? There was no place to hide in here. Besides the bed—too low to slide under—the room had only a dresser, a dressing table with a stool, and the low chair with broken springs that Jimmy'd been sitting in. Even my largest suitcase wasn't big enough to hold a woman.

I put my hand in my coat pocket, where I'd tucked my handbag. If it turned out that Jimmy Harrigan was crazy—a breaking-into-my-room-with-a-box-of-chocolates kind of crazy—I'd let Madame Savage scare him away.

Jimmy might know about Eleanor and Rutherfurd, but did he know about the red leather notebook? That's what I needed to find out. "Did you start on the champagne already, Jimmy? Because you're not making sense."

"I've never been so sober in my life. I've been looking for Mrs. Rutherfurd for the past two months, and I've finally found her." Jimmy's blue eyes pierced me like steel. "So close the door, take off your coat, sit down, and listen. Because the jig's up, Eleanor."

♫

I closed the door, but I didn't sit down. Instead, I stood ready to run from the room.

"Let me get this straight." I took a slow, deep breath. "You think I'm Eleanor Rutherfurd?"

"I know you are."

"You've lost your marbles," I told him.

"Let me tell you a story and then you tell me if I've lost my marbles." Jimmy placed the open chocolate box on the bed, inches from where I stood, before settling on the edge of the chair.

Just to show him I wasn't rattled, I took a piece of chocolate from the box. Raspberry cream.

"Eleanor," he began, "is from an old New York family. The kind that has a mansion on the Hudson, a house in the city, and lots of money in the bank."

"So, Eleanor's rich."

"But Thaddeus—he's one of Eleanor's distant cousins, did you know that?—wasn't rich. No mansions. No money. No nothing. Not until he married Eleanor and her father died and he took over the business."

"Don't forget the war," I insisted. "All of those contracts for guns and bullets and grenades. Thaddeus made millions in the war."

Jimmy continued as though he hadn't heard me. "After Eleanor's father died, it seems that she and Thaddeus had one of those rich-people marriages. In public, they acted very happy, but in private—"

"They were probably at each others' throats. Because it's hard to be rich, isn't it?" I inspected the candy box and slipped a chocolate-covered pecan into my mouth. "Enough with the history lesson. Why would you think I'm poor Rutherfurd's rich wife?"

For a moment I thought that Jimmy was going to admit it was all a joke. But he didn't. "Last August, Rutherfurd went to Washington for a week of meetings with President Wilson, and when he returned, his wife was gone."

"Like I said, why—"

"But Eleanor wasn't living in New York when Thaddeus went to Washington. She was stuck in a sanatorium he'd put her in a year earlier. Except that she ran away in July. No one knows where Eleanor was until October, when she caught the flu and was quarantined at St. Joseph's Hospital in Paterson."

"St. Joseph's . . ." A chill ran through my body and my knees trembled. Jimmy was off the chair and settling me into it before I could stop him. I folded my arms around my chest, trying to banish my painful memories. "St. Joe's was a hell of a place in October."

Jimmy kneeled on the carpet by the side of my chair. "Here's what happened. Eleanor Rutherfurd, runaway wife of one of the most powerful men in America, and Viola Vermillion, a singer in vaudeville"—he was inches away from me, and I looked at him as he spoke my name—"both caught the Spanish influenza last October. They were admitted to St. Joseph's around the same time and ended up in the same ward."

"Ward Five," I mumbled.

Jimmy pulled the coverlet from the bed and eased it about me. He found a handkerchief from somewhere and tucked it into my hand. Only then did I feel the tears welling in my eyes.

"Both Eleanor and Viola had it bad," said Jimmy. "But they held on, and despite their differences, they became friends. Confidences were made. Final wishes were exchanged. But then, Viola died."

I shook my head; the tears trickled from my cheeks. *No. I almost died.*

"Eleanor got better," said Jimmy. "When she was well enough to walk, she snuck out of the hospital in the dead of night."

Jimmy had been staring at me as he told his story. Now it was my turn to stare. "How . . . how do you know any of this?"

"Eleanor's maid told me. She's very worried that Eleanor might have brain fever."

"Her maid?"

"Hilda Braun." He peered at me as if the name meant something. It didn't. "She'd visited Eleanor in the hospital and saw Eleanor's fascination with Viola. She helped Eleanor leave St. Joseph's and brought her to her home. But Eleanor ran away from *her*, leaving a trail that ended in Viola's third-floor walkup."

I listened as Jimmy's story continued.

"Hilda came by weekly to visit Eleanor at the walkup, delivering groceries. Eleanor refused to leave Viola's flat and she sat for hours at the piano, playing through Viola's sheet music and singing along. She dressed only in Viola's clothes and demanded Hilda bring her red hair coloring. Mrs. Rutherfurd seemed possessed. Finally, she disappeared entirely, taking many of Viola's things with her. After I heard all *that*, I went to all of the booking agents in New York and found that Viola'd been booked on the Pantages Circuit."

"That's quite a story. Let me make sure I got it straight." I blew my nose into the handkerchief. Then I took as big a breath as I could. "You think I'm this Eleanor, that I've got brain fever or amnesia or something, and that I'm only pretending to be Viola. Is that right?"

"I do," said Jimmy.

"Sounds to me like you're dreaming up a new moving picture show."

"I'm not."

"Are you even listening to yourself? Do you know how crazy that sounds?"

"I know what it sounds like," he said. "But I asked the

questions and I did the footwork. I've been watching you since Seattle and it all fits together that you're Eleanor."

He'd been watching me? What did that even mean?

"Even if someone made themselves look like me, nobody *sounds* like me," I said.

"Eleanor had a voice, too. She took singing lessons as a child. Even sang in the Mount Holyoke College Choir."

"Ha!" I'd really had enough. "I've never sung in a choir and never will."

"Viola might never sing like Eleanor, but it wouldn't be hard for Eleanor to sing like Viola. All it takes is practice."

That was just too much! "Nobody sings like me and nobody moves like me. And nobody ever will. Once you see me on stage, you never forget me."

He had a ready comeback. "Funny you should say that. I've talked about Viola Vermillion to anyone I could find, and from what I heard, there's something different about her now. She's not the same singer she used to be."

I couldn't deny that. "We're all different these days. You can't be that sick, you can't almost die, without it changing you. It took months for my voice to be strong enough for two-a-day."

"Despite everything Rutherfurd said about her, I figure that Eleanor is a very smart woman. Unhappy, but smart. She probably thought vaudeville was a good place to hide since you're always on the move. You can change your name, henna your hair, raise your skirts."

"Sing in front of thousands of people a day," I protested. "Have your photograph plastered on theatre walls. Record your voice. Aim for the Big Time. How will that hide you?"

Jimmy's grin faded slightly. Still, he persisted. "If you're not Eleanor, who are you? Tell me about yourself, Miss Viola Vermillion."

I grabbed another chocolate from the box. "How does *Viola Clark* sound to you? Not quite as glamorous as Viola Vermillion, is it?" I bit into the candy as hard as I could. "Look at me. Look at me real good. Do I even look like an Eleanor to you?"

Jimmy did look at me. Pretty closely. And then he glanced at the almost-empty box of chocolates. "Rutherfurd had another name for his wife, besides Eleanor. A pet name."

"Which was?"

"Butterball." Jimmy smiled crookedly at the chocolate in my hand. "She had the sweetest tooth in New York State and weighed one fifty, two hundred pounds."

I licked my lips before tossing the chocolate into my mouth. I rose from the chair, placed the palms of my hands along the sides of my breasts, and ran my hands down my curves, clearly outlining my shapely but slender form. Jimmy had just lost his argument.

"And besides." I rubbed his nose in his defeat. "My booking agent knows where I am every week. Nobody runs away from their agent."

"Agents can be paid to keep their mouths shut," he replied. "Anyone can be paid off. With the right amount of money"

And there it was. Finally. "Is that what you're here for? You think I got the *right amount of money*? You want some of it?"

"I'm not here for money. I'm here to do a job." He sounded almost offended.

"Are you a cop?"

"I'm a missing persons man. And you have to admit I've done a great job. Better than the Pinkertons they hired."

"But you didn't! You only got it half right. There *was* a woman in the bed next to me at St. Joseph's. And she did ask a lot of questions, wanted to know almost everything about me. But she died. I'm the one who lived." Life had been so hard while I recovered; I didn't want to remember it anymore. I was determined to get Jimmy to finish his storytelling. "Why does Rutherfurd want his wife found? Do you even know?"

That shut Jimmy up, and once again, I had the upper hand. Because I knew exactly what Thaddeus Rutherfurd wanted from his wife. He wanted the red leather notebook that Eleanor gave me the night before she died. The red leather notebook where Rutherfurd recorded his secret dealings. The red leather notebook that someone stole from Stuart the afternoon he was murdered.

Yet Jimmy said nothing about the notebook. Was it possible Rutherfurd hadn't told him about it? Was it possible Rutherfurd only told Jimmy to find Eleanor, trusting that she carried the notebook with her and he could force it from her?

If Eleanor had left Thaddeus, if she'd deserted him, for whatever reason, he must be furious with her. If he even thought his wife was involved in something shady like vaudeville, he'd tie her up and hide her in the attic for the rest of her life. And if he ever heard she was involved in something as lurid as her lover's murder, he'd throw away the key to the attic door.

That would be something, wouldn't it? Telling Rutherfurd his wayward wife had been found, but, oh, by the way, she was locked up in jail for murder?

And once Detective Petersen told me to not leave town, jail seemed a looming possibility. Could I be put on trial for Stu's murder, found guilty, and, I don't know, hanged? I swallowed hard, feeling the noose tightening around my neck. It could happen, unless someone found Stu's murderer.

All at once I realized that Jimmy Harrigan, missing persons man, had to be that someone. If he'd really outsmarted the Pinkertons like he said, he could solve Stu's murder.

Couldn't he?

I knew what to do now, how to close this act. A smile curled slowly on my lips, the first smile since that last piece of chocolate melted on my tongue, but I forced it into a frown. I let my lip quiver. I allowed my shoulders to sag. I manufactured a tear. Two tears. Hell, I even sniffled.

"Well, you caught me."

"Huh?"

"I'm Eleanor. That's what you wanted to hear, isn't it?"

"Sure. I just expected . . . more resistance."

Had I miscalculated? Had I confessed too quickly? Nah. Jimmy believed me. Because he *wanted* to believe me. Just like he wanted to believe Eleanor's maid's tall tale.

"But here's the rub," I told him. "Dorothy Garrard—if you've been following me, you know who she is—got her father to convince the San Francisco Police that I might have murdered Stu. Detective Petersen even threatened to arrest me tonight. And if he does, Thaddeus isn't going to be too happy. And when he's not happy . . ."

Before Jimmy could imagine how my sentence ended, I said, "Wouldn't it be in your best interest to find out who really killed Stu? If you can hunt me down, you should be able to find his murderer."

"Whoa, stop right there. Your dead piano player is none of my business. My job was to find you and hand you over."

"You think the great Thaddeus Rutherfurd wants a wife tainted with a murder charge? The newspapers will have a field day." I waited, hoping that Jimmy was imagining the headlines. I certainly was. *Rutherfurd Shamed! Rutherfurd Humiliated! Rutherfurd Destroyed by Scandal!*

"Telling Thaddeus I've been working in vaudeville will be bad enough. If Stu's murderer isn't found soon, I'll be singing the blues in the San Francisco jail when he arrives. That'll make him real mad."

I saw Jimmy thinking it all through. Now to reel him in.

"So how about it?" I asked. "You gonna find Stu's murderer? You gonna keep Thaddeus Rutherfurd's wife out of jail? Or maybe you're just a runaway-wife kind of missing persons man. Not good enough to find a murderer."

"I'm plenty good." Then he snapped his mouth shut, as if he realized he'd nipped at my bait.

"Then why won't—"

"Because Rutherfurd hired me to find his wife and I have."

"But—"

"No *buts*. I've been looking for you long enough, Mrs. Rutherfurd." The name hung in the air. "And if your husband has to bail you out of the San Francisco jail, that's pretty much okay with me. Because I'm tempted to get you locked in there myself."

CHAPTER FIFTEEN

Not much later, Jimmy swaggered out of my room like he'd been practicing dramatic exits his entire life. I set the double locks against him and anchored a chair under the doorknob. Then I looked for something to kick, something to break, something to tear to shreds.

Jimmy's story had thrown me for a loop. Had he really been following me for months? No wonder he knew how to play the songs I'd sung in other cities.

He'd laid down the law before he left, warning me to not even think about bolting on him. I was being watched every minute of the day and night, he told me. The possibilities of what he'd do next drove me to pace the worn carpet. I stomped from the door (to recheck the doorknob) to the window (was someone out there spying on me?) to the bed (where I ate the remaining pieces of chocolate) and to the dresser (where I finished the champagne).

I charged into Stu's room, needing to know that Jimmy had not been in there. To my relief, the room looked unchanged. Every nerve in my body tingled to run away, and in a big city like San Francisco, there had to be a dozen ways to sneak out of town. Especially if I didn't care where I ended up. And I almost didn't care, because one thing I'd learned since surviving the influenza was that I could start over anywhere.

But as I stood in Stu's room, gazing at everything that belonged to *him*, I did care about his things. About abandoning them. Margaret Wilson had wound her way into my heart this afternoon and I wanted her to have everything that belonged to her son. But I wanted to give his belongings to her myself, not dump them with some policeman to drop off at Alcatraz. I also wanted to look through Stu's things again to make sure the letter Dorothy really wanted was not here.

Even more important than Stu's stuff was Stu's murder. The person who killed him needed to be caught, and then he needed to be punished.

"This would be the perfect time to tell me what to do with one of your lyrics, Stu," I whispered to his room. But all I heard was Detective Petersen's voice as we drove around San Francisco earlier tonight. *You knew him best*, he'd said. As if *knowing Stu best* meant I also could figure out who murdered him.

But as I stood in Stu's room, those words began to feel just right. I did know Stu best. I might be the only person capable of finding his murderer.

But there was no solving Stu's murder if I wasn't safe, so I returned to my room, picked up my handbag, and carried it back to his room. I pulled a chair to his small table and unloaded the contents of his leather pouch. Then I removed Madame Savage from my handbag.

Just as Stu'd showed me the night before we left New Jersey, I lined up his gun-cleaning tools, careful to keep everything in order. I carefully disassembled, cleaned, and reassembled my new gun and loaded the bullets from Stu's pouch. When my work was finished, I put the gun in the pocket in my handbag.

Even though I'd lost Mademoiselle Savage to the police, I never let Madame Savage leave my side.

♫

For the second time in three days, I left my hotel room at seven o'clock in the morning. This time, I peered around every corner looking for Jimmy Harrigan. Once in the lobby, I stopped to talk to Washington, the porter.

"I'm sure you've seen Mr. Harrigan. Blond-haired. Blue eyes. Long fingers." I resisted other descriptions that came to mind. *Smooth-talker. Liar. Spy.* "Someone let him into my room last night."

The porter was horrified. "That wasn't me, miss!"

I believed Washington at once, but now I wondered if Jimmy might have a key to my room. "What I wanted to know is . . . is Mr. Harrigan staying at this hotel?"

The porter nodded. "Room 701, miss. Just above you."

"How long has he been there?"

After a little consideration, Washington said, "He arrived the same day you did."

Almost a whole week and I didn't know it? I hadn't even seen Jimmy until that night at the Pan. "Is he still in the hotel this morning?"

"He's been gone about an hour now, Miss Vermillion."

I was tempted to let myself into Jimmy's room. After all,

two could play at this game. If I was going to talk Jimmy into helping me find Stu's murderer, I should know more about him. Like if I could trust him with anything besides playing my music in order and on tempo.

"There's Mr. Harrigan now." The porter nodded to the hotel entrance.

Jimmy was at my side before I decided what to do. He looked down at the small cloth bag in my hands. "You weren't running away, were you?"

"Of course not," I answered sweetly, letting my bag sway from side to side. "But I am going one place where you can't follow."

♫

In every city Stu and I played, I visited the Young Women's Christian Association at least once, hopefully twice, and sometimes every other day. The San Francisco Y I wanted was miles from the Pan, and today I enjoyed every minute of my solitary bus ride, knowing that even if Jimmy was following me in a taxicab, he'd never get into the place. That was the point of the YWCA: to provide a safe haven for women. Of course, the good ladies of the Y wouldn't allow a vaudeville trouper like me to rent a room from them, but they did allow me to use their swimming pool.

After changing into my bathing costume, I quickly headed to the pool. It was bigger than the stage at the Pantages, and the high-ceilinged room felt almost like a cathedral.

I stood at the edge of the pool and sang a scale. My voice bounced along the water, rolled onto the tiled walls, reverberated off the back wall, and returned to me. I repeated the scale a halftone higher. I ran through the major scales and then worked through some minor ones. The sound was glorious, much richer than any sound ever heard on a Pantages stage. Too bad I couldn't audition my act in a swimming pool.

I had goose bumps on my arms and legs as I wondered what it would be like to really let loose in here. Were my lungs truly healed from the ravages of the influenza? Stu thought they were, but I was doing the singing, and it felt like my lungs still held me back.

As I began my laps, I tried to put the last few days into some type of order. Someone had murdered my lover and stolen my notebook and taken seventy-five dollars from his pocket; another someone was egging on the police to arrest me; my livelihood was threatened; I'd found out my lover had a mother and I'd spent a lovely hour with her; and finally, my new piano player turned out to be a missing persons man accusing me of being the runaway wife of America's most successful munitions tycoon. If this had been a plot for one of Mary Pickford's moving pictures, I wouldn't have believed it.

And still the question remained: What was I going to do about it?

After completing my two miles, I swam another, the memory of last night's box of chocolates weighing heavily on me. At least I'd turned the tables on Jimmy and bought myself some time. By agreeing to be Eleanor, I'd made him responsible for getting me off the hook with the police. Of course, Jimmy hadn't agreed to help me find Stu's murderer, but he looked to have the earmarks of a prime hunting dog. Maybe all I needed was to give him was a scent.

I left the YWCA convinced I had the smarts to ferret out

who killed Stu. But until I found out who stole the red leather notebook from Stu's pocket, how to best Thaddeus Rutherfurd was going to be a lot harder to resolve.

CHAPTER
SIXTEEN

Jimmy strode through the reporter's bullpen of the *San Francisco Chronicle* toward the desk in the back, where his best friend, Erwin Stanton, pecked furiously at a typewriter.

Jimmy dropped into the chair next to Erwin's, knowing that even if he *could* interrupt, he *shouldn't*. Just like Jimmy shouldn't have told Viola last night that he knew she was Thaddeus Rutherfurd's runaway wife. Just like he should stop thinking of her as Viola. And stop looking at her, listening to her, and inching forward to smell her as though she were the sultry blues chanteuse she performed as on stage. He knew he should think of and address her only as *Mrs. Rutherfurd*, but he couldn't. He couldn't even call her Eleanor or Nelly. No, he'd always call her Viola, and he wasn't quite sure why.

He'd come to Erwin this morning for information that only his best friend could provide. The best friend whose six paragraphs about Stuart's murder had appeared in Tuesday's newspaper. And whose eight paragraphs reporting that Stuart Wiley was actually San Francisco's own thought-to-be-dead-in-1915 Stuart Wilson that ran on Wednesday. It was obvious that the investigation into Stuart's murder was stalled, and—despite what he'd told Viola last night—Jimmy needed to know why.

After all, Stuart'd been killed on Monday afternoon and here it was, already Friday. If the police hadn't arrested anyone by now—something Erwin would have reported in today's newspaper—they either weren't capable or they weren't trying. Jimmy figured it was some of both. And since the police weren't doing their job, he had to do it for them, because Viola wasn't safe until Stuart's murderer was caught.

Erwin continued his assault on the typewriter, now and then releasing his index fingers to send the carriage crashing back to a new line. Jimmy respected that Erwin had a job to do, maybe even a deadline, but so did Jimmy, and he tapped his hat against his fingertips to get Erwin's attention. It must have been a slow news day because Erwin stopped mid-peck and looked up.

"You know anything about a woman?" Jimmy asked innocently enough, even though he'd carefully crafted his opening salvo. "Maybe more of a girl. She's from here. Her name is Dorothy Garrard?"

"Jesus, Mary, and Joseph!" Erwin's eyes went wide. "When you hit San Francisco last week, you said you weren't working on anything big."

I'm not, Jimmy wanted to say. Except that he couldn't lie to his best friend. Scratch that. He couldn't lie twice—he'd already misled Erwin about his real reason for being in San Francisco.

As far as Erwin knew, Jimmy was in town doing a favor for an army buddy. Erwin didn't need to know that Thaddeus Rutherfurd had hired Jimmy to find his runaway wife. Or that he'd found her and her lover had been murdered. And he especially didn't need to know that Frank Cassady—Jimmy's own cousin—was working for Rutherfurd. No, Erwin didn't need to know any of that, at least not yet.

"I'm not working on Dorothy," Jimmy said lightly, because that much was true. He'd bet his stripes that Dorothy was on the periphery of Stuart's murder. All Jimmy needed right now was some context. "It's just that her name came up. So what do you know about her?"

Erwin stared at Jimmy as if he knew he was being kept in the dark. Again. "She's the daughter of the commandant at Alcatraz Island, and Daddy's a bosom buddy of the mayor. That's the first thing to know about her."

"What kind of girl is she, Miss Dorothy?"

"Not your kind, kiddo."

Jimmy put his right hand over his heart. "I promise that pursuing her never crossed my mind."

"It better not," Erwin almost growled. "You're getting married next month, and it's my job to get you to the altar. Miss Amelia will skin my hide if you call off your wedding. Or she'll poison me, or something. Trust you to fall in love with someone who knows a dozen different ways to do away with the people who cross her."

Jimmy knew full well that he was getting married next month, and how could he ever forget Amelia's temper? Or her skillful methods of retaliation, and how she smothered him with kisses afterward? But even those fine qualities paled in comparison to his fiancée's quick intelligence, bold desires, and raw possessiveness. Jimmy squirmed with longing.

Just to make sure he was back in Erwin's good graces,

Jimmy added humbly, "Yes sir, trust me to marry someone with talent and a temper."

Erwin must have been satisfied. "I don't read the *Chron's* society pages much, but I do know that Miss Garrard volunteered during the war, all of it on Alcatraz. She hardly leaves the island."

"So if Dorothy Garrard was at the Pantages about the time that Stuart Wilson was murdered on Monday, does that mean anything to you?"

Erwin sat back in his chair. "You're here about the Wilson murder?"

"I'm not." Jimmy felt a little rush that he was able to answer truthfully. "I'm just asking questions for a friend."

"Well, as your friend, I think you should come clean and tell me what you're really doing."

Jimmy thought so, too; it was unnatural not to share everything he knew with Erwin. Except that what Erwin didn't know might save his life. Because if Stuart's murderer was after Viola, Jimmy was in danger for protecting her. And if Erwin knew that Jimmy was in trouble, Erwin would put himself in danger to save him. And Jimmy wouldn't let his friend step in front of another bullet for him.

After remembering the shot that tore through Erwin's upper arm and probably made every keystroke on that typewriter a misery, Jimmy answered. "Can't."

"Then I can't tell you any more about Miss Garrard."

Erwin sat back in his chair, folded his arms, and seemed ready to wait until Jimmy yielded. Except that when there was a question to be asked, Erwin had to ask it. "You're sure it was Dorothy Garrard? How would you even know what she—"

"Because she was back at the Pan yesterday."

"The *Pan*? You mean the Pantages?" said Erwin. "Sounds like you're really getting around San Francisco. I've only been here a few months, but even I know that no one mentions Miss Garrard and a murder in the same breath."

"That's what I figured. She seems kind of high-and-mighty."

"The Princess of Alcatraz," said Erwin without irony. "The *Chronicle's* very careful about writing about ladies with fathers like hers. She's the commandant's only child and her mother died back in '09. That's all I know. Really."

Erwin's tone was almost apologetic, and Jimmy wondered if, after a lifetime of living in New Orleans, Erwin regretted his decision to move to San Francisco. Jimmy'd been shattered when his best friend didn't return to New Orleans after the war, although he certainly understood the allure of the vivacious Red Cross volunteer in Paris who lured Erwin to return to her home in San Francisco. Too bad that she dumped him a month later, right after Erwin landed a job at the *Chronicle*.

"What about this Detective Petersen?" Jimmy asked. "What's his story?"

"You want to know about Petersen? You sure you're not working this murder?"

"Like I told you, just helping out a friend."

"You can tell this friend that Petersen's honest," Erwin replied. "Seems to be a straight talker."

"How about your coroner? Will he talk to me?" asked Jimmy. "Off the record, so to say? About Stuart's death?"

"My reporting hasn't been good enough for you? You have read my columns, haven't you?"

"They were fine," Jimmy replied. "Fascinating, even. But

they didn't read like you actually saw the Pantages balcony or Stuart's body."

Erwin ran his fingers along the keys of his typewriter, as if he'd seen a sudden speck of dust. "I could have. Done both. But . . ."

As Erwin struggled, Jimmy replied, "I know what you mean. I've seen enough death myself."

"Doc Blakeney's our coroner, and he'll talk to you," Erwin replied softly. "I can call him. Tell him you're coming over."

"That's all I need. Thanks." Jimmy stood up.

"Whoa, son." Erwin plucked Jimmy's hat from his hands. "You asked a lot of questions today. How about you sit down and answer some? Like what's the case that really brought you here? Does it have any anarchists involved? Any communists or kidnappers?"

Jimmy grabbed for his hat, but Erwin held it behind his back.

"It's not that straightforward," said Jimmy.

"Which is why they called you in. Best missing persons man on the East Coast. So I'm guessing you're hunting down someone."

Jimmy sighed. "Don't know if I'm the best anymore, but I'm here. I made it back from France. *We* made it back."

"Yes, we did." Erwin tossed Jimmy his hat. "But before you go—"

"You're going to warn me about something, right?"

"Yes, sir, I am. And it comes down to this: be careful. No matter how alluring San Francisco is, it's not your town. And it's nothing like New Orleans."

Jimmy'd already figured that out. No matter how similar their tall buildings, speeding taxicabs, and weary inhabitants, most cities were nothing like each other. But he hadn't been in San Francisco long enough to know what made this one different. "What is it like, then?"

"I don't know entirely yet," Erwin admitted. "Except I get the feeling it's got a great *future.* As long as there's not another earthquake and fire."

"We've all got a great future. Until the next catastrophe comes along."

Erwin put his hand on Jimmy's shoulder. "All I'm saying is, be careful."

"You know me, Erwin." Jimmy eased his hat onto his head, hitting the top with his palm to make it stay put. "I'm the soul of careful, just like you. All I ever ask is one or two questions."

CHAPTER SEVENTEEN

THE CORONER'S office was deep in the basement of the Hall of Justice. Doctor Blakeney opened the door himself wearing a bloodied apron and wiping his hands on the white towel that was anchored by his suspender straps.

"You Harrigan? You're late. Erwin called an hour ago."

Jimmy silently cursed Erwin. "Thanks for giving me some time today, sir."

"You don't have to tell me how you know Erwin, I can tell by your accent. You from New Orleans too?"

"Yes, sir." Jimmy followed the doctor through the small, disorganized front office and into what appeared to be the workroom. He quickly sat in a chair, knowing it'd be more difficult for the doctor to push him out when he started asking too many questions. Like this one: "I don't suppose there's any chance Stuart Wilson committed suicide?"

"No chance at all," answered the doctor.

"I understand it was a double gunshot?"

"Correct. One to his right shoulder, the other to his heart. Both close-up, both from the confiscated Savage."

"Any other wounds?"

A shrill whistle sounded from behind Jimmy, and the doctor took a steaming kettle from a burner and poured water from it into a basin. Then he nodded to a closed door. "I've got some work back there. Do you mind?"

"Not at all." Jimmy followed Blakeney into the coldest room he'd been in since leaving France, not much surprised to see four covered bodies on shelves against the wall.

"My assistant's out sick today; I could use another pair of hands if you've got time." Blakeney put his basin down and went to one of the bodies.

"Yes, sir." Jimmy snapped to the other side of the stretcher the body was on and deftly assisted the doctor in carrying it to the large center table.

Blakeney studied Jimmy. "You've done this before, haven't you?"

Jimmy had, but army hospitals in France were the last thing he ever wanted to talk about again. Politely he asked: "About Stuart, sir?"

"You haven't taken any notes, so I'm guessing you're not a reporter like Erwin. Police? But not San Francisco police."

"Other wounds, sir?"

Jimmy stood silently as Blakeney added a clump of something to the hot water, then scrubbed his hands in the solution, giving so much attention to his fingernails that Jimmy thought he was going into surgery.

"There was one thing," the doctor offered in a stage whisper-worthy voice.

Jimmy was surprised. He hadn't taken Blakeney for a doctor who loved dramatics.

But evidently, the doctor did. As Jimmy's full attention

settled on him, Blakeney said, "Wilson had a very large love bite on his neck."

"Sir?" Jimmy took a second to regroup. "A love bite, sir?"

"You know what a love bite is, don't you?"

Jimmy knew all about love bites. Good Lord, yes, he did. He also knew about table girls, hand jobs, and almost-blinding absinthe hangovers. He hadn't honed his piano skills in a whorehouse to come away ignorant about sex. He just hadn't figured that Viola was a love biter, although he warmed quickly to the idea. Jimmy warmed so well that he gulped back the need for a drink of water. He nodded his understanding to the coroner.

"The right side," said the coroner. "About the size of a quarter. Yellowed, so it had been there a while. A few days, maybe."

"The police . . . do they know about the bites?"

"If they read my report, they will."

"About the police, sir. This Detective Petersen . . ." Jimmy lengthened his words, hoping the doctor would finish his sentence for him. But Blakeney stood solidly, as though he'd played this match before. Jimmy was forced to continue. "He's a straight one, that's what Erwin says. And honest."

"Nobody gets anything past him—police or public. He's already got one suspect, that girl Wilson was traveling with." The doctor looked sharply at Jimmy. "Is that why you're here? For the girl?"

Jimmy ground his teeth sharply and wondered if Erwin had slapped a sign on his back. A sign that said *LADIES MAN*. Or *FOOL FOR LOVE*.

Jimmy was only investigating Stuart because he was concerned that Viola would do something stupid and jinx his deal with Rutherfurd. Jimmy could set up Amelia in a very pleasant house in the Lower Garden District with what Rutherfurd was paying him, and for Amelia's sake, Jimmy ignored the doctor's question.

"So that's everything? Bullet to the right shoulder; kill shot to the heart; a large, yellowed love bite on the left side of his neck."

"Probably from a Saturday night of sex." The coroner's delivery was completely expressionless, but Jimmy was almost sure that Blakeney was attempting to make him uncomfortable.

"Where'd you serve, Harrigan?" The doctor removed his hands from the bowl and grabbed the towel under his suspenders. "Field hospital? You've got the temperament for it."

Jimmy much preferred the coroner this way: soldier to soldier.

"No, sir. It's not that. I've worked with some doctors before." When Blakeney seemed interested, Jimmy continued, "My fiancée's going to be a doctor."

"Most girls don't have the stomach for that type of work. She must be pretty special."

"She is. She ran the women's ward singlehandedly during the war." Jimmy watched as the doctor began removing the blanket that covered the corpse. He leaned toward the doctor and corpse just to confirm that he had no fear. "Erwin said you served here during the worst part of the epidemic."

"The worst part in San Francisco. It missed us in the spring but caught us good in the fall."

Jimmy's thoughts abruptly switched to Viola. "Did any of your patients have brain fever? I mean, the patients who survived. Any of them have amnesia afterwards?"

"Is this about your fiancée?" Blakeney asked cautiously.

Jimmy shook his head, unable to imagine Amelia falling victim to anything. "No, not her. But is it possible that surviving the flu could cause a woman to forget her past?"

"I haven't heard of a woman losing her memory from the influenza, but it would be convenient, wouldn't it?"

"What do you mean?"

"Everyone has something they want to forget," said the doctor. "Even you, I'm guessing."

♫

Jimmy left the coroner—but not without offering Dr. Blakeney a night on the town if he ever came to New Orleans—and made his way to the Western Union storefront. He was thinking about that love bite on Stu's neck, wondering if Amelia might test her teeth on his own neck. And if he'd like it.

He went up to the tall desk braced against the wall, grabbed paper and pencil, and began writing. The words came quickly enough.

Wife found. STOP. Suggest we meet San Francisco April 4. STOP. Confirm receipt. STOP.

If all of the wires across the country were working, Thaddeus Rutherfurd might know in less than an hour that his wife had been found. It would take him five days to travel from New York to the West Coast, which meant that Jimmy could collect his pay, leave San Francisco, and be in Amelia's arms in New Orleans in less than two weeks.

All Jimmy had to do between now and then was keep Viola safe and in San Francisco. And figure out how to tell Erwin what he was really doing here. And prepare to face

Frank, because as Rutherfurd's right-hand man, Frank would certainly be on that train.

But first, Jimmy needed to stop thinking about love bites and Thaddeus Rutherfurd's wife at the same time. Because, if Jimmy had learned anything in the past year, only a woman could throw him off his game.

CHAPTER
EIGHTEEN

Gripping the yellow telegram from San Francisco in his hand, Thaddeus Rutherfurd rolled back in his leather chair. He looked down from his office window at the men, mules, and wagons of the 27th New York Infantry Division parading below him. No building on this block of Fifth Avenue was as monumental as Rutherfurd Munitions, and as president of the company, he surveyed the street like the kingdom it was.

Every office building along the avenue was festooned with red, white, and blue bunting, their windows opened wide for men and women to lean out and shower the returning soldiers with confetti. Row upon row of marching men saluted as they approached Rutherfurd's building, and he returned their respect by flicking his cigar ash out the window.

Turning his head north, he saw the crowded reviewing stands, patriotically festooned with banners, flowers, and American flags. Thaddeus Rutherfurd, supplier of the American grenades, machine guns, and rifles that won the Great

War, had been expected to take his place on the reviewing stand over an hour ago. But the telegram from San Francisco had bolted him to his chair.

"Mr. Rutherfurd," Francis Cassady reminded his boss, "the parade chairman is waiting for you. The mayor's asked about you, too."

"Let them wait." Rutherfurd contemplated the telegram once more. "Let them all wait."

"Of course, b—"

"You're the one who suggested Harrigan. Do you think he's really found her?" Thaddeus tossed the telegram onto his desk.

"Jimmy's the best I've worked with. He's clever and fearless, not to mention lucky." Cassady's shoulder twitched suddenly, as if he hated praising the missing persons man he'd hired. "If he says he's found her, he has."

"And he won't be a problem for us." There was no question in his comment, for Thaddeus knew that Cassady was as capable with his knife and gun as he was with his fists.

"I'll make sure of it." Cassady retrieved the telegraph from his boss's desk. "How do you want to handle this, sir?"

Thaddeus wanted it all handled yesterday. He wasn't keen about leaving New York City just now, not with the newspapers and magazines all requesting interviews about how he won the war, but nothing was more important—or more delicate—than retrieving his red leather notebook.

"What's my schedule like?"

"Dinner with the general and his soldiers at the Armory tonight. Then it's the Follies."

"After tonight?"

"The usual dollars-and-cents meetings. All leading up to the dinner and the awards ceremony in Boston. I can get your private car hooked up to the twentieth century overnight and we can make Chicago in twenty hours. From there, we hook up on the UP. It's four days from Chicago to San Francisco. So five days out, one day in San Francisco, five days back."

Thaddeus stood up and his office butler appeared immediately with his overcoat. "Telegraph Harrigan we're coming out. We'll let him know our arrival later."

"There's one other item on your calendar." Cassady followed his boss on his walk to the elevator. "What about Miss Davenport? You told her you'd see her tonight."

"Send her flowers and a note. No, call the chauffeur to take her to Tiffany's. She can look over engagement rings and wedding bands. That should keep her quiet for now."

CHAPTER NINETEEN

DESPITE MAKING me feel like I was being watched every second, Jimmy didn't turn up at the Pan until fifteen minutes before curtain. I'd almost wondered if his story last night had been some type of practical joke, although there was nothing funny about being told that Thaddeus Rutherfurd was on my tail. Especially when I had no idea who stole the red leather notebook from Stu's pocket the day he was murdered.

Without a knock or a noise, Jimmy slid into the ladies' dressing room as easily as any magician. And he was definitely more dashing. He wore his tux well, and his blond hair was shined and sharply parted on the side.

I glanced around the room, surprised that we were alone and sure it wouldn't last long. "You've got some smile on you. What'd you get yourself into this afternoon?"

His grin deepened. "Just making the rounds of old San Francisco."

He was so pleased with himself that I grabbed his tux lapels, pulled him close, and sniffed him from his cummerbund to his collar. I liked a glass of gin as well as the next performer, but not before a show.

Our faces were mere inches from each other when he said, "Not a drop, I promise. You don't need to worry about me."

I pushed him away. "Took the pledge, did you?"

"Nope. But even if I was drunk off my—"

He stopped—perhaps remembering that I was Thaddeus Rutherfurd's wife—before continuing with, "I always get the job done. I'm a trouper."

At the mention of the troupe, I seized my chance to voice what I'd been worrying about since I'd returned from swimming, hoping I could make Jimmy solve Stu's murder. "Do you think one of the troupers murdered Stu?"

"You got someone picked out? Someone have it in for him?"

"No." I was still chilled at the thought that someone I'd worked with killed Stu. We weren't just a troupe; we were like a family. Well, at least like siblings who always competed with each other. "Who else could it be? If only Stu'd told me he was from San Francisco, I might—"

"I'm guessing he didn't tell you plenty about his past."

I hated Jimmy Harrigan right then. He might play the piano good enough and he might get along with Maestro Mitch, but he was so smug about . . . everything. The last thing I needed was to be reminded that Stu hadn't been honest with me. That maybe, despite our months of intimacy, he didn't trust me. And it felt unnatural talking about Stu to a stranger. Especially since Jimmy was holding me hostage for one of the richest men in America.

But Jimmy had no qualms. "He kept a lot of secrets from you. But they usually do."

"They?"

"Anyone involved in a murder. Murderer. Victim. Suspects. There's always a secret involved when someone gets murdered, and usually more than one."

"How—"

"I'm a full-fledged missing persons man, but I've done my share of detecting. Shootings. Poisonings. Divorces. Learned it at my Daddy's knee. Just like the song goes."

He was only a copper, my gallant Dad-dy.
Walking a beat, like so many Irish Pad-dies.
But he became a hero one day, yes sir, that's what
he told me.
So listen right now and hear what I learned
By sitting at old Daddy's knee.

The lyrics were so trite and his delivery so wobbly that I almost smiled, something I hadn't felt like doing since . . . since I'd found Stu's body. For a moment, I wondered if Jimmy was trying to make me smile.

"You made that up just now," I told him.

"So I did." He picked up my feathered fan and perched on the stool, looking at me just like one of Kitty's poodles expecting a biscuit. "What do you really think of it?"

"Stick to piano playing, kid."

Jimmy's smile soured, as though he had really believed in his verse.

"Stick to detecting, too," I added. "If you're any good at it."

"Oh, I'm good at it. Or did you forget that I found you?"

Jimmy leaned in toward me, so close that the feathers in my hair flicked at his presence. In the mirror, his pale cornflower-blue eyes reflected back at me. His lips came to within an inch of my ear before he moaned.

"Eleanor."

His nearness unsettled me. My heart raced and my breath sharpened. In that moment, I wasn't sure of much. Was Jimmy Harrigan trying to unnerve me right before going on stage? Was he making a pass at me? Hadn't I just told myself that I hated him?

I smelled the brilliantine on his hair and the faint aroma of lemon verbena that he must have used after shaving. His lips parted, as if he was going to repeat Eleanor's name. In that moment, still mourning Stu, still longing for him despite the carnation fragrance in his bed sheets, I wondered what kissing Jimmy Harrigan would feel like.

Our eyes held each other's in the mirror. I wasn't going to be the first to look away, and I hoped my voice was steady as I said, "All right then, Mr. Missing Persons Man. How are we going to find out Stu's secrets?"

Jimmy blinked. Then he stepped back.

"Or are you still eager to let the cops lock me up?" I asked. "How many times do I need to tell you? Thaddeus isn't going to like it if his wife's in jail and accused of murder."

"There's a lot of stuff that Rutherfurd isn't going to like about you." Jimmy removed an imaginary speck of something from his trousers. "Like you sleeping with Stuart."

Even though I was flustered by my sudden attraction to Jimmy's lips, my mind returned to Stu and how much I missed him. He'd been such an eager lover, his talented fingers never tiring of exploring and satisfying me. Even better, he encouraged me to give as good as he gave.

As much as my body ached for Stu, I missed our professional partnership just as much. Just a few days ago, we were a team, headed to the Big Time. Now it'd be up to me to reach for the vaudeville stars, to play the Palace in New York. But before I got there, I'd make damn sure the person who killed him never saw the inside of a theater again.

But right now, the person in my way was Jimmy Harrigan. "Why won't you help me find out who killed Stu?"

"For the same reason that I'm not going to let you do it yourself," he said. "It's dangerous."

"You're *afraid* of the person who murdered Stu?"

"One of us should be afraid, and I'm okay if it's me." He grabbed the stool, brought it close to my chair—although not too close this time—and plopped onto it.

"I'm warning you." He shook his finger at me like a disapproving nun. "Stop asking me about Stuart Wilson. Stop thinking about him. It'll only get you more trouble."

♫

Of course I wasn't going to let Jimmy stop me from doing anything. I just wished I could ignore the carnation fragrance that had saturated Stu's pillow. And I wished Kitty had never told me about hearing Stu having sex in Portland. I even wished we didn't have any other female performers in the troupe, because he must have been cheating on me with one of them. One of *us*.

Ouch.

It was true that our vaudeville troupe was one big happy family, but it was only true until two of us had to compete for the same spot. Then—just like Tuck had said last night—it was dog-eat-dog.

I played my two spot to very enthusiastic applause and

whistles, then lingered backstage to watch the rest of the show. I stood through eight acts of almost-first-class entertainment, increasingly unable to imagine why any trouper might want Stu dead.

At the beginning of the eleven spot, Maestro Mitch tapped his baton against his stand. The orchestra launched into a thinly veiled imitation of the "Hesitation Waltz," made famous a few years ago by Irene and Vernon Castle. A few bars into the waltz, Rocco and Jeanette glided onto the stage.

I had seen Irene and Vern a few times on stage and knew that Rocco and Jeanette had tried to incorporate most of the Castles' act into theirs. Calling it *incorporating* was generous because so many of us built our acts entirely of bits stolen from other acts. Most everyone got away with stealing *something* as long as they never crossed paths with the acts they poached from. Since Vern Castle was dead and Irene was retired, Rocco must have thought it was safe to use their headline dance.

Rocco and Jeanette weren't half as talented as the Castles, but they were an attractive couple. Rocco accentuated his exotic coloring by slicking back his hair with pomade, performing in a well-cut long-tailed tuxedo, and making frequent eye contact with the audience. Jeanette's big kohl-rimmed eyes and long blonde (from a bottle) curls (from multiple irons) were clearly her attempt to look like her idol, movie star Mary Pickford. Jeanette's legs were long (entirely her own) and her stride matched Rocco's like they were made for each other.

Yet as tightly as Rocco held Jeanette, as deeply she looked into his eyes, as much as the audience clutched their hearts in belief they were witnessing a stunning romance, it was all an act. I knew from knee-bracing experience that Rocco would mash almost any woman in his path, and I'd seen Jeanette flirt with any man who might give her a step up.

As the waltz wound down, Rocco deftly finessed Jeanette into the Castles' second specialty, the tango. He asserted his total control of Jeanette from his very first step, moving her only where he allowed. She was almost like a boneless ragdoll, forced to go in any direction Rocco commanded.

The couple easily slipped into their third dance, a fast-paced novelty foxtrot. When Rocco led Jeanette into their first dip, I stepped over to the stage door where Charlie the doorman was sleeping. The large ledger that both talent and guests were supposed to sign when they entered and exited was open in front of him. The last signature in the book was dated over a week ago—before Stu and I'd arrived in San Francisco—and I couldn't read it. Not that I expected Stu's killer would have signed in when he entered the theater. I mean, none of the troupe members ever signed in. But it seemed worth the look, and now I could tell myself that I'd done something to find out who killed Stu.

I suddenly realized that Charlie had a great view of backstage. In just seconds, I saw Officer Tuck cradling Champ in his arms, Ugo Baldanza slipping a bottle of hooch to a stagehand, and all ten of the Ling Ting Tumblers stretching their bodies into fantastic distortions. It didn't take a detective to realize that Charlie—if he ever woke up—had a front-row seat to everything happening in this part of the theater.

As Rocco and Jeanette's foxtrot turned into a rapid two-step, I left Charlie to join Jimmy, who was as close to the stage as he could safely get. The dance wound down quickly and applause rumbled up from the house. The couple held their pose for a few seconds, and then Rocco kissed Jeanette's hand and escorted her into the wings. They turned toward the stage, listening, hoping their applause would build and that Mr. Steccati'd signal them to return for an encore. But even as the orchestra launched into their encore song vamp, the applause shriveled to nothing, and Mr. S shook his head.

Rocco dropped Jeanette's hand and headed to the basement. She shook her head and shoulders as if she was glad to be rid of him. She stared at Audrey's dressing room, even crossing her arms in front of her as if her determination alone would cause the door to open. And maybe Jeanette's gaze did have some special powers because, within seconds, Audrey swept out of the room with Lionel behind him.

Coiffed in an elaborate auburn wig decorated with curls and tendrils, tightly corseted into an emerald-green ball gown, and delicately made up with the finest French cosmetics (so said his publicity materials), the Sensational Audrey Merrick might have been the most beautiful woman in the world.

If you liked your women from before the war, that was. No young woman I knew would ever again allow herself to be trussed like a turkey in a corset. Or wear dresses that hit just above her ankles. Or suffer the fussiness of long hair.

Audrey's in-between boys followed him like baby ducks. The tuxedoed boys were charming and personable during their time on stage, but their primary job was to make sure the audience forgot them as soon as Audrey came on stage. Oscar, the in-between boy I'd seen arguing with Audrey and Jeanette, kept his eyes on Audrey at all times.

The orchestra played Audrey's musical introduction, "She's Your Girl Tonight." Lionel was trying to hurry Audrey toward his entrance, but the headliner glided toward Jeanette. I eased toward her also, my curiosity getting the best of me.

I wasn't close enough to hear their conversation, and it was too dark to see much except Audrey accepting a handkerchief from Lionel and giving it to Jeanette. As Audrey looked on, Jeanette patted the cloth along her décolleté.

Three bars later, Lionel put his hand under Audrey's elbow and turned him toward the stage. Audrey sashayed to center stage and curtsied to the audience. As the applause settled about him, an usher ran down the right-side aisle to the front of the stage. He leaned over the apron to hand Audrey a huge bouquet of long-stemmed red roses. Although this floral delivery happened every show, Audrey always gasped deliciously as the usher bowed before him with the flowers, as though the gesture of admiration caught him by surprise.

Jimmy's voice broke through my thoughts. "You're just as good as he is."

"What?" I'd lost all pretense of a backstage voice and one of the stagehands shushed me. "I'm not just as good. I'm a real woman."

"I mean you're just as good at the impersonation business. Audrey's got everyone almost convinced that he's a woman. Just like you've got almost everyone convinced you're a vaudeville singer."

A shiver ran through my shoulders and I rubbed my hands on my bare arms. Last night I wanted Jimmy to accept the truth that I *wasn't* Eleanor. But I'd also accepted that the only way he might help me find Stu's murderer was if he thought I *was* Eleanor. I had to keep him thinking he was right. Which meant I'd need to keep up my impersonation until Stu's murderer was caught. I didn't like lying to the kid, but I had to.

I wanted to say something smart that would put him in his place, but the words didn't come. I was surprised to see Oscar a few feet away, staring at Audrey and mimicking his every move. Before he caught me watching him, Oscar paraded toward Audrey's dressing room, his posture capturing Audrey's stride and strut. I never doubted that Oscar and the other in-between boys watched Audrey's act closely, but to see Oscar impersonate Audrey so perfectly was a revelation.

Still at center stage, Audrey smiled at the audience, read the card included with the flowers, and whispered a kiss toward the most expensive seats, as if knowing exactly where his admirer was seated. The audience applauded with approval. Then Oscar appeared on stage, taking the flowers from Audrey. He escorted them backstage and handed them to Jeanette. The delivery of flowers was part of Audrey's act, of course. This particular bouquet would be delivered to Audrey twice a day until it shriveled.

Jimmy sniffed. "Bet you two bits those aren't even roses."

"You're on." Feigning interest in Audrey's bouquet—just like any woman might—I got close enough to see that a dozen red roses had been dried and repainted red. Maybe they'd never been real red roses; maybe they weren't even on real flower stems. But there was a floral scent about them. Not roses, but . . . carnations. Yes, definitely carnations. Not the sweet, early morning fragrance of a well-tended garden but a sultry, steamy, hothouse blue. The same spicy fragrance on Stu's pillowcase.

"Get your own flowers," Jeanette sneered. "Maybe your boyfriend"—she nodded at Jimmy—"will buy you some if you give him something sweet."

With a smirk delivered to me only, Jeanette carried the bouquet toward Audrey's dressing room. The handkerchief Audrey had given to Jeanette fell to the floor, and Jimmy swooped it up. He took a step toward Jeanette, but she closed the dressing room door before he reached her.

I snatched the cloth from Jimmy's hand and held it below my nose. Carnations.

"I'll leave you to return it," Jimmy said.

"What?"

"The monogram on the handkerchief. A. M. Audrey Merrick."

"But . . . it came out of Lionel's pocket."

"A. M." Jimmy repeated. "It might have come out of Lionel's pocket, but it belongs to Audrey."

"And Jeanette used it last."

As if he heard us talking about him, Audrey blew one more kiss to the expensive seats and, in a whisper-soft voice, began singing "She's Your Girl Tonight."

Then, as though a man could only watch a female impersonator for so long, Jimmy grunted, "I'll be back for you. Don't go anywhere without me."

CHAPTER TWENTY

"What did I tell you about slipping away from me?" Jimmy loomed over the empty seat at my table for two at Fong's Café.

I kept my gaze on my bird's nest soup and replied directly to a gooey sliver of nest. "A girl's gotta eat, Mr. Missing Persons Man." Although my thoughts were fixed on Audrey's carnation-scented handkerchief, I couldn't ignore the sensation of Jimmy peering down at me like a papa hawk. "And a girl would like to eat without being stared at."

He stood in place stoically, like he'd been used to holding his ground for hours on end, and I wondered what he'd done during the war. Had he been a sentry? A sharpshooter? Or maybe even a spy? That would certainly fit with his revelation last night. I only knew about spies from the *Illustrated News*, of course, but right now, they didn't seem too different from a missing persons man.

"At ease, soldier," I said. "Sit down and join me."

He extracted the chair opposite me and sat down, ramrod straight. Gone was the boy with the lazy Southern manner and sizzling syncopation. Gone was the sweet blue-eyed glint that he'd attempted to seduce me with in the dressing room earlier. Like the Jimmy Harrigan in my hotel room last night, this man seemed all business.

"Where I come from, nice girls don't dine alone."

I opened the lid of the rice bowl, spooned out a big portion, and slapped it into the remains of my plate of chicken chow mein. That got his attention. I shook my spoon at him to make sure he looked straight at me. "You rushed me on my second song this afternoon. The tempo needs to slow *slightly* between the verse and chorus. On the third song, you need to get the orchestra to pull it. That's my biggest laugh. That can't happen again. Whatever happened to you before the show needs to stay out of the Pan."

I added an eggroll to the plate and pushed it toward him. He pushed it back at me.

A few chairs scraped hard on the floor behind me. I watched a quartet of soldiers, dressed in uniforms and rubbing their stomachs in appreciation of the food, head toward the door. They passed by Jimmy without a look, but I wondered if last year, during the final months of the war, they all might have fought side by side. Perhaps they'd even addressed him as *Sir*.

But I couldn't dwell on the war when I had my own battles to fight. "What's bothering you, kid? You just captured the runaway wife of Thaddeus Rutherfurd. You should be on top of the world."

Jimmy's ramrod posture stiffened, as if he were delivering bad news. "You should know that I sent Mr. R a telegram today letting him know I found you."

"*Mr. R*, huh?" I pulled the plate of chicken chow mein toward me and arranged the chopsticks. I delicately selected a chicken liver. "How do you imagine this is all going to work? This heartwarming reunion between *Mr. and Mrs. R*? You think it'll be like the moving pictures? Like Lillian Gish and Wilfred Lucas in *Souls Triumphant*?"

I made fun of the movie—in which the wronged wife welcomes her conniving, unfaithful husband back into her arms—even though I had sobbed for an hour after seeing it. But that was two years ago. Today, I couldn't imagine that type of ending for two people.

The waitress brought a fresh cup to the table and poured my favorite oolong into it. Jimmy eyed it for a few seconds before taking a sip.

I also sipped. "Are we meeting Thaddeus here or are you taking me back to New York City?"

I picked up the menu that had been left on the table, wondering if I could eat another dinner special and still perform in three hours. Last night Jimmy had called Eleanor a butterball, and today I was ready to live up to that name. But before I ordered another six-course, dollar-fifty dinner, I saw the last, blank page of the menu and recalled another restaurant where Stu had spent our entire meal writing lyrics on the blank pages of the menus. Hotel stationery, the back of a flyer, the inside of a book, it didn't matter. When Stu was inspired, when he *had* to write, he used any piece of paper he could get his hands on. During one desperate time, he'd started writing on the backs of our publicity photos.

"Have you ever been in New York City, Jimmy? It's sure something to see. Especially the Rutherfurd Building on Fifth Avenue. Takes up an entire block. But the munitions factory and warehouses in Jersey are even bigger."

"You mean the factory that blew up in August?"

My heart stopped a little when Jimmy casually

mentioned the explosion that had ripped the factory apart. I had to concentrate hard to make even a few words come out of my mouth. "Yes. That one."

The menu drifted from my fingers and Jimmy quickly caught it. Then he looked at me as though expecting I had more to say. I did.

"The explosion caused the entire plant to burn down. He"—because there was only one *he* once Thaddeus was mentioned in conversation—"was in Washington and claimed a German agitator did it." I had to take a sip of tea to continue. "I was there when it all happened, did you know that? After the fire started, when it got really bad, when the ammunition ignited all over the place. I watched as the men and women were pulled out."

"I didn't know you were at the factory." Jimmy's tone softened. "All I knew was that you'd run away from the fancy sanatorium."

"Thaddeus was so consumed by the war he didn't even realize I'd escaped."

"You should be proud of his war work." Jimmy defended Rutherfurd as though the great man had personally protected him during battle. "Without his munitions, we never would have beaten the Huns."

"I'm proud of all the work those factory men and women did," I responded truthfully. "Did you know the Rutherfurd Building and the factories and warehouses all used to be named Vanderberg? Because my grandfather started the company."

Jimmy couldn't resist a satisfied grin. I'd just given him enough of Eleanor's background to prove that I was certainly she. Yessir, you've chased down Eleanor Vanderberg Rutherfurd. Well done, Jimmy Harrigan.

I sat back, pretty satisfied with myself. I *had* told him enough of Eleanor's information to keep him engaged. But was it enough to make him care about helping me find out who'd murdered Stu?

I gave up on eating another six-course meal, pocketed my almond cookies, and paid my bill. We left the restaurant together, stepping lively into the evening parade of workers on Market Street. If I'd been with Stu, I would have put my arm in his and we would have scurried down the street together, enjoying the hustle of the people, buses, and honking taxis.

We were one block away from the Pan when Jimmy caught my arm. He pulled me toward a building, as though he was going to check the directory. Taking a deep breath, he said, "You should know that Mr. R's coming out to San Francisco himself. To talk to you directly. I figure he'll leave New York tomorrow or the day after."

I'm not sure what alarmed me more, Jimmy's intensity or his actual news. Still, I was determined to play it casually. "He hasn't left already? He doesn't sound too eager to see his sweet wife again. Or maybe he doesn't believe you."

"He believes me, all right. He'll let me know when he reaches Chicago. After that, he'll be in San Francisco in four days. His train should be here next Friday."

"Friday, huh?"

I shrugged off Jimmy's arm and continued toward the Pan by myself. I had a week to recover the red leather notebook that had been stolen from Stu's inner jacket pocket, and once I had that notebook, I'd devastate Rutherfurd's life just like he'd done to mine.

♫

I entered through the stage door, smartly satisfied to find the backstage dark and our stage doorkeeper, Charlie, sleeping. It was the perfect opportunity to break into Audrey's dressing room. I tingled with excitement, not only because I'd shaken off Jimmy but because I'd soon know if Audrey owned any L'Amour Bleu. It might be a little risky, but on the slim chance that I got caught in his dressing room, I'd explain my presence by handing over the handkerchief that Jeanette'd dropped.

Of course, finding the carnation fragrance—either a whiff on another monogrammed handkerchief or a bottle on Audrey's dressing table tray—wouldn't prove anything. Because I could never imagine Audrey in Stu's bed. I couldn't imagine Audrey in anyone's bed, really, but I needed to do something to find out who might have killed Stu. The trail of L'Amour Bleu was all I had.

As I approached the dressing room, I saw that the door was already open a few inches. I stood as still as possible, listening to a recording of an orchestra playing "Oui, Oui, Marie." The tingle that had pulsed through me fizzled out. I had forgotten that Audrey often entertained audience members in his dressing room between shows. Then I heard a woman's laughter. When that died out, I heard only the clarinet section solo on the phonograph.

I eased the door forward, having no idea who was in there or if they heard me. But the handkerchief in my purse made me bold, so I pushed more to peek inside.

The light inside was low and natural, and it took me a few seconds to see Audrey, dressed in a white shirt and dark trousers, his dark hair slicked back like a moving picture star, seated upon his couch. On his lap—wearing Audrey's emerald silk dressing gown, her legs wrapped around his waist and her unmistakable blonde curls nodding up and down in agreement—was Jeanette. The dressing gown had slid down her shoulders, and she was displaying much more skin than she ever had in costume. It looked like she was holding the gown together to hide her breasts, and she might have been successful if Audrey hadn't reached under it like a soldier with a mission. I couldn't tell what Audrey's hand was doing, exactly, but as I watched Jeanette inhale sharply and bite her lip, I had a pretty good idea. She squirmed for a few seconds and then released her hold on the gown. As the silk drifted down her arms, Audrey pulled her toward him and kissed her full on the lips.

I'd been missing Stu's sweet touch, but watching Audrey and Jeanette's foreplay, imagining what would happen next if that was Stu and me, aroused me to the point of distraction.

Which is why I didn't see Lionel until he grabbed the doorknob and pulled the door shut, almost scraping my nose.

I scooted back and took a few breaths, sorry to lose my fantasies of Stu and doubly sorry to be caught by Lionel. He stared at me; I stared at him. Finally, I reached into my purse and handed him the monogrammed handkerchief. "I found this on the floor. I thought Mr. Merrick might want it back."

Lionel plucked the cloth from my hand. For a moment, I thought he was going to wave it at me and tell me to move along. Instead, he jammed it into a pocket, crossed his arms, and stood in front of the door like an army sentry.

Lionel could pull any posture he wanted, but it was too late. I'd already seen what I wasn't supposed to see—Audrey and Jeanette about to make love.

CHAPTER TWENTY-ONE

JIMMY DIDN'T RUSH any of the songs at my evening show and I delivered my set with perfect panache. I returned to the hotel as soon as my act was over. Bathed, brushed, and buffered from the horns and hoorahs of San Francisco, I fell asleep before ten o'clock.

I didn't wake up until twelve hours later, and I'd needed every second of that sleep. I was calling the musical shots for my act now, something I'd never done before. I had a lot to prepare today, especially since Mr. Z had put me back in the seven spot.

Jimmy waited outside my hotel room, looking like he hadn't slept a wink. We left the hotel together and walked almost in step to the Pan. I hugged Stu's large portfolio of sheet music against my chest, missing him more with every stride.

Even though I'd booked the rehearsal hall, I had to kick the Nolan Sisters out to get started. Jimmy took off his hat and jacket and lit a cigarette. I removed my coat and hat and stabbed his cigarette into the sand bucket. Time to get to work.

"Mr. Z is sending me out with some of the troupe to a private show tomorrow. It's a thank-you to the army boys who came home last week." I loosened up my shoulders and rolled my head back and forth. "I've got a twelve-minute spot so I'll need four songs and one encore."

Jimmy ran his right hand up the keyboard, playing one scale with ease before playing another scale in a different key. "Just you and me? Or are Mitch and the orchestra coming along?"

"Mitch is staying put, but part of the orchestra is coming. It's a place called Neptune Beach."

"A beach? In San Francisco? In March?" Jimmy hunched his shoulders toward his ears and pretended to shiver. "If everyone's at the beach, what's going to happen here?"

"Mr. Z's putting in some local acts, trying them out for a longer run. But don't worry. We'll still have a spot in the show tomorrow night."

My fingers lingered on the top of Stu's portfolio, remembering how possessive he was of the papers inside. And proud. Stu'd put all of his hopes and dreams into these songs, his stairway to the Big Time.

Some songwriters just strung words together—moon, June, tune, soon—but Stu wrote entire stories in sixteen bars. Love stories. Longing stories. Life stories. And my intonation, expression, and vigor brought those stories to life. I never thought I'd be planning my act without him, and I tried to be brave, but the tears welled up in my eyes.

"We can start with 'For Crying Out Loud' and then segue into 'I Hold Her Hand.'" I named two songs from my

San Francisco act. "Both of those should lighten the mood. For the third song, let's naughty up the romance with 'You're a Good Old Car'"—the middle number from our Portland weeks—"and for our finale, 'Back to My Old Hometown.'"

I'd named the last song before I realized that Stu really had come back to his old town. My heart sank with a thud. Had Stu written the song with San Francisco in mind? The first line told me yes:

There's a little gray-haired mother waiting there
for me.

Of course he'd written the song for his mother. Of course he was looking forward to seeing her. I wished I could take Stu in my arms and hug away the blues that had led him to write those lyrics. But with the same breath, I wanted to slug him for never telling me about his mother. Or who might want him dead.

As I thought about the rest of the lyrics, it was obvious that Stu adored his mother. Maybe San Francisco too.

Though I've caused her many heartaches, still
I know
That for me her heart must yearn and she prays
for my return
So that is why I'm longing now to go back to my
old hometown

I ruffled through the portfolio, trying to ignore Jimmy. My feelings for Stu were too fresh to share with someone I didn't know. And to Jimmy, I was just a fat finder's fee; I couldn't trust him any further than I could watch him.

I landed on a song I hadn't seen in a while. Oddly enough, it was another song about Mother. And now, knowing Margaret Wilson, I was sure that "Mother, May I Come Home Please" had been written for her.

Unlike most of Stu's stage tunes, "Mother, May I" was a tender ballad. He'd asked me to sing it in rehearsal before we joined the troupe—and I gave it all of the grand emotion it deserved—but he never put it into our act. It'd be perfect for tomorrow's encore, even though I already felt another heave of tears in my chest.

The song was sad enough as written, but now, knowing why it was written, it was sadder still. I silenced my sniffles, remembering Stu's mournful piano playing, and my heart yielded. If I didn't sing "Mother, May I Come Home Please" tomorrow, if I didn't sing it for my lost lover and his mother, who would ever hear it again?

Jimmy continued his piano gymnastics, this time confidently running both hands around almost every key on the piano. I handed him the sheets of music, hoping he wouldn't slaughter the song.

"Learn this song and we're good to go for tomorrow," I said. "Follow my lead. I'll show you how I like it."

Jimmy fumbled with lighting another cigarette, not even looking at the sheet music. I'd seen men stall before and he was nowhere near the best. "What's the matter?"

"I've never heard you sing this before."

"So?" I put both of my fists to my waist, the epitome of a frustrated woman.

"So, I don't read music."

Not the answer I expected. "Not even a line?"

"I play by ear." Jimmy slid over the piano bench and patted it with his free hand. "But if you play it through for me, I can get the idea. Once I hear it a few times, I'll be as good as you."

Was Jimmy testing me? Unlike me, Eleanor Rutherfurd had probably taken piano lessons from an early age. Probably played classics like Bach and Brahms and even new composers like Debussy.

I sat on the bench and bumped my hip toward Jimmy's. "Slide over, kid. I'll play it for you once, and you better listen good."

Reading from Stu's sheet music, I played it through slowly. The song was all about the lyrics so the music was simple, without any syncopation or rhythm changes. Jimmy left the bench and stood over the piano, looking at me—instead of my hands or the music—as I played. I ran through the song again, a little faster, this time adding the lyrics.

I'd been right. "Mother, May I Come Home Please" was the perfect song to end my act tomorrow. What could be more respectful to an audience of soldiers and their families and sweethearts than a song paying tribute to the women who loved them?

But Jimmy disagreed. "You sure you want to sing this tomorrow? Sure, it's beautiful, but—"

"Just you wait, kid. This heartbreaker'll stop the show."

Before I could convince Jimmy, Rocco barged into the room carrying a stack of recordings.

"Time's up, Viola. Get lost."

Jeanette followed in Rocco's wake and I attempted to pass by her, thinking once more of seeing her in Audrey's arms, hoping the fragrance of carnations might drift from her frock. But all I smelled on her breath was the sour odor of alcohol.

Our rehearsal time over, I made a trip to the ladies' room, where I sat on the commode for minutes, the memories of Stu and his ballad haunting me. I finally mastered my feelings, and Jimmy and I went upstairs for our stage rehearsal.

We found Audrey rehearsing in the pit with Mitch and the full orchestra. As much as it irked me, I understood the vaudeville pecking order and waited my turn, searching through Stu's portfolio for other gems.

Then Jimmy shoved me hard with his elbow. "You hear that, Viola? You hear what Audrey's singing?"

I hadn't been listening, but now I did. Still, I had to hear another four bars before I realized Audrey was singing "Mother, May I Come Home Please." Although he sang it as "Mama, Can I Come Home Please." The sweet, respectful, loving tune I'd played and sung for Jimmy had been changed into a bluesy tempo with a syncopated vamp.

Audrey had swiped Stu's music and lyrics. I stomped to center stage and stared down at Audrey in the orchestra pit.

"Hey! That's my song!"

Slowly, Audrey looked up at me. "I beg your pardon, Miss Vermillion?"

"You heard me. That's my song!" I stormed down to the pit ready to rip the sheet music from his well-manicured fingers. Lionel stepped in front of me, but I pushed him aside to confront Audrey. Nose to nose, toe to toe in his street clothes, Audrey didn't seem so sensational right now.

"If you lower your voice, Miss Vermillion," said Audrey, "I'm sure we can discuss this in a professional manner."

"There's nothing professional about stealing Stu's song. It's low-class and dirty and cause for dismissal." I was so incensed at Audrey's theft that I threatened him with the one thing that every vaudevillian feared most. "Maybe even blackballing."

Still standing beside Audrey, Lionel gasped and his eyes went wide. Blackballing was serious business in vaudeville. Once management in any theatre blackballed you, no theatre would ever book you again. Your reputation and livelihood were ruined.

Calmly, as though he hadn't heard any of my threats, Audrey turned the sheet music in his hand to show the cover. "Mama, Can I Come Home Please" was scrawled in thin black letters at the top and one of his small publicity photos was taped below it. At the very bottom of the cover was the sentence "Words by Audrey Merrick and Stuart Wiley. Music by Stuart Wiley."

I glanced at the piano, as though Stu would be sitting there, ready to come to my defense. But the round, pasty fellow on the piano stool couldn't even meet my eyes. Jimmy—who'd followed me into the pit—looked at me but said nothing.

Which left me with Audrey.

"This is my song," I told him.

"Did you write it?"

"No."

"Then it's not yours."

"Stu wrote it and gave it to me to sing," I said smartly. "Me and only me."

"It *was* Stuart's, but he wisely decided that it was better suited to me than to you."

"Prove it!"

Out of the corner of my eyes, I saw Lionel's hand reach under his jacket. Jimmy moved toward Lionel but held his ground as Lionel pulled out his handkerchief. Seconds later, someone strode through the house double doors. Since the house lights were lowered, it wasn't until he was almost at the pit that I saw it was Clipboard Clippy.

Clippy inserted himself between me and Audrey, forcing us both to move aside. "Mr. Merrick, Miss Vermillion, Mr. Zimmerman says that you'll be more comfortable discussing this business in his office."

I felt like I was being dragged to the principal's office at school. And just like those times, I was ready to make my case. Jimmy jabbed his arm through mine and together all five of us—Jimmy and me, Audrey and Lionel, and Clippy—trooped to Mr. Z's office.

Unlike my earlier visit to Mr. Z's office, there was no glittering stardust shimmering in the air, no magical possibility of promotion or stardom. It was only a dark, stuffy courtroom where Mr. Z. would play judge.

Before I said anything, Lionel presented Mr. Z with a piece of paper. "Here's the receipt for the song."

I stared at the blank back of the paper while Mr. Z reviewed it.

"This is robbery!"

"It doesn't look like that to me, Miss Vermillion. It looks like Mr. Merrick and Mr. Wiley had a business agreement."

"A deal, Mr. Zimmerman." Lionel pressed himself forward. "Mr. Merrick and Mr. Wiley had a deal to purchase this song."

Mr. Z took a few more seconds to review the paper before asking me, "Mr. Wiley wrote this music and it was Mr. Wiley's music to sell. Do you dispute that?"

"He gave me that song to sing. He wouldn't just sell it to someone else." I snatched the paper from Mr. Z's hands. The signature at the bottom certainly looked like Stu's, and the date was last Monday, the date Stu had been murdered. The receipt was for seventy-five dollars.

My heart started beating wildly because it was the same amount of money Stu'd had in his money clip the day he died. I remembered how stiff and fresh those bills were, and how he'd wanted to take me to dinner to tell me "all about it." Was *it* his first big song sale?

Jimmy spoke gently, just a few inches from my ear. "That all looks to be in order."

It might make sense, a receipt and money clip, both with seventy-five dollars, but I wasn't willing to give in yet. "What are you, an attorney?"

"I've seen a professional receipt before. Haven't you?"

Of course I had, but I'd also seen how lovingly Stu played "Mother, May I Come Home Please." He wouldn't change the lyrics or tempo for Audrey. Not even for seventy-five dollars.

He wouldn't. He'd rather die.

"Do you have any proof that you own this music? No? Well, since Mr. Merrick does, I have to agree with him." Mr. Z put out his hand for the receipt. "This bickering ends now, Miss Vermillion. This is Mr. Merrick's song and he has every right to sing it."

Jimmy put his hand on my shoulder. "It's done, Viola. There's nothing you can do about it."

But it wasn't done, and as I shrugged off Jimmy's touch, Audrey growled, "I'll let it pass once, but from now on, Miss Vermillion, remember your place."

Every man in the room looked at me as if daring me to

continue my dispute. I had plenty to say, all right, but I wouldn't waste my words on them.

I walked out of Mr. Z's office with as much sass as any siren could. There was nothing to do about Audrey's theft *now*, but I'd sure do something about it later.

♫

I clomped down the corridor from Mr. Z's office and dodged through the nearest double doors.

Stupid me—I'd escaped to the balcony. It was just as dark, just as still, just as odorous as the afternoon I found Stu. Once my eyes adjusted to the low lighting, I walked down the side aisle and to the railing. The orchestra must have gone on break when we went up to Mr. Z's office, and the stage curtain was closed.

I should be down there, rehearsing "Mother, May I Come Home Please." But even though I objected to everything that had just happened—Audrey's bawdy interpretation, Lionel's ready receipt, Mr. Z's dictatorial decision, even my own knowledge of the seventy-five dollars in Stu's money clip—I also knew how to survive in vaudeville. For the moment, I'd go along with Mr. Z's decision.

Of course Stu wanted to sell his songs. Songwriting was his whole life, and selling a song to Audrey would have been a dream come true. But if he had sold the song to Audrey, why keep it a secret from me?

Despite the dread shivering through my body—because the one thing every performer knows is that every theater is haunted—I sat down next to where I'd found Stu. The back and bottom cushions had been replaced with a bright velveteen, and the cement flooring smelled faintly of bleach. In only five days, all evidence of Stu's murder had been removed. Eventually, no one but me and the murderer would remember Stu'd been shot to death here.

Moments later, Jimmy slumped down next to me, spreading himself into Stu's seat. I jolted up, but Jimmy put out his arm out to prevent me from rising.

I pressed against his arm. "You've got one sec—"

"Maybe Stuart had a reason for keeping his sale to Audrey a secret."

"You think Stu had a reason to lie to me?" I dared Jimmy to disagree. "Because when you're with someone almost every minute of every day, when you sleep with them every night, when their success is your success, their happiness is your happiness . . . any secret is really a lie."

"Seems to me you kept your own secrets from Stu."

Okay, so I had. Secrets whispered from one dying woman to another. Secrets that Thaddeus Rutherfurd wanted awfully bad. But still—

"Like how you fell in love with him," Jimmy said softly. "That secret. I bet you never told him, did you?"

The boiling rage from the confrontation in Mr. Z's office dissolved into longing for Stu. Jimmy passed me his handkerchief and I pressed it over my tears.

"No. I didn't."

As we sat there—the three of us, really, since Stu was still present—the house lights came up. I cringed like a vampire bat. A few seconds later, the manager shouted, "House is open." It would be only a few minutes before people began moving into the balcony and taking their seats for the one-thirty show. As if that wasn't enough, an usher strolled through the balcony, running his flashlight between the rows. "Time to get out, folks."

"This is just a suggestion," Jimmy said as we walked out of the balcony together, "but you should probably keep that secret about being in love with Stuart from your husband when he gets here."

CHAPTER TWENTY-TWO

THADDEUS RUTHERFURD REPLACED the earpiece on the telephone set. It was a modern marvel, having a telephonic line brought into his rail car in New York City and getting an immediate connection to St. Louis. Without hesitation, he decided to purchase the local telephone company—perhaps every telephone company along the Union Pacific rail lines —when he returned from San Francisco.

He walked over to the sideboard and poured himself a large bourbon. It'd taken him an hour on the telephone, but he'd badgered the owner of the *St. Louis Gazette* into selling him the newspaper. Not even "the great" William Randolph Hearst worked as fast or as stealthily as Thaddeus Rutherfurd.

Munitions, newspapers, telephones . . . Thaddeus was on a buying streak, taking control of companies across America with no one stepping up to stop him. No one daring to stop him. It was impressive, really, his ambition and success. How quickly he took command and how quickly people obeyed him.

Everyone except his wife, that was.

Eleanor *had* been impressed with him once—in their early years together, almost fifteen years ago, when he went to work for her father. Thaddeus had been the exact opposite of Eleanor's keeper-of-the-status-quo father, and she adored him for it. Yes, he'd gone to Harvard, just like her father and grandfather, but he'd gone on a scholarship. A scholarship contingent upon him joining the school's Boxing Club and smashing all intramural opponents. Very quickly, his knockout wins not only brought glory to Harvard but also put money into the pockets of the students and professors who placed illegal wagers on him. Eventually, money flowed into his pockets as well, and once Thaddeus understood how the world of millionaires worked, he set his sights on joining their club.

Eleanor—just like the betting men Thaddeus made rich with his plaster of Paris-filled boxing gloves—had succumbed completely to him back then; to his relentless drive to succeed; to his animal instincts; his ruthlessness, even.

Everything was going according to Rutherfurd's plans until her father died and Eleanor suddenly wanted *more*.

She wanted to talk. She wanted to debate. She wanted to know where her father's money had gone. She watched her husband constantly, prying into things that did not concern her. She ate a plate of chocolates every day, and despite her four miscarriages, Thaddeus was sure she was using some method of birth control.

A month before the United States declared war, Thaddeus stuck Eleanor in a sanatorium in Rockland County. He forgot all about her as he negotiated contracts for the half-dozen (and growing) Rutherfurd Munitions factories across the East Coast. At President Wilson's request, he took on the job of Assistant Alien Property Custodian, where he was able to identify, capture, and regularly appropriate the substantial property of America's many resident enemies. So grew his empire.

He recorded all of this information—the facts that would turn his collection of businesses into a worldwide empire—in the red leather notebook Eleanor had presented to him on their Italian honeymoon. The notebook that Thaddeus stored in his New Jersey factory safe.

The World War solidified Rutherfurd's fortune. Only the explosion at the munitions factory last August had slowed him down. The hundreds dead and the dozens injured halted production in Paterson, of course, but he quickly sped up production in his other factories.

In September, the sanatorium notified him that Eleanor had escaped. In October, the director of St. Joseph's Hospital informed him that his wife, who had somehow found her way to Paterson, had died of the Spanish influenza.

When the war ended in November, Thaddeus had popped a champagne cork, counted his millions, and met with the Republican and Democratic bosses of the Great State of New York. Sometime in early 1919, he would plant a headstone for Eleanor in her family plot, and later in the year, he would marry another heiress.

He opened his finally cooled New Jersey safe in December and found everything intact, except that his red leather notebook was missing. That was the first time he suspected Eleanor must have stolen the notebook and triggered the explosion.

Two weeks later, the editors of the *New York Herald*—and *The Times* and *The Tribune*—informed him that a woman approached them claiming she possessed his personal diary and that she could prove he was an extortionist, a blackmailer. And worse. That's when he realized Eleanor might still be alive. Except that the red-haired woman who visited the newspapers looked or acted nothing like Eleanor.

Soon after that, he received a single blank page from the notebook in the mail, and that's when his hunt to find Eleanor and Viola Vermillion began.

He was sure that no one could ever decipher the entire notebook, but if they decoded even part of it, and if that information got to a certain man in Boston, Rutherfurd's ambitions would dissolve into dust. He'd be as much a failure as his father, and the praise he so depended upon would turn into ridicule.

What a shame, what a horror his downfall would be for the future of America, because Thaddeus Rutherfurd's ambitions for his country—like himself—were endless.

But now that he knew where his notebook was, it was just a matter of time before he had it back. Just a matter of time before America would be, once again, his for the taking.

CHAPTER TWENTY-THREE

Sunday morning, I walked down Market Street with Kitty, Stu's music portfolio firmly in hand. Kitty wasn't playing Neptune Beach, but she took any opportunity to exercise Romeo and Juliet, her largest—and despite Juliet's name—male dogs. Stunning, frisky, and downright personable, Kitty's dogs were the greatest advertisement possible for her act, and they trotted in front of us like a pair of carriage horses. Kitty passed out show flyers to anyone who stopped and complimented her, and despite the whorls of dust kicked up by the motor buses, the day seemed bright with promise.

Not to be outdone by Kitty's parading poodles, I strutted down the street in my silver-spangled gold costume topped by my brocade coat and raccoon collar. I carried a handkerchief, stage makeup, and my fully-loaded gun in my handbag.

Kitty kept up a constant chatter on our walk, sharing the latest troupe gossip—Was Gladys pregnant? Was Ugo brewing beer in his closet? What drove Jeanette and Rocco's fight this morning?—until we stopped for the dogs to do their business.

The Ferry Building was a few blocks away, and despite the exuberance of the elaborate arched entranceway, the American flag—waving at half-mast on the clock tower flagpole—sobered me quickly. The lowered flag brought Stu's murder right back to me, and my spirits drooped.

Kitty put her arm in mine. "I've saved the best news for last. I've heard that Audrey's leaving the troupe. Maybe before we jump to Oakland next week."

"Next week? Before his contract's finished?"

Right now, I couldn't imagine what would happen next week. Stu's murderer needed to be caught *now*, and then . . . Rutherfurd arrived in San Francisco. As I watched the buses and motorcars drive along the loop that stopped in front of the Ferry Building, I guessed that his train would stop at the Southern Pacific terminal where Stuart and I came in from Portland. But what if he arrived on the ferry? Or even a taxicab?

I wanted to walk up to the elevated footpath that crossed the street in front of the Ferry Building to see exactly how the land was laid out, but I couldn't budge. Because no one walked away from gossip about Audrey Merrick.

"The whispers about Audrey started last night," said Kitty. "Which means somebody needs to take his spot."

Despite my blues for Stu, a tickle of ambition came over me. Kitty and I grinned at each other, knowing that Audrey's departure could boost someone's career. Why not mine? If I won Audrey's twelve spot, I'd have forty-nine minutes on stage. Forty-nine minutes to delight the audience with my novelty songs, break their hearts with my ballads, enchant them with my love songs, and drive them to distraction with my red-hot mama blues. If I got the twelve spot in a Pantages lineup, it'd be a hop, skip, and a jump to a spot in the Orpheum circuit. The thought of being on an Orpheum stage cheered me, and I squeezed Kitty's arm.

She squeezed back. "It doesn't matter if Audrey leaves or not, I won't take another job in the one spot."

"You got to think big to get to the Big Time," I agreed.

Bursting with our dreams of success, Kitty and I sauntered along, two sleek women and two sleeker poodles, under the elevated walkway toward the Ferry Building.

Then I shared *my* Audrey news. "I looked into Audrey's dressing room after Friday's matinee and you know what I saw? Jeanette. Sitting on his lap." As Kitty's eyes widened in surprise, I added, "He kissed her." Just for good measure, I added, "And that's a fact."

"I've heard that it's good business," Kitty said, "for a female impersonator to have a lady around."

"It makes him look less like a lady himself, you mean?"

Kitty nodded. "Although I have been wondering about this in-between boy, this Oscar. If there's a *tendresse* between them. For weeks now, when I see one, I see the other. Audrey and Oscar. Oscar and Audrey."

"Have you ever seen Audrey and Jeanette together?"

"No. But perhaps Rocco did, and that's why they argued this morning." Kitty almost squealed with delight, and I couldn't blame her. For weeks, Rocco had been threatening to ruin her in vaudeville by poisoning her poodles. Now Rocco's own career might be in shambles.

"Jeanette's not a great dancer." I felt that I was reading Kitty's mind as I spoke. "But if he loses her to Audrey, Rocco could be out of the show."

We both took a moment to enjoy the idea of Rocco

leaving the troupe, but soon enough, Kitty nodded toward the Ferry Building entrance, where a navy man in a crisp white uniform waved at me. I finally realized the navy man was Mr. Z's secretary, Clippy.

Holding his ever-present clipboard and pencil, Clippy yelled, "You're late, Miss Vermillion. It's time to board the ferry. *Now.*"

Kitty and I walked arm in arm until we reached the lobby. She took one look at the slippery tile floors and called Romeo and Juliet to heel.

"We'll leave you here. See you tonight." Before she released my arm, she leaned in to say, "Knock 'em dead, Viola."

♫

The ferry was a long side-wheeler, and I moved inside on the lower deck. A few minutes from the pier, I caught a glimpse of Alcatraz Island, the prison and lighthouse illuminated in the midday sunshine. But despite the sunny glow, all I really saw were parched buildings, scrub brush gardens, and a miserable life for Stu. I didn't know how he found the gumption to leave his mother, but I was glad he'd escaped the harsh life on that rocky island.

Then I heard, "Thinking about going back there?"

I was ready to chew Jimmy out for being late, but seeing him dressed in his army uniform took some of my breath away. His khaki-colored officer's uniform was freshly pressed, his russet-brown boots polished to a high sheen. His wide-brimmed hat was perched squarely on his head, and two bright medals adorned his chest. I thought immediately of the covers of the sheet music for "Good-bye

Broadway, Hello France" and Cohan's "Over There," which both featured a dashing solder.

"Don't you look grand, kid." I hoped my tone sounded suitably sarcastic because I couldn't let Jimmy know how his spit and polish affected me. "All of those badges. What were you? A captain?"

"Second lieutenant. The lowest of the low." He offered to take Stu's portfolio from me and I gave it to him. He tried to stand at attention, but the ferry lurched and he widened his stance. As he took off his hat and held it under his arm, I saw his face slacken. Was the kid seasick?

I put my hand out to touch the badges on his chest, but he stiffened and pulled away.

"Pistol and Rifle Expert," he said.

"Were you—"

"In the army, just like them." Jimmy nodded to three men smoking cigarettes near the rails.

It took me a few moments to realize that *them* was Ugo, Lionel, and Oscar, all three of them looking sharp in US Army uniforms. None of them'd mentioned they'd been in the army, but I guess I shouldn't have been surprised. Looking farther down the long ferry, I saw that other Pan people—including Rocco and the skeleton orchestra crew—were in uniform. Only Audrey stood apart, dressed in civilian clothes, almost shriveling into his coat, like he was embarrassed about his lack of uniform.

I looked around for Jeanette, wondering about what Kitty had said. Was it *good business* for a female impersonator to have a lady around? I'd seen Audrey fuss over women, but they were the anxious older matrons who had been sold the idea—by Lionel, I was sure—that Audrey had special insights into how a woman might mesmerize her man. Which made some sense, because Audrey mesmerized men and women twice a day. But I'd never seen him kiss one on the lips. Or put his hand between their legs.

There was no sign of Jeanette, so I nodded toward Lionel, who also had a medal on his chest. "What's his for?"

"Pistol Sharpshooter," said Jimmy. "Means he's good with a gun, but not as good as me."

After a smooth ride over the bay, the ferry suddenly jolted. Jimmy slapped his hand over his mouth. He was getting sicker by the wave. I moved aside at the railing for him to join me, but he closed his eyes and stood at attention as though one move would finish him. When we were almost to shore, he pushed the portfolio into my arms.

As he slunk away to the back of the boat to be sick, I took another large gulp of bay breeze. Good thing Jimmy hadn't joined the navy. We'd never have won the war.

♫

Alameda, as it turned out, was a large island in the San Francisco Bay. After waiting ten minutes, Jimmy finally stepped off the ferry, holding a kerchief to his mouth.

Before he could take the portfolio, he faltered. There was nothing to do but put my arm around his waist. Then we both caught sight of a man in uniform with a jacket sleeve pinned up where his arm should be, and Jimmy shoved me off. I understood. Men had lost limbs during the war; Jimmy was only seasick. With a forced swagger worthy of Douglas Fairbanks, he offered his arm and escorted me to the train to Neptune Beach.

CHAPTER TWENTY-FOUR

CLIPBOARD CLIPPY HERDED our small troupe through the archway that marked the entrance to Neptune Beach. Although the inside of the park was a wondrous sight—I was instantly dazzled by the boxing ring, swimming pool, and tall diving platform, all decorated in an Egyptian motif—the true wonder was the Scenic Railway, a six-story, figure-eight-shaped roller coaster so vibrant and so loud that it drowned out Clippy's shouts. He took the challenge like a trouper, though, and waved both arms over his head for us to follow.

He led us into the massive Grand Ballroom and along the vast hardwood dancing floors toward a very low, very narrow stage. There were no steps from the floor to the apron, so Clippy went around to the side and then up a half-dozen narrow steps to reach the stage. It was the smallest stage I'd seen since playing the Elks Lodge in Millville—hardly wide enough to let the seven Nolan Sisters stand in a row.

Clippy gave us our instructions. "The show starts at two

sharp. There's no time for rehearsal, but everyone can come up and block their moves. There's no special lighting crew or stagehands today; they're all in the audience. Our orchestra"—Clippy nodded to a cluster of empty chairs and music stands—"sets up over there."

Clippy ran down the playbill as quickly as a track announcer calling a horse race. "The Seven Nolans are in the one spot with ten minutes. The diLorenzos are in the second with ten. Viola Vermillion plays third with twelve. Ugo Baldanza plays fourth with twelve, and Mr. Audrey Merrick has the five spot with sixteen minutes."

He fixed us all with a firm look. "Now that we're clear, ladies, follow me to the dressing room."

Clippy eased down the narrow steps—planks of wood without railings—and led us to a small room that wasn't big enough for two girls to sit and do their makeup at the same time. Before asking anyone, Jeanette plopped her case on the dressing table and moved a chair to the center of the mirror. The Nolan Sisters settled themselves to her left and right, trying to find any available light.

I did not want to squeeze myself into the mirror next to Jeanette, so I returned to the ballroom, watching as workers set up rows of chairs in front of the stage. That's when I saw Audrey walking out the main doors, and I followed him. I'd never believed Stu agreed to let Audrey claim credit for writing "Mother, May I Come Home Please," and I'd left the hotel this morning ready to force Audrey to tell me more about his "deal" with Stu.

The sudden sunlight blinded me, but as everything came into focus, I saw signs pointing to the midway, the movie theatre, and the dining rooms. But no Audrey in sight. So I followed the fragrance of popping corn and made my way down the midway, lyrically named the Street of Damascus. I found Audrey lingering next to a large *Shooting Gallery* sign, running his fingers along a gallery rifle.

"You weren't going to bother Mr. Merrick, were you?" Despite his wide-brimmed hat, Jimmy's pale Irish cheeks showed a tinge of sunburn. "Wouldn't you rather enjoy the sunshine and the sea air? I'll buy you an ice cream if you sit for a bit."

"'Sit for a bit'? You trying to write vaudeville tunes?" Despite Jimmy's intrusion, I kept watch on Audrey, who had moved on from the shooting gallery. "I can't have ice cream before I sing, but you can buy me one after."

But once at the ice cream counter, I settled for a single scoop of tutti-frutti. After accepting his butter pecan, Jimmy took my arm and steered me around the lines of people. And that's when I realized we were taking a stroll.

The sun was warm, a gentle breeze glided in from the bay, the path before us was carefree, and we had ice cream cones. It might have been the most tranquil, most lovely moment I'd had in years, and I didn't want to break the spell with talk about Stu's murder. I was still going to question Audrey, but every spark in my body exclaimed, *Not now*.

Although I banished Audrey from my mind, I couldn't dispel my thoughts about Thaddeus Rutherfurd. And once he came to mind, so did the red leather notebook. As Jimmy and I strolled in the fine sunshine of Neptune Beach, I wondered if it was time to tell him about the notebook—how important it was and how much I needed it. Wondered if it was time to beg him to help me find it.

But as we reached the beginning of the midway, I saw Clippy waving his board in our direction. It might have been a day at the beach for the crowds on the Alameda shoreline, but Jimmy and I had a show to put on.

♫

The ballroom was packed with people perched on wooden folded chairs, sitting at tables around the room's perimeter, and leaning against the balcony railing.

Backstage was half the size of an orchestra pit, which meant there was room for six people. Jimmy and I crammed into the space with Clippy and Rocco and Jeanette, who stood in costume as far apart from each other as they possibly could. Kitty had said the dancers were fighting this morning, and from the distance between them, it looked like they hadn't made up.

I'd put on my makeup and arranged my feathered headdress into my curls. Even though it was sunny and warm outside, it was cold backstage. I kept my coat on and clutched my handbag.

The front row was reserved for men in wheeled chairs and their families, and the second row was for men using crutches. Beyond them was an audience of men in uniform, women of all ages, many dressed in black, and children in spring pastels.

The mayor of Alameda led us in the Pledge of Allegiance and then welcomed all servicemen and their families. I was surprised to see that our small Pan orchestra had been buoyed by the addition of another dozen instrumentalists. I cringed at the idea of those unrehearsed musicians playing my music. So I prayed that the piano was in tune. I wished Jimmy and I'd taken a few minutes to block out my act, but it was too late now.

As Clippy commanded, the Nolan Sisters performed in the one spot. The audience went wild with their patriotic military drill and display of the flag—causing men in the audience to stand up and cheer more than a few times—and suddenly, I doubted if I'd chosen the right songs for my spot. My songs were fun and flirty, but seeing the wounded men, widows, and bereft mothers in the audience, I realized my lighthearted set might seem disrespectful.

Jimmy and I watched as Rocco and Jeanette hit the stage for the two spot. Rocco adapted quickly to the smaller stage, but Jeanette couldn't follow his lead and stumbled more than once. Rocco held her tighter, trying to lead her into the improvised steps, but she resisted him. He almost let her fall to the floor, but instead, he yanked her into his arms.

They finished their act, took a bow, and stumbled from the stage to the wings, landing just a few feet away from me. The mayor took to the stage once more, but my attention was on Rocco, who was breathing hard and dripping sweat, his right hand gripping Jeanette's wrist.

She attempted to walk away, but he tugged her back toward him. She landed almost in his arms, hissed out his name, and then slapped his face hard. He swore in Italian and slapped her back, just as hard. I was wondering, as I tried to give Jeanette and Rocco plenty of room, if this exchange would be a prelude to one of their legendary love-making sessions—until Jeanette stomped hard on Rocco's right foot. She pressed all of her weight into his foot before stepping off. Then she elbowed him in the ribs. Rocco tumbled to the floor and Jeanette sniffed in satisfaction.

Just then, Clippy must have realized it was his job to do something. So he pointed his clipboard at Jeanette and mouthed the words, "Leave the wings now."

The chaos might have stopped there, except the six steps from the stage to the floor were only wide enough for one person, and Ugo Baldanza was already coming up them. Even though he and his accordion took up the entire width of the steps, Ugo attempted to make room for Jeanette to pass. But she took the steps so quickly that, with no railings for support, Ugo lost his balance and fell onto the floor.

Jeanette huffed off without looking back.

Jimmy and I ran down the steps. Ugo lay curled on his left side and not moving, except to stretch his right hand out to his accordion, which had crashed to the floor with him. It had fallen silently and seemed to be in one piece, but Ugo was not so lucky. At least two fingers on his right hand were bloody. Together Jimmy and I lifted Ugo to his feet. At Ugo's insistence, I picked up his accordion and followed both of them up to the stage.

Clippy took one look at Ugo's bloody fingers and shook his head. "You're out."

"You," he nodded to Jimmy. "Get down to the orchestra. Now."

Then Clippy grabbed my handbag from me, pulled off my coat, and dumped them on his stool. As I watched my things fall to the floor, Clippy stepped over to the easel that held our program cards, and—I guessed—moved my card to the top.

He returned backstage. "You're on in one minute, Miss Vermillion. Break a leg."

As the mayor passed me backstage, I leaned out and saw Jimmy rolling the piano forward to get a better view of the stage. Then he started warming up by joining the orchestra in their between-acts rendition of "Alice Blue Gown."

Clippy put his hand to my lower back, but I brushed it

away. My heart might be beating wildly from witnessing Jeanette's ferocity, but I didn't need anyone to push me on stage. Not when I knew how lucky I was. I'd never have another chance to open for Audrey—the devil taking credit for one of Stu's most poetic songs—and I was going to give it everything I had.

I could have used the entire tiny stage, but after seeing how Rocco and Jeanette failed in the space, I decided to perform entirely on the apron, just inches from the orchestra and yards from the audience. Unlike the darkened Pan at show time, I saw the faces of everyone in the audience, from the row of wheelchaired soldiers directly in front of me to the boys leaning against the second-story railings. All eyes were upon me, and I witnessed more than one woman sniff into her handkerchief. As I looked over the ballroom crowd —barely realizing that Jimmy was leading the orchestra in a continued vamp of my first song—I almost succumbed to the love and loss that resonated throughout the room.

I still wasn't sure if my songs suited the audience, but I gave everything I had to "For Crying Out Loud," "I Hold Her Hand," and "You're a Good Old Car." I shouldn't have worried. This was one of the best audiences I'd sung to in months. Despite the sober occasion, they were eager for levity and humor and laughed easily at each of my novelty songs.

When it came time for my ballad "Back to My Old Hometown," I sang directly to a gray-haired woman in the fourth row.

There's a little gray-haired mother waiting there
for me.
Though I've caused her many heartaches, still

I know
That for me her heart must yearn and she prays
for my return
So that is why I'm longing now to go

Back to my old hometown where everything
is real
With its quaint old church and shady lanes
If you only knew how glad I feel just to be there
once again

I glanced backstage during the vamp to see Audrey lip-reading the sheet music of his "collaboration" with Stuart, "Mama, Can I Come Home Please," with Lionel and Oscar beside him. I wanted to tear the music from Audrey's hands. If he'd written any of those lyrics, they'd be entrenched in his heart. Nothing'd make him forget them.

I finished my set of four songs and one encore at center stage. The last note reverberated through my entire body, and when the applause died down, when I should have taken my final bow and exited stage right, I stayed put.

I walked the few steps to the edge of the apron and filled my lungs with the solid breath of intention. As silence settled in amongst the audience and Jimmy's forehead scowled in confusion, I began a second encore *a cappella*.

I've been so lost and so heartbroken
I'd pay any cost for just one token
Of your sweet love for me
Oh, mother dear

I sang Stu's stately and respectful "Mother, May I Come

Home Please" to the soldier who sat with his eyes closed in the second row, to the white-haired woman in the sixth row, to the pair of girls clutching each other's hands in the balcony, and to Stu's mother, wherever she might be.

Within a few bars, Jimmy brought in the piano accompaniment. It turned out that we were right in key with each other. The orchestra had no idea what I was doing, so it was just Jimmy and me. His confidence grew as we reached the chorus, and he added some tender flourishes on the piano.

Mother, may I come home please
I'm begging you upon my knees
I lied and deceived you
I shamed and mistreated you
But Mother I still love you so

If you take me back today
I promise that I'll never stray
I don't deserve you, that I know
But still I crave your sweet hel-lo
Because Mother I still love you so

For a few seconds, as my voice resonated through the ballroom with almost church-like reverence, every bone in my showbiz body wanted to belt the song out of the building. For the first time since recovering from the influenza, I knew I could do it. But I resisted. Audrey's version was all swagger; mine was all connection, reaching out directly to the audience and touching their hearts.

Jimmy's piano and I ended on the same note at the same time. The ballroom was silent, perhaps a little numb. And then applause rippled through the rows and aisles and across the balcony. My heart shattered a little to have the audience show their appreciation so ardently. I waved my hand toward Jimmy to rise and share the praise, but he remained seated.

With tears brimming in my eyes, I bowed once more and left the stage. I could have taken another encore, perhaps even two, but I'd never touched an audience like I just did, and I wanted to leave the stage a success.

Audrey stood in my path as I reached the wings. Despite the pale powder on his skin, his face raged with anger and his eyes filled with hatred. Lionel, standing next to him, looked like he would kill me on Audrey's behalf.

"Mr. Z will hear about this!" Audrey snapped.

"I brought down the house," I boasted. "You bet he's going to hear about it. Go ahead and sing your version, if you think anyone wants to listen to it now."

Despite my glee, I quickly stepped away from the two men and toward Clippy, who seemed dumbfounded. Jimmy must have run from the pit because he was already backstage, picking up my coat and handbag from the floor.

I wanted to celebrate, to crow in my triumph, but Jimmy rushed me out of the wings, into the narrow corridor, and then outside. I stepped into the sunlight like it was the glorious spotlight I deserved. I stood tall and soaked in the sunshine. It had been such a long time since my heart was so light and happy, since I'd felt so true to myself, and I wanted to enjoy it as long as I could.

Still tingling with the success of Stu's sweet song and the audience's response, I wrapped my arms around Jimmy and squeezed him tight. Then I kissed his cheek.

"I don't know about you, kid, but I'm going to dip my toes into the bay."

CHAPTER TWENTY-FIVE

Stunned by Viola's sudden display of affection, Jimmy caught up with her as she sauntered toward the bay shore. She'd been brilliant on stage—visually and vocally—and in the sunlight, with her bare arms and legs, red curls, and feathered headdress, she *looked* delicious. Despite the thousands of silver spangles on her dress, the fabric floated lightly about her legs, and as Jimmy's fingertips touched the spot where she'd kissed him, he wondered what it'd be like to float away with her.

Except that he couldn't. Because his job was to keep her down to earth, to protect her. Maybe she hadn't seen how Audrey's face reddened with anger, but he had.

He took his fingers from his cheek before bringing her to task. "That was a stupid thing to do. Audrey looked like he was going to tear your head off. Same with Lionel. You don't want to make enemies with men like that."

"Stu wrote that song for me! It's mine and I'll sing it whenever I like." Viola took Jimmy's right arm, as if she wanted to make sure he heard exactly what she said. "And I don't feel stupid. I feel just fine. Top of the world, as a matter of fact. Stu'd want me to sing it like that."

"Stuart would have wanted you to take care of yourself instead of angering Audrey."

"Why should I care how Audrey feels? You heard the audience's reaction. They loved the song. They loved *me*." Despite her words, Viola's bright glow seemed to fade. "I won't get that again after you hand me over to Thaddeus. Unless you've changed your mind."

Although the harebrained idea of spiriting Viola away from San Francisco before Rutherfurd arrived had crossed Jimmy's mind, he'd never admit it to her. With her kiss still sweet on his cheek, he pressed the question he'd been wondering about since he caught her trail in Seattle. "Why'd you run away from him in the first place?

"You really want to know?" Viola seemed to examine the swimmers shivering on the darkening shoreline before continuing. "It was the only way to get him to chase me."

"You wanted him to chase you?" Jimmy thought maybe he had an earful of wax. Maybe two earfuls.

"I certainly didn't want to confront him in New Jersey," she replied. "In New Jersey, in New York, anyplace back East, he's got hundreds of men working for him. Protecting him. Out here on the West Coast, at some point he's going to be alone and it's going to be just him and me."

"Him and you doing what?"

Again, she took her time. "Thaddeus needs to account for everything he's done. Not just to me, but to all of the people who trusted him to do the right things."

The excitement that had bounced off of her like sunlight faded from her face, and he helped her into her coat. It was his fault for ruining her mood, maybe ruining the rest of the day. But whether at the Pan or the beach, he needed to keep her safe.

"Like who?" He wanted to know. "Which people?"

She looked him straight in the eyes, not allowing him to look away. As though he ever wanted to.

"You remember the explosion at the factory in New Jersey?" she asked. "The one last August that killed over a hundred workers?"

"Sure, I heard of it."

"He was responsible for that." She studied the pebbled pathway at her feet before continuing. "It used to be a good factory, but he turned it into a monster of production, overworking everyone. Three shifts a day for years before the explosion. He needs to make it right again."

As Viola kicked the pebbles with the toe of her satin shoe, Jimmy's words wouldn't come. She had to be the first to speak, but he was surprised when she did.

"Why did you tell me that Thaddeus hired you to track me down? Did he tell you to tell me? Were you trying to trick me? Is *he* trying to trick me?"

"No, none of that. I—I wanted to give you a fighting chance."

"You did? That's more than he ever gave anyone." The dark clouds that had passed over as Viola spoke filtered away gradually and her high spirits seemed to return. "I'm going in."

"The water? Without a suit?" He stopped himself, unwillingly teased by the image of Viola swimming naked in the pool. She drove him crazy sometimes, behaving so boldly. How could he keep her safe? Even now, no one would blame him if he tossed her into the pool and she got a good soaking. Might even teach her a lesson.

But as he thought about lifting her up and throwing her in the water, another image of Viola—her thin wet costume clinging to her, exposing her breasts and thighs as she climbed out of the pool (because Jimmy was gentleman enough to remove her coat and secure her handbag before pushing her in)—stopped him entirely.

He shook himself free of the seductive images and went to deal with the real woman. Eleanor Rutherfurd, he reminded himself. Jimmy caught her just as she was going into a changing room.

"Water looks really cold." To verify his claims, he glanced along the shore and saw white caps foaming on the waters. "How about I buy you dinner on the midway instead?"

Viola snuggled her coat around herself, as though she'd been expecting Jimmy to prevent her from reveling in the bay. "How about another dish of ice cream? This time with some hot fudge on it."

♫

They'd almost reached the ice cream fountain when Viola nodded toward the shooting gallery. "What's Rocco doing over there?"

There—as the banner above it proclaimed—was the *Best Chance Shooting Gallery*, "the finest gallery on the West Coast, featuring over one hundred targets, all moving in different directions and speeds, and the highest challenge to hit." And it was obvious to everyone watching that Rocco, still dressed in his tuxedo, was demolishing every target.

After Jeanette and Rocco's scuffle in the wings, Jimmy wanted to keep clear of both of them. But Viola clearly wanted to see the gallery, so he escorted her toward the small cluster of onlookers.

Jimmy was more interested in the gallery than the shooters. The rifles chained to the counter—*No walking away with the merchandise here, folks!*—were Remington Model 12s, a pump-action gun that Jimmy was particularly adept at. And the gallery was stocked with enticing targets. Naturally, there were the standard target plates with gongs, but there were also two large slides running yellow ducks in opposite directions and two gnarled trees with squirrels—in progressively smaller sizes—running up the left and down the right sides of each tree. Finally, there was the pièce de résistance, a double revolving disc of tiny stars in the center of the gallery.

As Jimmy admired the bright centerpiece of rotating stars, five of them flopped over, courtesy of Rocco's rifle. When five more stars went down in quick succession, Jimmy realized that Rocco was alternating between two rifles to double his speed.

Viola must have noticed also, because she said, "Rocco's good, isn't he?"

So far Rocco'd hit every target he'd aimed at—including the tiniest, almost invisible squirrel—but Jimmy had no intention of praising him. "Anyone can get good at shooting." The targets were only ten yards away and anyone could hit them, but even so, Rocco's perfection was irritating.

Viola tightened her grasp on Jimmy's arm. "Are those bullets real?"

"Sure are," he replied. "The rifle's real too. But the bullets are made of soft lead that shatters to dust after hitting the target. Nothing to worry about."

But as soon as he replied, as soon as he saw the pain that

crossed Viola's face, he wished he'd said nothing. The bullets might be harmless, but they were still bullets, and Viola's lover had been shot to death only last week. He wondered if he should walk her away from the gallery. She hadn't seemed squeamish about guns and bullets, but no need to let her replay a painful memory.

An older man standing next to Viola took off his spectacles to peer at Jimmy's badges. "You had enough of this overdressed charlatan?" He nodded at Rocco's tuxedoed back. "Why don't you show him what an officer can do?"

Truth be told, Jimmy'd been straining to pick up a rifle since he heard the first target drop. Now that he'd seen Rocco shoot, Jimmy almost ached to compete against him. Unless it was the delight of Viola's hip bumping into his that really made him ache?

"Do it, Jimmy." Viola's hip was once more thrillingly close to his. "Show him how good you are."

Jimmy took the post to Rocco's right. He gripped the Remington in his right hand, testing the balance and sight, and found both to be adequate. He was ready to show Viola—and the others watching—that his Rifle Expert badge was honestly earned. Not only would he outshoot Rocco, he'd make sure Audrey and Lionel knew about it. Which should make them think twice about coming after Viola for singing Audrey's song.

"Five shots for five cents," the operator said.

"Five shots doesn't last long," Jimmy replied. "Fill it all the way."

The operator nodded smartly, as if he appreciated how much attraction a bona fide rifle expert brought the gallery. The original audience of a dozen had already doubled. "Yes, sir."

Jimmy plunked two dimes on the counter and nodded to the rifle on his left. "Load 'em both. Ten shots each. And make sure they're all .22 shorts."

Rocco had stopped shooting and was standing at ease, as if he was waiting to see what Jimmy had in mind. Now that Jimmy's intentions were clear, Rocco put down two dimes of his own. "Another twenty for me."

Jimmy heard scattered voices in the crowd. He knew that favorites were being selected and bets were being laid, most likely in his favor. All before he'd even fired his rifle.

As the operator took the first rifle to the side to load it, Rocco said, "I was a magician's assistant in Texas Jack's Wild West Show for three years. Learned how to shoot from Texas Jack himself, the surest shot in all vaudeville."

Jimmy had never heard of Texas Jack. "Well, I learned to shoot—"

Rocco picked up his remaining rifle and shot five of the yellow ducks in speedy succession. Rifle back on the counter, he turned to face the eager crowd behind him. "And in the army"—Rocco made eye contact with every person staring at him—"I was the best in my platoon."

The admission that he had been in the army gained Rocco a few cheers from the crowd, but Jimmy took it in stride. Once all four rifles were loaded and the operator positioned himself at the sidewall, they tossed a coin to see who shot first.

Jimmy's first twenty shots demolished every squirrel on the left tree; Rocco's first twenty did the same for the right tree. Rocco's second twenty shots collapsed every propelling target on the left side of the gallery; Jimmy's second twenty followed through for the right side.

Rocco waited until Jimmy put his second rifle down on the counter. "This could go on forever."

"Sure could," Jimmy agreed, not willing to end the competition as a draw. Viola needed to see how well he shot. She needed to know that he'd protect her. That she could trust him. And, Jimmy supposed, he enjoyed pumping that Remington in front of her, because there was no harm in her imagining—just imagining—what it would feel like to—

"In honor of Texas Jack." Rocco lit a cigarette, intruding on Jimmy's fantasy until it drifted away like smoke. "How about we use a mirror?"

"Mirrors?" The operator gulped. "You want mirrors?"

"You've got some?" asked Rocco.

"Mirrors came with the gallery," said the operator, "But I've never brought them out before. Nobody's ever—"

Jimmy knew about the mirror trick where the shooter put the shotgun on his shoulder, barrel pointed toward a target behind him, and used the mirror to site the shot. "Bring 'em out," he said. "We're using them today."

He saw Viola waving at him. He squinted at her and she came over to him, standing as far away from Rocco as she could. "Clippy just came by. We need to get on the next train. It leaves in ten minutes."

"Two more minutes," Jimmy replied, more casually than he felt, before nodding toward the operator. "He's bringing the mirrors out."

Viola scowled. "He is? Mirrors?" She came as close to Jimmy as possible, sending electricity through his veins as she whispered close to his ear. "You ever shot something behind you with a mirror before?"

He had, and the shot had saved his life, but he wasn't going to tell her that. He briefly wondered how Viola—

having only been in vaudeville for a few months—knew about mirror-trick shots, but he couldn't let the question distract him.

"Sure have," was all he said. Having delivered her message, Viola returned to stand next to the man with the spectacles.

Jimmy pointed his barrel toward a target no larger than the number on an eight ball. "How about those bluebirds?"

"Fine," Rocco grunted.

The operator wiped the dusty hand mirrors on his flannel shirt before handing them over. "I'm trusting you not to hit anything you shouldn't."

"Just to make this interesting," Rocco said, "How about we both shoot on the count of three?"

"Deal." Jimmy nodded at the operator. "Start at my signal."

Jimmy wondered if he should offer to shake Rocco's hand. After all, it'd been a long time since he'd been so evenly matched, and the dancer had proved himself to be one hell of a shot. Rocco had seemed equally content with their competition. He never congratulated Jimmy on his hits, but he didn't spit at them either. Whatever else Rocco might have done—and Viola had already said he hadn't killed Stuart—Jimmy had to credit his shooting skills.

Rocco stubbed his cigarette beneath his shoe, picked up his rifle, tugged at the chain that attached his weapon to the counter, turned around to position his back toward the gallery, and slung the rifle over his right shoulder, barrel aiming toward the targets.

Jimmy followed suit, using his left shoulder to anchor the gun. He held the stock steady and placed the mirror on the center of the butt, so he saw both sites. He located the line of bluebirds and counted out three from the side. He squirmed longer than he liked to, but there were so many moving parts involved, including his own shoulders. Also, he'd have to pull the trigger with his thumb instead of his finger, something that was sure to change his balance. For the first time since picking up the rifle today, Jimmy's heartbeat increased, his breath came harder, and he felt more alive, more *real* than he had for a very long time.

Jimmy raised his right hand to signal the beginning of the countdown.

"One," the operator called out, his voice loud and suitably excited.

Jimmy had his shot ready and he looked beyond the mirror, just for a second, to see Viola fixated on him with a combination of anxiety and awe that almost made him put down the rifle and rush to her.

"Two."

He was tempted to hold his breath, tempted to think it would steady him, but he kept breathing, just like he was taught. The mirror seemed to slip between his fingers for a second, but he secured it and reset his shot.

"Three!"

Just as Jimmy and Rocco shot, the chain that tied Rocco's rifle to the counter snapped off the rifle and clanged to the counter.

Jimmy kept his eyes on the mirror, took a fresh breath, and saw that his bluebird was down. He angled his mirror to check on Rocco's bluebird and saw that he'd shot high, about a foot above his bird.

Rocco didn't have to look in the mirror to know he missed. He let out a string of Italian curses and pulled at the inches of chain still clinging to his rifle. He swore again.

As though he'd heard all of those exact Italian curses before, the operator—who knew there were still nine .22 shorts in the magazine and preferred not to be shot by any of them—slid toward Rocco and put his hand out for the rifle. Rocco turned around and gave it to him.

The audience rewarded Jimmy with a smattering of applause, something that rubbed him the wrong way. Winning because of an equipment failure was not a win. He was about to propose another shot with Rocco using the other rifle, but he caught Viola glaring at him, then looking toward the midway entrance. Then glaring at him harder. If they were going to make the train to the ferry, there was no time to give Rocco a fair shot.

Nor did Rocco appear to want one. But he did want to shake Jimmy's hand, something Jimmy was glad to do.

We're both aces, Jimmy wanted to tell Rocco, but the dancer walked away before Jimmy found his words.

The gallery operator put his fingers in his mouth and whistled. "Winner! Winner!" He took the rifle from Jimmy's hands, pulled a brass trophy from under the counter, and pushed it into Jimmy's hands. "Take your prize, mister."

As Viola stepped up to Jimmy, as jubilant in his achievement as he was, the operator gave her an order. "Go ahead and kiss him, miss. He deserves it. He's the best at the Beach today. Maybe the whole season!"

With the applause surrounding her, Viola hesitated only for a second before kissing Jimmy lightly on the lips.

Jimmy came alive, dumping the trophy on the counter and taking Viola in his arms. He kissed her full on the lips, holding her closer and closer as her body yielded to his, until he was sure she was kissing him back.

Then he kissed her again to make sure it was all real.

CHAPTER TWENTY-SIX

JIMMY and I and the rest of the troupe just made the ferry to San Francisco. We should have been worn out from performing and we should have napped before tonight's show, but to a trouper, we were unusually restless, as though we couldn't wait to get back on a real stage in a real theater.

Despite their earlier blowup, Rocco and Jeanette held hands at the back of the ferry, as though to show they'd kissed and made up. Knowing they often used anger to fuel their passion, I wondered if they'd done more than kiss at Neptune Beach.

I thought again about that brief, intimate moment I'd witnessed between Jeanette and Audrey. I hadn't seen them together since; hadn't even caught them looking at each other. Had that intimacy been a one-time thing? An exploration? Or was it maybe the reason that Jeanette and Rocco had argued today? Or why Rocco blasted every target in the shooting gallery?

As Rocco kissed the top of Jeanette's hand, I thought

about my own kiss at Neptune Beach. I bit my bottom lip hard, trying to dull the sensation of Jimmy's lips against mine. No one ever made me tingle from my lips to my fingertips. Not even Stu. It was truly a cruel world when the kid who would deliver me to Thaddeus Rutherfurd kissed me so keenly that my toes curled and my cheeks flushed at the thought of his mouth on mine.

Jimmy walked toward me easily, then quickly double-timed past the side wheel to the nearest rail. He leaned so far over that one nudge would have pushed him into the bay. It was tempting to tease him a little by joggling him, but I resisted. Even though I was an excellent swimmer, I had no idea if Jimmy was. So while he lost his ice cream over one railing, I walked to the back end of the ferry even though Rocco and Jeanette were a few yards away, Rocco taking a quick swig from a silver flask.

Once more in the distance, Alcatraz Island shivered between drifts of fog, warmed only by the bright beam of the lighthouse. I thought of Margaret Wilson and how hard her life must have been, surrounded by the waters where her son drowned. My heart went out to Stuart, to his mother, and even to Dorothy and the army inmates. No matter why you lived there, Alcatraz was a prison.

The ferry seemed to slow, as if sending its regards to Alcatraz. Then Jeanette cried out, "Give it back, Rocco! Give it back!"

Rocco dangled a large paper high above Jeanette's head and moved his arm over the water. Jeanette struggled to reach the paper, going so far as to step on his toes as she grabbed at his sleeve.

"Damn you!" She beat her hands on his chest, as though that'd make him yield. Her girlish approach was almost humorous until I saw that Rocco wasn't just holding a piece of paper, he was holding a red notebook also.

A red notebook that looked an awful lot like the notebook stolen from Stu's pocket the day he was murdered. The notebook that I needed before I confronted Thaddeus Rutherfurd.

I inched down the railing toward them. Jeanette stomped her feet and grasped at the paper and notebook with both hands, like a desperate bridesmaid trying to catch the bride's bouquet.

As he saw me approach, Rocco—like he'd been waiting for a larger audience—announced in a flowery voice, "*The Remarkable Rocco*. Master of Magic Arts."

He waved the paper and book in a circle over his head. After one rotation, during which I verified the rich red color of the Italian leather, the thickness of the pages, and the little glint of gold stamp on the border, I was sure it was my notebook.

"Now you see it," Rocco intoned as mysteriously as possible. "Now you don't."

And with a flip of his hand, the items disappeared. I'd known that Rocco'd apprenticed with a magician—he'd boasted about it when he put his hand on my breast, offering to make my silk slip disappear—but I had no idea of his real skills. His current trick might have even been entertaining except that the notebook he was performing with was mine. Nothing would stop me from getting it back. Nothing.

He snapped the fingers on one hand and the paper appeared in his other hand. Jeanette snatched the paper from his fingers and clutched it to her chest.

"Where's the book?" I tried to ask calmly, even though my heart was thumping wildly.

"Yeah, Rocco," Jeanette demanded. "Where's the book? And don't say you dropped it in the bay."

Rocco snapped again and the notebook reappeared in his other hand. Seconds later, I heard a splash. He opened both hands wide to show they were empty.

"So I won't say it," replied Rocco.

I barged between Rocco and Jeanette to reach the railing. I searched the water, not seeing anything floating on the waves. I thought I saw—but, it wasn't. Again, something splashed in the bay, but again, nothing.

Then I saw something rustling on the waves. Something red, floating just under the surface of the waves, drifting farther and farther away.

Without waiting to think it through, I tore off my coat, kicked off my shoes, and climbed over the railing and into the San Francisco Bay.

♫

The freezing water hit me like an electric shock. I'd never been anywhere as cold in my life. I went under the water and stayed there for seconds. Then I began kicking and trying to swim. I kicked and grasped the water until I finally reached the top, gasping for breath. My jump into the water, the jump I'd made hundreds of times into a swimming pool, had almost pulled me into a watery death. As the waves sloshed about my head and I tried to move my arms in any direction, someone yelled through the low mist.

Fighting against the frigid water, I waved my arms and kicked my feet to stay afloat. I sank deeper into the water, forcing myself to keep my eyes open even though I couldn't see anything. Yet I kept reaching upward, fighting to keep my head out of the waters.

I poked my head out of the water and heard, "Woman overboard!"

I prayed the voice meant *me* and someone was coming to my rescue, because the little sense I had told me I'd freeze to death in seconds. I knew how to swim in rough waters, of course. I'd grown up challenging the brash East Coast surf. But I never expected the sun-drenched San Francisco Bay I'd admired from Neptune Beach to be so icy.

I also hadn't considered that my beaded chiffon costume would weigh me down so much. As my fingers stiffened into claws, I pawed at my dress, unable to grab any part of it. The harder I tried to pull it off, the heavier it got and the more I sank. With one last try, I stripped off my magnificent costume.

Still, I sank. I wanted to hug myself, to find some warmth, but I had to keep trying to swim. Trying to stay above the water.

I finally surfaced and cocked my head back, spitting water out to the side as I tried to breathe in. My head was just a few inches above the surface, and even in these calm waters, I saw and heard nothing.

I croaked out, "Help! He . . . lp!"

It seemed like an eternity, but something landed on the water, nudging against my head for seconds before drifting away. Seconds later, another something splashed in the water. I grabbed out in any direction, blindly grasping until my fingertips touched what felt like a thread of rough rope. I tried to pull it to me, almost unable to believe the resistance on the other end was a floating life preserver, but I had no strength in my fingers to pull, so I let the rope take me where it would, hoping that if I clutched hard enough, I'd stay afloat.

But my fingers fumbled and I lost the line. The cold took hold of me and again I sank, this time with less air in my lungs, this time going down deeper into the water.

As I fought to find the surface, that infamous enlistment poster, the one showing a woman and her infant drowning after the sinking of the RMS *Lusitania* by German submarines, floated through my mind. I'd had nightmares about that poster, not just because of the anguished mother and child but because their watery death looked incredibly peaceful.

Were the echoes of voices I heard floating through the air inviting me to join them?

But I couldn't let myself drift to the bottom of the bay. I wouldn't. I'd beaten the flu and I'd never give up my second chance at life. I'd never sink to the bottom of the ocean without a fight.

Voices again. Maybe even my name.

Wait! Was someone from the *Lusitania* crew coming to save me? Or was someone crying out for me to save them? I begged my body to move toward the sounds, but now my limbs, like my frozen fingers, were unable to move.

And yet, one white life preserver bobbed toward me. I scratched toward it with all ten of my frozen fingers. I couldn't reach it. I tried again, knowing that if I didn't, the cold would silence me forever.

I told myself that I could do it. I heard a familiar voice call to me from over the water as I struggled to remember why I'd jumped in the first place, and I made one last grab for the life preserver.

♫

"Do you know how lucky you are?" A woman's firm voice worked through my cocoon of fatigue. "Jumpers don't usually come out alive."

All I wanted was to drift back to sleep, but I forced my eyes open. I didn't recognize the woman before me, neither her voice nor her crisp, almost policeman-like uniform. The few clothes that I hadn't stripped off in the water—my camisole, step-ins, and slip—were in a pile on the floor. My exquisite, luminescent costume was nowhere to be seen.

I unwound the fuzzy muffler rolled around my throat before forcing my dry lips to speak. "Where am I?"

"Back on dry land, in the San Francisco Ferry Building." The voice was casual, as though people were almost drowned and rescued every day. "My name's Florence and your name's Viola. Is that right?"

Someone knocked and Jimmy slipped into the room, his uniform damp, dirty, and wrinkled. He carried a tray with three steaming mugs and took a flask from his hip pocket. Without asking, he poured generously and placed a mug between my mittened fingers. I clutched the mug, trying to absorb every speck of heat it held, trying to remember what had brought me here.

Florence gulped from her mug. "Thanks, soldier."

"I didn't jump in to kill myself," I said. "I had to—"

Suddenly, I remembered the red leather notebook. I'd jumped in to save the notebook, wasn't that it? But had I? Had I even really seen Rocco throw it in? I tried to stand, but the blankets weighed me down. The mug tumbled from my hand but Jimmy caught it. "I had to save something in the water."

Florence handed me a damp canvas sack. “Your clothes are inside. Your handbag, too.”

I looked inside the sack, amazed to see my coat, handbag, and one of my shoes. I already knew from the sack’s weight that Madame Savage was not inside my handbag.

“If there’s anything you need to talk about, to clear your head, so to speak, you can often find me here,” Florence said, not unkindly. “You should be grateful this boy pulled you out. A lot of jumpers don’t have it so good.”

“She’s not a jumper.” Finally, Jimmy spoke. “She fell overboard. It was an accident, and now I’m taking her home.”

CHAPTER TWENTY-SEVEN

JIMMY and I were silent as the taxi drove down Market Street, past the Southern Pacific and PG&E blocks and the pedestal clock in front of Samuels & Co. jewelry store, which seemed to read 8:05. My act went on at eight thirty-four, and for one second, I thought I could make my curtain. Or beg for a later spot. But with my throat raw from spitting out water, I knew my voice wouldn't carry past the first dozen rows. I set my head against the cool window glass, watching more illuminated signs and businesses pass by.

"I'm like a longshoreman in these trousers." After releasing me from the blankets, Florence had dressed me in men's clothing pulled from an old barrel. I was decent, dry, and warm, and knew I should be grateful. But if I couldn't perform, I wanted a hot bath and my own clothes.

Jimmy and I sat in opposite corners of the taxi until he slid toward me, stopping only inches away. "Are you going to tell me straight," he said, "or do I have to shake it out of you?"

What did he want me to say? That I was cold and sore

and didn't know if I'd ever hit a high A again, but still I wanted him to hold me tight, maybe kiss me, right now, right here in the taxicab?

His head, *his lips*, inched toward me, but a scowl spread across his forehead. "Why'd you jump into the bay? I need to know."

I needed to know about the red leather notebook. I'd been so sure I'd heard it splash in the waters, then equally sure I'd seen it floating along the waves. I'd been so sure I could retrieve it that I'd made the split-second decision to jump in after it. Now, I wasn't even sure Rocco had thrown it into the bay.

Rocco. He could tell me what I needed to know.

Jimmy grabbed my hands, forcing me to look into his eyes. "Rocco made you jump?"

I didn't even know I'd said Rocco's name, but Jimmy was like a dog with a fresh bone. "What did he do to you?"

"He didn't do anything. I jumped in myself. It's just like I told the lady at the Ferry Building. I had to save something in the water."

"What could you . . . ?"

He didn't finish his sentence, like he was waiting for me to complete it for him. And maybe I should have. Maybe now was the time to tell him about the notebook. Time to let him know that I really, really wasn't Eleanor. That I was only Viola, and that before Eleanor died, she had given me her husband's prize possession. Except that I didn't have the notebook now, and if Rocco had really thrown it into the San Francisco Bay, I'd never have it.

But if Rocco *did* have the notebook, Jimmy might help me get it back. Because for some inexplicable reason known only to men, he and Rocco'd seemed almost chummy during their shooting competition.

The taxi finally made it to the block with the broad Pantages marquee, proudly illuminated for the evening show. Yes, my name was just where it should be, third act from the bottom. At least something in my life was normal.

Just as the taxi turned the corner for the hotel, just as I was about to tell Jimmy the truth, he changed his tactics.

"You almost got yourself killed tonight."

I was touched by his concern. So touched that I was ready to relax against him for consolation. I turned to tell him so, and to tell him a few other things, beginning with *I liked your kiss*, but then he added, "Your reckless behavior almost got *me* killed."

I turned away and set my forehead back against the window glass. I wasn't always reckless, I wanted to tell him, but almost dying from the influenza . . . well, it made me vow to take every chance I could to get what I wanted.

Back at the Hotel Henry, the sixth floor was empty. I fumbled with the clasp of my handbag, missing the comforting weight of Madame Savage. Jimmy put his hand in his pants pocket and presented me with my door key.

"You'll feel better after you've had a wash and some sleep."

"I don't want sleep or a wash," I lied. "I want to come with you."

My intentions were earnest, even if my phrasing was evocative. But Jimmy hung back, thoughtful, as if for just a moment, he was contemplating something intimate.

"I'm not going anyplace except Stuart's room," he said almost gently. "To watch your door."

"Liar. I bet you're going to find Rocco. I could help you."

"Forget that. You're not leaving this room until morning."

But, to both of our surprise, when Jimmy pushed me into my room, we found Rocco waiting for us. Alone, on my bed, his dead eyes open, with my missing Savage in his lap.

CHAPTER TWENTY-EIGHT

JIMMY NEVER FIGURED Viola'd be the kind of woman to faint, but he was glad she did. He lifted her off the floor and set her in the chair in her room. He'd lock her away in *his* room, but not until he got a grasp on what happened to Rocco, which he could do only after he eased Rocco's eyes closed with his thumbs.

Just hours ago, Rocco had matched Jimmy shot for shot, losing their competition only because of an equipment failure. Still, he'd shaken Jimmy's hand and walked away from the gallery head held high. As Jimmy remembered those moments, he was surprised to find that he had a new admiration for Rocco even though he'd been at the top of the list of people Jimmy was going to question about Viola's near-drowning in the bay.

Jimmy secured the gun with his handkerchief. A Savage M1907, just like the gun that killed Stuart. He emptied the magazine, deposited the ten bullets in his jacket pocket, and put the empty weapon on the nightstand, barrel headed to the wall.

He'd seen that gun before, when he searched Viola's dresser in Seattle. This could be the gun that murdered Stuart—except it shouldn't be. The police wouldn't give back that gun until the murderer was found.

With a sinking feeling, enough to almost plunge him into the chair where Viola lay crumpled, Jimmy wondered if she had a pair of these pistols. He'd never considered it, that a woman would own two guns. Or maybe Viola owned one and Stuart owned the other. Or maybe she'd purchased a second Savage after the police collected the first gun from the balcony. This scenario seemed more likely but gave Jimmy no consolation because it meant that Viola had purchased the second weapon on his watch. Despite his surveillance, she'd escaped him.

If that were true, what else had he missed about her? What other important fact had he messed up?

How about allowing her to jump overboard? He suddenly wanted to plow the wall with his fist. *Where were you when she almost died today?*

He'd been mooning after her from the other side of the ferry, that's where. Hoping for some look or signal that she'd welcome another kiss. He hadn't been thinking about her safety at all; he'd been thinking of his own arousal.

Which meant that when he saw her approach Rocco and Jeannette at the rails, he was only mildly envious. He remained mildly envious until Rocco started teasing her. That's when his devil took hold and he started toward her, double-timing to separate them. He would have made it, except that just as she threw her coat to the deck and stepped out of her shoes, his stomach had almost exploded. He would have caught her, would have tugged her hard to keep her on the ferry, but his body had rebelled against him, freezing him in agony just yards away.

Seconds later, he'd lurched to the rails, ready to follow her in, but Rocco held him back. As he struggled against Rocco's bear hug, Jimmy could only yell, "Woman overboard! Off the stern! Woman overboard stern-side!"

It had all happened so quickly that Jimmy'd forgotten until just now that Rocco had held him back. Had kept him from possible drowning. And also from saving Viola.

"Maybe you are a bastard, after all." Without getting too close, Jimmy studied the whiskey-colored stain running down Rocco's chin. The setup suggested that Rocco had killed himself by drinking poison. Except the man Jimmy'd shot against earlier didn't seem like a quitter. Didn't seem like the kind to take his own life.

At least Viola had an alibi for Rocco's death. No one could suspect her of poisoning Rocco when she had the formidable Florence of the Ferry Building as her witness.

Right then, someone knocked softly on the hallway door.

"Viola, it's Kitty."

Jimmy knew Kitty, of course. Even though he must have seen her do her act eighty times at least, he still wondered how she'd trained two dogs to jump on her back at the same time. Officer Tuck's drunken dog act might be higher up in the Pan bill, but Jimmy'd always thought the two dog acts should change spots. Jimmy also knew that Viola and Kitty were friends of a sort, although that friendship seemed based entirely on Kitty talking and Viola listening.

From what Viola'd said, Kitty collected gossip like other French women collected lovers, and right now, gossip of any kind might help him understand how Rocco had gotten into Viola's room.

"I hear you in there," Kitty said. "I know something happened. I'm not going away until you let me in." Kitty's initial stage whisper grew louder with every word.

Jimmy cracked the door open. Kitty leaned into the opening, cradling a curly-haired white dog in her arms, her expression threaded with anxiety. She tensed slightly at seeing Jimmy and pushed into the room.

Jimmy stepped back, trying to position himself in front of the bed. Too late. Kitty stared directly at Rocco. She swayed slightly but did not back up. Nor, Jimmy noted, did she faint. Only slightly shifting the dog in her arms, she made the sign of the cross. Jimmy, brought up Catholic, resisted the reflex to cross himself. Then Kitty spit at Rocco's feet. Jimmy might have been tempted to spit at Rocco at one time, but now he just wanted to know how he'd gotten into the room.

"Rocco's been poisoned?" asked Kitty. "Arsenic? Like in rat poison?"

"Poison, yes. Arsenic? I don't know." He wondered how she'd known he'd been poisoned so quickly, although in the back of his mind, he remembered something about Kitty and poison. Or was it Rocco and poison? Or—his heart beat a little faster—was it Rocco and Kitty and poison?

Jimmy shut the door.

Kitty crossed herself again before going over to Viola. She caressed Viola's still-damp hair away from her eyes. "She really went into the bay? And you jumped in to save her."

"Yes." Once again, he felt the frustration of being held

back by Rocco. "And no. I jumped in a boat and helped haul her in."

"She'll be all right?"

"Too soon to tell," he replied. Then, because Kitty seemed genuinely concerned, he added, "She seems fine now. Just tired."

"Her voice? Can she still perform?" Kitty asked kindly enough, but the question irritated him. There was more to life than being on stage, more to life than applause.

Kitty returned to Rocco. "We all knew that he had *something*. He's been threatening to poison my dogs for months."

"Look, I have to call the police about this. It doesn't look good that he died in Viola's room. They're going to ask questions. Is there anything you can tell me?" Jimmy watched Kitty gather her thoughts before he continued. "How long have you been back at the hotel tonight?"

"About half an hour," she answered readily.

"Did you see anything . . . a door open . . . a light under the door . . . when you came up? In Viola's room? Or anything strange in the hallway?"

"Viola missed her spot tonight, so I knew something was wrong. I knocked on the door and then I tried it. It was locked."

"Any light?"

"No."

"Did you hear anything coming from her room?"

"When I was in mine?" Kitty ruffled the head of the dog in her arms. "With nine dogs and one boy?"

Jimmy was ready to believe her, except that Viola had fainted at the sight of Rocco's dead body and Kitty was so damn calm. Either Kitty'd seen a lot of trauma in her life or she was a woman without feelings. Or she'd already known that Rocco was dead. Even though Viola seemed quite taken with Kitty, Jimmy was almost hoping for the last possibility. Just to speed things along.

"You don't seem—"

"Hysterical about seeing a dead man?" Kitty nodded to Jimmy's army cap, still drying on his head. "Why should I? France was fighting Germans years before you Americans came over. I've seen much worse than a man looking like he's sleeping." She stood silently for a few moments, as if waiting for Jimmy's next question. When she'd waited long enough, she told him, "Bring Viola into my room. I'll take care of her."

Removing Viola to Kitty's care made sense. Despite the oversized men's clothing she wore, Jimmy carried her easily across the hallway, and, as he held her in his arms, he thought again of how he'd kissed her earlier. Despite his momentary guilt at kissing a woman who was not his fiancée, he was glad he had.

Kitty's dogs nestled in small packs all over the room. Jimmy dislodged a large black poodle before laying Viola on a low bed of cushions. He backed out of the room, but not before the poodle extended a protective paw over Viola's arm.

"She should sleep for a long time," he said. "But if she doesn't . . ."

Kitty was already removing the laced shoes and thick socks from Viola's feet. "Don't worry about Viola. I have something to help her sleep if she needs it."

Jimmy trod lightly across the empty hallway to Viola's room. He had been in this room at least twice—not just the night he sprang Eleanor's identity on her, but the night before, when he'd searched her room. But he couldn't remember exactly what the room had looked like before tonight.

He went through Rocco's pockets, finding only a money clip with three dollars, one used ticket stub to Neptune Beach's Scenic Railway, two quarters, and a small mirror and comb.

Then he searched the room for anything belonging to neither Viola nor Rocco, something Rocco's murderer could have forgotten. All he found—on the floor, a few feet from the hotel door, which made him wonder if someone inside the room had dropped it or if it had been pushed under the door from the hallway—was a small square of newspaper. The front had a ladies' hat advertisement. The back was Stuart's obituary, the same one Jimmy'd seen earlier this week in the *Chronicle*. Written in pencil across Stuart's burial information were two words: *I'm sorry*.

Jimmy walked down the stairs to the lobby to ask the night manager to call the police. If Jimmy was very, very lucky, the police would remove Rocco's body before Viola woke from her sleep.

If Jimmy was unlucky—which seemed more likely, inevitable even—he'd be running interference between Viola and the police all night long.

♫

"He's in here, officers." Jimmy opened Viola's door wider, allowing two patrolmen inside. They'd come prepared with a collapsible stretcher and a pile of blankets.

They'd dropped the stretcher as they came out of the elevator, picked it up, and dropped it again. As the noise reverberated through the floor, doors opened along the corridor and heads popped out, vaudevillians wondering what the ruckus was. There went Jimmy's hope of getting Rocco's body taken away quietly.

He'd moved most of Viola's things into Stuart's old room. Except for a pair of silver buttoned shoes under the dresser that Jimmy had missed, it would be difficult to say this was a woman's room.

He'd struggled with what to do about Viola's handgun, finally deciding that a second Savage would raise too many questions. So he deposited the gun in a hiding place in his own room.

He returned the *I'm sorry* note to where he'd found it on the floor.

As they stood in the hallway, Jimmy recited his story to the patrolmen, not giving them any room to interrupt. "I'd been away all day and found him here when I returned. Like I said on the phone, this is Rocco diLorenzo of the Darling diLorenzo Dancers. He's staying down the hall. Maybe the maid forgot to lock the door after she cleaned, you know how all of these rooms look the same."

Jimmy's story sounded good. He'd heard many such stories himself during his years of following his father in New Orleans. The trick was to make the story short and give the police something that sent them in a direction away from you.

A few minutes later, a man in plain clothes arrived, introducing himself as Detective Petersen. Jimmy knew who he was, of course, and was doubly glad that Viola was sleeping in Kitty's room. Jimmy heard one of the patrolmen report, "No note, sir." He stood in the hallway with the detective and repeated what he'd told the patrolmen.

Now was Jimmy's moment to explain that Viola had fallen into the bay, been rescued, and spent hours in the Ferry Building before they'd found Rocco here together. Except that he didn't explain because Viola could tell it better.

Still, because a detective always demanded more story than a flatfoot, Jimmy embellished his. "I don't know him well. Not at all, really. I just joined the troupe a few days ago." All that was true, of course, but it was small truths. To his surprise, Jimmy wanted to tell the detective what a great shot Rocco was. *Almost as good as me.*

"Which act?" asked the detective.

"Viola Vermillion, Red-Hot Blues Chanteuse, sir."

From inside Viola's room, Jimmy heard the struggle of moving a body onto a stretcher. He stood at attention, wishing he could attend to Rocco's body personally. Soldier to soldier.

"You play piano?"

"Yes, sir."

"And you were a Second Lieutenant."

"Yes, sir." Jimmy stood a little taller, despite his still-damp uniform.

Detective Petersen motioned for Jimmy to precede him into Viola's room, where the flatfoots were putting a blanket over Rocco's body. The newspaper clipping he'd found on the floor hadn't been moved.

"And this is your hotel room, connecting to Stuart Wilson's?"

"No, sir." Jimmy could only lie so much to a policeman. "It belongs to Miss Vermillion."

"Where is Miss Vermillion?"

Jimmy kept this response simple. "Sleeping. Just down the hallway."

"If that's the case," said Petersen, "it's time to wake her up."

CHAPTER TWENTY-NINE

JIMMY and the detective found Viola asleep in Kitty's room. The large black poodle, still settled at Viola's feet, growled, and Petersen demanded that Viola be brought back to her own room. Jimmy wrangled Viola awake, forcing her to walk when he really wanted to carry her off to his own room.

"Follow my lead and say as little as possible," he warned her.

It wasn't until they neared Viola's room that Jimmy realized Petersen's game. One of the patrolmen emerged from the room, obviously leading the stretcher holding Rocco's body.

Viola clutched Jimmy's arm but didn't remove her gaze from the blanket. For a woman who'd found her lover dead a week earlier and witnessed his body being carried out, having to view a similar stretcher was a mean maneuver. Jimmy'd thought better of the detective.

"It's Rocco and he's dead," Jimmy whispered into her ear. "You and I found him in your room. He's been poisoned." When Viola did not respond, Jimmy repeated, "He's dead."

Jimmy straightened his weary bones until he stood at attention, watching as Rocco's body was carried toward the elevator.

"Both of you," Petersen said grimly. "Inside. Now."

Jimmy positioned Viola's chair so that she couldn't see her bed. As she slumped into the cushions, he stood sentry at her side. Every nerve in his body was agitated and he could not relax. His uniform, almost dry, itched like hell.

Still dressed in the misfit men's clothing from the Ferry Building barrel, Viola looked like a down-and-out hobo in a comedy act, and she smelled, well, she smelled like she'd been sleeping with dogs.

Jimmy hadn't told Petersen about Viola's alibi—and his, now that he thought of it—but there was still time to get ahead of the detective's questioning. Yet Jimmy decided to hold back. Viola could not talk about her dunk in the bay without mentioning Rocco, and once she did, Petersen would look for any way possible to break that alibi and keep them here all night.

Why risk it, when Jimmy could quickly put Petersen on Kitty's trail?

"If I knew anything at all about Rocco's death, I'd tell you straight away," Viola responded to the detective's first question.

Petersen stood opposite Viola and Jimmy, notebook and pencil in hand. The newspaper clipping that Jimmy had returned to the floor—which looked like both a confession of Stu's murder and a suicide note at the same time—was gone.

"So, everyone in the troupe liked Mr. diLorenzo?" the

detective asked. "Nobody had hard feelings against him? Does that include you, Miss Vermillion?"

Viola answered readily. "Yes, that's right. No hard feelings here."

"Even though he tried to mash you more than once. Isn't that what you told me Monday?"

Viola cringed at the mention of Monday, when Jimmy knew she'd been questioned just after Stuart's murder. Still, she responded without rancor. "Me and every other woman in the troupe. Rocco's mashing never went far because we all knew how to stop him."

"How's that?"

"Stomp on his toes. A dancer only has his feet, and if he injures those he performs in pain. If he can perform at all."

Petersen restrained a grin. Jimmy did not. A sudden optimism lightened his worry. If Viola kept her responses entertaining, she just might walk away from greater scrutiny.

The detective continued. "You can't think of anyone who'd have a reason to murder Mr. diLorenzo?"

"No."

"How about a reason he'd take his own life?"

Viola shook her head.

"What about how he ended up in your hotel room?"

"If I don't know why'd he kill himself, I don't why he'd do it in my room." Viola scowled. "Why don't you just ask me if I killed him?"

"You'd tell me if you killed him, would you?"

"I'd tell you that I didn't. Just like I didn't kill Stu." When the detective didn't reply, Viola said, "Stu Wiley. Stuart Wilson. My piano player. Dead since Monday and you haven't found *his* murderer."

Petersen held his pencil and notebook just a little bit tighter, and Jimmy's optimism foundered.

Yet the detective kept his sights on Rocco. "How about poison, Miss Vermillion? Do you have poison in your room?"

"No."

"Anyone else in the troupe have it?"

Jimmy jumped in. "Rocco had poison."

"He did?"

Jimmy spoke before Viola could. "Because of Kitty LeBlanc's poodles." He knew Viola would never expose Kitty to the detective's questioning, but Jimmy had no qualms. "He threatened to kill Kitty's poodles."

"*Did* he kill any of her poodles?"

"Not that I know of."

The detective called the patrolman away from the door and gave him instructions. Jimmy was fairly sure the patrolman'd be knocking on Kitty's door in a moment.

Seconds later, the patrolman ran back into the room.

"You need to come now," he told the detective. "All hell's breaking loose down the hallway."

And then the screaming started.

♫

Petersen hustled toward the screams, but Viola stumbled getting out of her chair, her limbs stiff and slow. Still, she was faster than Jimmy, who'd been drifting to sleep on his feet. Petersen's trail led them to Rocco and Jeanette's room.

The narrow hotel hallway was packed with curious troupers: men in robes over pajamas, girls with long hair rolled in rags, and women with cold cream on their faces.

Audrey and his manager, Lionel, were dressed in the spiffed-up suits they often wore to dinner after the evening show, worried looks on both of their faces.

"I've been robbed!" Jeanette's frantic scream—surprisingly similar to her oft-overheard squeals of ecstasy—trilled through the closed door.

Everyone made way for the policemen, who tried the door, found it unlocked, and opened it widely. Jimmy leaned in behind the police and saw Jeanette in her street clothes, standing between the wall and the long side of the double bed. The mattress was pushed off the bed and hung almost on the floor. It was obvious that Jeanette'd lifted the mattress to look underneath. And found that whatever she'd hidden was missing.

"Mrs. diLorenzo, is it? I'm Detective Petersen with the—"

"I know who you are and I need your help!"

"What can I—"

"I've been robbed!"

"May I come in, Mrs. diLorenzo?" Even as he asked permission, the detective entered, the patrolman behind him.

Jimmy surveyed the scene like the son of an honest cop that he was, wondering if someone wasn't hiding under that overturned mattress, but knowing it wasn't his spot to suggest that. He couldn't believe that anyone—especially a performer who trooped from city to city—would be stupid enough to stash anything under a hotel mattress.

The detective took one step toward Jeanette. "I can help you, Mrs. diLorenzo, but right now, I have some terrible news to tell you. Your husband, Rocco diLorenzo, was found dead this evening."

Jimmy's father wouldn't have led with that information, especially with the entire troupe peering in from the hallway, but if Petersen was looking for a reaction, Jeanette gave him one.

"I know he's dead!" she screamed at him. "Kitty couldn't wait to tell me. Why do you think I'm checking on my money?"

"Shameful!" A man's voice called out from the hallway. "She don't even care about Rocco!"

"Maybe she murdered him for his money?" asked another.

Viola perked up enough to tell the detective, "She was fighting with Rocco all day. Even on stage. She was mad enough to murder him."

Upon that provocative suggestion, Jimmy would have shut the door to the vaudeville voyeurs. But it wasn't his call.

Petersen asked, "Is that right, Mrs. diLorenzo? Were you and your husband fighting all day?"

In an emotional switch so quick that little Mary Pickford would have begged for pointers, Jeanette's anger melted into sorrow, and she fluttered a sheer handkerchief at the corner of her eye.

The prospect of tears seemed too much for Audrey. He pushed through the troupe and inserted himself into the room. He offered his hand to Jeanette and settled her in the chair.

Audrey's focus was solely on Jeanette, but when he spoke, his voice reached the cheap seats in the back of the hallway. "Perhaps it's time to tell the police your little secret, darling."

At the word *secret*, everyone in the hallway pushed in on Jimmy and Viola, eager to be closer to the revelation.

"What secret is that, Mrs. diLorenzo?" asked Petersen.

Jeanette dabbed the handkerchief in the direction of her eyes and addressed the detective like a bereaved, broken-hearted widow.

"It's that me and Rocco weren't married, detective. But me and Stuart Wiley was."

♫

Jeanette's announcement was as deliberate and precise as a knife-throwing act. No one spoke that polished a phrase without rehearsing it, and no one rehearsed unless they had something to hide.

Although Jeanette was center stage, Audrey's lips moved in a way that suggested he had rehearsed Jeanette's explanation himself. Even written it, perhaps. Jimmy's intuition told him he should also pay careful attention to Lionel, who'd come inside to stand behind the pair. Such a touching trio.

And then there was Viola, huffing like a bull and so mad she could spit nickels. "What do you mean, you were married to Stu?"

Jeanette looked up from her handkerchief. "I was his wife. That's what marriage means, don't it? If you don't believe me, you'll have to believe this." She leaned toward Audrey, pushed a hand under her seat cushion, fished around for a few seconds, and came up with a folded piece of paper.

Jeanette offered the paper to the detective, but Viola snatched it before Petersen could take it. She backed away from Jeanette as if the dancer were contagious, unfolded the paper, and read it quickly. She frowned and read it again.

"It's a marriage record from New Jersey," said Viola. "According to this, Stu married Jean Hinckley on May 17, 1917." She stared at the paper, probably rereading it two or three times, but no one interrupted. Not even Jimmy, who would have throttled Stuart right here and right now. If he'd been alive.

"Jean Hinckley." Viola sneered at Jeanette. "Is that you?"

"It sure is," Jeanette nodded.

Jimmy expected Viola to fly at Jeanette with questions, but instead, she turned the paper over and read the back. It looked like there were phrases written in pencil, and even some musical notation. Stuart's handwriting?

"Did you marry Mr. diLorenzo, too?" Detective Petersen asked. "After you married Mr. Wilson?"

"Some girls married lots of soldiers, just for the monthly stipend. But I'd never do that, officer." Jeanette shook her head for emphasis. "Rocco just made it look like we were married. He said it made us more like Irene and Vernon Castle, and everyone loved the Castles."

"Did Mr. diLorenzo know that you were married to Mr. Wilson?"

"Not until today, when he found my marriage record. Rocco's been trying to get me to marry him forever, but I"—Jeanette's voice went quiet, as if she intended for only the detective to hear her—"I told him that I might already be married."

Jimmy considered shutting the door to remove the hallway audience, especially since he had the uncomfortable feeling that Jeanette relished the attention and wanted to tell her story to as many people as possible. But it wasn't his interrogation, so he left the door untouched. Maybe the troupe *should* witness all this.

"That's why we were fighting today. Rocco accused me of carrying a torch for Stuart." Jeanette finally responded to the detective's earlier question. "But I only married him because he was going off to war and he begged me. And then, after the war, he refused to give me a divorce, because . . ." Jeanette paused deliberately before gazing at Viola. "He said he couldn't stop loving me. That he always would."

Jimmy sensed Viola's anger rise. He didn't want to look at her, didn't want to set her off, didn't want to give her the opening to get into more trouble, so he blasted out at Jeanette for her.

"You were married to Stuart and you didn't think the police should know about it after he was murdered?" It felt good to question Jeanette. Good to force someone else to answer questions.

"I'm telling you now, ain't I?" Jeanette nodded to the paper in Viola's hands. "And now that I've proved I was Stuart's wife, that means I get all of his stuff." She looked at Audrey before continuing. "All of his papers. His music and his scrapbooks and his . . . his . . ."

"His entire estate," Audrey suggested.

"Yes, his entire estate," Jeanette parroted. She turned to the detective. "You can do that for me, can't you?"

"No, he can't," Viola spit out. "I've already given his things to his mother. She has it all."

Jimmy knew it was a lie, and he admired her for it.

"There might be some music she didn't hand over to Mrs. Wilson," he added coolly. "But it's at the Pan. We'll have to give it to you tomorrow."

Jeanette scowled. "But—"

"Tomorrow sounds reasonable to me," said the detective. "It's just a few hours away."

Jeanette nudged Audrey, who gracefully swanned toward Viola. He extended his hand for the marriage record and Viola released it readily, letting it float to the floor.

Outside in the hallway, vaudevillians gasped. That was not how any spot treated the headliner.

As Audrey picked up the paper and Petersen instructed his patrolman to shut the door, Jimmy put his arm around Viola and led her out of the room. They weren't even through the troupe when Viola protested.

"Stu would never—"

"Let it go." Jimmy shuffled her into her room.

She reached behind him for the doorknob. "I—"

"Just for tonight . . ." Jimmy backed up against the door; anything to keep Viola inside. "We can't talk about this here."

"But—"

"Not. Here." Jimmy opened the closet and removed the oversized men's coat from the Ferry Building. "You need to get away from here."

"I need a bath."

The rough-fitting men's clothing she'd been wearing had developed an unholy odor, some of it distinctly naughty poodle. He couldn't disagree with her about needing a bath, but he said, "You're fine for where we're going." Then he bundled her into the coat. "Just keep this on and no one's the wiser.

"Where're you taking me?"

"The safest place in the city." Jimmy prayed silently that he was telling the truth. "That's where we're going."

CHAPTER THIRTY

THE FARTHER JIMMY hustled Viola away from the hotel and the police and whoever might have killed Rocco, the easier he breathed. Even though Viola was far from safe.

"Viola," he gently commanded her. "Talk to me."

"You heard what Jeanette said," she grumbled.

Her fierceness almost made him lose his grip, and he redoubled possession of her. He spread his other hand against her back to keep her moving forward, expecting she'd have more to say.

She did. "Stu was married to Jeanette and he never told me. *Another* something he never told me." Then she added, "We saw Jeanette every day. *He* saw her every day. How does a man keep a secret like that?"

Viola's pain seemed to spiral into anguish, and she slipped from his arms, as though she had no energy remaining. He caught her and kept her standing. She hadn't looked at Jimmy since they'd left the hotel, and he wasn't sure he wanted her to now. Not because he didn't care, but because he had no answer for her pain. At least her pain asked a real question now: *How does a man keep a secret?*

He was ready to protect Viola from any physical harm, but he had nothing to soothe her emotional distress. Except that he agreed with her. Stuart's secrets—from running away from San Francisco to selling his song to Audrey to being married to Jeanette—piled up into one huge heap of hurt, each new secret inflicting fresh pain.

But now was no time to let his guard down with her. Not when they'd found Rocco in her hotel room with her gun in his hands.

That Savage still prickled at him. He'd been wrong to remove the gun from Rocco's hands, wrong to hide it in his own room. But he did not want the police finding it.

Viola stopped suddenly, refusing to go farther. "Where are you taking me?"

She plunged her hand into the coat pocket and withdrew her handbag, which Jimmy knew was empty. He suddenly realized where Viola'd been hiding her second Savage.

He maneuvered her into an alleyway and, despite the darkness, made sure she looked directly into his eyes. "You bought another gun? After Stuart was shot with yours?"

"I sure did. A girl's got to pro—"

"That's what I'm here to do. Protect you."

"I thought you're here to turn me over to Thaddeus." She pulled away from him. "You go ahead and take care of old Thaddeus. I'm taking care of me, and that means I need a gun."

"Do you even know how to hold a gun?" he asked. "Know how to shoot one?"

Before she answered, he led her down the alley, across a

street, and through another alley, until they reached a screen door with the words *Deliveries only Tadich* above it. He opened a narrow door, revealing a steep staircase. He motioned for Viola to go up, but she resisted. So he pushed her up the stairs, tempted to put his hands on her rear to make her move faster. On the door at the top of the stairs, he knocked twice.

"Let me make one thing clear, Mrs. Rutherfurd," he said before the door opened. "You're not getting that gun back and you will not buy another."

♫

"If you start from the beginning and tell me the truth this time"—Ervin topped off Jimmy's glass again—"I might be able to help you."

Erwin aimed the whiskey bottle at Viola, but just seconds after plopping onto his lumpy couch, proclaiming that she didn't want to be here, and saying that Jimmy couldn't make her stay, she'd fallen asleep.

For the second time since barging into Erwin's flat, Jimmy explained what had happened at Neptune Beach (where Viola had antagonized Audrey), on the ferry (where Viola had jumped overboard), and at the hotel (where Viola and he had found Rocco's dead body). In addition, Jimmy re-explained that Jeanette was not married to Rocco; she was married to Viola's lover, Stuart, and Jeanette had the marriage record to prove it. Yes, the same Stuart Wilson whose murder Erwin had reported in Tuesday's *Chronicle*.

Clearly, from his retelling, Viola was at the center of some ferocious storm. But since Viola wasn't really Viola, and since Jimmy still didn't want to confess Viola's real identity, he did not mention Thaddeus or Eleanor Rutherfurd.

Even though that omission only added to the guilt he felt about ruining Erwin's sleep. Sure, his friend's eyes had been open when he answered the door, and they'd opened even more when he realized the person in men's clothing was actually a woman, but Erwin had a reporter's second sense and knew Jimmy was holding out on him.

"You think Rocco was murdered, don't you?" Erwin asked. "And that Rocco and Stuart's deaths are connected. Right?"

"Two men sharing the same woman? How many times have you known that to work out? Three men, if you saw how Jeanette was attached to Audrey tonight. Yessir, these deaths are connected. I just don't know how."

"Any chance that Rocco really killed Stuart? Or himself? And maybe this time, you don't answer my question with another question."

Truth be told, Jimmy respected Rocco a lot more after their shooting competition and didn't see Rocco killing himself. Not with poison, not with a pistol. Not ever. "Viola alibied Rocco herself, so no. But Stuart's from San Francisco and it's possible he left some enemies here."

"Like Dorothy Garrard, Stu's childhood friend? You ever going to tell me what you wanted with her?"

"It was for Viola." He spoke her name softly; the last thing he wanted was to wake her up and have her start asking questions. "She's run into Dorothy once or twice. And . . . like I already told you, Dorothy was at the Pantages about the time Stuart was murdered on Monday. And she came back to the Pan days later."

"You tell the police about Miss Dorothy? Or are you keeping all of this evidence to yourself?"

"I haven't told the police about her *yet*," said Jimmy.

"Because you're going to tell Miss Dorothy yourself, aren't you? That's how you always go after something, by making people explain themselves. Which means that you're trying to close Stuart Wilson's murder. As well as Rocco's, I suppose. So what's your first step?"

"My first step was to keep her safe." Jimmy nodded toward Viola as he drained his glass. "Second step is to get some sleep. And the third step . . . well, I'll figure that out tomorrow."

♫

With Viola snoring in the big room, Jimmy and Erwin bunked in the smaller room, sleeping next to each other on the floor, just like old times.

Erwin punched his pillow twice before saying, "Miss Viola. She's really something, isn't she?"

"That she is."

"You got a handle on her?"

Sure do, Jimmy wanted to reply, even though *might have* was more likely.

"How about your fiancée, Jimmy? You got a handle on her, too? Because I told Amelia I'd watch out for you, keep you out of trouble." Erwin spoke plainly, even though each word resonated like fireworks. "You do remember Amelia, don't you? Brown hair, hazel eyes, steadiest hands in New Orleans, worth more than you and me combined?"

Jimmy did not deserve the amazing Amelia Oakes, that was true. He knew it, Erwin knew it, and everyone in New

Orleans knew it. But when a soldier goes off to war, he wants someone back home to care whether he lives or dies. And if that someone is the first girl you ever kissed, the prettiest girl you ever saw, you ask her to marry you.

"Has she called you?" Jimmy asked. "Is she looking for me?"

"She's got too much pride; you know that." Erwin waited long enough for that to sink in. "So I called her and let her know you were here. I even asked her to throw you over and run away with me. But she refused."

Jimmy knew Erwin was joshing about Amelia, but only just. More than Erwin knew, Jimmy wished his fiancée were here right now, beside him in bed. But since she wasn't, Viola was first in his thoughts.

"You should have been at Neptune Beach, Erwin. Should have heard Viola sing. She broke everyone's heart and made them feel fine about it."

Erwin punched his pillow again. "You ever hurt Amelia, you'll answer to me."

Jimmy snorted. They both knew Erwin could never take Jimmy. Just like they knew that Erwin would still try to wallop Jimmy if he thought he needed it.

"I've got everything under control," said Jimmy. "But just in case something goes wrong, in case something happens that shouldn't, when you talk to Dad, tell him *Rutherfurd*. He'll know what I mean."

"Son," Erwin extended the vowel all the way to the next room. "You say *Rutherfurd* and the entire world knows what you mean."

"You sound like you know something about him." Which shouldn't have surprised Jimmy, seeing that Erwin worked hard at his reporting.

"Thaddeus Rutherfurd is a steam roller and a tank all built into one, buying up newspapers all over the country, just like Hearst. Getting ready to buy some office. Governor of New York. That's the rumor."

"That so? Governor?"

"Is Miss Viola involved in this? With Rutherfurd? She is, isn't she? What are you still not telling me?"

"Just about everything." Jimmy was proud that he could at least tell Erwin that. "And you'll just have to trust me. Keeping you in the dark is the only way to keep you out of trouble."

Before Erwin could lob another question, Jimmy lay back on his pillow, ready to go to sleep like he did every night, thinking of a woman.

CHAPTER THIRTY-ONE

"As the crowd rose to its feet for the fifth time during Rutherfurd's magnificent speech, it was clear that Thaddeus T. Rutherfurd was not only the man of the hour but the man for our new American decade."

Thaddeus read the paragraph aloud again, deleted the word *fifth* and added *sixth,* and underscored the last three words with his fountain pen. From the soft leather chair at his train car desk, he lifted the paper toward Francis Cassady, who stood at his side.

Without looking up, Thaddeus said, "That goes in all of my newspapers after my speech at the legislature next month. You know how to send it out for distribution?"

"Yes, sir." Cassady took the paper from his boss. "And the train's prepared to leave Chicago, but the conductor wants to know if you're ready to depart."

"Indeed I am. Did he tell you how soon we'd reach San Francisco?

"Friday noon. If the weather holds up, we might even get in early."

From a special telephone secreted in a hidden alcove, Cassady passed the approval on to the conductor, and not for the first time since they'd left New York, Thaddeus congratulated himself on having such a well-outfitted private train car. Equipped with two bedrooms, two washrooms, and a dining room and kitchen, his office suite was the masterpiece of the entire car.

"Any news from Harrigan?" Then Rutherfurd asked what he really wanted to know. "Any news about *her*?"

"Nothing new." Still holding the to-be-published newspaper copy in his hands, Cassady said, "I still don't understand why you want to meet him in San Francisco instead of New York."

"The farther away from New York the better." Thaddeus settled back in his chair, nodding for Cassady to sit opposite him. It was just the two of them on this trip to the West Coast, and Thaddeus—missing his entourage of assistants, secretaries, and servants—required an audience. Perhaps he could share some of his hard-won wisdom with Cassady, who, despite his Southern accent and red hair, seemed a comer.

"You'll learn soon enough that no one cares what happens in California," Thaddeus told him. "It's hardly even part of the country."

As the train headed through the long maze of rails that crossed Chicago, Thaddeus wondered aloud, "Aren't you the least bit curious about Miss Vermillion? Don't you want to see her in the flesh?"

"I never thought you liked vaudeville, sir." Cassady squashed a smile.

"I don't, but I do like bold measures, and she's certainly been making them." She'd never succeed, of course. But she had thought up quite a scheme, and Thaddeus recognized a good scheme when he saw one.

"You sound like you admire her."

"Never! But I want to know what she thought she was doing by sending me a blank page of my notebook."

"And by going to the *Herald* and other papers," said Cassady.

"And that." That part of her scheme had been the most dangerous for him. If those editors had taken her seriously, if any one of them had a returning soldier on staff who understood encryption, the tables could have been turned. Disastrously. Instead of Thaddeus using the information in his notebook to blackmail his competitors across America, someone could now be blackmailing him.

But once again, he'd turned trouble into triumph. If Miss Vermillion hadn't gone to the New York newspapers, he might not be closing in on her now. "After I have the notebook, I leave everything up to you."

"You really want to give her all that money?" Cassady looked over to where the safe was hidden in the bookshelves. "Reward her for stealing your notebook?"

"I want this settled, and no woman like her is going to resist a big payday."

"What about Harrigan?"

"Give him a bonus, too. Whatever you think will buy his silence." Rutherfurd leaned back in his chair, satisfied. "But make sure they both know that if they ever mention the notebook to anyone, I'll make their lives a living hell."

CHAPTER THIRTY-TWO

STIFF AND SALTY, I wobbled into the small washroom. I turned on the tap, cupped my hands, and sipped the water. It was cool and fresh and nothing like the briny bay I'd jumped into yesterday.

My eyes were red, my skin was chapped, and my hair poked out at all angles. Makeup and a curling iron might make me look like a red-hot blues chanteuse once more, but did I have any voice left? All through my washup, I tried some deep breaths to test out my lungs, and now, with running water as accompaniment, I softly ran up and down a scale in an easy key. My tone was solid and I felt hopeful. But before I could really test my voice, someone tapped on the washroom door.

"Good morning, Miss Viola," said a male voice with a drawl like Jimmy's. "I wanted to see if you need anything."

I stopped mid-scale and peered at the door.

"Coffee's on the counter," the drawl continued. "And the newspaper is fresh."

I stared at my battered image in the mirror, trying to

remember what had happened after Jimmy pushed me into this flat last night. Someone had rolled the huge coat off of me, I remembered, and settled me onto a thin couch with lumpy cushions. I'd tried to stay awake and even heard a few words as I fell asleep. But the only words I remembered this morning were *marriage* and *record*.

And then I remembered holding Stu's marriage record in my hands. My Stu'd been married and hadn't told me. Worse yet, he'd been married to Jeanette, who always acted so superior to me. I guess now I knew why.

"Hello?" I called to the drawl. "Is Jimmy out there?"

"No, he is not," was the prompt reply. "He brought you here for your own good, if that makes a difference. My name's Erwin, by the way. Erwin Stanton. I'm an old friend of Jimmy's."

Once I completed my business, I came out into the hallway, and Erwin offered me coffee with hot milk. The newspaper was fresh—just like he'd said—even leaving ink on his fingers. That's when I remembered the *Deliveries only Tadich* sign, the high staircase, and last night's introduction to Erwin.

"Good morning, Mr. Stanton."

"Erwin." He held out a chair for me.

I sat, picked up the newspaper, and thumbed toward the back where the reviews usually were. From the way I brought down the house at Neptune Beach, my act should headline today's entertainment section. Although I wasn't in the first paragraph of the "Soldiers Concert at Alameda's Neptune Beach" story—the reporter did the right thing by focusing on the soldiers—my name was mentioned two paragraphs down.

"In case you're interested," said Erwin, "Rocco's death didn't make the morning paper."

Rocco. His name jolted me so hard the newspaper fell from my fingers. Like Stu, Rocco was dead. Even though he'd been brutish to me during our troupe's run, I never wanted Rocco dead.

"I'm sorry for your loss, Miss Viola."

Right away, I was back in New Jersey, being consoled after my sister's death. But how could this stranger know about Blanche? It took me a few seconds to realize that he meant Stu. Or maybe even Rocco.

"I reported on Stuart Wilson's death last week. In the *Chronicle*." Erwin spoke as though I should have known this, and I wondered if maybe I'd been told that last night but had forgotten.

"Did you know Stu?" I asked. "From before he left San Francisco?" *Did you know who wanted him dead?* was what I really wanted to ask. A sudden jolt of hope—or perhaps it was the strong coffee—cheered me on.

"No. I've only been here a few months." Erwin seemed genuinely disappointed that he hadn't known Stu. Then he reached over to his jacket and took out a long, thin notebook and a pencil, as though he was about to question me.

And that's when I remembered Rutherfurd's red leather notebook, which I'd jumped into the San Francisco Bay to retrieve. For the first time since being fished out, as I sat in Erwin's cozy, fragrant flat, I realized that if I'd been wrong, if Rocco hadn't thrown the notebook into the bay, he might still have it.

I took another sip of coffee. "Is . . . is Jimmy returning soon?"

"No, he's not." Erwin picked up the paper that'd fallen

from my hands. "He wanted to get a letter off to Miss Amelia Oakes. That's his fiancée. In New Orleans."

Erwin's eyes went to a collection of framed photographs on his wall. I was sure he wanted me to look at them, so I did. I immediately saw an informal photograph of Jimmy and a woman. With her soft eyes, sweet smile, and long brown hair, my sister Blanche would have called Amelia *a lovely girl*. From the way she and Jimmy held onto each other as they looked toward the camera, Blanche would have added, *They were meant for each other*.

"Yes, that's Amelia," said Erwin. "She and Jimmy are getting married soon."

Just as *Amelia*, *fiancée*, and *married* broke through my thoughts, Erwin handed the paper back to me. "I'll escort you to the hotel when you're ready, Miss Viola. Jimmy expects to meet you there."

♫

Back in my hotel room, I had just enough time to wash my hair and mold myself into a dress and my own shoes. As Jimmy and I walked to the Pan, I tried to concentrate on warming up my vocal cords, but I kept getting distracted by Erwin's pointed mention that Jimmy was getting married soon.

Jimmy'd never mentioned that he was engaged, although, why would he? I was just a paycheck to him. But fiancée or no fiancée, there was no reason for him to kiss me like he did yesterday. Except maybe he thought that Eleanor Rutherfurd could use one big kiss before she got returned to her husband. Maybe he thought he was doing the runaway wife a favor. Giving her a thrill.

He'd have been right about that, at least, because that kiss had thrilled me. Our lips and tongues touching and tugging, our bodies slipping so easily together, felt almost inevitable.

But what kind of woman was I to enjoy Jimmy's kiss? Stu and I had been lovers and performing partners for months, he'd been dead for less than a week, and there I was, mesmerized by the first attractive man I met. How could I betray Stu so quickly?

Well, hearing from Kitty that Stu'd made love with someone else in Portland helped. Just like finding out Stu'd sold Audrey the song that he said he'd written for me. Knowing that Stu'd been married to Jeanette—and didn't divorce her—seemed part and parcel of what I didn't know about him.

I might have loved Stu body and soul before he died, but how could I love him now? Now that I knew how many secrets he'd kept from me and how little he let me into his life?

I couldn't answer any of those questions right now, but I could present myself to Mr. Zimmerman and apologize for missing last night's show. I knew I'd have to persuade him that I could perform today, so I brought Erwin's newspaper with me, folded to showcase the glowing Neptune Beach review. I left Jimmy to wait in a chair by Clippy's desk.

Mr. Z sat behind his desk, charting my progress as I walked into his office. Before I handed him the newspaper he said, "It makes a hell of a story, Miss Vermillion. Vaudeville star breaks soldiers' hearts minutes before almost drowning in the San Francisco Bay."

All I really heard was *vaudeville star.*

"I'm moving you into the eight spot starting tonight. Mr.

Merrick has graciously consented to allow you to sing his "Mother, May I" song through the end of your San Francisco engagement. It took a lot of negotiation, but he realizes that what's good for the troupe is good for him."

I wished I'd seen how Audrey really reacted to Mr. Z's negotiations, and I pressed my good fortune. "About the money . . . "

"The money stays the same," Mr. Z responded decisively. "But offend Mr. Merrick again and I'll blackball you." He lingered on *blackball*, making sure I understood that he could throw me out of vaudeville forever. But he still wasn't finished scolding me. "After all the trouble you've caused this week, you're lucky I keep you at all."

I took a breath, trying to respond coolly. "I'm sure I don't know what you're talk—"

"I'm sure you do. I hear you've blamed everyone in the theater for Stuart's murder, and I could have blackballed you for that."

"But—"

"Rocco's suicide note puts an end to all that, and you'd better accept it. It's back to business for all of us."

I braced my hand on one of the wing chairs. "He left a suicide note?"

"Mrs. di—ah, Jeanette, found it this morning in their hotel room. He confessed to Stuart's murder."

Could the resolution to Stuart's murder be this easy, this sudden? A note found in a hotel room? If that was so, it had to be some note.

"What did the police say about the note?"

"How would I know?"

"Aren't the police keeping you informed?" I asked. "Did he . . . did Rocco give a reason for . . ."

Mr. Z stood up from behind his desk; this meeting was over. "Take the afternoon off, Miss Vermillion. I want you fresh and bright for the eight spot tonight."

"I'll be more than bright," I assured him. "I'll dazzle." I thanked him again for the opportunity before leaving his office.

Clippy didn't even look up from his paperwork as Jimmy hustled me into the corridor.

But once we were away from Clippy, I asked Jimmy, "Did you know Jeanette found a note from Rocco this morning? Saying he killed Stu and he was going to kill himself?"

Jimmy looked shaken. "No, I—"

"That's what Mr. Z said. Except Rocco didn't kill Stu, because he was with me the entire time."

"Someone must have written the note to make the police think Stu's murder was solved. And that Rocco wasn't murdered."

"Who would do that?"

Jimmy returned my question with a question. "You mean, who would kill Rocco just to make the police think Stu's murder was solved?"

But we both knew. Only Stu's murderer needed someone else to admit to killing Stu.

"I'm getting you out of town in the next hour," Jimmy told me.

"I just got the eight spot tonight. There's no way I'm leaving town."

But I did need to go shopping to replace everything I'd lost in the bay yesterday, and I started down the stairs.

Jimmy quickly came alongside me. "Two men you know have died in the last week. One of them in your bed. Don't you see the risk?"

No, I didn't. All I saw was the eight spot. And the need to find out if Rocco had the red leather notebook on him when he died.

"As long as the murderer thinks we think Rocco's note was true, there's no risk."

"I need to get you out of town before you get killed, too," he continued.

"I'm the only one who's going to kill today. Just wait until I get in front of that audience."

"But Viola—"

I hurried down the stairs, but he stepped in front of me. "Mrs. Rutherfurd, please—"

That got my attention. We'd rehearsed together, performed together, even kissed. But when it came down to it, I was just a job to him. A paycheck. "Mrs. Rutherfurd, is it?"

"Eleanor." His voice softened, as if he knew exactly how to get a woman to listen to him. "Your husband's—"

"Worried about my safety. Is that what you think? I know Thaddeus Rutherfurd better than you ever will, and I can guarantee you he's only interested in one thing, and it's not my safety."

Right then and there, as we stood toe to toe in the Pantages lobby, I almost told Jimmy about Rutherfurd's red leather notebook. From what Eleanor had told me, with that notebook, Thaddeus could build and control his burgeoning empire. Without it, he was lost.

I wanted to ask Jimmy if he'd searched Rocco's body, if he'd come across the notebook. Now that we were face to face, I didn't know how to ask. But I did know one thing. With Rocco dead, searching for that notebook should be easier.

But first, I needed a new pair of shoes. Maybe two.

♫

I'd never known a man to enjoy shoe shopping, and Jimmy Harrigan was no exception. He gave me the silent treatment through three shoe departments and one candy shop. An hour and a half later, I had two pairs of new shoes, one pair of flashy rhinestone buckles, and chocolate-covered fingers.

I also had a plan. Two plans, actually. One was to beg Kitty to refresh one of my second-best costumes; the other was to search Jeanette and Rocco's room for the notebook.

As we left the elevator on the sixth floor, Jimmy said, "I moved you into Stu's room."

I stopped cold until he explained. "I didn't think you'd want to sleep where Rocco died."

"Of course not." I couldn't imagine sleeping in Stu's bed, either, but I could sleep in his chair.

Jimmy unlocked Stu's door, and I went to the closet and pulled out my costumes, none of which came close to the sparkle of my gold-and-silver spangled dress. Even if I took the belt from the blue organza and put it on the green charmeuse, and added the gold ribbon sash along the square neckline, perhaps twisting it just so, I couldn't see a costume coming together. I hoped Kitty could.

While I was in my closet, my fingers fell on a hanger holding Stu's tuxedo. "How . . . how did this get here?"

"I brought it over from the Pan," said Jimmy. "Clippy said they needed the space in the men's dressing room."

I was sure there was more to Clippy's command—like

no one wanted to be reminded of Stu's murder every day—but I let it go.

Some of my best moments in vaudeville had been with Stu in his tux, and those memories flooded over me gently. Even though he'd lied to me about so many things, I still wanted to put my arms around his tux and feel those moments embrace me back. I stroked the silken lapels with the back of my index finger and ran my fingertips down the front. I dipped my hands into both of his pockets as though a lemon drop was waiting inside.

But instead of candy, there was an envelope addressed to Stuart at our hotel in Portland and stamped March 7, 1919, San Francisco. It'd been opened and I didn't hesitate to read it.

Dearest Stuart

I'm so sorry to let you know that your mother is dead, dying from the influenza last April. I was with her at the end, and her last words were of you, and how much she missed and loved you.

We are all so sorry to lose her, and your father is especially grieved. Your mother was buried next to your grave in Colma, as she requested.

Regretfully,
Your friend Dorothy Garrard

I READ IT AGAIN, suddenly feeling Jimmy perched over my shoulder, reading along with me.

He spoke first. "That bitch."

"I knew she was hiding something," I said. "But why would she lie to Stuart about his mother?"

Jimmy took the envelope from my fingers. He turned it over, looked inside, and even sniffed it.

I reread the note, this time out loud. "Do you think Dorothy killed Stu to keep him from telling his mother that she lied to him? That she lied to her about him writing from Portland?"

"That's a big leap, Viola. Besides—"

"It's a big lie, telling Stu his mother's dead. That's the kind of lie you can't get out of."

"It's also the kind of lie a young girl might make," he said. "The kind of girl who doesn't like sharing with anybody."

"What do you mean?"

Jimmy chose his next words carefully. "The day Dorothy was at the Pan with Stu's mother—"

"The day Stuart was buried," I replied. "When Margaret came to the Pan after his funeral."

"I knew right away that Dorothy was jealous of you. She put herself between the two of you like she wanted Margaret all to herself. You saw it too, didn't you?"

I had certainly felt Dorothy's cold jealousy that day. Just like I'd witnessed her possessiveness toward Stu's mother when I'd been on Alcatraz. I thought back to the other letter Dorothy must have written to Stuart—the letter where she sent him his own obituary. There should be some connection between the two letters and Dorothy's jealousy, but what was it?

As I reread the note a third time, I heard the poodles snuffling down the hallway, with Kitty coaching them forward.

"Kitty's back," said Jimmy. "But before you go, I need to tell you something. Dorothy was at the Pan the day Stuart was murdered."

"How—"

"I was watching the theater from across the street and saw her arrive by taxi and go around to the stage entrance. That was during the show." Jimmy's posture seemed a little straighter, as though he was reporting rather than talking. "Sometime after the matinee let out, she went through the front door. She came out a few minutes later. Then she got into a taxi."

"The matinee let out at five and the police thought Stu was killed between five-fifteen and six. You think Dorothy killed Stuart?"

But Jimmy didn't answer directly. "Wanting to keep someone from exposing your lies doesn't mean that you're able to shoot them."

I took the envelope from him and pushed the letter inside. "But if Stuart found out that Dorothy lied to him, she might have been scared enough—"

"Listen, Viola, it looks like the police accept that Rocco killed Stuart. They're not going to consider new evidence, especially if it's against the commandant of Alcatraz's daughter."

"But—"

"Aren't you in the eight spot tonight?" he asked. "Don't you have a dress that needs fixing?"

I knew he was trying to distract me, but it worked. Tonight's eight spot was the first in my career, and I needed a whole new costume before going on stage. I tucked the letter back into Stu's tux pocket, collected my dresses, and pushed Jimmy into the hallway. I headed to Kitty's room, crossing my fingers that she had time to make some magic for me.

And hoping that I could figure out if Dorothy's two letters meant that she killed Stuart.

CHAPTER THIRTY-THREE

"The eight spot! Tonight? *Quelle merveille*!" Kitty drew me into her hotel room, shooing away the dogs that clustered around her.

"It is." I was so excited to share my news with Kitty that I was grinning, something I wasn't used to. "But I go on in a few hours and I need to dazzle. Can you help me? Please?"

Kitty assessed the bundle of chiffon and crepe in my arms and took all but one dress from me. "That one. Hold it up, just under your chin, and don't move."

She backed up—careful not to dislodge Pascal, who was coaxing a large dog through a small hoop—and walked around me. She performed the same ritual for the other two dresses. "You want to shine and sparkle and show off your legs? The green one is best."

While I shimmied into the green dress, Kitty removed a collection of pharmacy bottles and black shoe polish from the nightstand next to her bed. She dusted some broken dog biscuits into her hand and emptied them into her pocket.

She pulled the stand into the center of the room, forcing Pascal to stop his training. "Now, up you go."

I wobbled for a few seconds—wearing new shoes a few feet off the ground will do that to a girl—as Kitty walked around me. She pulled my hem, fluffed my chiffon, and tugged at the ribbons below my waist. "It will take a miracle, but let's see what we can do."

I knew she traveled with a small, cranky sewing machine, but I didn't know she had a trunk stuffed with every type of costume embellishment imaginable. Kitty pulled out lace and silk and leather and feathers. Then came beads and buttons and rhinestone buckles. I'd seen some of those feathers and fancies on the poodles at least once, but with so little time to create my costume, I'd take what I could get.

It felt unnatural for Kitty and me to be together without gossiping, but this was no ordinary moment. I'd asked Kitty to create a masterpiece for me and she had no time for talk. So I looked around her room, watching Pascal draw a biscuit from a pouch on his waist to reward Lulu in almost perfect imitation of his mother when she performed.

As she played with a strand of sequins, I kept wondering about the letter I'd just found in Stu's tux. Why would Dorothy tell Stu his mother was dead when she wasn't? Did she know he was bound for San Francisco after the troupe left Portland? Maybe that's why she was at the Pan last Monday. To explain to Stu why she lied. Or to protect her lies by killing Stu.

But if Dorothy murdered Stu, how did Rocco have the notebook from Stu's pocket? Because I was sure I'd seen him dangling it on the ferry yesterday.

"A ribbon of rhinestones?" Kitty mumbled to herself. "Bugle beads would be *parfait*, but there's no time."

At her nod, I removed my dress and gave it to her. She sat down at her sewing machine without another word. As I put on my street dress, I kept thinking about the notebook. Rocco had it on the ferry, but did he have it on him when he died? Was it in the theater? Was it in his hotel room?

Once I got a hairpin from my room, I could pick the lock to Rocco's room in minutes. Except I couldn't, because as I stepped out of Kitty's room, Jimmy was closing the door to Rocco's room.

"What were you doing in there?" I stared at the box Jimmy held. It was large enough to contain multiple red leather notebooks. "What's in the box?"

"Detective Petersen left me a message at the front desk that the army had a spot for Rocco at the Presidio." Jimmy sniffed hard. "I thought he should be buried in his uniform."

"Shouldn't Jeanette be doing this?" I asked. "She was his partner."

"You'd think so," Jimmy shot back. "Seems she was eager enough to bring Petersen the suicide note she found this morning, but she couldn't be bothered helping with his funeral. Except to tell Petersen that Rocco was an only child and his parents were dead." Jimmy didn't try to hide his bitterness at Jeanette shirking her duty. "Good riddance to her."

"She's gone?" Of course, Jeanette had no act without Rocco, no reason to be in San Francisco anymore, but she'd seemed sure last night that she deserved Stu's music. "She's really gone?"

"Her things are."

"But Rocco's things are still there?"

"They are, and someone needs to box them up and decide where they go. The bill's paid up until Saturday, so I'm guessing it's gonna be me." Then, under his breath, I thought I heard him say, "Again."

"I'll do it," I offered quickly. "I don't mind."

"You sure?"

"I've done it for others." I squelched down the painful memories of going through Blanche's closet after she died. "I can do it for Rocco. Except it'll have to wait until tomorrow. You and I still have to figure out how we're going to slay 'em in the eight spot tonight."

♫

Jimmy and I got to the Pan with enough time to warm up and rehearse "Mother, May I Come Home Please" with the orchestra. They'd already learned the song—fast and frisky—for Audrey and it took some stern language from Jimmy before they played it at the tempo I demanded. We finished rehearsal just as the house manager opened for the seven-thirty show.

Kitty was in the dressing room when I arrived, and I saw a costume hanging on the wall, the top half covered by a sheath of muslin. The bottom half looked like the green chiffon skirt of my original dress, although my straight hem had been replaced with deep scallops.

Kitty removed the costume from the wall and undid the muslin cover. I gasped. And so did six of the Nolan Sisters, who were opening their makeup kits. Kitty'd used my simple green dress as the base, but she'd entirely changed the neckline (now square) and the arms (now bare). Most dramatically, she'd replaced the front of the bodice with a shiny new material, one that looked like it had silver Christmas tree tinsel woven into it.

I was mesmerized as I moved toward the fabric, delighted to see it reflecting the movement of the dozens of little lights that circled our makeup mirrors. If my dress shimmered like a holiday decoration in the dressing room, once the spotlight was on me, I'd sparkle brighter than any star in the sky.

Kitty encouraged me to walk, turn, strut, and shimmy and I gave it all I had, feeling bright and buoyant in my new costume. I couldn't believe what she'd done in such a short time or how confident it made me feel. With my new costume and headdress—not to mention those rhinestone shoe buckles and my peacock feather fan—I'd out-flash Audrey tonight.

I put my arms around Kitty. "This gown is so beautiful. How can I thank you?"

"I'm glad you like it, Viola. You deserve it after all you've been through." She knelt to clip a stray thread and whispered, "You heard about Rocco's suicide note, yes?"

"Yes," I whispered back, trying to not be overheard by the Nolan Sisters. "She found it this morning? In their hotel room?"

"She screamed for minutes, but she would not answer the door. When she finally came out, the whole troupe was in the hallway, so she had a full house watching her. She started to read it, but Lionel said it was causing her too much pain and she must stop. He said he'd escort her to the police station himself."

We were interrupted by the stage manager's assistant's knocks on the dressing room door. "Ten minutes before the one spot, Kitty LeBlanc. Ten minutes, please."

But before she left, she whispered, "One more thing. Jeanette's wearing a new ring. On her left hand. It looks like a diamond."

"An engagement ring?"

"Maybe Audrey asked her to marry him." She smiled knowingly before leaving the room, passing Jimmy as she walked out.

The scalloped hem of my new costume revealed a lot more leg than I'd shown before, and I could tell that Jimmy approved. I wondered how much leg Jimmy's fiancée showed, and whether she had shoes like mine with rhinestone buckles. I wondered if she was a performer—maybe attached to the Magnolia Voodoo Brawlers, the band he said he played in. Except now I realized that Jimmy'd probably lied about even being in a band. Just like he'd never told me he had a fiancée.

Jimmy leaned as far inside the dressing room as was decently possible before asking, "Do you want to go over anything else before the show? I can find us a piano somewhere."

As it happened, the large rehearsal room was open and I spent a good quarter of an hour in front of the mirror, fascinated by how my new costume responded to the choreography of my act. It'd been almost an entire day since I'd been gasping for air in the bay, and except for a pain in my shoulders when I shimmied, I was ready for whatever came our way. At least I hoped I was.

Later, as Jimmy and I passed Audrey's dressing room, I almost expected Audrey to step out and wish me good luck. Just to jinx me.

Instead, I was greeted by Officer Tuck, who raised his

cap in my direction and gave Champ the command to salute.

"Break a leg, Viola!" whispered Tuck. "I heard how you slayed 'em yesterday. Stu would have been proud of you."

I thanked Tuck and wished that I had one of Stu's biscuits to offer Champ. But I'd promised Mr. Z that I'd dazzle tonight, and with seconds until my first eight spot, I couldn't let my thoughts drift back to Stu.

Jimmy and I'd agreed that I'd do a love song, a novelty song, two more love songs, "Mother, May I Come Home Please," and two encores. But as I sang the early numbers, I wasn't sure I'd take any encores at all. Every performer knows that Monday night audiences are a little tired, a little dull, even a little reserved, and it was true tonight. I couldn't see anyone, and I could only hope someone was out there listening to me.

Two United States flags were positioned at the edge of the stage. I eased toward the one located stage left and stood next to it, ready to sing "Mother, May I Come Home Please" to my unresponsive, invisible audience. All I'd wanted earlier was to dazzle in the eight spot. Now I'd settle for not dying on stage.

Unlike my *a cappella* start yesterday, today the orchestra introduced the ballad. I started softly, almost a stage whisper, hoping to draw the audience in. After the first verse, I still had no idea if anyone was listening. Picking up the pace might get the song to sizzle, but I refused. I wouldn't jazz it up, wouldn't sing it Audrey's way.

I kept the tone reverent, giving the ballad all I had. And as I did, I watched a man drift down the side aisle to sit in the front row. So I sang to him—my audience of one, a glint of metal in the first row, a man who may have fought at the

Somme or flown with the dashing Lafayette Escadrille or saved lives by driving ambulances. Or maybe, like Stu, he'd spent his whole war years stuck at Fort Dix in Jersey.

There was nothing more important than giving that soldier the opportunity to know I cared about him. Maybe I imagined it, but the soldier eased toward me, as though he knew that I sang only to him and he wanted me to know that he cherished every lyric, every note of the song.

Although I'd started the ballad by the American flag, I slowly moved across the stage, holding my peacock fan closed. As I finished the final chorus, I ended up center stage.

Leaving you broke my heart
I never want to be apart
Mother, may I come home please.

The orchestra and I finished at the same time and silence filled the Pan. I crossed my right leg behind my left and bowed, keeping my head low for a few seconds. Seconds after that, the applause came. First in ripples from the audience, and then from the orchestra, something I'd never heard before. And for just a few seconds, I heard applause and cheers from somewhere in the darkened wings. Maybe even from the rigging at the back of the stage.

The applause brought me back for two encores. Buoyed by my success, I bowed and eased off stage, ready to celebrate with a double plate of chicken chow mein.

But I couldn't go anywhere because Jeanette stood directly in my path. She clutched several rolled-up sheets of music in her hand, pointing the roll at me like a sword. I knew she'd chop me to pieces if she could.

"What the hell is this crap?" She shook the music at me. "This ain't Stuart's music."

I wanted to throttle her for spoiling my special moment. But it was more than that. Last night Jeanette had made me feel like a fool, showing everyone that Stu'd been lying to me since the day we met. Sure, I wanted to make her feel as foolish as I'd felt, but not tonight. Tonight, I wanted to savor my success.

I dodged her, but she was at my heels as I went downstairs to the ladies' dressing room. I reached it first and shut the door before she could follow me in. I put my back to the door and held the handle, wishing the dressing room had a lock.

"You can't run away from me." She pounded on the door. "I want what's mine, and I'm going to get it!"

"Leave me alone! You don't even work here anymore!"

She pounded again. "You better let me in! I'm not going away!"

I would have outlasted her except I heard another voice outside the door. It was Gladys Nolan, telling Jeanette to get out of her way. Then Gladys demanded I let her in. Which I had to.

Jeanette followed Gladys into the dressing room, strutting like she was still in the show. She dumped the sheet music on my chair, and it unrolled with a splat. Of course I had to look at it, and from a brief glance, I knew that Stu hadn't written any of it.

"Where did you get this?" I asked.

"What do mean *where*? Your piano player gave it to me. He said it was from you. He said it was all of Stuart's music that you had and that I should leave you alone."

"You're lying." I'd never told Jimmy to do anything like that.

"And you're keeping Stuart's music from me, his wife." Jeanette attempted a pretty pout, a feeble attempt to get her way. It might have worked on a man, but never on me.

Still, that pout made me angry. Had Stu ever fallen for it? "I can't believe Stu ever married you."

"But he did. And he wasn't the only one who wanted me." Jeanette's irritation seemed to mend quickly. "All the men playing the Flatbush Theater begged me to be their girl. But Stuart, he had a way of making me feel special. Loved, you know?"

"He never loved you." I stood up to her, my heart beating.

"Oh, he loved me lots," she smirked. "And he loved proving it to me. Anytime and anyplace."

Her claim made me think about Kitty's story about Stu making love to someone in Portland. And of the L'Amour Bleu in Stu's bed at the hotel. All of the giddy effervescence from my performance drained from my body and I was suddenly so, so defeated. I slumped against my dressing table.

"That's right, Miss Eight Spot." Jeanette pressed toward me. "I'm talking about S-E-X."

For the first time, I realized that Jimmy was leaning against the doorway, just like he'd paid a premium price for a bona fide catfight and was not going to let anyone spoil it for him. It looked like Lionel was behind him, struggling to hear what was going on.

The last thing I wanted was an audience, but I had to ask Jeanette, "That was you in Stu's room in Portland?"

She shimmied her shoulders a little, as if luxuriating in the glow of post-argument sex. "What if it was?"

"And Tacoma and Seattle?" Kitty'd said nothing about those cities, but I had an idea now.

Jeanette winked at me, seeming to relish the role of vixen.

"And San Francisco? The night before you killed him?"

That question wiped the smirk off her face, and her eyes went wide. "I didn't kill Stuart! He was alive when I left him in the bal—"

Before she finished, Lionel was at her side. "Of course you didn't kill Stuart!" He put his arm around Jeanette's waist before turning to me. "Nor did she romance him like you're suggesting. Jeanette's engaged to marry Mr. Merrick. She would never expend her affections on anyone else."

I had so many questions swirling in my head but only got out one. "Not even her legal husband?"

"I didn't do anything she said. I swear, Mr. Fisk." For the first time tonight, she almost sounded sincere. "She put all of those words in my mouth."

"That's what it sounded like to me, Jeanette."

Lionel tugged Jeanette out of the dressing room waist-first. But she held firm at the door, delivering a final slap to my face.

"But even if I didn't do everything you said I did," her smirk returned. "I sure could have if I wanted to."

CHAPTER THIRTY-FOUR

INSTEAD OF CELEBRATING with a feast at Fong's, I returned to the Hotel Henry. I threw Stu's carnation-scented pillow against a wall and collapsed into bed. My sleep was ambushed hours later by someone banging on my door. It was Jimmy, telling me to meet him in the lobby in half an hour.

When I left my hotel room forty minutes later, just beginning to remember how much the audience loved me last night, I saw that Rocco's door was open. I was going to search his room for the notebook last night but hadn't. Was I too late now?

I reached his doorway to see a hotel maid slowly sweeping a broom over the worn carpet, her backside to me. The bed was made, the dresser top was bare, and one large brown leather suitcase waited just inside the door. Rocco'd carried this case as we jumped from city to city, so I knew it was his. Since the room was tidy and the suitcase was by the door, I figured it held all of his things, including, I hoped, my notebook.

There was only one thing to do. As the maid continued her deliberate sweep toward the far corner, I lifted the case, satisfied from the weight that it held *something*, and navigated it out the door.

In my room, I plopped it on the bed and flipped the lock open. Rocco's clothing was folded as lovingly as a baby's treasured baptismal gown. Suddenly, I felt a little guilty. Like I had no right to search through his stuff. I stared at his clothing—his folded white shirts and trousers; his bagged shoes; his drawers and socks, rolled into balls—and my spirits sunk.

This is it. All that's left of Rocco.

Even though he'd mashed and teased me, seeing Rocco's final possessions filled me with regret. Still, I plowed my hands through his tidy clothing. If the notebook was in there, I'd find it quickly.

Except I didn't. After feeling my way through the case, I dumped the carefully packed contents onto my bed. I ran my fingers along every inch of the suitcase, but there were no hidden pockets. No notebook.

"I said *thirty minutes*, Viola." Jimmy's voice cut through my door. "If you're not out here in the next minute, I'm coming in."

I almost wished Jimmy *would* come inside and that I could tell him about the notebook. If he was as good a detective as he claimed, couldn't he help me find it? But if he did, what would keep him from returning it to Rutherfurd himself? Nothing.

I didn't know if a minute had lapsed, but I heard the doorknob turn. I'd locked it when I returned, but I suspected that Jimmy could pick it quickly enough. I tossed Rocco's things back into the case, shut it, and slid it under the bed.

I opened the door just as Jimmy pushed in. We stood inches from each other, and as I stared into his eyes, I tried to read his expression: Concern? Exasperation? Whatever it was, nothing about it suggested *I want to help you find Rutherfurd's notebook.* So as we headed out, I kept my thoughts to myself.

Rocco'd had the notebook on the ferry, and if he hadn't dropped it in the bay and it wasn't in his hotel room, that meant he'd left it at the Pan before he died, he had it on him when he died, or Jeanette had taken it. But what good would Rutherfurd's cryptic shorthand do Jeanette?

Jimmy and I arrived at the Pan with time enough to work on a possible third encore. As I perfected my makeup and hair for the matinee, I did my best to put the notebook and last night's blowup with Jeanette out of my mind. But as Jimmy and I walked up the spiral staircase to the stage, I grilled him about the music she'd thrown at me last night.

"You heard her Sunday; she demanded Stuart's music," he said. "So I gave her a bunch of old sheets from the cupboard in the rehearsal room."

"Why would you give her anything?"

We passed Audrey's dressing room door, and I wondered if Jeanette was in there, smirking about having the notebook and scheming with Audrey about how to get her hands on the rest of Stu's music.

"She had a marriage record," Jimmy replied coolly. "Legally, his things probably belong to her now."

"She had a piece of paper tucked under a seat cushion." Even though I'd had that paper in my hands—and sure, it looked official—it was hard to admit it was real.

"Look," said Jimmy. "I know it was a big surprise, to find

out that Jeanette and Stuart were married. It must have hurt like hell."

"It . . . it . . ." It hurt worse than hell. Stu and I had been performing together, traveling together, sleeping together for weeks, and I thought I knew him. I thought I loved him. But every day since he died, it seemed like I hadn't known him at all. How could I trust any of my feelings for him anymore?

So I asked Jimmy, knowing that he hadn't told me he was engaged to be married, "Would you keep something like that, a *marriage*, a secret?"

He thought before answering. "I might. If I thought it had been a mistake. Maybe, if I could fix it before anyone got hurt."

"You think Stu didn't tell me about his marriage because I'd be hurt?"

"Or because he'd been trying to make it right with a divorce."

"But Jeanette said Stu didn't want—"

"All we know is that Jeanette has a marriage record," he said. "Anything else she says about Stuart could all be lies. You have to remember that."

"But how can I tell the lies from the truth?"

Jimmy paused like he was making a big decision, and then said, "I got a three-timing woman."

"You what?" I had no idea what he was talking about.

"That's the title of one of Stuart's songs." Jimmy took my wrist and drew me near to him. He nosed his way around my feathered headdress until his lips were so close they tickled my ear.

"I got a three-timing woman," he repeated. "And she's

so, so unkind. I got a three-timing woman, and she's stealing me blind. I got a three-timing woman, but the law still makes her mine."

A shiver ran down my spine. As Jimmy repeated the lyrics, I felt the cadence of the music; I knew the blues when I heard it. "Stu wrote that?"

"Yes."

So, so unkind. Stealing me blind. Could apply to lots of women. But *the law still makes her mine* could not.

"That song's about Jeanette!" I glanced back at Audrey's dressing room to make sure she hadn't come out. "You've been looking at Stu's music? Why?"

"I've heard enough about him to guess that his lyrics were more than lyrics. They were his life." Jimmy stared at me as if he was waiting for me to disagree. Except I couldn't.

"I only looked at a few sheets," he said. "Starting at the bottom of his suitcase."

"Because?"

"That's where I'd hide something I didn't want to be found. I thought he might too."

♫

I went on stage to the sound of vigorous applause, flushed with excitement to realize that the matinee audience had come for me, Viola Vermillion, Red-Hot Blues Chanteuse. They paid their money and jostled for a center seat to savor *my* performance.

And I didn't disappoint them. I sang them pathos, laughter, romance, and true love. More than that, I gave them room for their sorrows, assuring them with Stu's lyrics that they weren't alone, that their troubles were not larger than they were.

They seemed to love me, the applause growing after each song, becoming so vibrant I didn't want to leave the stage. I only wished Stu was here and could have heard how his songs connected to the audience.

Someone in the theater must have jolted from the electricity also, for as I took my final bow, a uniformed delivery boy ran up the center aisle with a bouquet of pink and white flowers wrapped in paper. Jimmy leaned over the orchestra pit to help the boy present the flowers to me. I was stunned by the tribute but quickly recovered and clutched the bouquet of roses and budding hydrangeas tightly, delighted and surprised.

"An admirer!" Kitty met me as I left the stage, beaming as though she had received the flowers herself. "You're a star now, Viola. Do you want me to put them in water so they can be delivered again tonight?"

I thought of Audrey receiving the same lifeless bouquet performance after performance and decided to keep the moment special and take the flowers back to the hotel.

"No thanks." I ruffled my fingertips amongst the pink roses, sad not to find a note attached. "I'm going to enjoy these today."

Kitty walked me down the spiral stairs to the dressing rooms, her voice suddenly low with caution. "Audrey and Lionel were in the wings during your performance. They saw your two encores. And your flowers. I heard Lionel say that he was going to put in a telephone call directly to Mr. Pantages. To complain about Audrey being neglected."

"Do you really think Lionel'd go over Mr. Z's head and protest to Mr. Pantages?"

"Grown men act like spoiled little boys when they don't get their way." Kitty pressed a drooping hydrangea back into the bouquet. "Please, Viola, watch your back."

CHAPTER THIRTY-FIVE

I LEFT the Pan soon after my performance, the long-stemmed roses and hydrangeas tilting against the rim of a chipped vase I found in a prop bin. The bouquet so beguiled me that I didn't notice Dorothy Garrard until she stomped toward me in the stage alleyway. I wondered if Margaret Wilson was with her, if maybe Margaret'd sent the bouquet, but Stu's mother was nowhere in sight.

Dorothy refused to let me pass. "I want my letters back. Now."

"Which letter do you want?" I shifted the vase in my arms, my lovely moment of stage triumphant eclipsed by Dorothy's petulance. "The one where you sent Stu his own obituary? Or the one where you told him that his mother was dead?"

That second letter had rumbled through my head since I read it last night. Stu must have written his mother that he was coming to San Francisco and Dorothy must have stolen the letter before Margaret saw it. And then Dorothy must have written to Stu, lying to him about his mother.

"You read them?" Her voice wavered, as though the possibility had never occurred to her. "How could you?"

"How could you lie to Stu and his mother?" If my arms hadn't been full of flowers, I would have shaken Dorothy until her teeth chattered. Even now my fingers itched to slap some sense into her. "How could you hurt someone like that?"

I'd seen enough stage tears to know the ones sliding down Dorothy's cheeks were real. But that didn't make me any more sympathetic.

"I can explain," she sniffed. "Can we . . . can we go somewhere? Just for a few minutes?"

Being with Dorothy was the last thing I wanted, but I did want my questions answered. I also wanted to see the marquee, to see if my name was higher up since I was in the eight spot. "Let's walk."

It was late afternoon and the April sunshine almost blinded me as we emerged out of the darkened alley. There was a taxicab in front of the Pan, and I half expected Dorothy to push me into it like she'd pushed Margaret in last week. So I turned away from the taxi, not caring if Dorothy joined me or not. But she did, huffing as she caught up.

I folded my arms around the vase. "I'm listening."

"What . . . what are you going to do with them?"

For a second, I thought she was asking about my flowers. Then I realized she meant her letters.

"Maybe I'll mail them to his mother." I couldn't help digging into the girl. "After all, don't Stu's letters really belong to her?"

Her head bowed, her shoulders clenched together, she seemed properly chastised, but I couldn't stop. "You kept a mother and a son apart for years. What kind of monster are you?"

Traffic cleared and I crossed the street. Dorothy kept pace at my side, but it was seconds before she responded.

She put her hand on my arm. "Please, can we stop for a moment?"

We walked a few more feet before stopping in front of the darkened window of a shuttered storefront. I looked over at the Pantages marquee, disappointed to see that my name was not higher up. I repositioned the vase in my arms. "Go on."

She was more than ready to talk. "Stuart hated living on Alcatraz. Hated working the lighthouse for his father. All he ever wanted was to write music. He tried to see the new shows at the Pantages and the Orpheum every Sunday. Did he ever tell you that?"

No, he didn't. Just like he didn't tell me he'd lived in San Francisco.

"All he ever talked about was running away to New York City, but it wasn't until the Expo that he decided to do it. We saw the Expo lights every night over at Alcatraz. Most nights we heard the music and the crowds having fun. It drove Stuart crazy to know there were so many musicians performing there and he wasn't one of them."

As angry as I was with Dorothy, I had to admit she knew Stu. And now she had my total attention.

"He decided to start a new life in New York and asked me to help him leave San Francisco. To run away so his father couldn't find him and make him come back. But we never ever thought a body looking like his would float up in the bay." She looked at the men and women passing by us. "The police weren't convinced the body was Stuart until his father testified that it was."

"You could have said something to somebody."

"I never saw the body. It could have been Stu."

"But you could have told his folks he planned to leave. And that he'd given you an address in New York City to write to him. He did give you that address, didn't he?"

She nodded. "I wrote him, but he never wrote me back. I thought the body in the bay *was* his. I never lied to Margaret."

"But you never told her that you helped Stu 'escape,' did you?"

"No. She was in so much pain already—"

Suddenly Jimmy was alongside us, holding my music portfolio under one arm. "Is everything all right?"

"Just a few minutes more." I thrust the flowers toward him and he took them with his free arm. "I'll meet you in front of the Pan."

Dorothy's lips quivered, as though she wanted to escape me by following Jimmy, but I wasn't finished with her.

"What about when Stu wrote you from Portland? You must have seen that Margaret had a letter from Stu and stolen it before she could read it." I could tell from her frown that I'd hit my mark. "And instead of being honest with her, letting her know that her son was alive, you kept it from her."

She shook her head. "I knew the moment I sent Stuart that letter that I did the wrong thing. And . . . I wanted to do the right thing. So I watched the newspapers to see if Stuart —if your act—was coming out here. I came to the Sunday matinee and saw him in the orchestra pit. I watched your entire show, but I couldn't face him. I talked myself into coming again on Monday, and I gave the stage manager a note asking Stu to meet me at Union Square after your act."

I thought of my last moments backstage with Stu and how he'd rushed out of the Pan. I'd thought he was going to check on Champ, but now it sounded like he was going to meet Dorothy.

"Did he?"

"Yes."

"You told him his mother was alive?" I imagined that scene playing out. How incredible it'd be for Stu to find out that his mother was alive but how devastating to realize his childhood friend had lied to him.

That childhood friend shook her head. "I—I watched for him from inside one of the shops. As soon as I saw him, I knew he'd hate me for lying to him. And he'd tell Margaret and she'd hate me, too. So I—"

"You what?"

"I watched him until he walked away. But after he left, after I saw how sad he was, I thought . . . "

"What? You thought what?"

"That if I told him about her funeral, he might feel better."

"But she never had a funeral." Despite wanting to scream *Because she's still alive*, I held my temper.

"I know that." Dorothy backed away from me, but I grabbed her hands to keep her close. "But funerals make people feel better. I saw it over and over again during the war. I thought if I told him about one of the funerals I'd been to—telling him that it was his mother's—if he knew how many nice things had been said about her, he'd feel better. That he'd let her go. So after thinking about all of the funerals I'd been to, I went up to the balcony."

"The balcony? How'd you know he was there?"

"That's where we always sat. Any show we saw. But the woman said the balcony was locked up between shows so I went away."

"What woman? What did she look like?"

"She had that . . . *look*. Like you have." Dorothy paused, as though she'd just caught herself from calling me *cheap* or *trashy*. "Like she was in vaudeville."

"Could you . . . could you recognize her if you saw her again?"

"Yes . . . I think so. I could try. If you give me back my letters first."

Before I responded, Jimmy rejoined us, flowers in the crook of his left arm, music in his right. "I've walked around the block once. I'm not doing it again."

He took my arm, and still absorbed by thoughts of who Dorothy might have seen outside the balcony—if she was telling the truth—I let Jimmy lead me away.

Dorothy caught up with us at the corner. "But—"

I'd had enough of her and let her know. "You didn't think I had the letters with me, did you? I'll let you know when I decide something."

"But—"

"When I decide," I repeated.

"You okay?" Jimmy asked as we crossed Market Street.

"She's a little liar, that one." I retrieved my flowers from him, letting their lush fragrance create some distance between Dorothy and me. "She helped Stu run away and never let his mother know that he might be alive. She even had an address for him in New York City."

I had known about that address for days, but I'd never told Jimmy about Dorothy's first letter to Stu, and there seemed little need to tell him more about it. "And that letter last night. What if she killed Stu to keep Margaret from finding out her lies?"

I pictured Dorothy finding Stu in the balcony, getting hold of Mademoiselle Savage, and turning her against him. As an army daughter, she must know how to shoot a gun, but was she cool enough to kill her childhood friend? Or foolish enough to think that Stu's real death would make Margaret love her more?

Despite the fine spring sunshine and the glorious bouquet in my arms, a sudden chill spread through me. I'd criticized Dorothy for lying to keep her secrets hidden, but the truth was that I had just as many secrets and had told just as many lies as she had.

Should I stop lying to Jimmy? Maybe take him into my confidence?

Both of those sounded like good ideas, but if I did tell him the entire truth about me and Thaddeus, would Jimmy be my champion or would he side with the man with the money?

CHAPTER THIRTY-SIX

Jimmy returned Viola to her hotel room, his heart pumping way too fast as she placed the vase of roses and hydrangeas on her dressing table. As she fussed with the flowers, he lapped up her satisfied sighs.

He'd written a card to go with the flowers but pulled it out when he took the bouquet from the delivery boy. He tucked the card—which had taken him fifteen minutes to write—deep in his pants pocket, but there was no reason he shouldn't tell her now that he'd had the bouquet arranged for her special.

Except that his mouth went dry and words eluded him.

What would Viola—*Mrs. Eleanor Rutherfurd*—say if he told her the whole truth, that he'd been stuck on her since the first time he saw her on stage in Seattle? That the sway of her hips mesmerized him and the tang of her voice clutched at his heart? That he was crazy about how she'd kissed him at Neptune Beach, teasing her tongue against his lips and licking the tender flesh inside his mouth?

Before the war, he'd never been tempted to mix the business of finding a missing person with the pleasure of love-making, but right now, he could hardly remember before the war. *Today* was what Jimmy lived for.

But before he gave Viola the card he'd written, before he held her in his arms, and before he betrayed his fiancée, the steadfast Miss Amelia Oakes, Jimmy needed to kiss Viola one more time. To be sure.

CHAPTER
THIRTY-SEVEN

STRUGGLING under the weight of my own secrets, I shrugged off Jimmy's escort to the theater for the evening show. But the kid was persistent, sticking to my side so closely that I saw the golden highlights at the center of his pale, cornflower-blue eyes.

A few doors away from the Pantages, he took my hand.

"Don't worry," he said. "I'm not going to bite you."

How I wanted to push all of my secrets aside and have him hold me in his arms. *Maybe you should,* I wanted to whisper. *Bite me.*

Holding our music portfolio in one arm, he slung his other around my waist and drew me to his chest. Against any sense I had left, I threw my arms around his neck. I held him tight as he nudged toward me. His eyes glowed with purpose and I wanted to linger in his embrace.

His mouth opened slightly and although I wanted to kiss him, I put my finger to his lips. I braced myself, surprised at what I really desired right now. And it wasn't the red leather notebook or catching Stu's murderer.

"Let's get one thing straight," I said.

"Here's one thing," he whispered. "I'm crazy about you,"

I forced myself to choke out the three words that would break the spell between us. "I'm. Not. Eleanor."

The glow faded from his eyes.

"*Mother of God.*" His arm fell from my waist. "Not this again."

"Yes. This again."

"If you don't want me to kiss you, just say so."

I want you to kiss me was on the tip of my lips, but I had to finish what I started.

"I'm *not* Eleanor, but—"

"I know exactly who you are, Mrs. Rutherfurd." He spoke the last two words slowly and deliberately, as if he could wake me from a deep sleep. "I'm sure you didn't want to be found—"

"But I told you at Neptune Beach—I did want to be found because I want to confront Rutherfurd."

Finally, I had Jimmy's attention. Not his hands-almost-on-my-behind, let-me-taste-your-tongue attention, but his real attention. I pinched his coat sleeve and pulled him into an alley a few steps away. It was a narrow, dark strip between two businesses, but there was enough light that we could see each other. He stared at me, maybe like he'd thought I'd lost my mind. Then he folded his arms. He'd listen, but not for long.

My heart was beating wildly, first from the almost-kiss and now from my need to make him hear my story.

"My sister Blanche—" I couldn't believe that even after all of these months, I still choked at her name. "During the war, my sister Blanche got a job at Rutherfurd Munitions. In Paterson."

I stumbled at the mention of Rutherfurd Munitions but recovered quickly. "When the war started, Blanche said that she had to do something besides performing. So she got a job on the line at Rutherfurd's factory. I was going to join her, but she wouldn't let me. She said it was too dangerous, and she made me promise to stay in vaudeville. For her."

This was where my narrative got trickier, and my throat began to dry. "Blanche was working the late shift on August 20, the night the Rutherfurd offices exploded. The second explosion ignited the buildings where the munitions were made, including Blanche's."

As often as I'd replayed that awful night in my mind, I'd never spoken about it to anyone. Not even Stu. I wanted to stop telling my story, stop feeling the horror of that night. I also wanted to find comfort in Jimmy's arms, which were still crossed over his chest.

"I was bringing Blanche her dinner pail when it blew up. I saw it all. It was a whole day before they found her. She was barely alive when they brought her to St. Joe's."

"Eleanor," Jimmy finally spoke. "Eleanor was at St. Joe's."

"She was, right after the explosion. She came in every day to visit the injured, and she even paid for some of the funerals. She sat with me and Blanche, trying to distract us, asking us about our lives in vaudeville. Happier days. Even when some of the patients started coming down with flu, Eleanor returned every day. She said it was her duty because her grandfather started the factory. On the day that Blanche died"—I was on shaky ground here because my memories were clouded by fatigue and fever—"I came down with the flu. A few days later, Eleanor also fell sick, and she ended up in the cot next to mine."

Jimmy's forehead settled in a scowl of disbelief. "You made up this story just because I wanted to kiss you?"

"I didn't make it up. It's true." I knew it sounded fantastical, like a melodrama playing at the Majestic, but he had to believe me. "The day before she died, Eleanor gave me a red leather notebook. She said it contained her husband's business notes about his war work. Notes about everyone he'd cheated and extorted and blackmailed. And people he *would* blackmail. Notes about the dud munitions he sold to the army knowing they were bad. She knew I blamed Rutherfurd for the explosion that killed Blanche, and that night, she told me I was right. She said he was responsible for the explosion."

"A red leather notebook?" He seemed almost scornful. "Why wasn't I told about it?"

"I don't know. All I know is what Eleanor told me."

I stopped to catch my breath, expecting Jimmy to respond, but he just stood there, listing slightly, as though I'd wounded him and in seconds he would crumble to the street.

Quietly, I said, "I told you the truth, that night in my hotel room. I told you I wasn't Eleanor."

His voice was equally low, like the growl from a dog about to turn on you. "You used me to get close to Rutherfurd."

I wasn't going to let him play the fool so easily. "You hunted me. You watched me every moment of the day and night. Or so you said."

"Is that why you got a gun? To kill Rutherfurd?"

"Blanche gave me the gun when she went to work nights. All I want is Rutherfurd to confess to everything he's done, and . . . a gun will make him do it."

"Coming after Rutherfurd with a gun is not the way—"

"I tried another way." And I had. "I took Rutherfurd's notebook to the newspaper editors in New York City. *The Herald, The Times, The Tribune.* I showed them pages of notes. I told them exactly what Eleanor told me about Rutherfurd's activities, about his thefts and confiscations. That the information in that notebook would send him to prison for the rest of his life. Even with the notebook under their noses, they wouldn't help me."

"You can't take the law into your own hands. Have you thought about that? Besides, I can stop Rutherfurd from coming to San Francisco with one telegram."

I wondered if Jimmy'd even been listening to me. "Do you think he's going to turn around and return to New York because you tell him I'm not his wife? All he wants is the notebook."

"Then I'll telegraph him that you don't have it. That'll turn him around."

Just then Clipboard Clippy hurried past the mouth of the alley, probably returning from dinner. He backed up and turned to us.

"Miss Vermillion," he said. "A moment backstage when you're available, please."

When you're available was shorthand for *right now*, but I needed to fix things with Jimmy. I got as close to him as he allowed me to.

"I don't have the notebook. It wasn't in Stu's pocket; somebody took it from him."

"Is that why you're telling me this? You think if you tell me a sad story, I'm going to help you find the notebook? Well, there are plenty of stories about the war and the influenza to go around, and yours is nowhere near the saddest."

"I—I thought you'd be glad that I wasn't Rutherfurd's wife." I surprised myself with those words, surprised myself to hope that maybe Jimmy liked me, Viola.

He stared straight at me like I was a stranger, as though we'd never meant anything to each other. Then he started out of the alleyway. "I'm sending a telegraph tonight."

"But we've got a show—"

"You can forget about the show and you can forget about me." He dropped my portfolio of music on the ground between us. "You're on your own now."

CHAPTER THIRTY-EIGHT

HEAD DOWN, shoulders hunched, Jimmy walked away from me. I gathered the sheets of music that were drifting away in the alley before trying to follow him. Finally, I stood in front of the Pantages like a department store mannequin, unable to move in any direction.

I wouldn't have taken back anything I said, but every bone in my body wanted to apologize to Jimmy for hurting him. Because I *had* hurt him. I'd watched his eyes lose their spark, his mouth fix into a line, and his confidence crumble. I wasn't used to hurting anyone, and it made me feel small and mean and useless. I searched the street for Jimmy for minutes, until a shiver of cold ran through my body and settled into my soul.

Kitty drew up beside me, grasping the leashes of three small poodles. "Are you all right, Viola? You don't look so good."

She put her arm in mine and walked me toward the stage door. "I'm putting Fifi's new trick in the act tonight!

The one we got from the Ling Ting Tumblers? It'll kill them dead!"

I barely heard Kitty chatting away, but I did hear a man's footsteps behind us. I hoped it was Jimmy with all my might, but after a few steps, I knew it wasn't. It was Lionel, almost careening into the dogs, not even raising his hat as he passed Kitty and me.

Kitty said, "Now Mr. High-and-Mighty can't even be bothered to extend a common courtesy."

"It's me he's mad at," I told her. "I told Clippy last night I wanted time for three encores tonight. Audrey's never done three before." But now that I didn't have a piano player, I wondered how I'd perform tonight. If I could sing past the ache in my heart.

"Remember what I told you, Viola! Be careful with Lionel and Audrey. They'll stop at nothing to stay on top." Kitty led her dogs up the stage door steps. "Come inside soon. Fifi's new trick will make the audience howl."

♫

I stayed out in the alley a little longer before heading inside. The stage door was cracked open and I heard the faint sounds of the orchestra warming up.

The feeling in my gut, my performer's intuition that I trusted so well, told me I'd seen the last of Jimmy Harrigan. It took me another minute of heartache, but then I rolled my shoulders to shake off the evening's gloom. So what if Jimmy couldn't take the truth? So what if he deserted me? I had a show to put on. I had an audience that loved me.

I stepped through the stage door with my head high and shoulders confidently square, ready to give my all to tonight's performance. First thing, I'd have to let Clippy know that I was without a piano player tonight.

It's an awful stomach virus, I'd tell him. *Poor Jimmy had to rush back to bed.* I'd need a few words with Maestro Mitch, too. Strong words like *don't rush that vamp* and *remember to let up on that chorus.* It'd take me a little extra oomph to perform without Jimmy, but I could do it. Hell, I'd shine even brighter tonight. No one would even suspect he'd walked out on me.

Clippy was waiting for me just inside the stage door. He guided me into Mr. Steccati's office and handed me a long white pay envelope. Stu'd been in charge of our paydays, so I had no idea how our money was delivered. I was slipping the envelope into my handbag when Clippy said, "Open it now, Miss Vermillion."

Something in his tone alerted me, but I was still surprised to see a pink slip with my name on it nestled against some dollar bills.

"You're out of the show, starting tonight." He looked at me kindly, but I'd seen him look just as kindly at other cut performers. "Mr. Z wants you and Harrigan out of the theater before Audrey takes to the wing."

I was stunned. It never even crossed my mind that I'd get a pink slip so soon after bringing down the house. This had to be a mistake. "But—"

"If not earlier." Clippy seemed to take a great interest in the wall behind me.

"But—"

Mr. Steccati barged into his office, muttering about a light that shouldn't be broken. Clippy put his hand under my elbow and steered me out. "We were just leaving, Mr. S."

Once in the wings, Clippy dropped his hand from my

elbow as though he'd touched poison. It reminded me of those days in the influenza ward when we were kept eight feet apart from each other and warned not to breathe on anyone.

"As quickly as possible, Miss Vermillion," Clippy informed his clipboard. "It's best for everyone."

"No," I replied, slightly surprised that I'd actually spoken.

"No?" Clippy scowled.

"I want to hear directly from Mr. Z."

"Mr. Z makes the decisions, I give the envelopes. You know how it works."

But I didn't know how it worked. I'd never gotten a pink slip before. Just like I'd never had my head buzz with such confusion or needed to clutch onto Clippy so that I wouldn't fall down.

Clippy must have been worried about my ability to stay standing because he grabbed my arm. Although he was already speaking softly, he lowered his voice further. "You didn't really think Audrey was going to let you upstage him, did you? As soon as you got those flowers, Lionel gave Mr. Z an ultimatum."

"He did?"

"Of course he did. You would, too, if you were the headliner."

I'd always said I'd do anything to succeed in vaudeville, and I was ready to be true to my word. Mr. Z could plunk me back to the two spot and I'd never complain. I just needed a chance to plead for a spot. Any spot.

"Please, can I go up and see Mr. Z?"

Now would have been the perfect time to try to dazzle Clippy with a bright smile or a sexy shrug of my shoulders, but my body didn't even feel like my body—it felt like coarse, heavy pudding stuck in one place.

"You're lucky Mr. Merrick didn't get you blackballed. But it could still happen if you don't get out of here. Or if you ever come backstage again." Clippy pulled a watch from his vest pocket. He had to move it around before he caught enough light to read it. "You and Harrigan need to be gone *now.*"

The mention of Jimmy's name prompted a fleeting image of the argument we'd just had. I wasn't worried about his things, just about ever seeing Jimmy again. But then, in the middle of wondering where Jimmy was, I heard Stu's voice, almost like he was right beside me.

Don't make them throw you out. Show 'em you got some class and walk out on your own.

I chewed on that for a few moments, more alarmed that the hands might throw me out of the theater than the realization that, once again, I was accepting advice from a dead man.

"No need for the hands to help," I replied to both Clippy and Stu. "I'll be out on time."

Clippy went one way and I went the other. I walked along the edges of backstage to avoid seeing any other performers, just in case they knew I'd been laid off. The last thing I wanted was for anyone to give me that sad look I'd given to other acts.

Outside the ladies' dressing room, I steeled myself to strut in, sit before my dressing table, and pretend that my world hadn't fallen apart. But how could I, when all seven Nolan Sisters were sitting at their tables? How could I hold my head up high when they might already know I'd lost my spot? That I wasn't anyone anymore?

I slumped past the dressing room and slipped into the rehearsal hall. Unlike the bright lights around the dressing room mirrors, the hall was lit by a single ghost light that hung from the center of the ceiling. I caught a shadowy reflection of myself—insignificant, slight, and defeated—in the mirror opposite the door. I couldn't look away quickly enough.

I locked the door behind me just as the ghost light began to flicker. I sat down at the piano and reached out to the lamp above the keyboard. One click and I could keep the room illuminated. Instead, I held the knob between my fingers as the ghost light sparked and died, leaving me in darkness.

It was quiet and chilly and comforting in the dark, and I wanted to hide here forever. If I stayed here long enough, my problems would solve themselves. Dying here would certainly solve all of my problems. It would be so easy right now to crawl into one of the bottom cupboards, close the door, and just let time and the rats gnaw me to the bone.

That'd be one way to make me forget I'd failed at everything I'd ever set out to do. Forget that not only had I lost my job in vaudeville, I'd lost Stu, and Jimmy, too. But most of all, I'd lost Blanche and the opportunity to avenge her.

I'd sworn to Blanche while she was dying that I'd make Rutherfurd pay, and now I'd lost my chance. I'd been relying on Jimmy to get me in front of Rutherfurd, just like I was relying on the notebook to make Rutherfurd admit his guilt. Without Jimmy or the notebook, how could I ever confront Rutherfurd?

If you feed yourself to the rats, I heard, *you'll never know, will you?*

I clicked on the lamp, blinking the light away from my

eyes. I'd been almost used to hearing Stu's voice guiding me, but this was the first time since her death that I'd heard Blanche talk to me.

I looked around the room, hoping against hope that Blanche was here. But I couldn't see her anywhere, and when I begged her to speak again, I heard nothing.

Someone had left four sheets of music on the music holder above the keyboard. "When Times Are Tough" was a rousing ballad that I hadn't heard in years and didn't remember anyone in the troupe performing. Maybe someone was thinking about adding it to their act now. I read through the lyrics, stunned by how they reflected the chaos in my heart:

When times are tough
When you've had enough
That's when you must dig in

The keyboard was open and I played a few bars, the ivories resisting my touch at first and then responding smoothly. Something about this tune reminded me of one of Stu's earlier compositions, "Don't Give In, Soldier," and so I switched keys and played four bars of that tune before moving on to another song. I played and sang snatches of songs that had comforted me through the years. Songs that Blanche and I had learned as children, tunes that Stu and I sang as we traveled out west, and even the melodies that floated through my addled brain as I lay in my bed at St. Joe's, feverish and soaked with sweat, my muscles assaulted with bone-deep aches.

But I didn't die at St. Joe's. I was still here, still breathing. Still playing the piano. Still singing. Once more working my way through the chorus of "When Times Are Tough."

Ignore the harsh whispers
Ignore their frenzied shouts
Just remember that I love you and
Forget all of your doubts.
That's when you must dig in.

Despite the raw pain of the chorus, a glimmer of hope seemed possible. Maybe there was still a way to expose Rutherfurd for causing Blanche's death. *And* find out who murdered Stu.

Maybe, if I could just *dig in*. I could collect my things, walk out of the Pan, and sink into my bed. Or crawl under the bed and never, ever come out.

It wasn't much of a plan, but it was mine.

I left the rehearsal hall and entered the ladies' dressing room ready to pack up my life at the Pan. The room was empty except for the two youngest Nolan Sisters, who were playing with every tube, tub, and carton in their older sisters' makeup cases.

While the young girls smacked their rouged lips at each other, I quickly cleared off my dressing table, tore the newspaper clippings from my mirror, and packed up my trunk. Gladys Nolan stuck her head through the doorway and whistled. Her sisters scurried past me and into the hallway.

Gladys glanced at my dressing table as though she wanted to claim my prime spot right now. "Tough break, Viola. See you around."

"See you around," I echoed. Moments later, I followed

the sisters up to the stage floor and paid one of the stagehands to deliver my trunk to the Hotel Henry.

I've walked out of plenty of vaudeville theaters, but saying goodbye to the place where Stu was murdered hit me hard. I swore to him—just like I'd sworn to Blanche—that I'd make things right. No matter how long it took.

CHAPTER THIRTY-NINE

Blindsided. Punched in the gut. Pummeled to pieces.

So torn up he couldn't think straight, Jimmy drifted along the streets of San Francisco like a speck of spent parade confetti. Barely noticing the ascending cable cars and the descending darkness, he walked until the odor of briny water woke him from his stupor.

If he'd walked this far in New Orleans, he could only reach one place: the Mississippi River. But in crazy San Francisco, surrounded by oceans, bays, and beaches, he could be anywhere. He continued on his path downhill, too numb to turn, too angry to seek directions. A horn blasted in the distance. Through the darkness, he saw a strong light revolve in a slow rotation, the way only a lighthouse could.

Jimmy cursed his unlucky feet for leading him to the exact place he'd followed Viola to last week: the path to the pier leading to Alcatraz Island. But he also saw the saloon where he'd had breakfast while he waited for her. Maybe it wasn't the end of the world after all.

Head down, soul beat, Jimmy plowed through the double doors of the Buena Vista Saloon.

♫

"Drink up, pal." The bartender filled Jimmy's glass to the brim for the fourth time. "Prohibition starts in three months. It's good to know who your friends are now."

Jimmy downed this whiskey more slowly than the previous three shots, finally realizing that if he was going to drink all night—which seemed a damn good idea right now —he'd better pace himself.

But no matter how much he drank, he couldn't ignore his gnawing failure: he was the biggest sap in the world. Equally worse, he was not the missing persons man he used to be. Somewhere, he'd missed a clue. Or he'd misread one. Or two, or two hundred. Or, as he thought back to meeting with Frank at a plush desk just outside Rutherfurd's private office, Frank had deliberately lied to and misdirected him. Even more than Jimmy had known he would.

But as much as Frank had played him, Viola had played him better. First, she protested, exactly as a runaway wife would, and then she fed him fact after fact about Eleanor's background.

I bet Viola played you, too, Stuart. But at least you got her back with all your lies.

They must have been quite a pair, traveling down the Pacific coast together: Stuart hiding his marriage to Jeanette, his life in San Francisco, even his own mother from Viola. And Viola hiding her connection to Eleanor Rutherfurd, the information in Rutherfurd's notebook, and her determination to avenge her sister's death.

As much as Jimmy wanted to blame Viola for everything, he kept coming back to Frank and why he'd sent him after Viola without telling him about the notebook. What did he have to gain?

Ever so slowly, another awful realization worked itself through the fog of whiskey. Frank must have known that Viola took Rutherfurd's notebook to the New York City newspapers, which meant that Viola was always his target.

At least Jimmy had the facts about the notebook now. He'd seen it, even tried to read it when he'd found it in Viola's closet in Seattle. It was so unlike anything else that she owned—so fine, so artful—that it almost declared "I belong to Eleanor Rutherfurd." Once he saw the tight code written on the thick pages, he knew the notebook was important, but he had no idea how much.

He'd been shocked to see the notebook when he searched Rocco's room for his uniform. Jimmy knew it belonged to Viola, so he'd taken it with him. It was in his pocket right now—tonight had seemed like the time to return it to her and let her find a way to be grateful to him for returning it. Instead, Jimmy didn't know what he was going to do with the notebook. Just like he didn't know who else would care that Rocco hadn't killed himself.

Jimmy'd tussled with determined women before, but never one as ambitious as Viola Vermillion. She was playing a foolish, dangerous game by trying to bring down America's biggest tycoon, and Jimmy wanted no part of it.

So good luck to her, because Jimmy Harrigan was bent on paying his bill at the Hotel Henry and sending one more telegraph before bidding *adieu* to Erwin and San Francisco. He'd return to New Orleans, agree to everything Miss Amelia

Oakes required of him, and forget that he'd ever kissed Viola.

But first, he had to see if he could stand up and walk out the saloon door.

CHAPTER
FORTY

I SHUFFLED to the hotel singing "When Times Are Tough." Except I couldn't remember the whole song, so I mumbled "that's when you must dig in" over and over.

Jimmy'd moved into my first room when we returned from Erwin's, and I stopped outside that room now. I was tempted to knock, but my arms froze around Stu's portfolio.

I slumped against the door of my current room, slowly unlocking it. I settled Stu's portfolio on my bed and shimmied out of my street clothes and into my kimono. The stunning bouquet of roses and hydrangeas I'd been thrilled to receive yesterday drooped despondently on my dressing table. Like me, the flowers had lost their luster. I gave them a mug of water before pulling Stu's flask from the dresser. The heavy flask held the promise of a long night of solace, but once I removed the cork, I could only peer into the alcohol's abyss.

Finally, I took a slug. Then another. I sank to the floor, ready to roll under the bed and cocoon myself away from the world. And I would have, except that Rocco's suitcase was already there and I didn't have the strength to move it. So I got up and plunked down on the bed. But instead of resting my head on Stu's portfolio, I fingered through the sheets of music, all of them penciled or inked in Stu's familiar hand. So many perfect songs; so many perfect moments. Not just on stage, but in the rehearsal hall, on the train, in restaurants, and in so many beds.

The more gin I sipped, the more I cherished my memories of Stu, and the more my tenderness toward Jimmy faded. How could he walk out on me when everything was really his fault? He was the one who'd kept insisting I was Eleanor when I told him that I wasn't.

I should hate Jimmy. I should forget I ever knew him. And I might have, except I couldn't forget him singing "Three-Timing Woman" to me. The lyrics were simple enough that I remembered them all:

I got a three-timing woman and she's so, so unkind.
I got a three-timing woman and she's stealing me blind.
I got a three-timing woman, but the law still makes her mine.

The title definitely pointed to Jeanette: her marriage to Stu, her false marriage to Rocco, and . . . whatever she was doing with Audrey. Maybe they were in love. Maybe they were meant to be. Or maybe they killed Stu, stole the notebook from his jacket, killed Rocco, and then wrote Rocco's I-killed-Stu suicide note.

Right now, I only had Jimmy's word about Stu's lyrics. I needed to see them myself.

But when I couldn't find Stu's suitcase in his closet, I knew Jimmy must have it in his room. Buoyed by another sip of gin, I didn't even knock on the door between our rooms. I didn't have to pick the lock either.

Stu's suitcase was next to the door so I brought it to my bed, popped it open, and took another sip of gin. The song that Jimmy'd whispered in my ear hours earlier was on top, but it was lyrics only. Stu hadn't set "Three-Timing Woman" to music, and he'd only written one verse.

So I went through the rest of the suitcase.

There were songs about San Francisco, including the one I remembered from Dorothy's grand piano, "We're All Fond of San Francisco." Then there were songs about other parts of the country. I figured these were written as Stu traveled east to New York City, especially since one of them—"It's Too, Too Hot in Hot, Hot Springs"—was more about being homesick than Hot Springs. There were soldier songs, Doughnut Dolly songs, love songs, and even two attempts at college fight songs.

I created piles of like songs and set them on the dresser. Then on the dressing table and nightstand. Then on the bed and the floor, even kicking Stu's carnation-scented pillow into a corner to make room for a pile.

At the bottom of the case, I found a bundle of papers tied together with a thick string. This was an entire act, from the splashy beginning to a playful novelty piece to a heart-breaking ballad that vamped into a grab-'em-by-the-throats finale.

I opened the music and looked at the key signature. Then I looked again. There were two sharps. The key of D, one of the absolute worst for me. Stu would never put a song for me in D major, but I knew right away who did sing in D. Audrey Merrick.

I took a generous swig of gin. And then another.

It sure looked like Stu was writing a new act for Audrey. Just one more secret he'd kept from me. I was caught between admiration for creating such a slick show and jealousy these songs hadn't been written for me.

Just to make myself feel more miserable—as I took another swig of gin—I sang one of the songs, slowly working my way through the words and music. I wished I was at a piano, or even had a ukulele to keep me in tune, but I did all right. The more confident I became, the louder I sang, until someone knocked on my door.

"I know you're in there, Viola." Jeanette's I-mean-business knocks escalated into fist-pounding. "Open up before I get the manager."

I got to my feet, clutched the kimono about me, and opened the door wide, as if I were welcoming guests to a swanky soirée.

Jeanette, wearing a fresh ensemble of pink silk, squared her shoulders. "I want Stuart's stuff."

I clutched the doorknob, huffing gin in her direction. "And I just want Stu."

I tried to keep my breezy bluff against her, but my insides were tearing apart. I really did crave Stu's company.

"You're drunk," she said.

"Not yet, but I'm trying."

"Give me Stuart's music or I'm going to the police."

"You want his music? Then step right in." I eased back carefully because the world around me was getting dizzy.

Jeanette burrowed into the room, almost tripping on a pile of music.

"What the hell?" She looked from floor to bed to dresser, gawking at the music I'd spread out. "These all have Stuart's name on them."

She soft-shoed a pile on the floor, revealing more sheets in Stu's handwriting. "That makes them all mine."

"Maybe; maybe not." I held the flask in my hand, feeling the gin rolling around, calling to me. From the way Jeanette eyed the flask, it must have called to her too.

Maybe there was a reason that my life had collapsed upon me tonight. Maybe it was all to get Jeanette and me together. Maybe I could prove she killed Stu.

"His music *could* be yours," I said. "If you answer a few questions."

"What is this? A game?" Despite the lure of the music and gin, she moved toward the door as if I might be dangerous. Which might just be true. I'd had a hell of a night between losing Jimmy and getting laid off. With nothing left to lose, I sure felt reckless. Maybe I was dangerous too.

She licked her lips like she tasted the gin already. That's when I realized I shouldn't taunt Jeanette. I should become her best friend.

"Want some gin?" I waved the open flask in front of her. "It's Stu's good stuff."

As she put out her hand, I pulled mine back. "One sip for every question you answer."

"First sip for good luck?" she asked the flask.

I shook my head and got down to business. "You were in the balcony the day Stu was murdered, weren't you?"

"Stuart made me meet him there." Her eyes caressed the flask in my fingers. "To talk."

"About what?"

"I really get all of this music?" she asked. "If I tell you stuff?"

"Yes," I said. I even nodded.

"Stu wanted a divorce," she said. "But he wanted his money first."

"What money?"

"He said I owed him $188.80, money that the army paid me instead of him. But that money was mine. I was his wife and the army knew it."

Jeanette put out her hand and I gave her the flask. After her second slug, I pulled it back.

"I was ready to get him his money," she said. "That's why I asked him to bring a gun. Rocco owed me back wages and there was only one way to get them."

"Stu gave you the gun?"

"Fat chance. He said he'd see Rocco with me and show him that he meant business. But I couldn't let that happen —couldn't chance Rocco finding out Stuart and me were married—so when Stuart showed me his gun, I grabbed it."

"You shot Stu?" I didn't believe she'd confess so quickly.

"No! I just wanted to point the gun at him and make him give me the marriage record. But he grabbed the gun from me and shoved it into his holster."

"What'd you do then?"

"What could I do? I broke in here and stole my marriage record."

I squelched the sudden desire to accuse Jeanette of stealing lots of personal things from the ladies' dressing room and handed her the flask instead. She drank.

"Did you take anything from Stu? Up in the balcony?"

"You mean like pick his pocket?" she asked. "Not when he already said he didn't have the marriage record on him."

"But he had a notebook with him. The same notebook Rocco was teasing you with when we were on the ferry from Neptune Beach." Remembering jumping into that frigid water to rescue the notebook made me shiver. "How'd Rocco get it?"

"That red notebook? He found it in his dresser on Sunday morning, and boy, was he surprised. Me too, because it had the marriage record tucked inside. He was so mad to find out I was married to Stu. You know, if looks could kill."

"If you were smart . . . if you really didn't want anyone to know you'd been married, you could have destroyed your record."

"I wanted to burn it, but after I heard Stuart was dead—"

"You thought you'd inherit all of his worldly goods?"

"Audrey said Stuart's music was mine."

"And if Audrey marries you, he gets all of this." I waved my hand over the piles of music but stopped cold when I saw Stu's pillow in the corner. I couldn't smell the L'Amour Bleu from here, but I still remembered when I'd first smelled it on the pillow, which must have been hours after Jeanette stole Stu's marriage record.

"Audrey'll get rich off of Stu's music." I told her.

"That's not why he wants it." She took a sip.

"Then what is it?"

Jeanette turned the flask upside down to show it was empty. "No more gin, no more questions."

But I was unable to look away from Stu's pillow and knew I wasn't finished. I grabbed her arm to make her look at me. "One more question. Did you have sex with Stu in this room? Or in Portland?"

"I'd never let Stu touch me again. Not here, not in Portland, or not anywhere. Not when I got Audrey." She followed my gaze toward the pillow and laughed. "You want to know about the L'Amour Bleu, don't you? I bet you found it after Stuart died. I bet it drove you crazy."

It had. It still did. But I was too proud to admit that.

But Jeanette wanted to rub my nose in the fragrance. "Stu bought a bottle of L'Amour Bleu on our honeymoon and wanted me to wear it every night. 'Cause it drove him crazy. So I thought if I wore it up to the balcony, it might soften him up, and I could convince him to forget about the money."

"But it didn't soften him up."

"No, it didn't. So, when I broke in here, I misted the perfume on his pillow. I wanted him to know I'd been here."

Instead, I was the one who got a snootful of L'Amour Bleu, and it convinced me he'd been cheating on me. That I'd been a fool to love him.

Jeanette pulled away from me, a satisfied smirk on her face. "I'll take my music now."

I plucked the flask from her hand and opened the door. "All you're getting tonight is gin. If Audrey wants Stu's music, he'll have to come for it himself."

"Don't think he won't!" Jeanette protested as I pushed her into the hallway and closed the door on her.

"This ain't over," Jeanette crowed. "Audrey, Lionel, and me, we're going to the police. They'll make you give me every last sheet and you'll have nothing left."

As I heard Jeanette walk away, I knew she was right. Despite everything she'd said about Stu and their marriage and the L'Amour Bleu and never letting Stu touch her again, it wasn't over.

Talking to the police seemed like a good idea, too. Although it wasn't as good an idea as shutting off the lights and crawling into bed.

So I'd wait until tomorrow to look for Detective Petersen's business card.

CHAPTER
FORTY-ONE

Bright and early Wednesday morning—at 11 a.m. on the dot—I carried Stu's two small suitcases to the location on Detective Petersen's business card: Central Police Station, Hall of Justice.

The desk sergeant woke up long enough to direct me to the detective, who was bent over a young woman shaking her head at a typewriter. I'd never been inside a police station before and was surprised at how much it looked like a booking agent's office: men barking into telephones, their desks overloaded with stacks of paper and photographs they'd probably never look through.

Except that these men wore blue uniforms and had guns on their belts. The room had tall ceilings, lots of windows, but—unlike the police station in the Keystone Cops moving pictures—there was no cell with prisoners against the walls.

"The keys are jammed again!" The girl under Petersen's gaze looked at me, pleading for help. I tried to look as sympathetic as I could, but I'd never touched a typewriter and never planned to.

Petersen patted the young woman on the shoulder and nodded to me to follow him. I set Stu's suitcases on the detective's office floor with a plop.

"I'm leaving San Francisco."

"Good morning to you, too, Miss Vermillion."

"Unless you've changed your mind about Stu's murder . . ." I wanted to give the detective every opportunity to talk about his investigation. "You still think Rocco killed him?"

"He explained it all in his suicide note. He killed Wilson and then himself."

"Did . . . did he say why?" I asked. "If he did, I deserve to know."

"He did not." Before giving me a chance to ask another question, the detective asked his own. "You leaving today? Now?"

"These are Stu's cases, with all of his things." Not *all* of course. I'd kept the big suitcase of music that I'd gone through last night. I'd also kept his gun-cleaning equipment, and—surprised by my own sentimentality—his pair of brown socks. But I'd packed all of the rest—his clothing, kit, pencils and pens, and uniform—into these cases. I'd have preferred to deliver them to his mother myself, but they were the perfect props for my visit to Petersen. "Can you take these to his mother?"

"His mother? Not his wife?"

"He'd want his mother to have his things."

"You think a mother's love outweighs a wartime marriage between a soldier and a gold digger?"

If I hadn't thought of Jeanette as a gold digger before, I appreciated Petersen's assessment now. And he was right. First Jeanette married Stu, then she latched onto Rocco, and now she had her claws into Audrey. Maybe none of them gave her fur coats or motorcars, but they'd each kept her out of the unemployment line.

"I do," I said.

"All right. I'll get them delivered. Might even take them to Alcatraz myself."

"Thank you," I said honestly, before shifting into my second reason for being here. "Are you doing the same for Rocco's grandmother?"

"He's got a grandmother?"

"In Italy," I launched into the story I'd concocted earlier this morning. "I'm sure she'd want his notebook back."

"Notebook?"

"It's small and covered with red leather. He told everyone she'd sent it to him. It'd been blessed by the Pope." I crossed and uncrossed my fingers quickly.

Petersen pulled a file from his lower drawer and swept over the top paper before reporting, "He didn't have a notebook on him."

"Hmmm . . . maybe I was wrong."

"Maybe you were." Which, from his inflection, really meant *Maybe you were wrong about a lot of things.*

"If you wait here," he said, even though I made no move to leave his office, "I can release your gun. It was a Savage M1907, right?"

"The gun that killed Stu?" My chest tightened. "You want to give it back to me?"

Shouldn't you throw it in the bay? Or bury it in an underground vault? How could anyone want to see or touch or think about a gun that killed someone they loved?

"The case is closed," he replied. "The gun belongs to you. Do you want it or not?"

I hadn't had breakfast yet, hadn't even had a cup of coffee, but I had to tighten the muscles in my stomach to keep from retching.

"I—I—never want to see it again."

"You sure?" he asked.

I nodded.

He plucked a paper from a file, handed it to me, and nodded to a pen on his desk. "Sign that."

I scribbled my name without looking and dropped the pen.

"Do I need to see you out," he asked, "or can you find—"

I was out of his office and threading my way through the policemen and their stacks of papers before he remembered some archaic law forcing me to accept my gun back.

At least I knew for certain the police had closed their minds to finding Stu's real killer. A job that was all up to me now.

♫

Nine blocks away, at the offices of the *Chronicle*, I talked my way into a huge room of desks and typewriters, very much like the police bullpen I'd just left, except these men were barking into typewriters instead of telephones.

Erwin Stanton and a gaggle of reporters watched as I sauntered through the narrow path to his desk. I might have been laid off from the Pantages, but it wasn't because I'd lost my sizzle. I could still attract an audience.

But could I get Erwin to help me expose Stu's murderer?

Erwin grabbed his jacket from his chair and stabbed his arms inside it. Then he tightened his tie against his collar. Despite my discomfort at being in his flat on Monday morning, he'd seemed the model of intelligence and information. Just the man I needed now that Jimmy had abandoned me.

"Miss Viola Vermillion, welcome to the *Chronicle* editorial offices." Erwin's New Orleans accent was as lush as Jimmy's, and it pierced my heart.

"Mr. Stanton, it's a pleasure." I shook his outstretched hand. "I was hoping you'd remember me."

"You are not a lady I would soon forget." He brought his head close to mine in confidence. "Even if you hadn't bedded down on my couch Sunday night." He looked past me to the editorial room entrance. "You're alone?"

"That's right. All by my lonesome, Mr. Stanton, and hoping you can help me." It was a risk to trust him outright. I could have vamped him, I could have entranced him, but I kept it straight. "I've come to you for a favor. Is there somewhere we can talk privately?"

I followed him into a small office with large windows and we sat at a table. "How may I help you, Miss Viola?"

"I have a story for you. An exclusive." I performed my best sly smile, but despite my enthusiasm, Erwin remained nonplussed. I'd have to work a little harder. "Tomorrow, I'm going to expose the person who really murdered Stu. Stuart Wilson."

"His real murderer?"

"That's right. Rocco didn't kill Stu." Although I hadn't read a newspaper since Monday, I assumed Erwin knew that Rocco confessed to Stu's murder.

His quick reply confirmed he did. "You've got evidence about who really killed Stuart?"

"I've got knowledge. About our troupe. Much more knowledge than the police ever had."

Erwin played it straight. "As much as I love a good

scoop, it is my civic duty to encourage you to discuss this information with the police."

"I've just come from the Hall of Justice, but Detective Petersen's made up his mind that Rocco killed Stu and then himself." I gave Erwin a few seconds to absorb that before adding, "I don't expect you to just write what I tell you."

"That's good, because—"

"I want you to witness when I confront—"

"You're confronting a murderer yourself?" Finally, Erwin seemed genuinely interested. As though he imagined the *Chronicle*'s front page with his name just under the headline: *Vaudeville Star Unmasks Lover's Murderer! An Exclusive!*

For the first time since getting up this morning, I had a real hope of succeeding. If I got Erwin on my side.

"It's happening tomorrow?" he asked.

"It's got to. The troupe jumps to Oakland after tomorrow night's show."

"I might be able to help you out, but on one condition."

Erwin had my entire attention and he knew it.

"You leave Jimmy alone."

Erwin's condition stopped me hard. "What do you mean, *leave him alone*?"

He looked me straight in the eyes. "You and I, Miss Viola, we're both adults. Jimmy might seem like an adult, but he's just a kid. He's got a great girl back home who's going to marry him, and I promised to make it happen. But she's in New Orleans and you're here. And you're very distracting." He stopped to take a breath. "So here's the deal. I'll help you out tomorrow if you agree to leave Jimmy alone. Forever. Starting now."

I was so surprised by Erwin's request, and so irked to hear Jimmy's fiancée described as *a great girl*, that it took me seconds to realize that this was the easiest decision I had to make today. Besides, after abandoning me last night, I never expected to see Jimmy again.

"Don't worry," I assured Erwin. "I'm the last person Jimmy wants to see. He wouldn't even look at me again."

"We have a deal?"

"We do." We shook hands, Erwin and I, both of us pretty pleased with the bargain we'd struck.

Until we saw Jimmy frowning at us from the doorway.

♫

I'd seen boys after a bender, but Jimmy beat them all. His blond hair was strung over his eyes, his cheeks were cherry red, his collar was unbuttoned, and his tie limped down his shirt. The odor of booze drifted from his every pore. The best thing I could say was that he was in one piece. The worst thing was that he was still sore at me.

"What the hell is she doing here?"

Erwin answered for me. "She's going to expose Stuart Wilson's murderer."

"She is?"

"I am." To prove to Erwin that I agreed to his terms, I added, "And it has nothing to do with you."

"But it concerns Erwin, right? Otherwise you wouldn't be here."

"Come inside, Jimmy," Erwin said. "Take a load off." There were no more chairs in the room, so Erwin offered his to Jimmy, who scuffled into it. "Just don't breathe on either one of us. Now, Miss Viola, tell us what you're up to."

I didn't want to tell Jimmy anything, but somehow my plan came tumbling out. Some of it, at least. And it all sounded pretty good to me, even if I stretched the truth here and there.

"So," said Erwin when I was finished. "Let me see if I have this straight. Tomorrow at the Pantages, you'll break into Audrey Merrick's dressing room and find something which will prove who killed Stuart. Is that right?"

"That's right," I replied. Although I was really planning to look for several things, including—if I didn't find it at the hotel tonight—the red leather notebook.

Jimmy suddenly spoke up. Or maybe he woke up. "You think if you find Stuart's murderer, you'll find Rocco's?"

I'd been wondering how closely Jimmy had been listening. It turned out *not very*, because I hadn't said anything like that. "I don't care about Rocco. I only care that he didn't kill Stu."

"How's that?" asked Erwin.

"The police know that Stu was killed between five-fifteen and six, while I was with Rocco."

"You were with Rocco the entire time?"

"Yes. I was outside the hall while he rehearsed from five to five-thirty, and when it was my time to rehearse from five-thirty to six, he showed me some new steps. We both left at six." That was all true enough. I didn't want to go into how Rocco started mashing me, so I left that part out.

"You're sure he was in there when you were outside?" Jimmy asked.

I nodded. "I opened the door and watched him dance." However awful he was, Rocco was also one of the most graceful dancers I'd ever seen, and watching him rehearse was like getting a private show. So I'd watched him rehearse, never suspecting what he'd try on me later.

Erwin cuffed Jimmy on the shoulder. "You know what

that means, don't you? If Rocco didn't kill Stuart, then he didn't write a suicide note saying that he did. Which means that someone poisoned Rocco. You were right."

"I know I'm right," Jimmy replied. "Rocco wasn't the take-poison type."

Erwin was on a roll. "So, what do we have here, Jimmy? Two murders and one murderer, or two murders and two—"

"My money's on one," said Jimmy. "Stuart and Rocco were murdered by the same person."

But Erwin wasn't buying it. "One murderer for two men killed a week apart, one with a gun, the other with poison? You sure?"

"What does that matter, gun or poison?" I'd read somewhere that poison was easy for women to use, but so was the Savage, which was made for a woman's smaller hands.

"It could be the difference between something planned and something that happened quickly. Someone could have been planning to poison Rocco for a while, and Stuart could have been—"

"Stu would have been surprised that anyone wanted him dead. Unless," I had to admit, "he realized someone was desperate to be rid of him."

"Hold on!" said Erwin. "Just so I'm clear, you think Jeanette murdered Stu and then she murdered Rocco?"

"She's got a ring on her finger." I didn't know what the ring meant, but her having it so soon after Stu's death irritated me. "Kitty thinks it's a diamond from Audrey."

"And a girl needs to get rid of husband number one before she can marry husband number two, is that what you're thinking?"

I had been thinking that, although I hated how Erwin reduced Stu to *husband number one*.

"There's something strange going on between Audrey and Jeanette." I hadn't told them that I'd caught the two together in an intimate moment, hadn't suggested the romance might be real. "Kitty says Audrey's leaving the troupe. And when I went through Stu's music last night"—I looked at Jimmy, who was not looking at me—"I found he'd written a whole act for Audrey."

Erwin didn't even give me a chance to take a breath. "How—"

"Because none of the songs are in my keys. They're in Audrey's."

"Then why are we even bothering with Jeanette?" Erwin asked Jimmy.

"You think Audrey killed Stu?" Jimmy asked me.

"What a headline that would make," said Erwin.

"Here's what I want to know," said Jimmy. "What are you going to do if you find that something in Audrey's dressing room"—he paused, almost melodramatically—"and you decide you know who the murderer is?"

"I'm going to get a confession." *Just like I want Rutherfurd to confess to Blanche's death.* "That's why I need Erwin to bring a policeman with him, so we can get a confession."

"But the San Francisco Police hate Erwin." For the first time since sitting down, Jimmy had the ghost of a smile on his lips.

"Hate is a little strong." Erwin returned Jimmy's smile. "They haven't all tried to get me fired."

"You're saying you've got a friend on the force?" asked Jimmy.

"One you can bring with you tomorrow?" I crossed my fingers, wishing for luck.

"Maybe, Miss Viola. I might just."

"Hold on. Before you agree to help *Miss Viola*," Jimmy spoke the last words with deliberate scorn, "There are a few things you should know about her. Do you remember the other day when I mentioned Rutherfurd?"

"I do."

"Then forget all about lunch, Erwin, because I have a story to tell you and it's a long one. About Rutherfurd and his wife and Miss Vermillion here."

Jimmy's decision surprised me, but if he was going to share any secrets with Erwin, he needed to share them all.

"My sister Blanche," I added, determined she would not be forgotten. "You should know about my sister Blanche first because—"

"Take a seat, Erwin." Jimmy stood up unevenly. "All of this storytelling is going to take a while."

CHAPTER FORTY-TWO

Jimmy'd been raised to be respectful toward women, so he sat silently as Viola told Erwin about her sister's death. He even listened as she spoke, hearing much more than he had last night, when his anger had drowned out much of her story.

"Now that we've heard from Miss Viola," Erwin said, shoving his foot against Jimmy's to get his attention, "how about you speak your piece?"

Erwin's request came out lightly, but Jimmy saw the concern in his eyes. Damn. There was no reason to make Erwin worry any more than he naturally did. And there was no reason that Erwin should be involved in Viola's scheming.

Swallowing hard and wishing that he'd never left the Buena Vista Saloon, Jimmy told Erwin how Frank had hired him to hunt down Thaddeus Rutherfurd's runaway wife. And how Jimmy'd deduced that Eleanor Rutherfurd was eluding her husband by pretending to be Viola. And how Jimmy'd followed Eleanor-as-Viola from Seattle to San

Francisco, and how he'd arranged for Rutherfurd to arrive in San Francisco this Friday to collect his wife.

Except, Jimmy sneered, he didn't have Rutherfurd's wife. No, he had a manipulative vaudeville singer who claimed she had the one thing in the world Rutherfurd really cared about, a red leather notebook. Except that Viola didn't have the notebook, because someone stole it from Stuart before, during, or after his murder. (Jimmy didn't tell Erwin and Viola that he had the notebook now, and that he'd hidden it in the same place where he'd stashed Viola's gun.)

Viola hadn't interrupted him, hadn't tried to explain herself to Erwin. She just nibbled her lips to keep from speaking. Jimmy kind of liked her lips that way—rough and rosy—but her duplicity still stung, would always sting, and he would never forgive her.

That didn't mean he would ever forget kissing her or, God help him, didn't want to follow after her right now as she strutted out of the editorial bullpen, obviously satisfied that Jimmy and Erwin were going to help her tomorrow.

Once Viola passed the newsroom gate, Erwin smacked the back of Jimmy's head. Hard, like he meant it. "What the hell were you thinking, taking a job from Frank?"

Erwin sat Jimmy down in the chair Viola'd vacated, hunching over him until they were eye to eye. "Well?" Erwin asked in a voice hauntingly like his father's. "Speak up, son."

"I—I wanted to buy Amelia a house. Make a home for her." And he would, as soon as he got back to New Orleans.

"How much money are we talking about?"

"Lots of it. In advance."

After a silent few seconds, Erwin asked, "Rutherfurd gets in on Friday, right? Is there time to tell him to turn around?"

"I don't want him to turn around. I want to be on the

platform when his train arrives. Frank lied to me about this whole business and I'm going to stomp him until he crumbles into dust. And I want to do it here, not in New Orleans."

"Frank's coming to San Francisco with Rutherfurd? Your idea sounds just as crazy as Miss Viola's." Erwin shook his head. "Do you think hers has any chance of working?"

"It might. These vaudevillians are her people and she knows how they think, how they react. She might be right about this being the only way to get the murderer to confess. Or it might blow up in her face. I can't tell." He took a breath. "Can you really bring a policeman to the Pan tomorrow?"

"I've still got a few tricks up my sleeve."

"Don't try to pull out too many tricks, Erwin. I don't want you getting into trouble. This is my mess, and if it gets dangerous, I'll handle it."

"What about handling Frank? You still got your Colt?"

Jimmy nodded. "You still got your medic bag?"

"Haven't used it since the war, and the last thing I want to do is patch you up again. So you and Frank need to keep it civil. Although"—Erwin allowed himself a smile—"I'd pay just about anything to see you give Frank the whupping he deserves."

CHAPTER FORTY-THREE

I SEARCHED through the hotel's telephone directory and, after charming the clerk, made one call. I spent the next hour pacing the worn lobby floors as I waited for Kitty to return from her evening performance. She, her dogs, and her son finally arrived, and as we took the elevator upstairs, I asked for a big favor.

She was immediately agreeable. "Let me make sure I have this straight. Tomorrow before the matinee, while Audrey and Lionel are in Mr. Z's office, you're going into Audrey's dressing room. After you've been in there for fifteen minutes, you want me to find Jeanette—who should be in the lobby being interviewed by a newspaper reporter. I should tell her that Audrey needs her in his dressing room?"

"Yes, that's right."

She shook her head in disbelief. "You *want* Jeanette to find you in Audrey's dressing room?"

"Yes." I was so overwhelmed by my plans for tomorrow that I couldn't answer her. Or look at her.

"Don't worry, Viola." Kitty took my hands in hers. "I won't let you down."

The elevator hit the sixth floor and I shared something else with Kitty. "I was at the Orpheum today, trying to get an appointment with their booker. I overheard that an Orpheum talent scout would be at the Pan tomorrow. At the matinee."

Kitty's face lit up like a child with a fresh lollipop.

"I didn't hear *who* he was coming to see," I apologized as I unlocked my door. "But I wanted to let you know."

Kitty and I said goodnight, and minutes later, she knocked at my door. Only it wasn't Kitty. It was Jimmy, cleaned up from head to toe, his pale hair darkened with brilliantine, sporting a fresh shirt and collar.

Hours ago in the *Chronicle* bullpen, as Jimmy had told Erwin our story, I'd forced myself to remain mute. Now, I didn't know what to say.

"What are you doing here?" he asked, as though knocking had been a formality to entering my room. "It's show time."

"I got laid off last night."

Even though it'd been a full day since I'd gotten my pink slip, the words caught in my chest. I looked past Jimmy to the peeling wallpaper in the hallway, trying not to give in to the heaviness of my heart.

"I guess Audrey didn't like you singing his song after all," he said.

I almost expected a hint of glee in Jimmy's voice, but he spoke matter-of-factly. "Maybe you should invite me in?"

Had Jimmy forgiven me? Was he ready to go back to *before*? I remembered *before* quite well, being kissed and wanting more. And yet, hours earlier, I'd shaken Erwin's hand and agreed to leave Jimmy alone. Making that agreement was much easier when I thought I'd never see the kid again. Much harder with him in front of me.

I stepped back and he closed the door. Before I realized what he was doing, he pointed a gun at me. Well, not quite pointed. And not just any gun, he was holding my own Madame Savage.

"*You've* had her?" The heaviness in my heart turned to sheer irritation. "When did—"

He pointed Madame Savage to the carpet. "Rocco had it in his hands when we found him."

"He did?" My throat suddenly went dry. "I don't remember that."

"Not surprising, since you fainted when you saw him."

Jimmy put the gun on my dresser. "You really get laid off last night?"

"Right after you left me." I didn't say it to feel sorry for myself; it was just the truth.

I took Madame Savage from the dresser. Despite having her in my hand, I suddenly felt fearful, as if something bad was going to happen. "Last night, you said you'd telegraph Rutherfurd and stop him from coming to San Francisco. Did you?"

"I was going to, until I realized he already knows you aren't Eleanor. He figured out that Eleanor gave the notebook to you before she died and that you're the woman who went to the newspapers. No telegram is going to turn him around."

"How . . . how do you know all of that?"

"I figured that once you left the newspapers, their editors called Rutherfurd and told him everything. What you looked like, what you said. What the notebook looked like."

I remembered how I'd felt when I left those newspaper offices: frustrated, cowed, all of my hopes dashed. But I never imagined the newspapermen would inform Rutherfurd.

"From that moment on," Jimmy continued, "Rutherfurd's men were tracking you. Once they had a name, Frank came to me. Although he never told me to look for *you*. He hired me to find Eleanor."

I leaned against the wall, begging it to support me. My legs went weak and I slid to the floor, overwhelmed by it all. "If Rutherfurd's been wanting *me* all along, why would he hire you to search for Eleanor?"

Jimmy gazed down at me. "I've never met Rutherfurd. Frank hired me. He knew I'd be game to hunt down a rich runaway wife but that I wouldn't hunt down a struggling girl singer."

I didn't like being called struggling, girl, or even a singer, but all of my energy was gone. "You mentioned Frank this morning. Who is he?"

"We got history, Frank and me. Something you need to stay out of." He added, "This is Frank's golden moment, though. Getting Rutherfurd his notebook and making a fool out of me at the same time." Jimmy straightened up. "But I'm not letting either of those things happen."

"How are you going to stop it?"

Instead of responding, he took Madame Savage from my hands. "The first thing I'm going to do is stop you from shooting anyone. Especially me."

Somehow, I found the steam to stand up and face him.

"Don't worry about me. Blanche made sure I knew how to shoot."

I remembered how we'd practiced shooting targets with the gun a few miles away from our house and how, after shooting two dozen rounds against Blanche, on my last shot I winged a bird that got in my way. It fluttered in the weeds for minutes before it gave up, and I hadn't shot a gun since. But I'd pull the trigger on Rutherfurd if I needed to.

"You won't need a gun at the theater tomorrow. You know that, don't you?" Jimmy said, "Even if you find Stu's murderer, you won't need a gun."

"Will you have one?"

"No."

I wanted to ask him *why not*, but he folded his arms and looked anywhere except at me.

"Why are you giving her back to me?" I asked.

"It belongs to you. That's all. And . . ."

When Jimmy wouldn't finish his thoughts, I realized I could finish them for him. Except the words stuck in my throat, and when they finally came out, they were soft and slow. "We're not going to see each other again, are we? After tomorrow?"

His silence confirmed that Jimmy was finished with me. I knew I'd hurt him, but I had to be honest with him about who I was and what I wanted. Didn't that honesty mean anything?

But even if it didn't, I wouldn't take anything back. The moment I saw my sister bandaged from her feet to her forehead at St. Joe's, I'd vowed to make Rutherfurd pay. I couldn't stop for Jimmy now; I'd never stop until Rutherfurd confessed.

I put my hand out to Jimmy. "Just give me the bullets and get out of my room."

♫

Minutes later, there was another knock at my door. Tuck held Champ in his arms and the dog extended his paw to greet me.

"I heard what happened last night." Tuck paused as though he was too superstitious to say the words *laid off*. "I'm real sorry."

"Thanks."

Champ yipped twice, as if offering his own condolences.

"I got your money," said Tuck.

"Money?"

"From last week when Champ was sick. Stu gave me seventy-five for the animal hospital."

"Stu gave you money?" I knew Stu was crazy about Champ, but . . . "Seventy-five dollars?"

Tuck held a roll of bills out to me. "It saved Champ's life, this money. That doc made me pay up front."

I shook my head, not because I didn't want the money but because I'd thought the person who killed Stu had stolen my notebook and his money.

"Did Stu know Champ was poisoned?"

"I never got a chance to tell him," Tuck said softly. "But he knew right away that Champ needed a doc and a hospital. He knew it was serious. He put us in a taxi and made me take the money. That was the last I saw of Stu." He extended his hand closer to mine. "Take it, will you?"

So I did, finally realizing from the tears in Tuck's eyes how important it was for him to repay Stu's kindness.

But I needed more. "I didn't talk to Stu much after Champ got sick. I just wondered if he said anything to you. I mean, if he said anything about me." It was awkward to ask, but I wanted to know what Stu was thinking that day. Especially since it looked like he'd rushed our spot to meet Dorothy in Union Square.

"He did say one thing," Tuck replied. "But I don't think it was about you."

"What was it?"

Tuck seemed to debate with himself. Should he tell me?

"He said, 'I'm not going to let her get away with it.' Something like that. He sounded pretty angry, and I know you never made him angry."

"'I'm not going to let her get away with it'?" That couldn't mean me. But could it mean Jeanette? Or Dorothy? And what was *it*?

Champ pushed his paw at me again, like he wanted to say goodbye. Tuck seemed eager to move on also, so I said "good night" and let them leave.

I closed the door and threw the money on the dresser.

"I'm not going to let *her* get away with it." I murmured. "I'm not going to let her get away with *it*."

I retrieved Stu's gun-cleaning materials and sat at the dressing table. Cleaning Madame Savage was slow work, made slower still since I kept wondering what woman Stu had planned to stop. And if maybe she'd killed him before he could stop her.

CHAPTER
FORTY-FOUR

"Miss Vermillion! What the hell are you doing backstage?"

I wasn't happy to run into the Pantages stage manager, but I forced a smile. "I'm working for Kitty now, Mr. Steccati."

From out of nowhere, Gladys Nolan sidled up to us. "You better watch her, Mr. S. Make sure Viola doesn't sneak on stage. Pretend she's a poodle or something. No telling what she'll do with an Orpheum scout in the house."

"There's a scout in the house?" My eyes lit up as though I hadn't created the rumor myself.

"See that, Mr. S?" Gladys continued. "She acts all innocent, but she'll rush to the peephole to find out where he's sitting. Even though everyone knows that Mr. High-and-Mighty Orpheum Scout won't arrive until the fifth or six spot."

Gladys might be right about when a real scout arrived, but when I looked through the curtain peephole minutes later, I found Erwin Stanton—wearing a black Homburg such as the Orpheum Scout always wore—in the center of the house, sitting next to a woman.

A woman! So much for bringing a police officer with him.

Kitty joined me at the peephole, bouncing from left to right, her nervous energy on full display. "He's here all right! Not like last week. Today he's really here."

I stepped back from the curtain feeling a little sad I'd lied to Kitty and given her hope she had a chance to play the Orpheum. But I had to do it; she needed to think it was real to sell it to the rest of the troupe.

And sold it she had, eagerly telling me that even Audrey seemed nervous when he arrived at the theater. Of course, Audrey might have been nervous about his interview with the across-the-bay's *Oakland Tribune* reporter. Erwin'd called in a favor so that Audrey and Lionel would be busy in Mr. Z's office while I was in Audrey's dressing room.

Where, I told Kitty, I was ready to break into. Except I didn't tell her that I had to speak with Owen Tuck first.

"In fifteen minutes, I'll tell Jeanette that Audrey wants her." Kitty glanced toward the dressing room. "Break a leg, Viola."

As Kitty bobbed away, I wished myself luck. Lots of luck. Because I needed Jimmy's help today, and I had no idea if he would come through for me.

I easily picked the lock on Audrey's dressing room door and slipped inside. It was smaller than I'd expected, but compared to the dressing rooms downstairs, Audrey's place —with rugs, a sink, and illuminated mirrors galore—felt like a high-class hotel suite.

I forced aside my envy and started my search, made a little tricky since I was searching for two things: the red leather notebook and any piece of Stu's handwritten sheet music.

Since Jeanette had hidden her marriage record under her seat cushion, I started with the closest chair. I lifted the cushion and dug into every spare spot. No sheet music. No notebook. I did the same with two other chairs and one chaise but came up with the same: nothing.

I quickly went through Audrey's dressing table, forcing myself not to linger on his Parisian cosmetics or boxes of jewelry. But I did read a bunch of telegrams positioned in a corner of his top drawer. Their abbreviations and stilted sentences didn't sound like any vaudeville business I knew, but a few words stood out: Chaplin. Studio. April 19.

I searched through everything else: boxes, trunks, hatboxes, even the umbrella stand. Same results: no notebook, no sheet music.

Audrey's clothes rack was my last and most unlikely chance. As I started through his costumes, I was confused—and envious—to realize he had two of each of his gowns. He even had two striped bathing costumes for his *sur la plage* sketch.

Audrey's shoes were equally curious. Each pair had a mirror image next to it, except each second pair—looking like they hadn't been worn—was larger and wider. I'd love to have roomier shoes to choose from every now and then. What woman wouldn't? But as I picked up a new sparkly pair with Parisian heels, I caught myself. Audrey wasn't a real woman, so why did he need the same shoes in different sizes?

He didn't. And that's when I realized these dresses and shoes were made for two different—

"You?" Jeanette huffed from the doorway. "What are you doing in here?"

She rushed across the room and tried to grab the sparkly shoes in my hands by their T-straps. I held on to them, knowing they were too precious for her to ruin. So I tugged them and she came along, until our faces were inches apart.

"I want my red leather notebook." I spoke slowly and directly, like I was explaining to a child. "Now."

"What notebook?"

The one I asked you about two days ago, was on my lips. But instead, I said, "The one Rocco had on the ferry."

"Oh, *that* notebook." She stepped back from me, her hands still on the shoes. "It's at the hotel. The last—"

"It isn't."

"Of course it is. How would you—"

Her eyes went wide with understanding, and she looked like she wanted to clobber me with the shoes. "You were in my room? You b—"

"You broke into Stu's room; I broke into yours." My reply was more gleeful than I felt since I hadn't found the notebook when I searched the room she shared with Audrey this morning.

Just as Jeanette took out her frustrations by tugging on the sparkly shoes, the door opened. But instead of Jimmy warning me that Audrey and Lionel were leaving Mr. Z's office, it was Audrey himself, with Lionel at his heels.

Audrey reached Jeanette in two steps and took the shoes from both our hands. He growled at me, his voice lower than I'd ever heard it before. "Get out of here this instant!"

Before I made my next move—which definitely was not out the door—Jimmy rushed in, glanced at the four of us, and shut the door. He turned his attention to me, and it wasn't kind. His intensity alarmed me until I realized that at least he was here. He hadn't abandoned me.

From the few moments the door was open, I'd heard the orchestra suffering through their pre-show numbers. Which meant Kitty was about to start her one spot.

Still glaring at me, Jimmy angled his head toward Jeanette. "Did she confess yet?"

"Confess?" Jeanette's eyes went wide. "To what?"

"That's why we're here, right?" Jimmy sneered. "To get her confession for killing Stuart and Rocco?"

Jeanette latched onto Audrey's arm. "But I didn't kill—"

"Of course you didn't, dearest," Audrey replied.

"No, she didn't," added Lionel.

"That's right." The agreement seemed to pop from my lips.

"What the hell, Viola?" Jimmy snarled.

It was a fair enough question, and I explained quickly.

"She argued with Stu in the balcony, but she didn't kill him. Instead, she broke into his hotel room and stole their marriage record."

"*My* marriage record," Jeanette insisted.

Jimmy ignored Jeanette's protest, his eyes locked on mine. "You can't take her word she didn't kill Stu."

"I'm not. But if she knew he was dead, why didn't she steal his sheet music too? You know how much she wants it." I knew Jimmy'd realize the answer eventually, but with Kitty about to start the show, I couldn't wait. "It's because she expected Stu to return to his hotel room after the evening show. She knew she could get away with stealing the marriage record, but there'd be real trouble if his music was missing. Which means she expected Stu to be alive."

"He *was* alive when I left him," Jeanette pouted, as if she didn't understand I'd just given her an alibi.

But Jimmy understood, and he nodded toward Audrey and Lionel. "How about them?"

"Us?" asked Audrey. "We wanted Stu alive more than anyone."

I watched as Audrey looked longingly at his clothes rack, at the pairs of costumes and shoes in different sizes. I had enough experience in vaudeville to know one reason why he'd have duplicates in different sizes. Then I remembered Kitty's news from Sunday morning, news that I'd only taken for gossip.

"You're leaving the troupe, aren't you?" I asked. "But someone's taking over your act. That's why you've got two sets of costumes. And shoes in different sizes."

"Audrey's going to Hollywood to direct pictures and I'm going with him," Jeanette blurted out. "He's gonna make me a star."

I thought about the telegrams I'd just fingered through. Were they about Audrey getting work in Hollywood?

"You're leaving the troupe, but Audrey Merrick is staying on stage?" It came out as a question, but I was sure of the truth. Including, "Stu was writing music for the new Audrey?"

"The Sensational Audrey Merrick has bookings into next year," said Lionel. "We intend to keep them."

"You're taking over?"

"No," Lionel replied roughly. "Oscar's stepping into the role."

"Oscar?" asked Jimmy.

"One of their in-between boys." The one who mouthed Audrey's lyrics and mimicked his moves in the wings. Who spent so much time with Audrey that Kitty thought they were having a love affair.

"Oscar agreed to perform under my name, but only if Stuart wrote new songs for him," explained Audrey.

"We signed a contract in Portland for him to produce a new revue," added Lionel. "'Mama, Can I Come Home Please' was the first song he delivered, but it was too good to wait for Oscar to premiere."

Jimmy scowled, but I was livid.

"If you really had a contract, Stu would have told me about it." Except the pitiful looks Audrey and Lionel gave me confirmed that they did, and Stu didn't.

"None of us could trust her to keep a secret, and we couldn't risk Mr. Z finding out," Lionel explained to Jimmy. "So Stuart agreed to keep her in the dark until our first payment."

Jimmy shook his head. "But after he died and you suspected he had more music for you—"

"They still didn't trust me," I realized. *They thought I'd steal the music for my act.*

Lionel looked only at Jimmy. "If Mr. Z found out we were putting an untried chorus boy into a headliner's role—"

"With a headliner's salary," I added.

"Mr. Z'd cancel our Pantages contract," finished Audrey.

"And blacklist us with the other circuits," added Lionel. "None of us would work in vaudeville again, and—even though Audrey's jumping ship—I need to keep working."

"Maybe you did want Stuart alive," Jimmy conceded. "But what about Rocco?"

But no matter how much Jimmy glared at them, Lionel, Audrey, and Jeanette looked at us blankly.

"Two murders, one murderer?" I reminded Jimmy of

what he'd said at the *Chronicle* yesterday. "If they didn't kill Stu, they didn't kill Rocco?"

Jimmy shook his head. "You think Rocco would let Jeanette walk off with Audrey without a fight?"

"Rocco was not that upset about it." Lionel avoided looking at Jeanette as he spoke. "He was already looking around for a new dance partner."

"*After* I told him Audrey and I were in love," added Jeanette.

After a long pause—it was a lot to take in, as I knew—Jimmy said, "Fine. But if nobody here murdered Stuart or Rocco, what are we doing here?"

"Getting my notebook," I told him.

"How many times do I have to tell you," said Jeanette. "I don't have it."

"You're lying!"

"No, Viola. She's not," said Jimmy. "I've got it. I found it in Rocco's dresser the day I secured his uniform." Jimmy removed the notebook from his pants pocket and—just like it was any book off of any library shelf—he handed it to me.

I grabbed it and quickly fingered through the pages, my heart beating a little faster to be reunited with the strange combinations of letters, numbers, and symbols. But then I saw the crumbs stuck between the pages. Lots of crumbs. Dry dog biscuit crumbs. I guessed right away where they came from.

Stu must have kept Champ's daily biscuit and my notebook in the same pocket. Except I knew he never would. He kept the notebook in his inner pocket and Champ's biscuit in his outer pocket. And Rocco and Jimmy never carried biscuits.

"Viola, what are you doing?"

I was putting the crumb up to my nose, that's what I was doing. And it didn't smell like the biscuits that Stu bought for Champ. It smelled beefy. I was about to taste it when Jimmy pulled my hand away from my mouth and opened my fingers so the crumb fell to the floor.

Jimmy's move got everyone's attention. Except mine. Because all I thought about were the bits of dog biscuits Kitty kept in all of her pockets and how they smelled like the crumbs between the notebook pages.

Jimmy grabbed my arm and pulled me out of Audrey's room like I was a misbehaving child. He put his lips to my ear.

"You don't care about who killed Stuart and Rocco at all, do you? All you care about is that damn notebook."

He snatched the notebook from my hand and plunged it into his pants pocket.

"Of course I care about them. Why do you think I asked Erwin to pretend he's an Orpheum scout?"

As Jimmy stumbled for a reply, I was drawn to a huddle of troupers against the wall and the unmistakable sound of someone retching.

Once more Jimmy's mouth was at my ear. I said, "If you think I'm letting you have this notebook—"

"I don't want the notebook right now." Glancing around Jimmy, I saw Mr. Steccati join the huddle, which was my real cue to action. "I want you to keep it safe while I solve Stuart's murder."

CHAPTER
FORTY-FIVE

I PUSHED through the knot of performers to see what was happening. It was eerily similar to the last time an Orpheum scout was supposed to be in the house, except the players were reversed. Instead of Tuck crying over an almost-lifeless Champ, today Champ pawed anxiously at Tuck's knees as his master aimed his head into a waste bucket.

And today, instead of finding Stu dead in the balcony, I was going to find his murderer.

"What happened?" I asked.

"What are you doing here?" Ugo Baldanza demanded. "Aren't you laid off?"

"What happened?" I repeated.

Gladys broke through the huddle to hand Tuck a wet washcloth. After pressing the cloth against his neck Tuck murmured, "I got sick."

"Sick like Champ last week?"

Tuck nodded.

"We should call an ambulance," said Gladys.

Jimmy edged in between me and Ugo, glanced at Tuck, and said, "Maybe we should call the police."

"The police?" asked Ugo. "What for?"

Mr. S spoke before Jimmy could. "I'll decide who gets called, and when."

Tuck looked up from his bucket, his face slack and his eyes blurry. I swore he winked at me, but before I knew for sure, his head was down again.

"He's in no shape to perform," I said. "Who gets his spot?"

"Not you," said Mr. S.

"But who's taking it?"

"Kitty," he replied coolly.

"You're putting a dumb act in Champ's nine spot?" Ugo didn't bother hiding his disgust.

"She's not dumb any longer. Seems Kitty's been pitching a new act to Mr. Z," Mr. S informed us. "Since we're down an animal act today, he's agreed to go with Kitty in the ninth."

"Does Kitty know yet?" I asked.

"Of course she knows. I was going to pull her from the one spot, but none of the tumblers are here yet." He looked me over. "I thought you were assisting her, Miss Vermillion. Because if you're not—"

"Yes, Mr. S, I'm on my way right now."

I hustled to the edge of the stage, watching Kitty and her poodles performing in front of the curtain. I kept thinking about what Stu had said the day he was murdered: *I'm not going to let her get away with it.* And in addition to that, now I had the biscuit crumbs in the notebook to think about.

Jimmy joined me. "You have a visitor."

I turned to see Dorothy standing nervously next to the stage door. As she searched the darkened backstage, I wondered if Stu had any inkling about what *she* was trying to get away with. Because I sure did.

"I waited outside like you asked me to last night," the girl said as soon as I reached her. "Do you have my letters or not?"

I dug into my handbag and held up the envelopes. She tried to snatch them, but I kept them out of reach.

"Not yet," I told her. "First, tell me why you wrote them. You wanted Margaret all to yourself, didn't you?"

Dorothy pulled her hand away, her glare hard and direct. "Stuart didn't deserve her. Running away broke her heart."

"And when Stu returned to San Francisco, you realized that the only way to keep his mother's love all to yourself was to kill him."

She frowned. "No, I—"

"She didn't, Viola," Jimmy edged in before I got my answer. "She told some awful lies, but she's not a murderer."

I hadn't realized Jimmy was next to me. I wished he weren't. I didn't like him defending Dorothy. "You don't have proof she didn't kill him."

"Maybe not, but I'm as sure about her as you were about them." Jimmy nodded toward Audrey and Lionel and Jeanette, who were leaning almost into the stage light, probably searching the audience for the Orpheum scout. "And like you just said, 'Two murders, one murderer.' No one would believe Dorothy killed Rocco. Not even you."

Then he spoke so quietly that only I could hear him. "Besides, you already know who murdered Stuart."

"I don't." I almost hated Jimmy then. Because after agreeing that Dorothy and Jeanette were innocent, only one *she* remained.

"You may not want to know who," Jimmy said. He almost seemed like a mind reader. "But you do."

I turned my attention back to Kitty, who was setting up her poodles for their big finale.

Dorothy followed my glance. "That's the woman I saw outside the balcony. The one who said it was closed."

It was the perfect distraction, and as I stared dumbly at the stage, Dorothy snatched the letters from my hand.

Kitty strutted off stage toward us, looking triumphant. All nine of her dogs walked on two feet behind her, with her son Pascal completing the dance line. Kitty's chest heaved with excitement as she U-turned and led her dogs back toward the other end of the stage. But as she reached center stage, she turned around and saw Dorothy.

"I know Kitty's your friend," Jimmy said. "But you don't really know her, do you?"

Jimmy was so, so wrong, because I knew Kitty very well. I knew the long hours she put into training her dogs and working on her act. I knew she wanted to make it to the Big Time just as much as I did. I also knew she wouldn't let anything or anyone keep her in the one spot.

I wanted to tell Jimmy that I'd warned Tuck to be vigilant today and that his wink was to let me know I'd been right, that Kitty'd offered Champ another poisoned biscuit. I wanted to tell Jimmy that I'd been replaying everything Kitty had said or done since Stu's murder.

But all I said was, "Kitty must have poisoned Champ last Monday—like she thought she did today—and Stu must have seen her do it." The more I thought about it, the surer I was. "That's why he told Tuck he wasn't going to let her get away with it."

It made sense—awful sense—but then Jimmy turned

Devil's Advocate. "You think Kitty shot Stu because he saw her poison Champ? Then why didn't she poison Stuart, too?"

"I don't know. Maybe because he had a gun and shooting was easier than poisoning?" Then I realized something else. Something easier for Jimmy to believe. "But maybe she used the same poison on Rocco. Maybe she wanted Rocco blamed for Stu's murder all along, and that's why she stole the notebook from Stu's pocket and put it into Rocco's dresser drawer." I looked down at the bulge of notebook in Jimmy's pocket. "It's got crumbs between the pages because Kitty had it in one of her pockets."

"But couldn't the crumbs have come—"

I shook my head, still watching Kitty perform. "They didn't come from Stu because he kept his biscuit in his outside pocket and the notebook in his inside. And Tuck was at the pet hospital when Stu was murdered, and Rocco would never buy biscuits. And . . ." I took a breath, "They smell and look just like the biscuits Kitty gives her dogs."

Just when Kitty should have been lining up the dogs to take their final bow, when she should have been relishing the applause, she twisted around and dashed stage left, sprinting into the wings.

Jimmy tensed. "That's not part of the show, is it?"

It wasn't, and there was only one reason for her dramatic exit. "She's getting away!"

Without their mistress, the poodles scrambled over each other. A few beats later, Kitty's son Pascal emerged stage right and attempted to corral the poodles. The orchestra played on, even increasing their volume and tempo, as though they might entice Kitty back for an encore.

"You stay here." Jimmy ran through the wings. As he

plunged onto the stage, three small poodles raced toward him. They grabbed onto the bottom of his pants, one dog on his left trouser leg, two on his right, pulling at the fabric and keeping Jimmy in place. He tried to shake them off, but they pulled him in three different directions, keeping him in one spot. The orchestra accelerated their number as if Jimmy's plight was part of Kitty's act.

"Get those mutts off the stage!" Mr. S ordered. "And get ready for the two spot."

As a stagehand lunged toward the dogs, I followed after Jimmy, grabbing a wooden rifle from Gladys Nolan's hands. I ran to Jimmy and shoved the rifle under the poodles' short legs. Between Jimmy's foot and hat and my rifle butt, the dogs loosened their grip on Jimmy's trousers. Two of them backed off, still snarling at him. But one jumped up to Jimmy's hand and latched onto his fingers. Jimmy tried to shake the dog off and it finally fell to the stage, where it reattached itself to his trouser cuff.

I heard snickers from the audience, and then a series of boos. Why not? As far as everyone in the audience knew, Kitty and her dogs had done no wrong. Jimmy and I were the troublemakers, bursting on stage and fighting with the poodles.

From stage right I heard Kitty yell out, "*Venez ici*!"

The dogs ran toward her voice, and Jimmy raced after them. I dropped the wooden rifle and raced after Jimmy. Backstage, we almost tripped on the youngest Nolan sister, who was picking herself up from the floor. She pointed to the back of the theater before bursting into tears.

"Let me do this," Jimmy almost ordered.

"No. She's . . ." I swallowed back *my friend* even though I was besieged by memories of our gossipy camaraderie.

Jimmy and I ran into two stagehands moving a grand piano, and I jagged right and he jagged left. As I cleared the piano, I was greeted—tails wagging, heads cocked happily—by the poodles who had just attacked Jimmy. They sat neatly in front of me and I stepped around them.

Jimmy crouched as he moved forward, as if listening for Kitty to reveal herself. I stepped quietly also, reaching the backdrop—set fifteen feet from the back wall—at the same moment Jimmy did. That's when I realized Kitty had two escape options: Out the double doors behind the backdrop and into the street-wide alley behind the Pan or out the stage door to Market Street.

A door slammed shut backstage, and even though we were chasing a murderer, my first instinct was to hope the sound hadn't carried to the audience. Jimmy's instinct was to run toward the sound of the doors.

As I decided to make for the stage door, I realized Kitty had a third option—she could climb up into the rigging that held the drops and lighting. I'd never been up on the catwalks that overlooked the stage, but I wondered if Kitty had, and if she knew of a door or window that opened to the outside. I peered into the above-stage darkness to look for her, although I was listening more than watching.

Sure enough, I heard something and turned to see Kitty walking toward me, stepping as precisely as one of her poodles. She pointed a knife at me. The blade was a few inches in length and so shiny I saw the brutal sawtooth edge. I imagined her lunging at me, aiming at my heart, the tip hitting just where she'd shot Stu.

Here was the woman—the *friend*—who'd sympathized as I cried over losing Stu. Who'd supported me when I tried to get back on stage. Who'd sheltered me after finding

Rocco's dead body. Who'd fashioned the dress I wore in my first eight spot.

The woman who'd killed my lover and looked like she was ready to kill me now.

I knew I could scream and one of the stagehands might rush to chastise me, but I wanted Kitty's confession before I captured her.

"You'll never get away with Stu's murder," I told her. "I know you killed him."

"Oh, Viola." Despite raising a knife to me, Kitty's tone was surprisingly comforting, as though we were sharing confidences over tea at Fong's. "I've already gotten away with it. No one will believe I killed Stuart. Not after Rocco's confession."

"Then I'll prove you wrote—"

My words were gone, muffled completely as the orchestra blasted out the first bars of the Nolan Sisters' opening number. Kitty and I were both distracted by the sisters' fourteen feet and seven wooden rifles drilling sharply on stage, their rhythmic pounding resonating backstage. I knew this opening; I'd watched it many times. I also knew they could only perform so precisely for thirty seconds. If I could distract Kitty that long and yell out afterward, someone would rush to us, and together we'd catch Kitty.

"I'll prove you wrote Rocco's confession," I repeated. "And poisoned him. Probably with the same poison you used on Champ."

I knew Kitty was taking me seriously now; she realized she couldn't tell me what to believe or do or hope for anymore.

"I know you killed Stu," I yelled, even though I was sure

no one could hear me. "You gave Champ the biscuit that made him sick, and Stu knew it, and he was going to do *something* about it."

"That fool!" She yelled back at me. "He threatened me! He was going to get me blacklisted! I had no choice! I had to kill him!"

Kitty's last words landed just as the Nolan Sisters finished their drill and before the audience applauded. Her scream resonated between us, horrifying and almost destroying me. Yet I still held out hope someone had heard our argument and would reach us before Kitty escaped.

And someone *had* heard her.

"*Maman*?" Pascal's scream cut through the silence. "Maman, where are you?"

At the sound of her son's cry, Kitty eased past me and toward the front of the stage, the blade extended out to keep me from her. I carefully followed behind her. She took the quickest route to Pascal's voice and ran on stage, plunging into the Nolan Sisters.

But Gladys saw the knife and aimed her rifle butt right at Kitty. Suddenly, the stage lights went down and the curtains swooshed to a close. I heard the orchestra launch into something bright and lively, attempting to distract the audience, and then I thought I heard Kitty's knife hit the stage.

Pascal screamed again.

Kitty pushed Gladys to the floor and ran toward her son. But instead of stopping to comfort the boy, she ran past him, the poodles straining on their leashes to follow her.

I darted across the dark, Nolan Sister-strewn stage as Kitty ran to the stage door. I skidded into the wings, dodging people and poodles, racing to reach the door before she did.

I was just yards away when Kitty pushed open the door. She was moments from escaping, and she might have made it out of the theater, except that she ran straight into Erwin, his lady companion, and two uniformed policemen.

"Stop her!" I shouted to Erwin. "She killed Stu!"

CHAPTER FORTY-SIX

Erwin heard me—as he told me later, the cheap seats in the balcony probably heard my scream—but it was his lady friend who blocked Kitty from escaping. With exquisite dramatic timing, Erwin's companion crisply announced, "I'm Florence Eisenhart, San Francisco Police Female Protective Officer."

Kitty seemed stunned by the policewoman's declaration, but just for a moment. Then she revealed the knife still in her hand, as if expecting it'd give her passage out the stage door. Officer Eisenhart revealed her own weapon, a small gun pointed straight at Kitty.

Kitty froze, as if assessing her chances of success. She dropped the knife and put up her hands. The policemen tackled her to the ground anyway.

Erwin stepped away from Florence's side and nodded at me to join them. "Tell her, Miss Viola. Tell Officer Eisenhart everything you know about Stuart's murder."

Only then did I realize that Florence Eisenhart, Female Protective Officer, was Florence from the Ferry Building. She seemed to recognize me, too, even though I was nothing like the chemise-clad girl she'd brought back to life after plunging into the bay.

"That's right, Viola." Jimmy was at my side now, his cheeks red and his handkerchief soaking up sweat from his forehead, like he'd run miles. "Tell her how Kitty killed Stuart."

As the men brought Kitty to her feet and handcuffed her, I realized that everyone backstage—troupers, stagehands, even wide-eyed Dorothy—was watching Officer Eisenhart, her policemen, and Kitty as if they were the afternoon show. Only Gladys Nolan—shepherding a tearful Pascal away from backstage—ignored the drama at the stage door.

After a few seconds of surveying her open-mouthed audience, Florence said, "Let's go outside and let everyone else get back to work."

Once we gathered outside the stage door, Florence said, "I know the facts about Stuart Wilson's murder, and that someone confessed to killing him. What makes you think that this woman—"

"Kitty LeBlanc," Jimmy said. "She's got a poodle act—"

"—that Miss LeBlanc," said Florence, "killed Mr. Wilson?"

"She admitted it to me a few minutes ago," I answered loudly, glad to be freed from the hushed tones required backstage. "After she ran offstage to escape me. She ran because Dorothy Garrard"—I could only wish that Dorothy's name meant something to Florence—"told me Kitty'd been outside the balcony the same time Stu was in there. And I'd figured out that Kitty kept Dorothy from going into the balcony because she'd just killed Stu."

I gave the officer a moment before I continued. "Jimmy

and I followed Kitty after she ran offstage. And when I found her, she said she killed Stu because he threatened her."

"He threatened her?" Florence seemed to study Kitty. "Was it self-defense?"

"No," I said. "It was murder. She shot Stu because he knew she poisoned Champ, one of our dog troupers."

"And why would Miss LeBlanc poison a dog?"

Because it's dog-eat-dog, I wanted to say. But I settled for, "Last week, there was a rumor an Orpheum scout was in the house. Someone we'd do anything to perform in front of. But scouts don't usually show until the five spot, and Kitty's in the one. But Champ—our other dog act—performs in the nine spot." I wasn't sure how familiar Officer Eisenhart was with spots on a vaudeville show, but I sensed she understood ambition. And possibly a woman's desire to climb the ladder of success.

Kitty had been silent and stunned as we talked around her, but now, she erupted. "My poodles are more talented than any dog act in vaudeville! Even the nine spot is not good enough for them!"

Her poodles *were* talented, but none of that excused the horrible things Kitty had done.

"The only way to get Champ's nine spot was to make him too sick to perform," I continued. "So she put poison on a dog biscuit and Champ ate it. He almost died, and when Stu realized why, he must have confronted her about it."

"It was not even poison," Kitty told Florence. "It was just Veronal."

"Veronal?" asked the officer.

"It's a sleeping elixir," I told her, remembering the labels of the pharmacy bottles I'd seen on Kitty's nightstand when she helped me with my new costume. "She's got a bottle in her hotel room."

"It's supposed to give you a good night's sleep," added Jimmy. "Unless you use too much. Then it will kill you."

"But I only coated one biscuit to make him sleepy," Kitty protested. "The same as I've done for my own dogs."

"It almost killed him." I still remembered Champ's almost-lifeless body and how distraught Stu'd been. I thought about that biscuit and the crumbs I'd found in the red leather notebook. I knew those crumbs had to be from Kitty's pocket, but I didn't want Florence to know about the notebook. I didn't want her to ask questions about it, and I especially didn't want her to demand to see it.

So instead I said, "Like I said, she confessed to me."

"I'd like to hear for myself," said Florence. "Well, Miss LeBlanc?"

"Stuart confronted me when I was watering the poodles in the alley," she said boldly. "He said he'd turn me in to Mr. Z if I didn't do it myself."

"Which you didn't," I said. "Because Mr. Z would have cut you from the troupe."

"Not just the troupe! I'd be blacklisted from vaudeville," Kitty cried out. "I'd never work again, and I have a son to support! I thought if I talked to Stuart, if I told him how sorry I was, if I *begged* him, he might see things my way."

It seemed for a moment that Kitty might manufacture a tear to make herself look more sympathetic, but she remained dry-eyed. "I didn't even know Stuart had a gun."

"But he did." I thought of Mademoiselle Savage and how sure Stu'd been about her that day. How I'd trusted her to keep us safe, and how brutally she'd failed. "You shot him with it. Twice."

"I had no choice! He was pulling on me, trying to make me confess to Mr. Z. I had to get the gun from him."

Florence seemed satisfied with Kitty's confession, but I wasn't.

"You lied about Stu's lovemaking in Portland, didn't you?" Jeanette had said twice that she hadn't slept with Stu, and the realization that Kitty'd tricked me into distrusting Stu still clutched at my heart. I leaned against the railings for support.

Kitty seemed about to respond, but Jimmy inserted himself between me and Kitty.

"What about Rocco?" he demanded. "Did you poison him with Veronal too?"

"Rocco diLorenzo was a dancer in the troupe," Erwin informed Florence.

"The suicide at the Hotel Henry?" she asked. "The one who left a note saying he'd killed Mr. Wilson?"

"That was always a lie," Jimmy said. "Because Rocco was with Viola when Stuart was killed. Kitty must have written Rocco's confession so no one would suspect her of killing Stuart."

"Miss LeBlanc," Florence spoke sternly. "Do you have something to say about Mr. diLorenzo?"

Kitty sure did. "Rocco'd been threatening to poison my dogs for weeks! So I told Mr. Z that he poisoned Champ."

"That had to make Rocco mad." I spoke directly to Florence because I could hardly look at Kitty.

"Rocco had a gun when he came back to the hotel Sunday night, and he pointed it at me," Kitty told Florence. "He'd found out what I'd told Mr. Z. He said was going to shoot me."

"So you poisoned Mr. diLorenzo? How?"

"He couldn't stop drinking, that's how. He had a bottle of whiskey when he threatened me in the hallway, and he finally drank so much he had to use the washroom. The bottle was almost empty so he left it in the hallway, and when he did—"

"You put Veronal in it?" Jimmy asked.

"I mixed it in with his whiskey. When he came out of the washroom, he drank it all in one gulp."

I was worn down by Kitty's confession. All I wanted was to walk away. But I had one more question. "Why did you put Rocco in my bed?"

"I tried to get him in his own room, but he kept falling. Then I heard the elevator coming up. Your room was the quickest place to put him, and once he got on your bed, there was no moving him."

"Enough," said Florence. "We'll finish this up at the Hall of Justice. We need a secretary to take down your confession."

"Confessions," Jimmy and I said at the same time.

All I wanted was to see Kitty pushed into the back of the police car, but she would not go gently. She jerked away from the policemen to face me. "I wrote Rocco's suicide note for *you*, Viola. So you would stop worrying about who killed Stuart. So you'd get your mind back on your act."

How dare she! Suddenly, Jimmy's arms were around my waist, and he pulled me away from Kitty. Still, I lunged at her, satisfied as her eyes lighted with fear.

"You didn't do it for me, and you know it," I spit my words at her. "You did it for yourself and the nine spot."

CHAPTER FORTY-SEVEN

My heart was pumping wildly as the police took Kitty away. I'd found Stuart's murderer, and Rocco's. I'd put everything together. Mr. Z would have to re-hire me now.

But first, Jimmy needed to give me Rutherfurd's notebook. Or stand still long enough for me to snatch it from his pocket.

I picked up his hand, alarmed at the dog bites and puffy skin. "I've got something back at the hotel to fix this."

He walked me to the street, hailed a taxi, and pushed me in. The ride was short and not to our hotel.

"Third and Townsend, Southern Pacific Train Station," the cabbie announced as he stopped. "Twenty-five cents, pal."

Jimmy paid the driver and tugged me toward the door. I tugged him back until he sat next to me.

"What are we doing here?" I demanded.

He put his arm around my shoulder and pulled me out. We stood on the sidewalk in front of the squat stucco building, which was almost overrun with men, women, and children hurrying in and out. A sharp whistle sounded and Jimmy scowled. He pushed me into the station and to a just-opened ticket counter.

"One ticket for the first train out of here." He pulled a roll of bills out of his trouser pocket. "How soon does it leave?"

The agent slapped a ticket on the counter but kept it under his hand, making sure I didn't grab it without paying. "Twenty minutes."

"Jimmy—" I moved to put my hand on his but stopped, alarmed at his swollen fingers. "What's going on?"

He pushed the money toward the agent before replying. "Rutherfurd'll be here tomorrow, so I need to get you out of town today."

I smiled at the news until I realized all the power I had over Rutherfurd was in the notebook in Jimmy's pocket. I had to get it from him.

"Where's the ticket to?"

Jimmy checked the paper in his hand. "Tucson."

With stops somewhere in California, I guessed. Knowing that Rutherfurd was arriving tomorrow, I had no problem agreeing to get on that train. Because I'd get off at the first stop and come right back to San Francisco.

Jimmy folded three bills around the ticket and pushed them into my hand. "After you reach Tucson, take the next train to New Orleans."

He hurried me through the waiting room and outside to the covered platform colonnade that faced six railroad tracks, three of them occupied by trains.

"New Orleans," I parroted back to him, knowing I'd never take that train. "What happens there?"

"You wait there and I'll find you."

"I do?" I couldn't keep the surprise out of my voice. "You will?"

"That's right. No matter where you are in New Orleans, I'll find you."

"How's that?"

"Because I love you, Viola Vermillion." Jimmy kissed my cheek in the chastest way possible. "But just a little."

I hadn't expected a declaration of love, and it set me back some. No, it set me back a lot. I'd be a real heel now to play on Jimmy's emotions, but I had no other choice. I cozied up to him, half of me wanting to beg for another kiss, the other half preparing to dip into his pocket.

"You'll find me in New Orleans?"

"That's right." He looked at my lips as if the peck on my cheek had been a warm-up. "But before you get on that train, give me some sugar."

He came in to kiss me, and it took all the resolution I had to turn my head away.

"I can't." I raised my hand to come between my ear and his mouth, wanting to move my fingertip to the full center of his lips, wanting his tongue to caress my finger. "Because I promised Erwin."

"Promised Erwin what?" His tone, which had purred sweet and low, turned into a growl.

"That I'd leave you alone." I hated myself for baiting him, but as he stood against me, watching me lick my lips, I lifted the notebook from his pocket and slid it into mine.

Suddenly, we weren't alone anymore, and it wasn't Erwin disturbing us. A red-haired man whose suit pocket was stuffed with fresh newspapers stood a few steps away. He aimed a gun at us.

No, not us. Me. And we were the only three people on the platform.

My breath caught in my throat. Then in my lungs, and then I couldn't breathe at all, expecting the gun to shoot at any second.

"Frank!" Jimmy jostled me aside so that I was behind him. He widened his feet and squared his shoulders, blocking my view. "What the hell are you doing?"

Despite Jimmy's protective stance, I twisted myself around to see Frank Cassady, the man Jimmy "had history" with. With his blurry eyes and stubble beard, Frank looked like he'd been awake since New York City and wanted to take it out on the world.

"Jimmy, you idiot." Frank's voice carried the same drawl and cadence as Jimmy's. "It looks like I have to bring Miss Vermillion in myself."

"This isn't Miss—"

"Stop the stories. I know what she looks like." Frank's gun made a lazy circle motion toward my pocket. "But first I'll take that notebook."

Jimmy eased his swollen hand to the pocket where the notebook had been. His eyes twitched, and he must have realized that I had it now. He raised his empty hands into the air as though he was being robbed, and that's when I figured Jimmy didn't have a gun.

"You weren't expected until tomorrow," he told Frank.

"We had the tracks cleared for us." Frank motioned with the gun for Jimmy to lower his hands. He holstered the gun under his jacket, and before I knew what was coming, Frank socked Jimmy under the jaw with his right hand and punched his cheek with his left. The newspapers tilted from

Frank's pocket and hit the platform hard, exploding out in every direction.

Jimmy staggered back, trying to form fists as he raised his swollen hands in front of his face. He jammed a bloated fist into Frank's left shoulder, and they circled each other, neither one paying attention to me.

I expected a station agent to come and tear them apart, but they fought without interruption, smashing, kicking, grabbing, and head-bumping each other. I backed away, horrified yet curious. If Jimmy and Frank had history, how had they not killed each other by now?

"Get out of here," Jimmy shouted at me. "Go find Erwin."

But I wouldn't leave Jimmy. I opened my handbag, ready to retrieve Madame Savage and protect the man who'd just said he loved me. But my fingers froze on the rim of the bag, and my hands were as cold as ice. Could I even hold the gun without shaking?

A man's elderly voice pierced through the punches. "Now, now, gentlemen! There's no reason to fight. Especially not in front of this young lady."

Stooped over in his ill-fitting uniform and sun-bleached hat, the porter trailed a luggage cart behind him. I tried to get his attention by shaking my head, but he kept coming towards us. As Frank caught his breath, the porter reached a hand out to Frank's shoulder as if this was a schoolyard fight he could easily break up. Frank elbowed the porter hard and he crashed to the ground.

That's when Jimmy unmercifully punched Frank's stomach, and we all heard Frank's gun drop to the platform.

The four of us stared at the gun, but only the porter reached for it.

Jimmy was faster, racing over and swooping down to retrieve it. Then Frank came down on top of him and neither one could reach it. So I grabbed for the gun—and almost had it—when Frank lunged for it.

Jimmy pulled Frank away from me, but not before Frank poked his face in mine. I don't know what I expected, but I knew instantly that Frank was ready to kill us both.

Jimmy's struggle to reclaim the gun only pushed it farther away. It slid along the pavement, stopping feet from the tracks and inches from me.

As Frank barreled toward it, I did the only thing I could think of. I kicked the gun into the empty train tracks, cringing as I heard the gun screech on the tracks. If Frank wanted his gun badly enough, he'd have to jump onto the tracks to get it back. But before he tried, he'd have to face Madame Savage. I savored a second of satisfaction.

Frank ran toward the track and stood on the edge, as if weighing what was more important, Jimmy or his gun. He chose Jimmy, but by the time he turned around, Jimmy was right on him with another barrage of punches.

I would have stayed to watch Jimmy, except the porter showed no signs of rising. I ran from the platform into the waiting room, saw a middle-aged man in a station uniform, and planted myself in front of him.

"Two men are fighting by the tracks." I gulped a breath. "One of your porters needs help."

But by the time the station agent and I reached the tracks, Jimmy and Frank were gone. Only Jimmy's crushed fedora and the mess of newspapers suggested that anyone else had been there.

Frank's gun was still on the track where I'd kicked it.

The downed porter came to life. "Craziest thing, those two . . ."

"Where'd they go?" I asked.

"One took off and the other followed."

I glanced from track to track until my gaze reached the last track in the yard. That train was six cars long with the final car painted a resplendent royal blue. Some type of light shone from the interior, and I saw what looked like golden velvet curtains draped against the long line of windows. It had to be Rutherfurd's private car.

"Did they head over there?" I asked.

"No." The porter shook his head. "Yes. Maybe."

"Which is it?"

"Good riddance, it is." The station agent eased the porter onto a bench. "They'll both be arrested if they do something like that again." He shot me a look that said, *And we'll arrest you too.*

The agent's threats meant nothing to me; I was worried about Jimmy. But since he wasn't *here*, I couldn't help him. Sure, he'd told me to go to Erwin, but what could Erwin do?

I thought about the ticket to Tucson Jimmy'd given me, about finding that train and jumping on it. It'd be so easy to run now, to tell myself that I couldn't help Jimmy, that I didn't have to fight for Rutherfurd's apology.

Except that I heard Blanche's voice once more, just like she was at my side, like we were waiting in the wings together. Just like she knew how nervous I was. *"You can do it, Viola. You're the only one who can."*

With Blanche's words pushing me on, I rolled my shoulders back, took a deep breath, and headed to the royal blue train car. Seeing a shiny brass *Rutherfurd Munitions* plaque bolted to the side of the entrance, I knew I was in the right place.

I stepped into the car and grabbed for the handle that would close the train door. I pulled it quickly, setting what looked like a lock.

I drew Madame Savage from my handbag and stood for seconds in the dim light, my body tingling from head to toe, just like it did before I went on stage. Which is exactly what I was doing, of course. Standing in the wings, about to make my entrance upon the stage of Thaddeus Rutherfurd's ruination.

CHAPTER FORTY-EIGHT

I'd rehearsed my confrontation with Rutherfurd a dozen times, but I'd never run through this exact moment, just before I surprised him. Only a pair of velvet curtains—as opulent and heavy as any I'd seen on stage—separated us.

Then I heard a voice. Male, middle-aged, and moneyed, his tones reflecting the educated swells that commanded Wall Street. I strained to hear if anyone responded, praying I was his only audience.

I nudged my gun between the curtain panels, creating a small peephole. Within seconds, Thaddeus Rutherfurd—looking exactly like his strong-jawed, robust, well-heeled newsreel image—strutted into view, reading from a paper in one hand, holding a cigar in the other.

"And so, gentlemen," he trumpeted. "I accept this nomination and will vigorously—"

He paused mid-stride to slap the paper on the desk that separated us. He used his fountain pen to slash through a line and scribble something else. With the paper back in his hand, he continued pacing.

"I *humbly* accept this nomination and *vow* that I will vigorously prosecute all miscreants."

I tilted my gun to widen my peephole. This was certainly a rich man's office, furnished with plush high-back chairs, built-in shelves holding leather-bound books and bottles of booze, and the broad carved desk he stood behind. Yet it was still a train car with long rows of windows on each side and another door at the far end. I imagined that behind this room was a bedroom, and beyond that, a door to the deck at the back of the car.

But nothing else mattered except the here and now. It was time to take the stage. I parted the curtains and made my entrance, Madame Savage aimed straight at Thaddeus Rutherfurd.

♫

Ignoring the curtain's murmur, Rutherfurd continued his monologue, promenading between the rows of windows, apparently so enthralled by the sound of his own voice that he never looked up.

Until I pulled Madame Savage's hammer, producing a solid, unmistakable *CLICK*. Just to introduce myself.

He stopped mid-stride and gave me his full attention. It took him a moment, but he recognized me. Jimmy'd been right. Rutherfurd was coming after *me* all along.

He began lowering his papers to the desk, but I shook my head *no*. For that, I was rewarded with an expression I hadn't seen on the Rutherfurd newsreels: pure irritation. He wasn't used to being refused anything. Just like he wasn't used to having a gun pointed at him.

I relished his upheaval. I savored the moment. I prayed

that somewhere in heaven, Blanche was watching us and enjoying the show.

"Miss Vermillion." Rutherfurd nodded as though we were being properly introduced. "You surprised me."

It didn't matter how polite he was, he wasn't getting any pleasantries from me. He figured that out quickly.

"Give me my notebook right now and I'll let you go."

"Let me go? I'm walking out of here when I'm ready to."

I spoke lightheartedly, although in truth, my heart was beating wildly. The scenarios I'd pictured for months were now real, and the imaginary stage I'd rehearsed on seemed to turn into a moving picture. The movie where the plucky heroine fought the fight of her life.

"What do you want, Miss Vermillion? Money? Jewelry? It's yours for the asking. But first, let me see my notebook."

His words came out so smoothly that I wondered if he'd rehearsed this meeting also. My breath stopped for a moment. If he had, if he was just as prepared as I was, did I have a chance of getting what I wanted?

Not allowing my aim to relax, only looking at Rutherfurd's luxurious silk tie, I dug into my handbag and held the notebook high. I had what he wanted, and I wanted him to know it.

He inhaled sharply, as though he hadn't believed I had it, the notebook that Eleanor assured me would enable him to manipulate and destroy powerful men around the world.

"How much do you want for it?"

That line *was* in my script, and so was my response. "I don't want *money*." I infused the word with loathing. "I want my sister Blanche back. I want Blanche to come home. My sister worked at your factory in Paterson. Did you know that?"

Rutherfurd might have, since he knew who I was, but his calm expression betrayed nothing.

"Return all of the workers you killed in the explosion to their sisters and brothers and wives and husbands," I continued. "Return every one of them and the notebook is yours again."

It was an impossible request, but I had to make it. He needed to know how many lives he'd destroyed. Not just his workers' lives, but their families' lives also.

"Who do you think you're talking to?" He roared like a lion that had been suddenly stuffed into a circus car. "I moved mountains for America and saved the Allies from destruction. I'm an international hero."

He paused, as though recounting his victories. "But I'm not the Almighty; even I can't change the past."

"Even you can't resurrect the dead? Then a public apology will do. A full-page advertisement in every paper in the United States. Telling everyone what a bastard you are and how your greed killed my sister."

"I wasn't even in New Jersey when it happened. I was in Washington, with the president."

I'd anticipated this denial, and my response was swift. "It was your factory and you were in charge."

"The police investigation concluded it was Germans."

It was almost like we'd rehearsed this. "It wasn't Germans. It was you cutting costs to make more money faster."

"It wasn't me," his protest continued. "It was Eleanor. *She* did it."

"Eleanor?"

I never imagined he'd blame his wife. Madame Savage faltered ever so slightly. The excitement that had seen me through Kitty's capture and launched me into Rutherfurd's train car was seeping out of me.

Suddenly, I strained to hold Madame Savage.

Rutherfurd spewed out his denials. "I had an investigation done after the explosion. The only person who could have gotten in there that night was Eleanor."

I rested my right arm on the top of a chair, lowering my gun just an inch. Rutherfurd set his cigar into his ashtray. Then he sat on the corner of his desk.

"Did Eleanor tell you where she got my notebook? *How* she got it?" He leaned toward me like we were longtime confidants. "She stole it from my office safe in Paterson. Then, she blew up my factory to make it look like the Germans did it. It was months before the safe cooled enough to open it. Months before I realized the explosion had been set to keep me from finding out the notebook was stolen."

I thought back to the moment in October when Eleanor pleaded with me to take her notebook, how she pushed it into my hands and told me it would ruin the man who killed my sister.

"Eleanor wouldn't have done that," I protested. "She told me she loved the factory in Paterson, that her grandfather started it. She had tears rolling down her face when she talked about how you destroyed it."

"I'm sure she was crying. She was always very good at tears." He watched me closely, as though expecting me to be very good at tears also. "Who says you can't love and destroy something at the same time?"

I'd thought Rutherfurd would confess as soon as he saw a gun pointed at him, but the scenario I'd envisioned was fizzling away. I couldn't allow that. "You know that I can shoot you at any time, don't you?"

"I won't confess to something I didn't—"

His words were drowned out by the sounds of someone pounding on the train door behind me. I must have really locked it; at least I'd done one thing right.

I looked toward the long row of windows, wanting to inch over to see who was outside the car, hoping it was Jimmy and that he'd find another way inside.

"That'll be Francis Cassady." Rutherfurd spoke like a man used to being protected. "If he sees you pointing a gun at me, he'll shoot you down."

"Frank's gun is gone." *Kicked on the train tracks.* That hadn't been in my original script, but I wanted to wipe the satisfaction from Rutherfurd's smirk. And it worked. But hearing that Frank was weaponless, that his rescue wasn't assured, only sobered him some.

Still, I was doing better than the heroines in the moving pictures. They got dropped into waterfalls, tied onto train tracks, and trapped in burning buildings before the hero rushed in to rescue them. But despite hoping that Jimmy was just outside the train, I didn't expect him to rescue me.

The pounding on the door stopped, and the silence unsettled me more than the noise. I motioned for Rutherfurd to walk in front of me to the windows. Keeping him between the window and me, I saw Frank limping beside the train car, holding his hands to his lower ribs.

Through a partially lowered window, I heard Frank yell, "Stay dead this time."

That's when I saw Jimmy. Alive, but taking every step in pain. Then I couldn't see either of them. I guessed they were racing each other to the back of the train.

Rutherfurd picked up his cigar and inhaled leisurely, as though I didn't have a gun leveled at him, as though he knew Frank would soon grab the notebook from me.

Sure enough, Frank crashed into the office, tripping as he came in. Despite my need to avenge Blanche, I thought only of Jimmy. Had he made it inside also? Or was he crumpled and bleeding on the tracks?

Rutherfurd's eyes flinched at the sight of Frank's bloodied hands and face, but his words to me were steady. "This is your last chance to give up the notebook."

Frank doubled over, then put one hand on the wall to anchor himself. Suddenly, he had a gun in his hand. His grip was not too steady, as if one of his fingers had been broken.

Frank aimed the gun at me.

I refused to give in. I lifted the notebook to my mouth, tore a page out with my teeth, and began to chew.

"Stop!" Rutherfurd cried out as though the notebook were a living, breathing thing to him. "A hundred thousand dollars for that notebook!"

But I kept chewing.

"Shoot her!" Rutherfurd yelled.

"No!" Jimmy stumbled into the car, his voice low and fractured. He'd lost his hat and jacket, his collar dangled from a single button, and his face was mottled with blood. He lunged to grab Frank, but he crumpled at Frank's feet instead.

Frank pulled Jimmy up and hugged him to his side, like they were bosom buddies. Then he pointed his gun at Jimmy's temple.

My heart stopped. I'd come here to avenge Blanche, and Rutherfurd was threatening someone else I . . . I . . . loved?

I spit the chewed page into my fingers and displayed the

round pulp. "You shoot him and you'll never get the notebook. I'll chew it all, every page, right now."

"Shoot *her,*" Rutherfurd commanded again. "But for God's sake be careful of that notebook."

As Frank took aim at my chest, I jammed the notebook between my teeth to free both my hands. At the same time, Jimmy pushed into Frank's side, punching him in the ribs. Jimmy grabbed the gun, and he and Frank struggled for possession.

I tried to keep my aim on Rutherfurd but was pulled toward Jimmy. My hands wavered and Madame Savage shook.

Rutherfurd's roar resonated off the walls of the train car. "Shoot her, dammit! Shoot!"

So I shot Madame Savage. Twice.

CHAPTER FORTY-NINE

I'd seen more than one moving picture where the film got stuck in the projector. Where all the action stopped; all the characters froze in place like statues.

It was just like that when I pulled the trigger. Everything stopped.

Rutherfurd stared at me open-mouthed, Frank shut his eyes, and Jimmy—well, Jimmy didn't freeze. He collapsed to the carpet with a horrifying thud.

Frank fell to the floor beside him a few seconds later.

"He's dead!" Rutherfurd yelled. "You killed him!"

I stood numb, still clutching Madame Savage.

Rutherfurd reached Frank in a few steps. He pulled at his jacket lapels, trying to lift him. "Get up, Francis! Get up, son!"

Inches away, Jimmy began to rise. Putting his weight on an armchair to his side, he was almost upright. A bright-red stain blossomed on his right shirtsleeve. My bullet had struck him.

I wanted to run to his side, but I couldn't move. He'd

come to rescue me and I'd shot him. Jimmy's look of surprise, of being overwhelmed and in pain, of realizing that he'd failed, clogged my chest, and I couldn't breathe. The notebook dropped from my mouth and the tears that Rutherfurd had tried to tease out of me earlier welled up in my eyes.

Rutherfurd kicked the chair out from under Jimmy, and Jimmy fell back onto the floor. I couldn't see him anymore. Rutherfurd got Frank to his feet and steadied him against the desk. Frank looked at his right hand, which still held the gun, and then at his left arm, which Rutherfurd was attempting to bandage with his handkerchief.

For the second time, Jimmy tried to rise. Frank pulled away from Rutherfurd, grabbed the shoulder of Jimmy's vest, and dragged him to his feet. Leaning Jimmy against the chair, Frank took aim at him again.

This moment in Rutherfurd's train car wasn't about Blanche anymore. It was only about Jimmy. Getting him out alive was more important than getting Rutherfurd on his knees. So I scrunched down, felt around on the floor for the notebook, and grabbed it. Then I dangled it directly in front of Madame Savage's barrel.

"Come any closer and I'll shoot the notebook. I mean it. Hurt him again and I'll shoot it to shreds." I had no idea if I could shoot the notebook in my hands, but I was desperate for Frank to leave Jimmy alone.

"Or." I took a deep breath. "We can make a deal."

"Put your weapon and my notebook on the desk, turn around, and walk out of here," Rutherfurd replied. "That's the only deal."

"I'm not leaving without Jimmy."

"We'll push him out when we leave the station."

I shook my head, imagining how bruised and banged up Jimmy would be if Frank had another minute with him. Not to mention being pushed out of a moving train.

"Here's *my* deal. Jimmy comes with me now and I'll give you one page."

"The entire notebook or nothing."

"I've got eight more bullets. I'll shoot again."

"No, you won't," Rutherfurd sneered. "You could hardly pull the trigger the first time. Give me the entire notebook *now* and I'll let you walk out of here."

"If I give you the notebook, you have no reason to let us walk out."

He put his hand to his heart as if he was leading the Pledge of Allegiance. "I am an honorable man. It's a well-recorded fact that I live up to my deals. I can be trusted."

"That's not what your wife told me." The influenza might have robbed me of some of my memories, but I'd never forget the most horrible of Eleanor's stories. "You promised to love and cherish your wife, but instead you threw her into a sanatorium."

But Thaddeus Rutherfurd wasn't a man to consider his own sins. He was a man who thought he could get away with everything.

"Trust me, Miss Vermillion, or your friend bleeds to death in minutes."

Shivers crept down my spine. I couldn't see Jimmy well enough to know how my bullets had struck him. I'd seen blood on one arm, but what if I'd hit him twice and the second shot was worse?

I'd never trust Rutherfurd, but I had to keep Jimmy alive. "One page only."

Rutherfurd finally relented. "I choose the page."

My fingers were frozen. I couldn't cock the gun. I couldn't even heave the gun at his head like I wanted to. I had to make the deal.

So I did. "I choose the location."

♫

We walked solemnly along the platform to the waiting room in one wary, ragged line. Me, Rutherfurd, Frank, and Jimmy. Not quite shoulder to shoulder because Jimmy was leaning hard against Frank. And not just four of us, because I held Madame Savage in my coat pocket, just like Frank had his gun somewhere.

"You love a large audience, don't you, Miss Vermillion?" Rutherfurd's voice was light and energetic, as though our notebook sparring had invigorated him.

I didn't care a hoot about an audience, but I sure wanted witnesses. I wanted heads to turn in my direction if I screamed. Which made the waiting room ideal for the swap.

I also needed to know how much I'd injured Jimmy. Frank had made him wear a jacket from Rutherfurd's closet to hide his bloody shirt, so I still didn't know how badly I'd hurt him.

But I did know that people on the platform were looking at us.

A few seconds into the waiting room and more people were staring at us. Men put down their newspapers, women stopped feeding their babies, and the shoeshine man even stopped buffing. I was used to being ogled on stage, but this was different. And then I realized the attention wasn't for me, it was for Rutherfurd. I thought a standing ovation and three encores were Big Time, but the world stopped entirely when Thaddeus Rutherfurd appeared.

As a stout man wiped his hands on his pants, clearly about to approach us, Rutherfurd grabbed my wrist.

"Give it to me now," he ordered.

I fought to squirm free of his hold, but failed. "I won't do anything until you release me."

He let go of my wrist only when the stout man demanded to shake his hand.

Mr. Stout pumped Rutherfurd's hand as though it were an oil well. "I can't believe I'm meeting you, Mr. Rutherfurd. You're my hero. You're everyone's hero."

Three more men came up and offered their hands, ignoring me, even bumping into me, as they jockeyed to get closer to their idol.

And then men and women from all corners of the waiting room surged toward us. A hostess with menus in her hand rushed out of the restaurant, ticket clerks shut their sales windows, people scurrying to their trains suddenly pivoted in our direction. In seconds, we were surrounded. The questions came quickly.

"When are you declaring for president?"

"Are you building a factory here in California?"

"Can you hire my boy?"

"What about Wilson's League of Nations?" A woman's voice jolted out of the men's chorus. "Will it save the world?"

Rutherfurd noticed me being pushed away, but he would not abandon his audience. Nor it seemed, would Frank leave his boss, even if it meant that Jimmy and I slipped away.

Jimmy limped to my side, his right arm hanging awkwardly. "Let's get out of here."

"Wait until he's surrounded."

"*Now*, Viola. The police will be here soon."

So as Rutherfurd stood firm with Frank beside him, Jimmy and I allowed the crowds to push us away.

I leaned over to put my arm around Jimmy, but he pulled back. "I can walk. I just wanted to make Frank work harder."

On our way out, we brushed past a cluster of people—including a few patrolmen—rushing inside. Jimmy's sudden energy failed as we reached the street, and he slumped against me. I searched the streets and saw a taxi coming to the corner. Jimmy eased himself inside and I followed.

Blood seeped through Rutherfurd's jacket and I removed it to see that one bullet had burned a line into Jimmy's upper arm. I scrambled through the taxi for anything to stop the bleeding and finally pressed the jacket sleeve against it.

I leaned over the seat to give the driver instructions. "Take us to the nearest hospital. Fast."

"No," Jimmy croaked before falling against me. "Take us to the *Chronicle*."

His body went limp and I lowered his head into my lap. As the taxi took off, I saw a police car parked on a side street. We moved forward and they turned to follow us.

I tried to tickle the large roll of money out of Jimmy's pocket, planning to throw it all at the driver to get him to outrun the police. But before I got the money, the police car turned onto another street.

"You shot Frank." Jimmy opened his eyes as if he knew his pocket was being picked. "You really shot him."

"I shot you too." I looked at the arm I'd shot, having no idea how serious his injury was. But his hands—his beautiful piano player hands that he'd crossed on his chest as if he were laid out in a casket—were swollen and flecked with dried blood, forever scarred by dog bites. "I'm so sorry."

The taxi driver pulled up sharp. "The *Chronicle,*" he said.

I handed the driver the money Jimmy had given me to get to New Orleans and he helped me get Jimmy out of the taxi. We limped into the editorial offices, relieved that no one looked up from their typewriters. Even Erwin was reluctant to leave his desk until he saw the blood.

"Jesus, Joseph, and Mary!" Erwin caught Jimmy as he slipped out of my arms. "What the hell have you messed up now?"

CHAPTER FIFTY

"I WANTED to get him to a hospital," I told Erwin as he retrieved a bag from under his desk. "But—"

"Best medic in the Second is right here," Jimmy insisted softly.

Erwin removed bandages and bottles from his bag and stripped Jimmy down to his sleeveless undershirt. With his muscled arms and shoulders, Jimmy would have been the perfect specimen of male beauty, except for the still-bleeding gash on his right arm. And the bruises on his chin. And the dog bites on his hands.

"Just looks like a lot of blood," said Erwin. "How'd it happen?"

After extracting a promise that nothing we said would get reported in any newspaper, Jimmy asked for a drink. Erwin pulled a brown bottle and a coffee cup out of his desk and poured Jimmy a large one. He raised the bottle toward me, but I shook my head. Jimmy took a gulp, and then another, and told Erwin how Frank Cassady had surprised us at the train station.

As Jimmy described his down-and-dirty fight with Frank —in phrases that kept Erwin howling with appreciation—I remembered my pledge to Erwin. Yesterday, in this very office, I'd said I'd leave Jimmy alone. And here Jimmy was, explaining how he'd protected me from Frank. Erwin hadn't seemed irritated that I was by Jimmy's side, but now that Jimmy's arm was bandaged, should I honor my pledge? Should I slide out of the *Chronicle* offices and Jimmy's life for good?

But I couldn't. Not when—

"Done." Erwin slapped the scissors on the desk. "And this is nothing. Frank must be losing his aim."

"It wasn't Frank," I said. "It was me."

Erwin seemed to study me for a moment. "If that's so, Miss Viola, we need to get you some shooting lessons."

I found Jimmy studying me too, as if he was reliving the moment I shot him. He hadn't yet told Erwin anything about what happened in Rutherfurd's private car; now, he changed the subject entirely.

"What happened at the Pan after we left? Your girlfriend is a real police officer, isn't she?"

"She's not my girlfriend. Not yet. But she is a real police officer all right, even though they keep her assigned to the Ferry Building. And you can find out what happened by reading the front page of tomorrow's *Chronicle*. Now, Miss Viola," Erwin settled on me. "I know that any publicity is good publicity for show folk, but how much of your detecting do you want mentioned in the newspaper?"

"None." I'd already been branded a troublemaker and laid off from the Pantages Circuit. If I had any hope of staying in vaudeville, my newspaper mentions needed to be strictly professional.

But I was concerned about how Erwin's newspaper article might affect Margaret Wilson. "Do you think Stu's mother knows? I guess she might, since Dorothy was there."

"Mrs. Wilson knows," was all Erwin said.

Jimmy reached out to Erwin. "I need to warn you about Frank. He's mad, and he might still be in town. No telling how long."

"That's one thing *I* can tell *you*," Erwin replied. "After your big story yesterday, I started looking into some of the claims you made about Rutherfurd."

"Claims?" Jimmy sounded almost insulted. "What'd you find?"

"His schedule for the next month, for one thing." Erwin picked up a pencil and notebook. "Rutherfurd's giving an important speech in Boston in six days. I called someone I know at *The Globe* who said the event's still on. The way I figure it, Rutherfurd needs to make tonight's express to make Boston in time for his speech.

"You think Frank'll be with him?" I asked.

"Why wouldn't he?"

"Because I shot him, too," I answered. "Maybe worse than Jimmy."

"You shot Frank?" Erwin mimicked cleaning out his ear with his pencil. "Maybe you don't need lessons after all."

"Frank will be fine," Jimmy responded easily, as if Frank got shot and survived every time he and Jimmy met. "He's no worse off than I am, and all I needed was a medic."

But I wanted to hear from Erwin again. "You're sure Jimmy doesn't need a doctor?"

"What he needs is a bed and ten hours of sleep," Erwin replied. "But since I've got a deadline, taking care of Jimmy is all up to you."

♫

With the hotel porter's help, I got Jimmy up to the sixth floor and into bed. Into *my* bed, because I couldn't bear to put him in the bed where Rocco had been murdered. My bed had been Stu's bed, of course, but his presence no longer lingered in the room.

Outside in the hallway, troupers were shutting doors and lugging suitcases, scurrying to make tonight's jump to Oakland. I envied them all—the Nolan Sisters, Tuck and Champ, even Audrey—for knowing where they'd be playing next week. I had no idea where I was going. Or if I'd ever get back on stage.

Jimmy stirred, saw me listening at the door, and reached for the trousers I'd folded at the edge of the bed. "You weren't leaving me, were you?"

He fell back into bed, his flash of energy drained. I went to his side to see that his color was calm and his forehead was cool. I straightened his mussed linens, but my hands lingered on his chest for a second too long, and he grabbed them and pulled me to him.

If I was going to perform again, I needed to get out of San Francisco. And if Jimmy was going to return to his fiancée in New Orleans, he'd better let me go.

Just not tonight.

♫

Market Street on Friday morning was overrun with buses and delivery trucks and workers hustling into offices, but the sky was blue, the clouds were fluffy, and the sun warmed my face.

I gazed up at the Pantages marquee one last time, saddened to see it entirely bare. I imagined one of the workers pulling out the letters for my name and hooking them into the top of the marquee grid. They'd repeat it on the other sides of the marquee, of course, so that everyone approaching the Pantages would see that I was headlining.

It was a fine fantasy, seeing my talent recognized. So fine that I might have gazed at the marquee for hours, except I felt Jimmy standing by my side.

"Your suitcases and trunk are gone," he greeted me. "You running away from me?"

I guess I was. After leaving my hotel room, I'd tipped the manager to keep my cases and trunk for the day. Then I'd reached Stu's mother on the telephone and we'd made plans to meet this afternoon. I'd suggested we visit Stu's grave together—I wanted to apologize to him for believing he'd cheated on me—but Margaret declined, saying that she and Dorothy were going tomorrow. Margaret also hinted that Dorothy had confessed her part in Stu's disappearance.

Still, I wanted another hour in Margaret's company, another hour to tell her how special her son's music was. And if she wanted to know anything about Kitty's confession, I wanted to be the one to tell her. Knowing Stu's murderer had been caught had eased my sorrow; maybe an honest talk would help Stu's mother also.

But all I told Jimmy was, "It's time to leave San Francisco."

"Yes, it is, and I want you to come with me."

My thoughts drifted back to last night and how easily our bodies had fit together, how quickly we'd fallen asleep. But despite Jimmy's all-night hold on me, Thaddeus Rutherfurd had invaded my sleep like an unwelcome stage-door Johnny.

It had been the luckiest of breaks that Rutherfurd had been swarmed by admirers yesterday and that Frank had stayed to protect him. I knew Rutherfurd wouldn't stop pursuing me, and I was thinking about heading south, maybe as far as Mexico City. But I couldn't tell Jimmy.

"I can't," was all I said.

"I might know someone who can break Rutherfurd's code," he offered. "Someone we can trust. But you'll have to come to New Orleans to get it done."

Or I could give Jimmy the notebook and take off on my own. Except that'd put a target on Jimmy's back. So I couldn't give him the notebook.

At the same time, I knew that I could never convince Jimmy that I could take on Rutherfurd myself. Not when yesterday he'd fought to protect me. Even after I shot him.

A rogue tear crept into my eye as I remembered how my bullet had torn into Jimmy's arm. Before I flicked the tear away, Jimmy put his hand inside his jacket. His fingers fumbled and his handkerchief drifted out of his hands and to the ground. Two small photographs landed on top of the handkerchief.

I collected his things from the ground. One of the photos was the same image of Jimmy's fiancée that I'd seen in Erwin's flat, and I handed it to him right away. But when I saw the other image, I froze.

That was me in the second photo, a girl with a charming smile and eyes that dazzled. Yet I almost didn't recognize myself because the war and influenza and Blanche's death had worn me down so much. I hadn't been that bright, buoyant Viola for a long time.

"Where did you get this?" I'd had this photo made just for Blanche. It made no sense that Jimmy had a copy.

"Eleanor's maid gave it to me."

My memories of Eleanor were hazy enough; I certainly couldn't remember her maid. Or could I? Slowly, an image of a small, dark-haired woman came to mind. "Hilda? Was that her name?"

When Jimmy nodded, I said, "When did you see her?"

"Frank said Eleanor burned every photograph ever taken of her, so I thought Eleanor's maid might have one. As a memento."

"Eleanor's maid gave it to you." I released each word slowly. My heart was still heavy with memories of how much Blanche treasured this image of me. "Why would Eleanor's maid have this photograph of me and say it was Eleanor?" I took another hard look at the image. "This is me, isn't it?"

"It's you all right. Your eyes, your nose, your lips." He took the photo from my hand and used his thumb to smooth out a bent corner. "I can think of at least one reason *now* that Hilda'd misdirect me. Because she wanted me to find *you*, and not Eleanor."

"But why?"

"Viola." Jimmy's tone alerted me to the change in his thoughts. "It's not you Hilda wanted me to find. It's what you have."

"Rutherfurd's notebook."

As much as I'd tried to forget those days at St. Joe's, now I wanted to remember everything about them. And finally, I remembered a conversation I'd overheard when Hilda demanded to take Eleanor to a private hospital. And then I knew.

"Hilda doesn't want to find me. *Eleanor* wants to find me. Because Eleanor's alive and *she* wants the notebook back."

Jimmy shook his head. "You're not making sense."

"How did you start your search for Eleanor?" I asked. "Someone must have told you she was alive. Someone trustworthy."

"They did. At St. Joe's. The same time they told me the red-haired woman next to her had died."

"It makes sense they'd keep track of Eleanor," I said. "Since she was *someone*. But me . . . I wasn't anybody. Especially with so many people dying."

"Son of a bitch." Jimmy shook his head. "Hilda said that Eleanor had a brain fever and thought that she was you. Hilda begged me to send her a telegram once I found Eleanor so she could come out and 'bring Eleanor back to her senses.' Or something like that. I never sent Hilda a telegram and never planned to."

Despite the warming sun, Jimmy pulled his jacket close and folded his arms stiffly.

"You should go back to the hotel," I told him. "Back to bed."

"Only if you come too."

"I can't," I lied. "I have an errand."

"Do it later." He unfolded his arms and hooked them both into mine, careful not to lean on me with his injured arm. "Lead the way."

I walked with him to the Hotel Henry. To keep from thinking of our night of cuddling, I forced myself to concentrate on how to get Rutherfurd's notebook to someone who could use it.

"Rutherfurd said Eleanor set the explosion at the

factory, just after she stole the notebook from his safe. I didn't believe him, but what if it's true?"

Then, "Since Hilda asked you to send her a telegram when you found Eleanor, what if we send her one now? Once she knows where I am, she'll come out here. Probably with Eleanor."

"You really think Eleanor's alive?"

"You thought she was, didn't you?"

"I did," he said. "I've gone over everything I did—all of the questions, all of the witnesses—trying to discover where I went wrong. And it comes down to Hilda. I shouldn't have trusted her. I *could* telegraph her that I've found you, and Hilda and Eleanor *might* come to San Francisco. But then what?"

"We force Eleanor to tell us if she set the explosion that killed Blanche."

Jimmy seemed to weigh my every word. And then his own. "That might work, but we can't do it here. We need the upper hand, which means we have to do it in New Orleans."

"I can't go to New Orleans with you." And then I told him why. "Erwin said that you're getting married soon. Is that true?"

"That's the plan."

I was transported back to yesterday and the train platform, remembering exactly how he'd kissed my cheek.

"Yesterday you said you loved me," I reminded him. Although I didn't add his *But just a little bit.* "Is that why you want me to come to New Orleans? Does it have something to do with your fiancée and your wedding?"

"I want you to come with me so that we can finish what we've started."

I didn't know if he was talking about keeping the notebook from Rutherfurd or our attraction to each other. "What will your fiancée say if you bring me to New Orleans?"

"You leave Amelia to me."

"What will everyone else say?"

"We have an Orpheum in New Orleans. Did you know that?" Jimmy had no shame in not answering me directly. "And a couple of other vaudeville houses, too. We even have a legit playhouse, if that's what you're interested in."

I'd heard a lot about New Orleans from other troupers, about the festive and carefree Mardi Gras, and the music, and the food. I'd even been told that the acoustics of the New Orleans Orpheum were perfect for a singer like me. So it wasn't the city that had me concerned. No, it was my sudden envy of Jimmy's fiancée.

But Jimmy wouldn't give up. "Think about it, Viola. I can introduce you to the booker at the Orpheum, the stage manager at the Crescent, and the guy who buys the sheet music for everyone in the city. I can even help you find a new piano player. Or your own band."

He took my left hand, almost as though he were proposing. "I'm not going to let you say no. I can't leave you all alone."

I'd never be free of Rutherfurd or Eleanor until I confronted them directly, and I'd read enough newspaper battle stories to understand Jimmy's point. We were at war against Thaddeus and Eleanor Rutherfurd—and Frank Cassady—and the stronger our army, the better our chances.

And there was something Jimmy wasn't telling me about his fiancée. Something I guessed that even Erwin didn't know about. Something that might make Jimmy's being "a little in love" with me not such a bad thing after all.

Unless, of course, it turned out to be the worst thing in the world for both of us.

—THE END—

ACKNOWLEDGMENTS

Many years ago, I inherited the scrapbooks, recordings, and theatrical ephemera of vaudeville songstress Elsie Clark, and I used this treasure trove to create Viola Vermillion, the smart, sassy, and bodacious vaudeville heroine of THE RED-HOT BLUES CHANTEUSE.

While Elsie's memorabilia inspired me to write RED-HOT, so many friends and family have assisted me in completing the book. And so I thank my critique buddies Margot Abbott, Terry Shames, Peggy Lucke, Gayle Feyrer, and Kate Wyland, and my beta readers Kerry Brunson and Deanna Doherty. For helping me finalize and launch this book, I give special thanks to my fellow Paper Lantern Writers. Special thanks to Edie Cay for her formatting expertise.

As always, I am entirely indebted to my husband, Tim, for his support, his transcription of Elsie's phonographic recordings, and his knowledge of Alcatraz Island.

About the music

After You're Gone, 1918, Turner Layton and Henry Creamer, songwriters.

Back to My Old Home Town, 1910, Jack Norworth & Nora Bayes, songwriters.

Naughty! Naughty! Naughty! 1916, Joe Goodwin, Nat Vincent, & William Tracey, songwriters.

Till We Meet Again,1918, Richard A. Whiting & Raymond B. Egan, songwriters.

ABOUT THE AUTHOR

Ana Brazil has a master's degree in American history and loves to read and write historical fiction about curious, ambitious, and bodacious women. Her Gilded Age mystery FANNY NEWCOMB & THE IRISH CHANNEL RIPPER won the IBPA Gold Award for Historical Fiction, and her short stories have been published in multiple crime fiction anthologies. She is a founding member of the Paper Lantern Writers Authors Collective, and her short story "Trust No One" appears in the PLW's UNLOCKED anthology.

THE RED-HOT BLUES CHANTEUSE is the first book in Ana's Viola Vermillion Vaudeville Mystery trilogy. For a closer look at Elsie Clark, American vaudeville, historic San Francisco, and other historic insights, visit Ana's website @ anabrazil.com.

Ana, her husband, and Cappy-the-wonder-cat live in the beautiful hills of Oakland, California.

ALSO BY ANA BRAZIL

NOVELS:

Fanny Newcomb and the Irish Channel Ripper

SHORT STORIES:

Fault Lines

Me Too Short Stories

Unlocked

Beneath a Midwinter Moon

Book reviews are greatly appreciated!

www.anabrazil.com

Printed in Great Britain
by Amazon